PRAISE FOR OLIVIA CUNNING'S
RED-HOT SINNERS ON TOUR SERIES

DOUBLE TIME

"Snappy dialogue, dizzying romance, scorching hot sex, and realistic observations about life on tour make this a winner."

—*Publishers Weekly*

"Whether you like rockers or not, this story will get you thinking about becoming a groupie!"

—*Night Owl Reviews*

"Hot rock stars, hotter sex, and some of the best characters I've read this year."

—*Guilty Pleasures Book Review*

ROCK HARD

"The sex is incredible and the love is even better. Each rocker has a piece of my heart... an excellent read."

—*Night Owl Reviews* Reviewer Top Pick

"Readers will love the characters and enjoy their scorching love scenes and passionate fights."

—*RT Book Reviews*, 4 Stars

SINNERS ON TOUR

Hot
TICKET

OLIVIA
CUNNING

sourcebooks
casablanca

Published by Sourcebooks Casablanca, an imprint of Sourcebooks, Inc.

P.O. Box 4410, Naperville, Illinois 60567-4410
(630) 961-3900
FAX: (630) 961-2168
www.sourcebooks.com

Library of Congress Cataloging-in-Publication Data is on file with the publisher.

Printed and bound in Canada

WC 10 9 8 7 6 5 4 3

Chapter 1

WITHIN SECONDS OF MEETING a man, Aggie could assign him to one of two lists.

List A: *Men Not Worth My Time.*

List B: *Men I'd Like to Fuck.*

List A grew in length every hour she worked at the nightclub, Paradise Found. She couldn't remember the last time a man had landed himself on List B.

That might explain why Aggie dropped her bullwhip when *he* caught her attention. Whoever he was. Potential List B strode across the floor as if he owned the place. He had that stereotypical bad boy look—leather, tattoos, and a giant chip on his shoulder—which was contradicted by the sweetest face she'd ever seen. When he took a seat at the table closest to her stage, he leaned back in his chair and crossed his legs at the ankle, as if he planned to stay for a while.

Interesting. And entirely fuckable.

Sipping his beverage, Angel Face gazed up at her with an odd gleam of challenge in his dark eyes. Something about him had her instantly thinking naughty thoughts. Only half of them involved inflicting pain on his tight body. Oh, the guy was a looker, no denying that, but that wasn't his main appeal. Strange thing was she didn't know what set him apart from the other nightclub patrons. Perhaps she needed a new list just for him.

Temporary List C: *Men I Can't Instantly Label.* She had no doubt that this list's only assignee would quickly land himself on List

A. In no way would she ever consider a customer List B potential. It didn't matter how attractive he was.

Aggie retrieved her bullwhip from the stage floor (how embarrassing) and cracked it next to Hottie's cheek. He didn't flinch. His body tensed, but not with fear. From the slight gasp he emitted and the flutter of his lashes, she could tell her threat turned him on.

Most men liked to watch Aggie's routine from the shadows and think they could take her abuse. Trying to show their toughness, they chose the dominatrix in leather to entertain them at Paradise Found, but few sat within striking distance of her bullwhip. Not that she'd actually hit anyone at the club. If a man wanted her to punish him for being born with a Y chromosome, he had to pay extra.

Aggie drew her arm back and lashed her whip at the new arrival's cheek again. The leather snapped centimeters from his skin. She was satisfied when he didn't flinch this time either. Oh Lord, he'd be fun to break. It had been forever since she'd had a real challenge in her dungeon.

He stared directly into her eyes as she danced closer. He looked quite young—midtwenties, maybe—but he had eyes wise beyond his years. She'd bet he'd seen a lot of tragedy in his life. Many of those who sought her for release had.

The young man beckoned her closer with a crooked finger. Surprised, she arched a brow at him and glanced at Eli, the bouncer who stood near the stage. She wasn't supposed to discuss her side business at the club. As far as her coworkers were concerned, Aggie's dominatrix routine was entirely an act. Later, when she moved to the floor to interact with customers on a more personal basis, she would slip her card to potential slaves, but her stage set wasn't over yet. She needed to concentrate on her dancing and not daydream about making some tough-looking übercutie her bitch.

Aggie hooked her leg around a silver pole and twirled around it, her long, black hair flying out behind her. When she stopped, she found the guy had vacated his chair and was standing against the stage at her feet. He pulled a bill from his back pocket and held it out to her between two fingers. *Hello, C-note. Mama needs a new pair of boots.*

Holding onto the pole with one hand, she leaned toward the customer, offering the tops of her full breasts to his view. His gaze shifted to her bare skin, and he drew his tongue over his upper lip. Usually, one guy looked as mundane as another to her, but she took in every inch of this one, from his heavy black boots to his spiked platinum blond hair. Dark eyes. Dark eyebrows. Dark beard stubble. The hint of a tattoo revealed itself above the neckline of his T-shirt. A studded leather band adorned his right wrist. He looked hard and tough, yet saccharine sweet at the same time. A hell's angel, heavy on the angel. She wondered if his beard stubble was an attempt to cover up that undeniably cute face of his.

He slid the bill between Aggie's breasts and into the bodice of her black leather bustier. As his fingertips brushed her skin, her nipples tightened. Totally unusual reaction for her. Customers typically gave her the heebie-jeebies when they touched her. This one had all her systems set to go. The small silver hoop in his earlobe caught a strobe light. Aggie gnawed on her tongue, wanting to nibble on his ear instead. She did have a thing for ears.

Um, wrong answer, Aggie. Customers were never fair game for action in the sack.

"Do you do private dances?" he asked, his chocolate-brown eyes locked with hers. His voice was deeper than she'd expected and so quiet, she wouldn't have heard him over the throbbing club music if she hadn't been leaning so close.

"You mean like a lap dance?"

"If that's what you do. How much?"

"Fifty bucks."

He handed her another hundred. The guy must have had a good

day at the casino. He didn't look rich. He wore a plain white T-shirt, worn black leather jacket, and snug blue jeans, which clung to the huge bulge in his pants. *Well, hello there, big guy.* She was glad she wasn't the only one thinking her next dance should be the horizontal mamba.

Aggie, pull yourself together, woman. He's a customer. No can do. Oh, but she so wanted to. Do. Him.

His gaze lowered to the floor, and he flushed. "Do you offer *other* services?"

Whoa, buddy. Brakes engaged. "I'm not a prostitute, if that's what you're asking."

He shook his head. "That's not what I meant. I want you to hurt me." He drew a deep, shuddering breath into his expanding chest. "Hard-core."

Oh yeah. Can do, sugar.

Aggie glanced over at the bouncer again to make sure he wasn't watching her side transaction. Eli's attention was on the far stage, where Paradise Found's newest dancer, Jessica, a.k.a. Feather, was dancing in her white feathers and silk scarf. Men were mesmerized by her. Even though Jessica had a fantastic body and knew how to move it, she simply didn't have the right mind-set to be an exotic dancer. None of the drooling men who surrounded Feather's stage with slightly bulging eyes and excessively bulging flies would agree with Aggie's opinion. All they saw was her beautiful outer package—not the severely broken heart within. Aggie saw it though. She'd recognized it the instant she'd met Jessica and helped her land this job. Poor lamb. So confused and conflicted.

Aggie returned her attention to the guy at her feet. She didn't have the same sympathy for men. "I do indulge for a price," Aggie told him, "but no sex."

"I don't need sex."

She nodded. He wasn't new to this. Which made him so much

more fun than her usual victims. She had a few regulars who visited her dungeon, but most of her customers were guys visiting Vegas who wanted to explore their darker sides for a night. She never saw most of them again, which suited her just fine. Many dommes preferred regulars, but Aggie would rather turn over a quick buck and avoid growing fond of one of her submissives.

Her current interest's body held tension in every line. When he glanced up at her, the deep emotional pain in his gaze made her belly quiver. *Yeah, blondie, you're exactly the challenge I need right now.* "I can work you over, angel, but not here. I'll slip you my card later, and you can call me. If you're lucky, I'll show you my dungeon."

He shuddered, his breath coming out in an excited gasp.

Maybe she should take him backstage and give him a taste of what she had to offer. He looked ready to explode with the strain of containing his pain. He needed the release she could give him. And she needed to see him grovel at her boots so she could dismiss him as not worth her time. The sooner he joined the thousands of men on List A, the better.

Aggie dropped down on her knees on the stage to continue dancing as she talked to him. "When do you need this?"

"As soon as possible."

"I think I have an opening in a few days."

"Tonight. I've got money. Name your price."

Name your price? He was definitely speaking her language, but making him wait would do half her work for her. She ran her bloodred, pointed nails down the side of his neck, leaving light scratches in their wake. "I'll check my calendar and see if I can squeeze you in. Maybe tomorrow. Or the next day."

She was eager to raise welts on his flesh and hear him cry out in pain. Wanted the ultimate prize he would gift her: begging her for mercy, begging her to stop. That sweet instant he gave her all of his power and she *owned* him. That's what she wanted. What she needed to keep herself elevated from that deep, dark pit she'd once resided in. But it was too soon to indulge him. He'd attain greater fulfillment if she put him off a few days. Let the anticipation settle into his body and his thoughts until he could think of nothing but the delicious agony she promised.

A commotion on the other side of the room drew her attention. Eli, Aggie's bouncer, darted toward Feather's stage. Some big, good-looking customer had captured Jessica in his arms. She was wrapped in a leather jacket with her arms trapped helplessly. Several bouncers were trying to secure her release. Several others were escorting some tall, thin guy out of the club. A third guy standing next to Jessica's captor shook his head in disgrace. All three customers had a similar look to them. Like they were in some rock band or something. Come to think of it, the cute guy at the end of her stage had a similar appearance. A matching set. She looked down to find her potential good time had vanished.

"Motherfuckers!" her blond angel yelled as he launched himself onto the back of one of the bouncers.

When Jace saw that a bouncer was dragging Sinners' drummer, Eric, toward the exit, he didn't think, he just acted. All thoughts of the beautiful, black-haired dominatrix and what glorious things she could do to his body fled his mind.

Jace raced across the club, hurdled a chair, and landed on the bouncer's back. He knew he wasn't big enough to take him down, but Jace could fight. If things had turned out differently, he might have become a professional boxer, instead of the bass guitarist for a rock band.

He didn't mind an occasional brawl—he was good at fighting and knew how to knock a man out in one punch—but Jace wasn't even sure why they were engaging with a bunch of bouncers at Brian's bachelor party. They were supposed to be celebrating, not stirring up shit. Eric had better have a good reason for making eight club bouncers pissed enough to hit anything that moved. As the fight moved to the sidewalk outside the club, it escalated. Jace took out a couple of guys with one punch, before pausing to assess the situation.

Tall and wiry, Eric was putting up a fine fight, but was outnumbered four to one. Surrounded on all sides with no way out, Eric unexpectedly pointed to the sky. "Look, the Flying Elvises!"

All four bouncers stared up at the dark sky like turkeys in a hailstorm. When their attention turned skyward, Eric crashed into one of the bouncers at waist level, trying to escape the circle of muscle, but as soon as they realized there were no parachuting icons to entertain them, all four bouncers pounded Eric in rapid succession.

Jace decided to even the odds. Two uppercuts and a couple dozen jabs later, two more bouncers lay on the sidewalk: one out cold, the other attempting to rise, but failing to regain his equilibrium.

Eric wiped the blood out of his eye, his surprised gaze shifting from the human debris at his feet to Jace. "Jesus, little man, you're a one-man wrecking crew."

Distracted by Eric's compliment, Jace found an unexpected fist against his jaw. Pain radiated up the side of his face. His ears rang. Vision blurred. The pain he didn't mind, but the jar to his senses left him unbalanced. He took another hit to the jaw before he could focus well enough to knock his adversary out with one hard punch under the chin.

Breathing hard, Jace spun and saw some guy whack Sinners' rhythm guitarist, Trey, in the back of the head with an aluminum bat. Trey hadn't even been in the club when the fight broke out. Why had he been targeted? "Fuckin' queer," the bouncer growled.

Trey dropped to the sidewalk, instantly unconscious. Eric went after the fucktard with the bat, yanking the weapon out of his hands, and tossing it into the road beyond the sidewalk.

"No one." Eric punched the guy in the face. "Calls him." Hit him again. "A queer." And again. "Ever." Eric continued to pummel the guy until he stopped getting up.

Their lead guitarist, Brian (when in the hell had he joined the fray?), had a one-on-one fight going with the last bouncer standing. The two of them went back and forth with blows down the sidewalk. Brian took a hard fist to the nose, which pissed him off enough to take the guy down with a couple of quick punches.

Jace took a deep breath. Glad it was over. Now maybe he could finish his whiskey and make that appointment with that hot-as-blue-flames dominatrix. Sinners' vocalist, Sed, burst out of the club. Apparently, he'd gotten tired of the stripper he'd captured off the stage and was ready to fight. They could have used him earlier. Sed was huge. A bodybuilder who would have made a good bouncer had he not been gifted with a voice from the heavens. Sed glanced around, looking for someone to hit, but every bouncer was already down.

Unfortunately, so was Trey.

Sed crossed the sidewalk in two strides and bent over Trey. Sed took him by both shoulders, lifted his torso off the ground, and gave him a gentle shake. Out cold, Trey's head lolled loosely. "Trey? Trey! Trey, open your eyes." Sed glanced at Eric. "What the fuck happened to him?"

"That douche bag whacked him in the back of the head with a ball bat." Said douche bag was groaning in the middle of the sidewalk. Eric had made a mess of the guy's face.

"What the fuck?" Sed eased Trey down to the sidewalk, dropped to his knees, and put his ear to Trey's chest. "His heart's still beating. He's breathing."

"Well, duh. You didn't think he was dead, did you? He isn't even bleeding."

Brian staggered his way back up the sidewalk to join them. He massaged the knuckles of his right hand, his dark brows drawn together in an angry scowl. "Damn it, Eric, why do you always have to start shit?"

"It was Sed's fault. He's the one who grabbed Jessica off the stage."

Jace's gaze swiveled toward Sed in astonishment. *Jessica?* Sed's fiancée who'd dumped him almost two years ago? Small world. Jace hadn't recognized her without clothes.

"Who cares who started it? It's over," Sed said. "Let's get the fuck out of here before the cops show up. I doubt Myrna will want to bail Brian out of jail on their wedding day, and then there's the concert tomorrow. Kind of can't miss it."

They probably should have thought about that before they messed up their hands, faces, and bodies in a brawl that seemed pointless now that it had ended. While a world record contender for the Shortest Bachelor Party Ever, Brian's last night as a single man had definitely been one to remember.

Jace glanced at the club's door and released a frustrated sigh. He hadn't gotten that wood-inducing dominatrix's card, and he so needed to see her in private. Fighting tended to release some of his tension—that's why he continued to box for recreation, even though he had a better gig in a rock band now—but getting in a bar fight didn't sooth his soul's turmoil. Not in the same way being whipped to the limits of his tolerance by a woman in spiked heels and black leather would.

Sed scooped Trey off the sidewalk, tossed him over one broad shoulder, and headed to the pink '57 Thunderbird parked at the curb. The sound of sirens grew increasingly loud.

"Jace, let's go!" Eric shouted.

After one last look of longing at the club's swinging doors, Jace climbed on his Harley, waited for Eric to settle down behind him, and then followed the car back to their tour bus behind the Mandalay Bay Hotel. Surely someone would report their vehicles. There were plenty of witnesses to the fight. Every member of his band was probably screwed. Busted. In huge trouble. Their manager, Jerry, had told them if any of them were arrested again, not to bother calling him. He refused to bail them out. He also threatened their stage crew with immediate termination should they lend their aid. Jerry didn't make idle threats.

When Jace pulled to a stop behind the tour bus, Trey stumbled out of Myrna's car and leaned against the fender. At least he was conscious now. Jace rocked the bike back on its kickstand, shut off the engine, and went to check on Trey.

"You all right, man?" Jace asked.

None of his bandmates were what Jace would consider tan, but Trey looked downright ghostly.

"Yeah. Just a little dizzy." Trey pressed on his temples with both hands. "Fuck, my head hurts."

Brian leaned out the driver's window. "Get back in the car, Trey, and we'll take you to the hospital."

"Fuck that. You know I hate hospitals. Why do you think I never followed in my father's footsteps?"

"Because you're too dumb to be a doctor," Brian said. "Now get back in the car."

Sed unfolded his six-foot-four frame from the little car. "Listen to Brian, Trey. Get back in the car." He grabbed Trey by the shoulders and tried to force him.

Trey pulled out of his grasp. "Eric's bleeding all over the fuckin' place, and you aren't threatening to take him to the hospital."

Sed shrugged. "Whatever. It's just Eric."

"Thank you very fucking much for your concern, Sed," Eric said. "Really. Appreciate it." From the gash on the side of his head, blood continued to drip down Eric's face and onto his black T-shirt.

"Do you need stitches?" Jace asked.

Eric's brows drew together. "Do you?"

Jace shook his head. "I'm not bleeding anywhere."

"And why is that, little man?"

Jace shrugged, shifting his gaze to the ground to prevent Eric from recognizing that he'd managed to push his buttons. Again. He just couldn't win with Eric. Ever. And he respected him too much to knock him on his ass. Jace took a deep breath and released it slowly as he stared at the ground. He took a lot of shit from Eric, but if that's what he had to do to stay in this band, he'd continue to take it. Nothing else on this whole fucking planet meant more to him than these four brilliant musicians.

"Sed, give me your sunglasses," Brian said, now standing in their little huddle and waving a hand at Sed.

"What the fuck do you need sunglasses for? It's almost midnight."

"Just hand them over."

Sed retrieved his shades from his jacket pocket, handed them to Brian, and then took a deep breath. "Okay, I'm going in. Myrna is going to kill me for letting Brian get his ass kicked the night before their wedding."

"I didn't get my ass kicked."

"You've looked better, my friend. Trust me on that."

Sed headed up the tour bus steps, followed by Eric.

"You sure you're okay, Trey?" Jace asked.

"Yeah. I just need some ice." Trey fingered the back of his head and winced. He followed Eric up the steps, only veering slightly to the left.

"You go next," Brian insisted of Jace.

Jace grinned at him. "Afraid of Myrna?"

"Hell, yeah, I'm afraid of Myrna. I hate arguing with her. She always wins. And she has every reason to be pissed at me. Who wants to stand at the altar with a guy who has two black eyes?"

Jace's grin widened, and the warmth of embarrassment spread across his face. "Myrna does. She loves you."

Brian took a deep breath. "I hope you're right. God, I can't get that ring on her finger fast enough. Okay, Jace, go. Sed's probably broken the news to her by now. I need multiple obstacles in her path, and I don't think she'd actually hit you. She thinks you're the sweet one." Brian almost choked on his laugh.

Jace had never given Myrna a reason to think otherwise. "Everything will be okay. Just grovel."

"Grovel?" Brian looked reflective for a moment, and then nodded. "Can do."

Jace climbed the steps to find Myrna, still wearing her business suit and looking all prim and proper, when she was decidedly *not* prim and proper by any stretch of the imagination, fussing over the cut near Eric's temple. Eric ate up every minute of her concern. He had a little, make that *big*, crush on Brian's woman, so any attention she paid him made him giddy and stupid. Trey was searching the freezer for ice. Sed stood next to the dining table looking like he'd robbed a bank.

It didn't even take two minutes for Myrna to put Brian in his place. She was conscious enough of the lack of privacy to take their argument to the bedroom at the back of the bus, but even with the door closed, Jace could hear Brian's groveling. He was doing a fine job by Jace's estimation, though Myrna still didn't sound too forgiving about her fiancé's matching black eyes.

Jace rubbed his swollen knuckles, wondering how he was going to play the next night. He couldn't let himself get into any more fights. If he hurt his hands, Sinners would undoubtedly get rid of him. He didn't want to give them a reason to fire him from the band. Not after he'd worked so hard to become a part of it.

Sed retrieved a bottle of aspirin from the bathroom and grinned as he handed it to Trey. He nodded toward the thin bedroom door. "I guess they made up."

No more sounds of Brian groveling. Just the unmistakable cries of ecstasy that Myrna produced on a very regular basis.

Trey laughed. "Who can stay mad at Brian?" He swallowed several pills and passed the bottle to Eric.

"I'm glad they made up," Eric said, holding a bloody dish towel to his temple. "I'd have felt terrible if she called the wedding off."

"You should feel terrible," Jace said, staring at the floor, as he knew his gaze would hold a challenge. Through all the *lessons* his father tried to teach him, keeping defiance out of his gaze had never stuck. "You started the whole thing."

"Well, I didn't ask for your help, little man, now did I?" Eric said.

Nope, he hadn't. Jace should have stayed out of it and let those bouncers rearrange Eric's face.

Jace pursed his lips and nodded slightly. He left the bus without a word, not in the mood for another confrontation. Not with Eric. The man who had no idea how much of a positive impact he'd had on Jace's life. If he'd thought of Eric as anything less than his hero, he would have punched him in the face years ago.

Jace climbed on his Harley, secured his helmet, and started the bike. The engine roared to life beneath him. The freedom the sound represented instantly brought him peace of mind. He headed off, not really knowing where he was going, but his thoughts had settled on a black-haired beauty with a whip. That woman was exactly what he needed.

He wondered if she was still at the club. He needed to pick up that card she'd promised him and make an appointment for her perfect abuse.

Immediately.

Chapter 2

JACE PULLED INTO THE alley alongside the strip club. He shouldn't even be there. While he'd always been good at remaining unnoticed, he knew he had a distinctive appearance, and bouncers didn't take kindly to getting their asses kicked. If they caught sight of him, he'd probably spend the night in jail. Or worse, the hospital. Participating in a fight was one thing, being jumped by a group of musclemen, another thing entirely. But he was willing to risk it to see *her* again. Her. Whoever she was. Hell, he didn't even know her name.

Jace turned off the Harley's ignition, shifted the bike backward to engage the kickstand, and climbed off. Leaning against the side of the seat with his helmet on, he waited outside the back exit for his beautiful demon in black leather to emerge. He hoped he hadn't missed her. He needed her. In a bad way. He'd wait all night if he had to. It wasn't as if he had anywhere else to be.

Over the next half hour, several people, mostly other dancers, exited the club through the back door. Jace earned a few curious glances, but no one questioned his motives.

When she finally emerged, his breath caught. She wore a long, black fur coat over her leather bustier, black satin panties, and thigh-high boots. Jace suppressed a shudder of primal longing. She paused at the bottom of the steps and reached into her pocket, searching for something. A cigarette, perhaps?

Jace patted his pockets looking for a lighter, but she pulled out a pack of gum and popped a piece in her mouth. She turned her head in his direction.

Noticed him.

His cock stirred with excitement. Anticipation. Every inch of his skin tingled with longing.

Her full, red lips curled into a sexy smile.

Did she recognize him? He didn't know how. He still wore his helmet with its black face shield down. Maybe she smiled like that at every guy. He wasn't sure why that thought bothered him. He just wanted to buy her services for a few hours, not make her a permanent fixture in his life. But as fixtures went, she was in a class all her own. Dear God, the woman was positively luscious.

She walked toward him, moving gracefully, like a prowling cat. The closer she got, the harder his heart thudded and the faster it raced. Jace stood straight, stepping away from the bike.

She stopped directly in front of him. He could feel her body heat through his clothes. It caressed his skin. Heightened his awareness of her.

He leaned toward her. Wanting to touch her. Taste her. Experience everything she was.

But mostly, he wanted her to beat the ever-loving shit out of him.

"I thought you might show up," she murmured. "I still owe you a dance."

In her three-inch, thigh-high boots, she stood a couple inches taller than him. Without them, he probably had an inch on her. Her height didn't bother him. Looking up at her excited him. Her long white neck excited him. The sharp angle of her jaw. Smooth cheek. Full eyelashes. Thick, black bangs. The musky scent of her perfume mingled with leather and spearmint gum. The soft, husky sound of her voice. Everything about her excited him. He needed her. Now. It took every shred of his willpower not to drag her body against his.

"How did you know it was me?" he asked.

She lifted the visor of his helmet and stared into his eyes. Her cerulean blue irises stood in shocking contrast to her jet-black hair and porcelain-white skin. "Besides the fact that you're still wearing the same clothes?"

Oh.

"It's the way you carry yourself, angel. The tension in your body. It pulsates off you. How long has it been since you've had release?"

He knew what she meant. She didn't mean sexual release. He could have that any time he wanted. She meant how long since he'd gotten what he needed. The release *she* could give him. "Almost a year."

She pursed her lips with sympathy. "Poor baby. I'll fix it." She touched his cheek. "Make it all better."

Ripples of delight snaked along his jaw, down his neck and belly. Grabbed him by the balls. He shuddered. Reached for her. Needing *it*. Her.

She slapped his hand away. "No."

He clenched his hand into a fist and lowered it to his side. He knew she was a domme and used to men taking her orders, so he allowed her to retain her power. For now. "Let's go."

"Now?"

"Yeah, now. Right now."

She laughed. The rich, husky sound made his spine tingle.

"I've got to go back to work, sugar."

His breath came out in a frustrated huff. "Then when? When?"

"Tomorrow night. Ten o'clock."

Jace's stomach tightened. He shook his head. "I can't wait that long."

Her hand cupped his crotch. His breath caught. She squeezed his balls. Not too hard. Just enough to gift him with delicious agony. It hurt so good, he bit his lip to stop himself from crying out in ecstasy.

"You will wait," she said evenly. "Say it."

He resisted.

She squeezed harder. "Say it."

He drew the horrible, sweet pain inside, craving more of the same.

She removed her hand, and he winced. His stomach roiled, but he wanted more pain. Lots more. And he knew she wouldn't give it to him, ever, unless he obeyed her. "I will wait."

She smiled and slid something into his hand. A business card. "This is the address. Be on time, or I won't answer the bell."

He glanced down at her plain black business card. There was just enough light in the alley to make out the blood red text.

MISTRESS V

SPECIALIZING IN CORPORAL PUNISHMENT

Corporal punishment? Lord, he almost came down his leg, just seeing it in print.

Jace took a steadying breath to clear his thoughts. He had other responsibilities to consider. Sinners had an important performance the next night. Would the concert be over by ten? Though they usually headlined, Sinners was opening tomorrow, so their set started earlier than usual. They should be done by nine thirty, so he'd have to hurry. "I'll be there," he said.

"I look forward to making you beg for mercy," she murmured.

"Then you'll be disappointed." He slid her card into his pocket and climbed onto his bike. He turned the key, and the engine roared to life beneath him. "Until tomorrow."

Chapter 3

JACE MOVED HIS ICE pack from his left hand to this right. The swelling was starting to go down, but he knew he wouldn't play for shit tonight. They were opening for Exodus End, in front of a sold out crowd. In fucking Las Vegas, Nevada. This should be a huge boost to their music careers, and they were all but guaranteed to suck. Sinners was moving up in the business, but Exodus End was at the top of the genre with no signs of slowing down. Could Sinners have picked a worse concert to be off their game? Not likely.

Rock star hair wet from a recent shower, Eric sank onto the sofa beside Jace. "How's the hand?"

Jace shrugged. "I'll live."

"Yeah, but more importantly, can you play?"

Jace looked up at Eric, who had three thin strips of tape on his temple holding his wound closed. "Should be able to. How's Trey?"

"He's taking a nap."

Jace drew his brows together. "A nap?" That didn't sound like Trey. Shouldn't he be out finding some girl to fuck for a couple hours? Or some guy? Trey didn't care either way. "Maybe we should take him to the doctor."

"I think he's kind of down about Brian getting married this afternoon. He won't say anything, of course, but Brian isn't going to have as much time for his best friend now that Wifey Sinclair is in the picture."

Jace guessed that made sense. Trey and Brian had been best

friends for almost twenty years. They were even roommates. Trey was bound to feel left out now that Brian was married. "Yeah."

With no warning, Eric slapped Jace on the back of the head. "Why didn't you ever mention that you fight like a UFC champion?"

Jace glanced up at him. "You never asked."

"Where did you learn to kick ass?"

The cabin of the tour bus seemed to close in on Jace. He did not like to think about his past, much less talk about it. He stared at the ice pack on his hand and shrugged. "I dunno. How about you? You were kickin' some ass."

Jace hoped to change the focus from himself to Eric. It usually worked to dissuade prying. Especially with Eric, attention whore extraordinaire.

"I had no choice but to learn to fight. I was shuffled from foster home to foster home for fifteen years. I didn't get the benefit of being matched with a sponsor who wanted to help kids or make a healthy family. They were all just looking for an easy paycheck. Half of them didn't even feed me." He shrugged, his blue eyes brightening as he effortlessly abandoned thoughts of his past. Jace wished he was capable of doing that. "Knocking heads together is fun though, right?"

Fun? No, not really. Validating? Yeah, totally. "I guess. What started that fight anyway?"

"You didn't see that bouncer put Sed in a choke hold? He didn't even release him when I told him he was a professional singer. I had to deck him one."

Jace would have probably decked him one too. Sed's voice was one of those things that made Sinners so unique. Jace smiled slightly. "I'm glad we kicked their asses then."

"We should go rehearse." Eric launched to his feet. "Our set is about half the length it usually is. I just know I'll end up kicking off with the intro to 'Twisted' when I should be playing 'Good-bye Is Not Forever.'"

Jace chuckled. "I have the feeling we're gonna suck tonight anyway." He climbed from the comfortable leather sofa and tossed his melting ice pack in the tour bus's small freezer.

"No one will notice. The fans will be too excited to see Exodus End to give a rat's ass what we do."

"I think they'll notice that we suck."

Eric chuckled. "Don't worry. No one ever listens to the bass guitarist. Suck as much as you want."

Jace bit his lip to prevent himself from telling Eric off. The tension was really starting to get to him, and he needed an outlet. How many hours until he could visit Mistress V? He glanced at the clock on the stereo. *Shit.* Four hours too many.

After rehearsal and a quick bite of leftover wedding cake, Jace stood backstage off by himself, trying to psyche himself up enough to play live in front of twelve thousand people. The swelling in his hands had gone down, but his fingers lacked their usual flexibility. He feared that they'd let Exodus End down and do a piss-poor job as their opening band tonight. It made him sick to think that he might disappoint them. He owed that band a world of gratitude. Especially their lead guitarist, Dare.

Something poked him in the left shoulder, and he turned to find Eric grinning at him, while using his drumstick as a prod. "You gonna hide out by the drum kit again tonight?"

Jace shrugged. He didn't like the performance part of playing live. He just wanted to play his bass guitar with all the skill he could muster and leave the crowd entertainment to Sed, Brian, and Trey. The three of them were naturals when it came to interacting with the audience. Jace wasn't. He felt like an ass whenever he forced himself from the security of the back half of the stage.

"There's a problem with that idea tonight, little man."

"What problem?"

"We're opening, which means we're working with half a stage.

There's no room for you near the back. My drums take up too much room. It's front and center for you tonight."

Jace's stomach plummeted into his boots. "Shit."

Eric laughed at his misery. "This should be entertaining. Though I do remember a show when Brian was distracted with Myrna, and you took up his slack. You can be entertaining when you want to be."

Problem was he never wanted to be. He was there for the music. No other reason. He didn't require the ego trip of fan adulation. A loud crash startled Jace out of his reverie. Travis, one of their long time roadies, extended a hand into a pile of empty guitar cases and pulled Trey to his feet.

"You okay?" Travis asked.

Trey stumbled sideways as he regained his footing and held onto Travis's arm for a long moment. Still unnaturally pale, Trey nodded slowly. "Yeah, just lost my balance."

Jace moved to stand next to their unsteady rhythm guitarist. "I think you should go get checked out. Head injuries aren't something to mess around with."

"I'm fuckin' fine. I wish everyone would stop treating me like I'm severely injured. Where in the hell is Brian?"

"I think he's getting in a quickie with Myrna," Sed said, chomping down red licorice ropes by the yard. He used the candy's glycerin to lubricate his vocal cords, or so he claimed. His throat must still be bothering him.

"Jesus, all he does is fuck that woman these days," Trey grumbled. "Doesn't he realize we're onstage in ten minutes?"

"Seven minutes," Dave, their front of house soundboard operator, corrected before jogging out into the audience to work his magic on their audio equipment.

Trey stumbled against Jace, who grabbed him by both arms to steady him. "Take deep breaths."

Trey closed his eyes and obeyed without argument.

"Better?"

He nodded slightly and then winced in pain. "Fuck, my head hurts."

"Why don't you sit down?" Eric said. "You're going to break something."

"Probably your neck," Brian said as he finally joined them and lifted his guitar strap over his head.

"Done boning Myrna?" Trey asked, shaking his head at the pussy-whipped disgrace his best friend had become.

Brian chuckled. "Not by a long shot. The real honeymoon starts in forty-six minutes."

Sed scowled and grabbed Jake, their Mohawk-sporting, guitar-tuning roadie, by both arms. "Yo, Jake. Find me two real hot ones for tonight." Sed's scowl deepened. "Make that three hot ones."

No one needed to ask three hot whats. Sed meant groupies. He'd been in a mood since he'd run into his ex, Jessica, the night before. Whichever three groupies Jake selected for Sed's entertainment were going to get fucked. Fucked long, hard, and good. Sed was in all-out predatory mode. Jace was doubly glad he'd be spending the time after their concert in Mistress V's dungeon. The bite of her whip was sure to be less painful than watching Sed's groupies cry and beg for his attention, after he'd finished with them and sent them on their way.

The stadium lights went down, and the crowd cheered, knowing it meant it was time for the band to take the stage.

When Trey stumbled over the bottom step in the dark, Brian took him by one arm and helped him climb up to the stage. "You sure you're okay, buddy?" Jace heard Brian say over the crowd noise.

"Like you care." Trey wrenched his arm free of Brian's hold and trotted over to his usual spot stage right. There wasn't much light for Jace to find his own yellow X taped on the floor. At least he was behind the front line and somewhere in the middle. Here he could probably hide behind Sed's broad, muscular form.

The first thump of Eric's bass drum kicked Jace's heart rate up a notch. He entered the first song, "Twisted," with his steady bass line progression. His bruised and swollen fingers protested every note. By the time Brian entered his solo, Jace could scarcely force his fingers to move at all. Trey found a speaker to sit on. He typically strummed his rhythm guitar shreds with great enthusiasm, but several stumbles into his mic stand had him seeking a stable place to rest. He did manage to play without problem, as long as he didn't move around much. When Sed roared into the mic at the end of Brian's somewhat screwed up solo, the singer broke off mid-note with a cough. He cleared his throat and tried again with no success. Jesus, what a disaster.

When the song blissfully came to an end, Jace rubbed his stiff and aching knuckles while Sed called to the crowd and told them they were the best audience ever. Same thing he told every crowd. He made no excuses for the band's unusual suckatude. The only one who was performing anywhere near normal was Eric. As Eric was the main reason they'd gotten into a club brawl in the first place, it didn't seem fair that he didn't suck as much as the rest of them.

Since Sed's singing was subpar, he apparently decided additional showmanship could make up for it. He dove into the crowd in the middle of their set's second song and seemed oblivious to the fact that he missed singing the vast majority of the lyrics, as the crowd passed him hand-over-hand above their heads. If Jace had tried that crazy shit, he'd probably have been tossed on the cement and trampled to death. Security rescued Sed from the writhing crowd, and he eventually made his way back to the stage.

"Hell yeah. You crazy muthas know how to rock!" Sed cried into his microphone. "Who's here to see fucking Exodus End?" He thrust a fist in the air as the crowd erupted into cheers. He cleared his throat. Winced. Turned his volume down to a lower roar. "My throat's a bit sore tonight. Note to self, do not get into fights in strip clubs the night before a show, no matter how fucking hot the chick is."

The audience cheered Sed's debauchery. Jace couldn't help but smile. The more trouble Sinners got into, the more their fans loved them. Occasionally, they had to act like, well, sinners and maintain their mostly fabricated, dark image. They waited while Brian and Trey traded their usual electric guitars for acoustics to play their next song, "Good-bye Is Not Forever." This song always put a fucking knot in Jace's throat. It reminded him of Kara Sinclair. They'd had a secret relationship as teenagers. The more reckless, lawless, and out of control Jace had been, the more attracted to him she'd become. One reason he couldn't forget her was Kara was Brian's younger sister, or had been, before a car accident had taken her life. Brian had no idea that Jace had once dated her. Stolen her innocence. That was a secret he planned to keep to the grave. No reason to tarnish a man's pure and cherished memories of his perfect little sister.

Trey and Brian flanked the sides of the stage, sitting on platforms, as they strummed the intricate riff of the band's one and only ballad. Sed sat on the front of the stage, his legs dangling over the edge, and sang his heart out. Requisite knot in his throat, chills raced down Jace's spine at the sound of Sed's amazing voice.

The only one standing, Jace felt incredibly exposed. He took a deep breath, his fingers finding the thick, metal guitar strings and appropriate notes by memory. Concentrating on producing the perfect sound—which wasn't easy with his knuckles so swollen—he approached the front of the stage, standing between Sed and Trey. His eyes scanned the crowd, taking note of the sudden enthusiasm of several young women in the audience as he entered their view. Jace saluted a particularly excited twenty-something with two fingers, and she grabbed the hem of her T-shirt. She lifted both hands over her head, screaming at the top of her lungs, as she exposed her naked breasts to the band. Sed glanced up at Jace and grinned. Not to be outdone, Sed lifted his shirt and flashed a pair of hard pecs and his washboard abs to the Lady Sinners in the first few rows. The squeals of the women in the audience made Jace's ears ring, even over the music filtering in through his earpiece.

Sed tilted his head at Jace, as if to say, your turn. Jace shook his head and took several steps backward, his temporary desire to interact with the crowd completely obliterated. He kept in good shape, but was no match for Sed's body-builder physique. No sense in embarrassing himself in front of twelve thousand people.

By the time the concert ended, Jace's fingers refused to move, Trey could barely stand at all, Sed was singing at a whisper, and Brian was so distracted—by thoughts of his honeymoon, no doubt—that he walked offstage without removing his guitar. It produced a series of discordant sounds as he headed backstage at a run until a roadie managed to stop him long enough to claim the instrument from their eager lead guitarist. All things considered, Jace couldn't remember a worse performance. If the crowd noticed, you couldn't tell by their cheers and the chanting of "Sinners, Sinners, Sinners" ringing through the entire stadium.

"Wow, you all sucked," Eric commented as he tossed a drumstick into the crowd at the front of the stage.

Jace flicked his guitar pick to the flasher chick in the front row. When it landed in her outstretched hand, she drew it to her lips, kissed it, and then started jumping up and down.

"I think you have a fangirl, Jace," Sed commented, wiping the sweat off his face with the hem of his shirt. "Maybe you should invite her backstage. You look like you need a blow job."

Jace felt his ears turn red. That fangirl had nothing he needed, but a black-haired dominatrix dressed in leather did. Thinking about Mistress V and the needs she was about to fulfill forced Jace to adjust his fly behind his bass guitar.

"I know *I* need one," Sed added.

"I get to watch, right?" Eric asked.

"You know I perform best in front of an audience." Sed winked, took another bow, and headed offstage.

Jace handed his instrument to Jake, who carefully carried it to the collection of guitars along the side of the stage. Jace dug the black and red business card out of his pocket. Now he just had to find her address. Nothing short of death would prevent him from arriving on her doorstep at precisely ten p.m.

Chapter 4

AGGIE'S DOORBELL BUZZED AT five minutes to ten. She smiled. Lit another candle. Flicked her fingers through the flame. Made him wait.

The bell buzzed again, longer this time. Looking in the mirror that covered one entire wall of her dungeon's outer room, Aggie smoothed her long, straight hair with both hands. Checked her makeup. Ran her tongue over her teeth. Made him wait.

Buzz. Buzz-buzz. Buzzzz.

She stroked the handle of her favorite whip. Traced the floral design she'd embroidered on her leather corset. Glanced at the clock. Two minutes until ten. Not yet.

He laid on the buzzer. *Buzzzzzzzzzzzzzzzzzzzzzzzzzzzzzzzzzzzzz.*

Aggie chuckled.

She left the soundproof room and walked through the foyer to answer the door.

On her doorstep stood the tough angel she couldn't get out of her thoughts. His name was Jace. Jace Seymour. Jessica, Sed's ex-fiancée who had privilege to such information, had spilled that sweet tidbit to Aggie earlier that day. Yeah, Aggie had swallowed her tough bitch facade long enough to ask Jessica about a guy. Not her proudest moment. She didn't think Jess would tell anyone that she was interested in someone she shouldn't be.

Jace met her eyes and took a deep shuddering breath. "I thought I was late. That you wouldn't answer."

Just as cute as she remembered him. If he'd lose the piercings, spiked hair, and tattoos, he could have made a comfortable living as an Abercrombie and Fitch model. How did a guy this fine end up with a pain fetish? None of her business, she decided. She was just trying to make a living here. And hell, she might as well enjoy her work.

"Come in."

He entered. Glanced around, looking excited and anxious.

She took his hand and led him to the zebra print love seat just outside the open door of her sanctum: the room where men spent most of their time on their knees. Aggie and Jace sat side by side, inches separating their thighs. They needed to talk business so she knew what he wanted. How he wanted it. And for how long. Each customer was different. "What do you want me to call you, sugar?"

"Jace," he said.

"Is that short for Jason?"

He tensed, and a flash of deep emotional pain stole across his even features. "Never call me Jason. Never."

"Whatever you prefer. I'll call you dog, slut, slave, pussy, bastard, Batman, whatever you like."

He grinned and shifted his gaze to his hand, which rested on his knee. "Jace is fine."

That brief glimpse of his smile had her belly quivering. She'd never been this stupid over a guy before, especially not one of her submissives. What was wrong with her? She was going to hit him extra hard for making her want him.

She lifted her free hand and stroked the dark, rough beard stubble on his cheek, trying to get him to look at her. His mouth fell open, and he tilted his head in her direction, shuddering with contained desire. Oh fuck, yeah. She needed to get to work.

"Your safe word is *mercy*. Mercy, Mistress V."

"I don't need a safe word."

She bit her lip to hold back her snort of amusement. "I specialize in corporal punishment."

"That's why I'm here."

She decided this guy was into the kind of stuff she was too squeamish to perform. "There's something you should know before I start. I refuse to break the skin. I don't do hooks or barbed wire. I won't nail your nut sac to the floor. If you get off on that kind of thing, I have a couple colleagues I could refer you to, but I won't go that far, no matter how much you pay me."

He shook his head. "I just want you to hit me."

She laughed. "That I do. And do it well."

"Can we get started now?"

Yeah, they could. "Do you want me to restrain you?"

"No."

"Gagged, hooded, collared?"

"Just fuckin' hit me, okay? I don't want to talk about it."

She would make him regret that disrespect. "You pay half your tribute now. Half when we're finished."

"How much?"

"Two hundred for ten minutes."

"How much for two hours?"

Her eyes widened. "Two hours?"

He nodded curtly, avoiding her gaze.

"Sugar, I don't think—"

"How much?"

The longest she'd ever gone was forty minutes. He must not know what he was in for. Some dommes spent the majority of the session teasing, but she liked to get right down to business. Her theory was spare the whip and spoil the slave. She didn't tie guys up and leave them in the middle of the floor for two hours while she painted her fingernails, and then spanked them for three minutes before sending them home. She spanked first. Whipped second. If they made it that far. But if Jace wanted to pay her for two hours, she was more than happy to take his money. "Two grand." Hot guy discount.

He opened his wallet and retrieved ten crisp one-hundred-dollar bills.

She folded the cash and slid it into her leather bodice. "No refunds."

"Fine." He stood. "Where?"

A man of few words. She was really starting to like this guy.

"I want to make it clear that I'm not a prostitute. You aren't buying sex. I don't have sex with clients."

"I know how this works."

"Good." She climbed to her feet and took his hand. "Follow me."

She led him to the sanctum and slid the heavy door closed behind them. It clanged shut. She bolted it and checked the panic button to make sure it was functional. She'd never had to use it and doubted she would now, but even a girl who was an expert in self-defense and knew how to use a whip *might* need assistance from the police or a paramedic at some point.

Jace glanced around with interest. The room was perfectly square, with padding on three walls to muffle sound. The mirror on the fourth wall was for clients who liked to observe while she inflicted pain. If they didn't want to watch themselves cry and beg, she could slide the heavy, velvet curtain across it. There was a second room where she stored extra instruments and cleaned and sanitized the tools of her trade after each session.

Jace examined the implements on a table against one wall.

"Something there catch your fancy?" she asked.

"I'd like to try them all." He glanced at her over his shoulder, his brown eyes meeting hers unflinchingly. "Repeatedly, and in excess."

Aggie covered her surprise with a laugh. "You're going to regret giving me complete freedom, Jace. I'm known for my viciousness."

"I look forward to it."

He smiled, and her heart skipped a beat. My God, he was probably the cutest guy she'd ever encountered anyway, but when he smiled... She swallowed and gave herself a mental shake. She couldn't afford to be attracted to a client. Not even one who made her wet on sight.

"You ready to start?"

"Yes."

She stepped close to him, her nose inches from his. "Yes, Mistress V." Her voice was hard.

He shuddered, watching her through half-lowered lids. "Yes, Mistress V."

"Take your clothes off."

"All of them?"

She gritted her teeth and poked him in the center of his chest with one finger. "Don't question me. Never fucking question me. Understand?"

"Yes, Mistress."

He removed his leather coat, T-shirt, boots, and socks. Nice body. Lean with sculpted muscles. Decorated here and there with tattoos. She wished she had time to examine them more closely, but she had to pretend she held no regard for him. That he was insignificant. That he was privileged to get *any* attention from her. Even her abuse. *Especially* her abuse. It was one of the most important components of the game they played.

Jace hesitated, clutching the waistband of his jeans. "I don't wear underwear."

"What? You think I care about seeing your cock? Do you think it's special? That it might hold my interest?"

He trained his gaze on the floor. "No, Mistress."

"Then strip."

He took off his jeans. It turned out his cock was something special. Enormous. Beautiful. Thick. And hard as granite. Her pussy throbbed at the sight of it. Okay, so she *was* interested, but she couldn't let him know that.

"Do I excite you, Jace?" she asked with a sardonic grin. It had been a long time since she'd wanted to fuck a man. Any man. And she'd never wanted to fuck a client.

Until now.

"Yes, Mistress." He gasped. "You make me hard. Punish me."

"Down on your knees."

He hesitated. He didn't look at her when he said, "No."

"No?"

So he wanted to play. She did like a challenge. She rarely got one.

"I just want you to hurt me. I don't want to grovel or be humiliated." When he tilted his head to look at her, there was defiance in his eyes. Defiance? He wasn't a submissive? Then why was he here? What in the hell did he need her for?

She watched him struggle to repress his defiance and decided that he *did* want to submit. He just needed more encouragement than most. Her typical clients would already be crawling around on their hands and knees, begging for pain, and then crying for mercy.

"If you want me to hurt you, you'll do as I say," she said in a dangerous growl. She slid her hand over his lower back, and he tensed. She tried to ignore the thrill of excitement that trembled in her belly when she touched him. "And if you think you can talk to me without addressing me properly, I'm going to fucking gag you. You will *always* address me with respect. As Mistress V." She grabbed his nipple and twisted. What she really wanted to do was knock him off his feet and drive his massive cock into her pussy for about an hour. It was the look in his eye. The strength. So unlike what she was used to. It made it difficult for her to stay in her dominant character. Made her want to submit to him. And that was entirely unacceptable. Without even trying, he had managed to throw her off her game, and she didn't appreciate it. It pissed her off.

She gritted her teeth. "Don't look at me like that, Jace."

The defiance never left his eyes, but he lowered his gaze. To hide it. When she released his nipple, he took several deep breaths. "I apologize, Mistress V."

His unusual mix of strength and weakness drove her crazy.

"If you want to feel the bite of my whip, Jace, you'll get down on your knees."

Struggling with his pride, he dropped to his knees at her feet. He didn't look at her. Kept his eyes downcast. No doubt he was still hiding his defiance from her. She'd relieve him of it soon enough. She lifted her foot and pressed her spiked heel into his chest. "Kiss it."

Again he hesitated. This one would be so fun to break. She couldn't wait to get started.

She waited patiently. The minutes ticked by slowly. Her leg was getting tired by the time he pecked the sole of her boot. "Forgive me, Mistress V."

"Stand, Jace."

He stood. No hesitation there.

She grabbed a thick, red rope that was hooked to a ring in the wall. She pulled it out straight and handed it to him. He wrapped it around his left wrist and gripped the taut rope with a bruised left hand. She handed him a second rope affixed to the opposite wall. He wrapped that one around the black leather cuff on his right wrist and gripped the rope with his right hand. With his arms extended to the sides, it left his back exposed for her work, and gave her a wonderful view of his hot body. He wasn't tall, but had a perfect physique. Especially that tight little ass of his. Damn, her one major weakness when it came to men. A perfect ass. And it couldn't get any better than his. A gentle curve. Tender cheek. Slight indentation on the lateral sides. She could write sonnets about that ass, but he hadn't paid her to ogle his gorgeous naked body. She had work to do.

Aggie would start light and increase the intensity until she found his happy place. She didn't know his tolerance for pain and had to seek his threshold before she could do her real work. Finding his edge and driving him just beyond it. Not too far. Never too far. But taking him exactly where he wanted to be. Beyond pain. Where euphoria ruled.

Selecting a smooth, round, wooden paddle from her table, she moved to stand beside him. Their eyes met in the mirror.

"Have you been naughty, Jace? Do you need a spanking?" The musky scent of his excitement engulfed her, and her nipples tightened.

"Yes, Mistress V," he said breathlessly.

She dropped the Mistress V act for a moment to whisper to him. "Yell all you want, Jace. The room is soundproof. No one will hear you. I will hit you until you say, 'Mercy, Mistress V.' Do you understand?" She slapped his ass with the paddle, careful to make it sting, but not leave a bruise.

He didn't even flinch, much less yell.

"What do you say to get me to stop?" she prompted.

When he didn't respond, she rubbed her hand over his ass, his hip, his thigh. The firm muscle of his flank quivered beneath her touch. "Tell me, Jace, or I'm finished."

"I don't need a safe word."

She dropped her hand and stepped away. "Then I'm done. Put your clothes on."

"Mercy, Mistress V," he said.

She smiled to herself. She was starting to understand how this one ticked. She touched her paddle to his ass. "That's good. Say it again so you don't forget."

"Mercy, Mistress V," he whispered.

"Now don't say it unless you mean it. The second you say it, I promise to stop no matter how much I'm enjoying your agony."

He swallowed hard and nodded.

She struck his ass with her paddle, watching his reaction to determine when he was near his limit. Harder. In the same place.

Again. Again. She knew the sweet spot. That tender place on the buttocks that stung like the dickens when swatted. He glanced at her as if to ask her when she was going to start.

"You've been very naughty, haven't you?" she said, rubbing his ass with her bare hand. She usually did that to ease the sting so her client could take more pain, but in his case, she just really wanted to touch him.

"Hurt me, Mistress V. Please, hurt me."

She moved to something more vicious. She skipped the riding crop and selected the three short whips attached to a handle. She struck his back with a loud crack. Most guys would have cried out. Jace didn't even twitch. In the mirror, she saw his eyes were glazed with pain. Not physical pain. Emotional pain. Deep and scarring. Why did she have the sudden, ridiculous urge to hug him? She struck him harder. Harder. Harder than she normally would, watching the welts rise in threes on his skin. She didn't usually take a man this close to bloodletting. Why did he refuse to cry out or beg for mercy? Could he even feel pain?

Feeling twinges of frustration, she tossed the short whips aside and grabbed her bullwhip from the table. It cracked loudly as the tip snapped and left a red stripe along his side. A second strike wrapped around his body and left a welt on his belly. His thigh. His chest. His back again. He didn't react. Not once. The only indication that he felt anything was the occasional twitch above his left eye. He wasn't even gripping the ropes very tightly.

Where the fuck was this guy's threshold? She wasn't sure how much harder she could hit him. And the usual signs she recognized to help her locate a man's limit were all missing.

"Am I hurting you at all?"

"Not enough," he whispered. "Make me bleed."

She refused to make him bleed, but there were other things she could do to break him. And that's what he needed. He needed to be broken. She would drive him to his knees. Make him beg her to stop. He *would* submit to her, even if it took all night.

Mistress V tossed her whip aside and returned to the table. She blew out a candle. Tested the melted wax with her fingertips and jerked them back. Hot! She stared him in the face and splashed the wax up his chest and neck. "How's that?" she sputtered. "Did that hurt?"

"Do I make you angry, Mistress V?"

She'd never met a man she couldn't break, and yes, his silent suffering—his *stoicism*—angered her. He had to be in a lot of pain, but for all he showed, she might as well be tickling him with a feather.

"I'm not angry. I'm trying to figure out how to make you submit."

"No one ever has before," he told her, "but you're doing a fine job trying. Don't stop now."

"Don't patronize me."

"Do you have a flog? With knots?"

She flogged him, first with her nylon flog with its three dozen, foot-long, stinging strings. And then with her knotted leather flog that left his skin a mess of crisscrossed welts. He didn't flinch. Didn't protest. She took up a thick wooden rod and caned him more than a dozen times against his already raw back. Careful to avoid vital organs, such as his kidneys, she grunted with exertion as each strike landed between his shoulders. *Caned* him. She never resorted to such vicious caning. Didn't use the cane very often, as it wasn't usually necessary. And still he made no protest. She wasn't even enjoying this. The feeling of power that usually infused her when she served her slaves was nonexistent. Her temper flared.

He glanced at her over his shoulder. "If you're getting tired—"

"Shut up."

She took up her bullwhip again and vented her increasing frustration on his back. She wasn't even in her role as dominatrix as she cracked her whip. She just wanted him to cry out. Just once. Any indication that she was getting through to him would be appreciated. She needed that. To know she was in control. She didn't want to admit that she wasn't. Or that as long as she let him get to her, *he* was the one in control. She struck the backs of his thighs, realizing how much that fucking hurt, but he took it. He took it and calmly waited for her to continue.

"Damn it, Jace! Work with me." She struck him across the back again. An angry red stripe appeared. Not a welt. Blood.

He gasped softly.

Aggie dropped her whip. She prided herself as a professional in causing all the pain, but never drawing blood. What she'd done to him hadn't been professional. She'd been frustrated. *Angry.* She'd never become angry during a session before. Of course, she'd never met a man she couldn't break in ten minutes or whose threshold for pain was this far above normal. Maybe he was juiced-up on painkillers or something. He didn't look stoned, but she couldn't think of any other plausible reason for him to accept so much pain so easily. Aggie paused behind Jace, gently touching the raw skin above the bleeding gash that ran diagonally from shoulder to spine.

"I'm so sorry, Jace. I didn't mean…"

"Thank you, Mistress V, may I have another?"

"No." She shook her head vigorously. "*No!* Your session's over."

"I paid for two hours."

"Then I'll give your money back."

"You said no refunds."

She circled his body to face him and stared into his eyes. Never had she seen so much pain in a man so young. He wasn't using her for release. He was taking her abuse and internalizing it, adding it to what already existed and building upon the ache inside him. She knew he'd felt every lash of her whip. Knew she had hurt him far more than he'd been letting on. Why did he refuse to crumble? She didn't get it.

"Whatever it is that's eating you alive, you have to let it go," she murmured, stroking his brow, his stubble-rough cheek, and his angled jaw with tender fingertips. "Let it go, Jace."

His jaw set. He shook his head slightly. "I'd rather be gutted alive."

Her hand still cupping the side of his face, she tilted her head and eased closer until a fraction of an inch separated their lips. She shouldn't kiss him. She wanted to, but... Leaning away slightly, her eyes searched his. As much as she wanted him physically, it was more important to help him. Take that anguished shadow from his gaze. Take it away.

Take it.

Her lips brushed his, light as a feather. He shuddered, emitting a huff of air, and his lips parted to coax her closer for a deeper kiss. She devoured his mouth, intoxicated by his taste, his scent. A deep longing hollowed her core, leaving her empty and wanting. She pressed her leather-clad bosom against his hard chest, her free hand circling his back to press him closer. The stickiness of his blood against her fingertips reminded her of what she'd done to him.

She pulled away, knowing that kiss had been all her idea. She couldn't lay any of the blame on him. He was still holding on to the ropes, his fists tight and knuckles white.

"I want you, Mistress V," he growled.

Her lips parted, her nipples tightened, and her pussy swelled until it throbbed relentlessly. She wanted him too, but she never had sex with clients. She sighed with remorse. "The name's Aggie." She uncoiled the rope from his right wrist, and he released his grip. "Let's go take care of that wound."

"It's nothing," he insisted. "Finish me."

"It is something, and I am *finished* with you. You paid for professional treatment, and I got carried away. I apologize for breaking your trust. I drew blood. That is unacceptable."

"I don't think so, but fine. If you're not into this, I'll go." He released the second rope and moved to the edge of the room to find his clothes.

She didn't want him to go. His cock still stood at full attention. She wanted him inside her. Inside Aggie, not Mistress V, but it was Mistress V he wanted. He'd said so himself.

Before he could slide into his pants, she took his hand and yanked him toward the bolted door.

"You're not going anywhere until I dress that cut," she said.

He didn't protest, allowing her to open the door and lead him through the foyer to a second part of her domicile—her private living quarters. She'd never brought a client into her personal home before, but now that their business transaction was over, she wasn't thinking of him as a client. She tapped a code into the lock's keypad and pushed open the reinforced door that separated her home from her dungeon.

After securing the door behind them, she led Jace to her bedroom and urged him to sit on the edge of her bed while she went to the connecting bathroom for antibiotic ointment, bandages, and… a condom. She slid the condom into her bodice and found the cash he'd given her still there. She pulled the thousand dollars out, tossed it into the sink, and carried the first-aid supplies back to her bedroom. She found Jace where she'd left him, with his eyes closed, breathing deeply through his nose. His cock grew softer with each exhalation.

"What are you doing?" she asked.

He started and turned his head to look at her standing in the doorway. As his gaze drifted over her body, his cock grew stiff again. Good. She wanted it hard. Hard and uncomfortable, so she could soothe him with her flesh. And he could take care of that deep ache between her thighs.

"I'm trying to calm down." Jace grabbed his cock in one hand and flinched, sucking a breath through clenched teeth. He was probably already too excited to be any good, but that didn't stop her from wanting to take that huge cock of his deep. And hard.

"You don't want to fuck me?"

"You don't fuck clients," he reminded her.

"True. Mistress V never fucks her clients." She climbed up onto the bed behind him. He watched her over his shoulder as she applied antibiotic ointment and a few bandages in places that were still seeping blood. She hoped it didn't scar. He had such a beautiful body. She'd hate to think she'd caused it permanent damage. She pressed a kiss to his skin, just above the gash. "I told you, your session is over. If you want to fuck Mistress V, she's off duty, but if you want to fuck Aggie, she's willing."

She slid her arms around his body, loving the solid feel of his hard pecs and rippled abs beneath her palms. He had the sexiest strip of hair running down the center of his lower belly. She enjoyed the coarse texture against her fingertips while she sucked his earlobe and the silver earring that decorated it into her mouth. Ears. Another weakness of hers.

"Aggie," he whispered.

The sound of her name on his lips wrapped around her heart and squeezed. She shouldn't get tangled up with this one. She could already tell she'd be sad to see him go, whether he left in thirty minutes, thirty days, or thirty years. Damn it anyway. She had a soft spot for these tragic, quiet types. And a defiant submissive? Good lord, how was she supposed to resist that combination? She almost hoped he sucked in bed. That he was a minute man who climbed on top of her, thrust into her twice, and came with some stupid look on his face. It would make it easier to discard him. She had no use for a man. Any man. Not even this one, who seemed custom-made to her specifications.

Aggie released his earlobe, and he turned, crawling up on the bed to face her. He tugged her against him and kissed her, sucking on her lips with tender abandon. If he fucked half as good as he kissed, she was done for. She clung to his ruined back, opening her mouth to accept his exploratory tongue. He didn't probe and thrust like some uncouth animal. He stroked and caressed her lips and mouth so tenderly it made her heart swell. While he kissed her, his fingers methodically worked at the clasps on the back of her leather bustier. Unhurried, he released the fastenings one by one, his fingertips brushing every inch of her spine as they moved downward. He loosened the garment until nothing held it in place but the proximity of their intertwined bodies.

His fingers found the smooth skin of her back. They dug into her flesh as he ground her body against his and then his touch softened, gently stroking, coaxing a soft sigh from her throat. He eased her onto her back, robbing her mouth of his, as he lifted his head to look down at her.

"Your beauty steals my breath," he murmured.

"Your kiss steals mine."

He smiled and cupped her face in both hands. He kissed her cheeks, the tip of her nose, her eager lips. She spread her thighs for him, and he settled between them. One strong hand moved to the margin where the leather of her boot ended and the flesh of her thigh began. His mouth moved over her chin to her throat, where he suckled and kissed her sensitive flesh until she thought she might cry from the care he showed her.

He shifted onto one elbow and peeled her bustier from her body. He tossed the stiff garment aside, found the condom resting between her breasts, and grinned crookedly. "What's this?"

Her heart thudded. That smile of his. If she hadn't already been utterly seduced by the man, that would have done it.

Jace slid the condom into the top of her thigh-high boot. Her nipples pebbled beneath his heavy gaze. He didn't touch or kiss her excited flesh, only stared as if in utter awe. She felt like the most beautiful woman in the world at that moment. And then he slid down her body to suck her nipple into his mouth.

She gasped, her fingers stealing into his spiked blond hair. She held him to her breast. Her back arched and she shuddered with pleasure. His hand moved to her free breast, and he cupped it gently, caressing the nipple with his thumb. He used a rhythm that matched the strokes of his tongue. No awkward plucking and brutal squeezing from this guy. The man knew how to please a breast.

"Jace," she murmured. "Jace."

She squirmed, wriggling her hips from side to side, wanting him to fill her body with his. His shaft brushed the inside of her thigh, and she cried out.

Oh God, Jace. Take me.

She was ready for him. Probably had been the moment she'd noticed him striding across the room back at the club. He lifted his head, blessed her with a gentle smile, and then shifted his head to take her other breast in his hot mouth. He sucked hard, and then rubbed the flat of his tongue against her budded nipple. Sucked hard again. Rubbed. Sucked. She quivered beneath him, the throbbing ache between her thighs unbearable.

"Jace," she cried desperately.

His hands slid over her rib cage, and he moved down her body, trailing tender kisses down the center of her belly. He made love to her navel with his tongue until she thought she'd explode. Sliding farther down, he shifted until his face was even with her crotch. Her thighs trembled in anticipation. He must smell her sex and feel the heat coming from it. She was so hot. So wet.

Waiting.

Wanting.

"Jace, please."

"Shhh, Aggie. Don't rush it."

He lowered his head and kissed the inner surface of her thigh.

She gasped, her pussy clenching, so close to release she knew she'd explode the second he finally possessed her. But he didn't claim her. He kissed a trail down the inside of her thigh. When his mouth reached the top of her boot, he fished the condom out and tucked it inside her other boot. He then started his slow journey down her leg. Unzipping her boot as he went, his lips and tongue forged a gentle path of pleasure from thigh to toe. When he finished, her boot lay discarded somewhere on the floor, and she was clinging to the bedclothes.

"Jace, you're driving me crazy."

He chuckled. She loved the sound of his laugh. Deep and rich. Happy. Could a man so consumed by pain feel happiness?

She lifted her head and gazed down at him as he crawled his way up her body to work on her other leg. He was smiling to himself as he pulled the condom from her remaining boot and tucked it into her panties, as if to say, this is next on my list of things to pleasure with my sinful mouth. Her breath came out in an excited huff.

Yes, Jace. There. She couldn't wait. Couldn't wait to feel his tongue against her clit. Stroking her fluid-drenched lips. Writhing in her pussy. *Oh! Please, hurry.*

He worked his way down her other leg, his beard stubble rough against the inside of her thigh. He soothed the rawness left behind with tender kisses. She was panting and thrashing with excitement when he moved back up her body. He ran his finger under the elastic of her black satin panties. She shuddered.

The condom tumbled free over her hip and landed somewhere on the bed beside her. He took it between two fingers and inserted it into her mouth. She fought the urge to bite into it, not wanting to compromise its integrity and have it break when he finally opened the package, unrolled the condom over his massive cock, and thrust into her. Her back arched at the thought of him inside her. Filling her. Pounding her. *Oh God, Jace, I need you. Inside me. Immediately.*

He slid her panties off, his hands skimming her thighs, the backs of her knees, calves, and ankles. He tossed the undergarment aside and spread her legs wide. Cool air bathed Aggie's hot, aching flesh. His warm breath stirred against her wet skin. She groaned.

She was glad she'd waxed every bit of her pubic hair when he drew one exposed and swollen labium into his mouth, sucking until she thought she'd go mad, sliding his wicked tongue over the slick inner surface until her hips bucked. He suckled his way to her mound. His tongue brushed the hood of skin that covered her clit, and she cried out in delirious torment. He suckled her other swollen lip, swirled his tongue in the empty, wet well between them much too briefly, and scraped his stubble-rough chin over her tender asshole. He plunged his tongue inside the puckered orifice and then slid it up to bury it inside her throbbing pussy. Her mouth fell open, the condom sliding from between her lips and down her face.

"Jace, Jace!" She grabbed his hair, yanking upward hard.

He shuddered and then fucked her with his tongue, thrusting it as deep as possible and withdrawing, before thrusting inside again. He slid the tip of one finger in her ass, removed his tongue from her pussy, and replaced it with two fingers on the same hand. Her body strained against his hand as he burrowed his fingers deeper, deeper, wriggling them inside her, spreading her wide. And then, he sucked her clit into his mouth.

She exploded with ripples of unparalleled delight.

"Yes, yes, yes!" she screamed as he sucked her clit, his tongue stroking the engorged flesh, his fingers writhing inside her clenching pussy and her delighted asshole.

Too quickly, he pulled away and moved up her body until they were face-to-face. He licked her juices off his fingers, murmuring delighted sounds in the back of his throat.

He retrieved the condom from near her shoulder and tore it open with his teeth. He lowered his head and kissed her, before rolling onto his side to apply the condom. It was too small. He struggled to stretch it over his thick shaft, biting his lip with concentration—should have brought him a Magnum. She'd been with only one other guy who needed them, but that had been years ago. She knew she didn't have one on hand.

He used his hand to guide himself into her body, and every concern vanished.

His strokes began shallow as he wet his cock with her juices and allowed her to grow accustomed to its glorious thickness. When he finally possessed her completely, she arched her back to take him even deeper. Ah God, she'd never felt so deliciously full in her life.

"You're beautiful," he murmured, brushing his lips against hers. "Your body—*bliss*."

She didn't know how he managed to make her feel so loved. *Love?* Now there's a sentiment she didn't typically consider when a guy was between her thighs.

Jace pulled back slowly and thrust forward again. He watched her closely. Seemed to be gauging her responses to determine what she liked. It was as if his own pleasure didn't matter to him—only hers. Jace's rhythm, relentless and perfect, tugged her willingly up the slope toward release, spiraling closer to nirvana. His deep strokes were neither too slow, nor too fast. Just right. And deep. Oh so deep.

Once he found her rhythm, he kissed her neck while he made love to her, brushed the backs of his hands over her skin, rubbed her nipples between his thumb and forefinger, and drove her utterly mad with desire. She'd never known a guy to continue with foreplay throughout the entire experience. Jace worked every pleasure point on her body as he moved within her. Going so far as to rub his big toe over the instep of her foot every so often, after he discovered it made her shudder with unexpected delight. She closed her eyes and let him have complete control. She'd never given her power to a man so effortlessly. She always struggled with this, but not with Jace. Why? She was too delirious to consider the reason.

After a long while of inflicting his perfect pleasure, Jace's breath hitched, and Aggie opened her eyes to find him biting his lip. "I waited too long," he gasped. "Can I come now?"

He was *asking* her?

"Yeah, go ahead." He'd more than earned his release.

It was as if something inside him snapped. He tore into her like an animal. He wrapped his arms around the backs of her thighs and folded her in half. He fucked her hard, driving his thick cock into her body. She cried out, unable to distinguish between pleasure and pain, knowing only that she loved it and didn't want him to stop. She liked the harsh contrast of being fucked after the considerate, tender lovemaking he'd showed her before.

"Yes, Jace!" she screamed. "Fuck me."

"Hurt me," he countered.

Aggie's nails dug into his chest. He groaned.

She drew her hands down, leaving eight parallel scratches down his chest. He shuddered, his head tilting to the side, his mouth falling open in ecstasy. "God, yes," he growled.

She grabbed his nipple, twisting viciously.

He lowered his head to kiss her. She bit his lip until she tasted his blood. He didn't resist her cruelty, but rose up on his knees so he could fuck her harder.

She cried out, close to orgasm.

His lip now free of her bite, he lifted his head and looked down at her. "Do you want to come hard?"

Well, of course she did. What kind of a question was that?

"Yes, Jace. Make me come hard."

"Don't take your eyes off mine."

He continued to thrust into her, driving her closer to the edge.

She stared at him, lost in his intense gaze. He watched her as if looking for the exact moment to let go and join her in bliss.

She felt a connection to him—deeply personal, more than sex. More than she wanted to experience with some guy she scarcely knew. Her heart thudded hard in her chest. For a short instant, he let her see him. That internal part of his troubled psyche he hid from the world. Her breath caught, and she held it even after her lungs began to sting in protest.

Unexpectedly, her womb contracted. A spasm gripped her pussy. Ripples of release sent her body into convulsions, and she couldn't keep her eyes open any longer.

Oh God, she was coming. And coming. And coming. He pumped into her harder. "Aggie, hurt me. I need…"

The instant she dug her fingers into his raw back, his body shuddered against hers as he spent himself inside her. He rubbed his face against the hollow of her neck as he called out. They clung to each other, bodies writhing in mutual bliss.

He paused and lifted his head. His voice sounded distant. "Breathe, baby. Take a breath."

Breathe? What did he mean?

"Aggie!" He shook her by both shoulders.

She gasped, glorious air filling her stinging lungs, and came again. Came even harder than when that first orgasm had gripped her in that intense moment of personal connection she didn't quite understand. Aggie cried out, rocking her hips to work against his softening cock. Her entire body writhed with ecstasy, twisting her into an involuntary spasm of delight.

That had been fucking amazing.

When her body stilled, Jace moved his arms from the backs of her thighs so she could stretch her legs out straight. He rubbed her hips to alleviate the ache, and then cupped her face in both hands to gently kiss her lips.

"You okay?" he whispered. He rubbed the tip of his nose against her cheek, his lips tickling the skin near her ear. "I think you forgot how to breathe there for a second."

"I'm more than okay," she said deliriously. "What *was* that?"

"What?" He rubbed his lips over her jaw.

"I can't explain it. I don't know if it was how hard you were fucking me or the way you were looking at me or something else. It was…"

"Exciting?"

"Exciting? That was fucking unbelievable. Do it again, please."

He lifted his head and stared down into her eyes. He looked utterly stunned. "You don't hate me now?"

"How could I hate you after that? I've never experienced anything like it in my life. It was wonderful."

"Even though I couldn't come until you hurt me?"

"If that's what you need to get off, I'm perfectly fine with it."

He smiled. "This is usually the part where the woman calls me a sick bastard, grabs her clothes, and runs out of the room naked without a backwards glance."

"I'm not running."

His smile widened, causing her heart to stutter stupidly in her chest. "I noticed. Will you whip me again? I'll take it better now that I'm not so sexually frustrated."

She grinned. "I'd be happy to. Will you fuck me again when you've had enough pain?"

He kissed her and pulled out. "If I'm still capable of moving."

He stripped the condom from his cock, glanced around the room, and got out of bed to dispose of it in the small trash can near her desk. She dragged herself from the bed, not ready to shake the afterglow still coursing through her body.

She sighed and reached for her panties.

"You're getting dressed?" he asked.

"Don't you want me to whip you again?"

"Yeah, I want *you* to whip me—Aggie, not Mistress V. I want you naked. I want the body I'm learning to please exposed while you hurt me."

"I can't, Jace. I'm not capable of hurting you as myself. I have to be in the domme role."

He cocked an eyebrow at her and ran his hand down the scratches on his chest. "Oh really?"

She ducked her head. She had hurt him. And something about it excited her. "This is usually the part where the man calls me a crazy bitch, grabs his clothes, and runs out of the room naked without a backwards glance."

"I'm not running." He held a hand out, and she crossed the room to take it.

He led her through her home, back into the foyer, and into the soundproof room. A cell phone was beeping in Jace's pile of clothes. He had a voice mail. His brow furrowed. "Who could that be? No one ever calls me."

He retrieved his phone from his leather jacket and listened to his message. She watched his expression change from confusion to horror. He reached for his clothes and started to dress.

"Sorry, but I have to go."

"Is something wrong?"

"Trey's in the hospital."

"Trey?"

"Sinners' rhythm guitarist."

"Is it something serious?"

He stomped his foot into one boot. "Yeah, sounds like it. Head injury. Can I see you again?"

She crossed her arms over her naked breasts. "If you have an appointment."

"Tomorrow night? Same time?"

"I have another client scheduled for ten tomorrow."

His entire body jerked, the way it should have responded when she whipped him. "Oh," he murmured breathlessly.

"How about five in the evening?"

His smile rivaled the sun in its brilliance. "Even better."

She tried to hide a grin, but failed. "I'll pencil you in."

Chapter 5

IF THE WAITING DIDN'T kill Jace, the dark cloud of doom surrounding Dare Mills just might. The long hair and leather identified him as the infamous rock star he was, but the worry twisting his face with concern was a staunch reminder that he was only human and an utter wreck over his little brother's hospitalization. It was almost five a.m. Trey had been out of a successful surgery for a few hours now, but he was still sleeping off the anesthesia.

"Why won't they let us in to see him?" Dare asked for the twentieth time. "I just want to see him."

"He needs his rest," Eric said. "That's all." He produced a lion-sized yawn and scrubbed his face with both hands.

"It's not like I'm going to yank him out of the hospital bed and take him for a cruise down the Vegas strip. I just want to see him. To know he's still fucking breathing."

Jace patted the back of Dare's hand. He understood all too well what Dare was feeling. Not that he could express it. Every time he opened his mouth to tell Dare how it had felt to sit in a hospital waiting room while a loved one's life was in the hands of strangers, the white walls seemed to close in on him, and a paralyzing anguish stole his breath. None of his experiences with hospital waiting rooms had ended well. Dare didn't need to hear that, and Jace didn't want to revisit it, so he just patted the back of Dare's hand every so often, hoping that he somehow realized that Jace was there to support him. He owed Dare his success—his entire livelihood.

None of the guys knew how Dare had helped him become a part of Sinners. It had been Dare who had arranged Jace's audition with the band. Dare who had talked Trey into having the Sinners' original bassist, Jon, fired for drug abuse. Dare who had invented that bullshit story about Jace being considered as a replacement for Logan—Exodus End's bassist. Logan had never considered quitting Exodus End. It had been a setup. Dare claimed to have intervened because it was best for his little brother's band. The dude had a strong protective instinct when it came to Trey. Jace wondered if Trey realized how much his older brother cared about him, and how it would feel to have someone love you that much.

"I'm about to crash," Eric said. "When is Brian supposed to get here and give us a break?"

"In a few hours," Jace said.

"You can go, Eric," Dare said. "You've done enough for him."

Eric smiled and then jumped to his feet. "I'm not pussing out now. Who needs coffee?"

"Yeah," Dare said absently.

"I'll take a cup," Jace said. He expected Eric to twist his words into a barb, but he headed out of the room to find another dose of caffeine. Jace decided Eric must be completely exhausted if he'd given up on wisecracks.

"I didn't talk to him about Brian," Dare said.

Jace looked at him in question. "What about Brian?"

"I should have talked to him. I should have checked on him to make sure he was okay."

Another thing Jace completely understood. A case of the "should haves." *I should have ridden the bus to school that day. I should have pushed Kara away. I should have never climbed out that window. I should have never been born.*

"I should have talked him into going to the doctor sooner," Dare said.

"We tried to talk him into going to the doctor, Dare," Jace said.

"But he listens to me." Dare stroked his eyebrow with his middle finger. "Sometimes."

"We should have insisted. We knew he was hurt," Jace said.

More should haves.

Eric returned with three Styrofoam cups between his long fingers. "What are you two grumbling about?" He handed a cup to Dare and then one to Jace, before taking a sip from his own.

"We should have gotten Trey help sooner," Dare said.

"Well, we didn't. Now we have to deal with the consequences. No sense in beating yourself up over things you can't change. You have to make the best of the current situation," Eric said.

"The current situation blows," Dare said.

Jace patted Dare's hand again. He understood. He still beat himself up over things he couldn't change years after they occurred. He couldn't imagine ever letting that guilt go.

Chapter 6

Obnoxious pounding on Aggie's front door woke her before noon. She grabbed a pillow and buried her head beneath it. It muffled the persistent knocking, but not enough to let her go back to sleep. When the pounding intensified, she huffed loudly, kicked her covers aside, slipped a robe over her naked body, and stormed to the front door. Her mother stood on the threshold, glancing over her shoulder nervously.

"What are you doing here?" Aggie asked.

Mom pushed her way over the threshold, slammed the door behind her, and locked it. "I'm staying here for a few days. You got coffee?" She eyed the open door of the soundproof room where Aggie worked over her clients. It had stood empty since Jace had left the night before.

Aggie took Mom's elbow and led her through the connecting foyer into the living room. She continued through the family room to the kitchen, which was separated from the large, open room by a breakfast bar. "Why do you need to stay here? What did you do now?"

"Some men are looking for me. No big deal—just better if they don't find me. Mind if I smoke?"

Mom reached into her purse and pulled out a pack of cigarettes. She thumped one out of the pack and put it between her bright pink lips.

"Actually, I do mind. Go smoke outside. I'll put on coffee."

Mom glanced over her shoulder toward the closed front door.

"I need to quit anyway." She put the cigarette back in the pack and went to close the reinforced door that separated the living room from the foyer. Aggie usually left it open, unless she was expecting a client, but if it made her paranoid mother feel better, she'd keep it closed for added security.

Mom followed Aggie to the kitchen and perched herself on a stool at the breakfast bar. Yawning, Aggie started a pot of coffee brewing and leaned against the counter across from her mother.

"What's with you?" Mom asked. "You get laid or something?"

"Huh?" How on earth would her mother know that?

"You're walking all bowlegged."

"Shut up," Aggie said. "I am not."

"If you say so." Mom gave her an appraising look, reached into her purse, and retrieved her pack of cigarettes again. "Men. Jackasses. All of them."

Normally, Aggie would agree, but she'd found one last night she kind of liked. One who apparently made her walk bowlegged. "They're not all bad."

Mom thumped another cigarette out of the pack, put it between her lips, and lit it. "Shit, you found a man, didn't you?"

Aggie shrugged. "Not really."

Mom took a deep drag off her cigarette, smoke curling around her head as it floated to the ceiling. Aggie really wished she wouldn't smoke in her house, but with this woman there were so many battles, Aggie had to pick the ones she was willing to fight.

"Not *really*?" Mom lifted her penciled eyebrows at her. "What's his name? Is he nice?"

"There's no guy, Mom." Aggie said, shaking her head. She was unwilling to tell her mother anything about Jace. Not even his name. She wouldn't describe how attractive she found him or how his rare laugh warmed her heart. And would especially never mention how he fulfilled her sexually in a way no other man ever had. She knew if she confided even the tiniest detail, her mother would point out everything negative, until Aggie lost sight of how wonderful he was. Mom always did that.

"So what's going on with you?" Aggie asked. Mom never showed up unless she needed something. Even when Aggie had been a kid, her mother had been more absent from her life than present. The woman was always chasing one unlikely dream or another. Having a kid had never been a dream—more of a burden. She was far more likely to run from her parenting obligations than embrace them. Aggie had come to terms with that years ago.

The coffee pot gurgled as it spewed the last of the brew into the carafe. The heady aroma of strong coffee perfumed the cozy kitchen. Aggie turned to fill two mugs. She shoveled several spoonfuls of sugar into her mother's cup, taking her own black.

Her mother accepted the mug between her bony hands and took a sip. "I had this great idea to finally get you out of that strip club."

Aggie rolled her eyes. "How many times do I have to tell you? I like working there. I don't dance because I have to. I dance because I *want* to."

"Don't be ridiculous, Agatha." She shook her head dismissively. "I bought a book on the Internet."

"A book? What kind of book?"

"On how to win at slots. Guaranteed."

"You didn't."

"Yeah. And I tried out the method." She smiled brightly. "I won a couple grand."

"That's great. You can pay down your credit cards."

Mom took another drag off her cigarette. Slurped some coffee. Took her time about getting to the point. "So I thought if I can start with fifty bucks and make two thousand, then if I start with fifty thousand, I could make two million." She pointed her cigarette at Aggie and offered her a wink. "I was always good at math."

Aggie's heart sank. "What did you do, Mom?"

"Well, what do you think? I took out a loan and went to the casino. I kept thinking I would get ahead. I followed the book to the letter."

Oh shit. "How much did you lose?"

Mom stared at the glowing tip of her cigarette. "Well, after I lost the first fifty grand—"

"Fifty grand!"

"I borrowed another fifty and…" She shrugged, took the last drag off her cigarette, and finding no available ashtray, crushed it on Aggie's granite countertop.

"You lost a hundred thousand dollars in slots!"

"Oh, no no no no no," Mom said, shaking her head vigorously.

Aggie sucked in a deep breath of relief.

"I only lost fifty grand in slots. The other fifty I lost at roulette." She smiled sweet as syrup.

"What is *wrong* with you?" Aggie shouted.

"I wanted to get you out of that club, sugar. That's all."

"*Mother!* Don't you dare try to make this my fault." Aggie rubbed her face with both hands. She had a few thousand dollars in the bank and another grand in the sink in her master bathroom, but she'd just remodeled this house for her side business, so her liquid assets were minimal. No way could she come up with a hundred grand to pay off that loan. "Wait a minute." She pinned her mother with a hard stare. "Who in the hell would loan *you* money? Your credit is shit."

Mom shrugged, twisting her garish red hair around one finger. "Oh, some guys."

"Some guys?"

She scrunched her eyebrows together and pursed her lips. "I think they're members of the Mafia," she whispered and glanced over her shoulder, as if expecting to see them standing behind her with sandy shovels.

"*What?*"

Mom flinched. "Don't you yell at me, young lady!"

Aggie paced the galley area of the kitchen, chewing on the end of her finger. "When are you supposed to pay them back?"

"Soon."

"How soon?"

Mom cringed. "I do not like your tone, Agatha. Don't forget who you're talking to. If it wasn't for me, you wouldn't even exist."

"How soon?"

"Three weeks ago." She tapped another cigarette out of the pack and lit it.

Aggie found it impossible to close her mouth. Or breathe. "And you tell me this *now?*" she sputtered finally.

"I know how busy you are. I didn't want to bother you with my little problems."

And now Aggie was hyperventilating. "Little! I suppose you owe them interest as well."

"Of course. Who gives loans without charging interest?" Mom said and took a deep drag off cigarette number two. She pulled the butt from her mouth and stared at its glowing ember as she slowly exhaled and drew smoke into both nostrils.

"How much?"

"Twenty percent."

"Annually?"

Mom laughed, a billow of smoke erupting from her mouth. She lifted her blue-eyed gaze to Aggie's. "They don't do annual loans, sugar. I really thought I'd be a high roller right now, with no problem paying everything back and setting up both of us for life—somewhere other than Vegas. I'm tired of Vegas. Aren't you?" She shrugged and took another drag off her cigarette. "How do you feel about Tahiti?"

"They're going to kill you, you stupid woman."

"How are they going to get their money out of a dead body? I'll figure something out. I always do. But until then, I don't want them to know where I am, so I'm visiting for a while. Okay?"

No, it wasn't okay, but what could she do? This was her mother—her ridiculous, stupid, exasperating mother. If she didn't love her so much, she'd strangle her.

And then she had that little problem of Jace coming over that evening. How was Aggie going to hide him from the nosy woman? The last person on earth she wanted to introduce him to was her mother.

Chapter 7

JACE RANG AGGIE'S DOORBELL precisely at five. He stuffed his guilt trip to the back of his mind. He should be visiting Trey in the hospital, not seeking hot, all-encompassing sex from the most desirable woman on the planet. Trey had woken a few hours ago, but he wasn't back to normal just yet. He'd lost much of the mobility in both hands. Jace wasn't sure how to deal with that. He just needed to get Aggie out of his system one more time, and he'd be fine. With her help, he could concentrate on something other than the ache in his soul that was already building again. The matching ache in his groin was only a minor consideration.

The middle-aged, red-headed woman who answered the door looked him up and down suspiciously.

"What do you want with me?" she growled. Her eyes were the same cerulean blue as Aggie's, but this tough-looking broad was no Aggie.

"Uh…" Thrown off his guard, Jace had lost his tongue.

"I ain't got it yet, Maynard. Keep your dick in your pants."

She slammed the door in his face.

Jace scratched his head. Checked the house number to assure himself this was Aggie's house.

Who?

What?

The door opened again. Lovely Aggie appeared wearing her leather dominatrix costume. The embroidered design on the corset was different. Last night it had been red roses. Today it had mint green humming birds.

Aggie rolled her eyes at Jace. "Sorry about that. My mother is visiting. Unexpectedly. Against my will. And better judgment."

That half hard-on he'd been sporting most of the day shriveled. "Your mother?"

"You're just a client." She gave him a stern look.

Just a client. So that incredible intimacy they'd shared the night before, that connection he'd never experienced with anyone, hadn't meant anything to her? Why did that thought cut into his heart? It wasn't as if he gave a shit. He didn't. He didn't give a shit about anything but his music. It was the only thing in his life that never let him down.

Aggie took his hand and led him toward the soundproof room where she'd whipped him so spectacularly the night before. And drawn blood. He shuddered at the memory.

"You know him?" Aggie's mother stood in the foyer with her arms crossed over her chest, watching her daughter with disapproval.

"I told you I had a five o'clock appointment. Go back into the house."

"I don't trust him, Agatha. He looks suspicious. Like a member of the Mafia."

Mafia? Probably the leather jacket. Jace hurried into the room where Aggie served her clients.

"He's not Mafia. Go away, Mother." Aggie slid the sanctum's door closed behind her and bolted it. She turned to face Jace. "Sorry about that. She has… *issues*." She fluttered a hand.

Jace shrugged and looked at the floor. He wanted to leave. He couldn't do this with her mother in the house, especially not after the woman had told him to keep his dick in his pants. The sole reason he was here was to put his dick in her daughter. Repeatedly and in excess.

"I should go," he said quietly.

Aggie moved to stand directly in front of him. Her large, succulent breasts entered his line of sight. He licked his lips. His cock stirred in his pants. This woman was positively luscious and chased every thought from his head. She cupped his face in both hands and eased his gaze up to hers. "What's the matter?"

"Trey…"

"The guitarist in the hospital?"

He nodded. "I should go visit him."

"How's he doing?"

"He made it through surgery, and he's awake now. I should be with him."

"So he's okay then?"

Jace shook his head slightly. "He can't move his fingers right, or something."

"You can go see him later. He's probably resting."

"Yeah." Jace lowered his eyes to her full, ruby red lips. "Resting." He stared at her lips, mesmerized by their sensuality. "Can I kiss you?" His hands moved to rest on the flare of her hips. He shifted her closer.

"Are you staying for a while?"

He nodded. Even if he was just her customer today, he still wanted to be with her.

"Then, yes. Kiss me, Jace." She said his name like a gentle caress. It made his heart ache.

Don't pretend you care. Just don't.

He brushed his lips over hers. Her lips were soft. Yielding. He kissed her again. More deeply. He leaned away and looked into her eyes.

"I thought about you a lot today," she murmured, wiping at the corner of his mouth with her thumb. He was probably wearing half her lipstick now.

He smiled. It felt natural to smile when he was with her. He never felt that way with anyone. He always felt on guard, but not with her. With her he felt... safe? Comfortable? Understood? Something. "Oh, yeah?"

She nodded. "Did you think of me?"

"Constantly."

She tugged his shirt over his head and bent to press her lips to his collarbone.

"I'm afraid to look at your back. Are you sore?" Her fingers trailed gently over his skin.

He'd had a hard time crawling out of bed that afternoon, but he was ready for more now. "Not really. You're not going to take it easy on me, are you?"

"Whatever you want, baby. You'll do the same for me, won't you?"

She wouldn't ask him to hit her, would she? He didn't have it in him.

"What did you have in mind?" he asked.

"Whatever you want to do to me—I trust you."

Jace's heart stumbled over a beat. She'd give him the freedom to do whatever he wanted to her? He needed to get her to the tour bus. His suitcase of pleasure-inducing implements was stored in a closet there. He'd been collecting things to inflict pleasure on a deserving lover for years. And every woman he'd tried to initiate had ultimately disappointed him.

Aggie unbuttoned the fly of his jeans. She squatted as she pushed his pants down his thighs. She placed a tender kiss on the head of his cock. It twitched, rapidly engorging, growing thick, long, and hard. Wanting to be buried in her voluptuous body—in her slick warmth—where it belonged.

Aggie wandered over to her table and selected a paddle. She turned to look at him and winced when her gaze fell on his back. "You're really bruised," she murmured. She moved to stand behind him and traced the thick bands of damage along his upper back. "The cane. Why didn't you tell me I was doing that much damage to you? I would have stopped."

"I didn't want you to stop. I needed it."

"I'm not hitting you with a cane again," she said. "You'll have to settle for a good paddling this evening." She kissed his shoulder and circled his body to face him. She caressed his bare buttocks and then struck him on its fleshy cheek with her paddle.

It cracked against his tender flesh. Stinging pain shot through his ass, settling as pleasure at the base of his cock. That other pain—the pain in his heart, his soul—eased slightly. The only time it left him was when he was distracted by physical pain. The physical always hurt so much less than the emotional. It became a reprieve. Aggie struck him again. His toes curled in his boots. Again. His nipples tightened.

Ah God, Aggie. Hurt me.

Take the pain away. Hurt me.

Watching his face, she struck him again and then kissed him deeply, her tongue mingling with his. He didn't usually experience a blend of pain and pleasure. In the past, he did his best to keep the two separate. But even the night before, Aggie had given him what he needed and hadn't judged him for it. Jace's excitement mounted quickly. He wrapped his arms around her, tugging her against him and deepening her kiss.

He groaned in her mouth when she struck him again. Fuck, he was hard. He wanted her. No, more than that. He needed her.

Like he needed air.

She turned her head, breaking their kiss, and spanked him again. "You like that?"

He couldn't form a coherent thought. "Huh?"

"A touch of pleasure with your pain?"

"Yeah."

She slid down his body, settling on her knees at his feet. She licked the head of his cock. He shuddered, pleasure rippling through his flesh. She drew his cock into her warm mouth and sucked gently. When she struck his ass again, he cried out. She sucked him harder, rapidly bobbing her head to rub her plump lips over the sensitive rim. She paused frequently to swat him, before returning to pleasuring him with her mouth.

The sweet pain blended with agonizing pleasure until he couldn't take it anymore. He twisted his fingers into her thick, silky, black hair and held her head still. "Aggie," he whispered. "Don't. I can't. Too much."

She reached between his legs, cradling his nuts in one hand. She squeezed. His stomach roiled as the pain left him breathless. She loosened her hold, and while Jace breathed through the pain, she sucked him deep into the back of her mouth and worked her throat muscles and tongue around his cock. He forced his hands from her hair, knowing he'd pull and hurt her if he got too excited. And she was quickly getting him way too excited.

He looked down at her, submissive at his feet, his cock down her throat.

"Oh fuck." He gasped, his breath catching. He shifted his gaze to the mirror across the room. Her waist-length hair swayed against her back as she pulled back, sucked him deep, and pulled back again.

Setting the paddle on the floor, she released his cock from her mouth. She reached into her tight leather bustier and retrieved a condom. After ripping the package open with her teeth, she unrolled it over his cock. It wasn't one of those little ones he'd been forced to use the night before.

He grinned down at her. "Thanks for considering my comfort this time."

"Went out and bought some larger condoms just for you, big boy." She slapped his ass with her bare hand.

He chuckled. "I think you should know the drummer of my band calls me little man."

"*Little* man?" She eyed his cock appreciatively. "Hardly. What do you call him? Blind?"

Jace didn't want to talk about Eric. He wanted to put the condom to good use. He tugged his boots off and kicked his jeans aside. He glanced around. "There's no bed in here."

"No, but there's a table."

He grabbed her around the waist and pulled her across the room. After he removed her panties, she perched on the edge of the table. He squatted between her legs and suckled her clit until she was dripping wet. Her scent drove him crazy. He inhaled deeply through his nose while he lapped at her sweet nectar, his tongue dancing over her slick flesh. Her excited breaths, hitching in the back of her throat, alerted him to her impending orgasm. He stood and carefully inserted his cock into her body. Her back arched, and she shifted her hips off the table to drive him deeper, holding most of her weight with her arms. Her heat engulfed him. He groaned, bracing himself with his feet wide apart to hold her on his throbbing shaft. She shifted back onto the edge of the table, and he surged forward to fill her again.

"Jace," she whispered breathlessly.

He thrust into her slowly and watched her reactions as he methodically increased his tempo. When he found her perfect rhythm, evident by her writhing and mewing, he maintained it relentlessly, drawing on the same consistent cadence that served his music.

She reached behind her and grabbed a flail off the table. She struck him lightly across the chest. Each of the dozens of slender strands released delicious stings in his flesh. His breath caught. He drove into her harder. She met his thrusts with lashes—matching both his rhythm and his intensity. The harder he fucked her, the harder she struck him. He pounded into her harder and harder. He let the excitement carry him, losing all conscious control of his motion, giving his craving for pain full control over his attainment of pleasure. How did she know exactly what he needed? Quickly, his need for release built to the breaking point. His balls ached with heaviness.

He forced his eyes open to look at her. Was she close to orgasm yet? Her entire body shook with each hard thrust, her beautiful tits jiggling each time their bodies came together. His chest was raw and red from the lashes of her perfect retaliation. Her mouth fell open with wonder as he watched. She was closer than he'd realized.

"Look at me," he demanded.

She pried her eyes open, and their gazes locked. He slid one finger down her slit, rubbing her clit and sending her flying over the edge.

"Jace!" she screamed.

As her pussy clenched around his cock in orgasm, he let go. His body tensed, pumping his seed into her with spurt after glorious spurt, while her body shuddered uncontrollably. He held her gaze the entire time, knowing how emotionally vulnerable that made him, but with her, it seemed right.

Spent, he collapsed against her trembling body. She wrapped her arms around him and rocked her hips back and forth, continuing to find pleasure in his cock.

"Oh God, Jace," she murmured. "I'll never get enough of you."

He'd never get enough of her either, which was a problem as far as he was concerned. He tangled his hands in her long silky hair, knowing she deserved far more pleasure than he'd given her. With her flailing him like that, he'd gotten too excited to treat her with proper care and attention. What he had in mind for her next would make up for that, he hoped.

"Do you wanna go somewhere with me?" he asked, leaning over her to kiss her shoulder.

"Yeah, okay," she said. "Where are we going?"

He rose up on his arms above her and stared down into her flushed face. She pouted when she saw the mess she'd made of his chest. Her gentle touch was intoxicating as she traced the crisscrossing welts on his skin, drawing memories of the pain to the forefront of his mind again. He caught her wrists, and she looked up at him.

"The tour bus. I want to show you true bliss."

"True bliss? Wasn't that what I just experienced?"

He chuckled. "Baby, that was just a warm-up."

Chapter 8

AGGIE SNUGGLED CLOSER TO Jace's back, her hands pressed flat against his abdomen. She loved motorcycles. Especially low-pitched, rumbling Harleys. Foreplay on wheels.

They drove down the Vegas strip. The summer evening air was stifling, yet the crowds were still thick on the sidewalks and the traffic heavy. The tourists would really come out to play after dark. Aggie had lived in Las Vegas her entire life, and the city's ceaseless excitement still stirred her. Jace turned into the area behind Mandalay Bay at the southern end of Las Vegas Boulevard and stopped next to a set of three tour buses. Jace parked beside a silver and black bus and held her hand while she climbed from the bike.

She removed her helmet, her long, thick hair cascading over her shoulders and down her back. She flipped it out of her face impatiently. "We need to drive into the desert and have an orgy on this bike."

He removed his helmet, smiling to himself. "I think that can be arranged."

"Now?" she asked breathlessly.

"I have other plans for you now. Next time."

Next time? She wasn't big on planning the future, especially if it required relying upon a man, but she'd make concessions for Jace.

He swung the bus door open and climbed the steep steps. Glancing down the corridor, he ushered her inside with a wave. The inside was nicer than she'd expected. A plush, leather sofa faced two captain's chairs, a flat-screen TV, and a stereo system. Farther down the main corridor, a kitchenette stood opposite a small, square table and booths. Beyond the dining area, there were two stacked curtained compartments on each side. As Jace continued down the hallway, he swept each curtain aside to reveal four empty bunks.

"I don't think anyone's here," he said.

The bathroom door stood partially open. No one in there either. He knocked on the door at the end of the hall. When there was no response, he opened the door to reveal a small bedroom. He switched on the light, and Aggie entered the room, glancing around. A comfortable-looking queen-sized bed filled over half the room. A closet, overflowing with clothes, bedding, and towels filled one wall. A long dresser stood next to the door, and a small window was situated on the wall opposite the closet. A hook in the ceiling caught her eye.

"That's for you," Jace whispered into her ear.

"For me?"

"You'll see. What do you want to drink?"

His dichotomous personality always surprised her. He had a gentle, considerate side that so completely contrasted with the animal just beneath the surface. An angel and a devil. Strange thing was, she liked both—the side that warmed her heart with affection and the side that burned her body with lust. "Do you have any wine?"

He grinned. "A woman after my own heart. I hope you like it sweet."

"Is there any other kind?"

"I have some port on the other bus. I'll be right back. Make yourself comfortable." He kissed her cheek and left her to herself.

Aggie removed her leather jacket, folding it carefully and setting it on the dresser. She contemplated removing her clothes and waiting for Jace naked, but decided she liked him to undress her. Slowly. Seductively. With great care and tenderness. In the silence, a faint hum came from the side table drawer. Her brow knitted with confusion, she went to investigate. Pulling the drawer open, she found it full of sex toys. Dildos of all sizes and thicknesses. Vibrators. Condoms. Flavored oils. Cock rings. Butt plugs. Was this why he'd brought her here? She found the humming vibrator and turned it off before dropping it back into the drawer.

"You like that kind of thing?" Jace asked from behind her.

She spun around. "Sorry to pry. One of the vibrators was humming. I followed the sound." She nodded toward the drawer. "Is all that stuff yours?"

Jace shook his head. "It's Brian's. He likes toys. He doesn't mind sharing though, if you want to borrow something."

"Who's Brian?" She accepted the glass of wine he held out to her.

"Our lead guitarist. I take it you're not a Sinners fan. Everyone knows Brian 'Master' Sinclair. He's a rock god. Sed, our lead singer, is a notorious womanizer. Trey plays rhythm guitar and any person— male or female—who catches his attention. And then there's Eric, who… is our drummer. I'm obscure by comparison."

"You sure about that? You're awfully cute."

He flushed. "Sed's the one all the girls scream for. He's a beast."

"Like you?" Aggie grinned, taking a sip of wine—perfectly chilled, full-bodied, and sweet. She'd never tasted anything more delicious. "Mmmm." She looked down into her glass. Thick, the wine clung to the inner surface of her glass. It reminded her of blood. She took another sip, holding the cool liquid in her mouth. Its flavor soured as it warmed on the surface of her tongue. She swallowed.

"I'm a whole different type of beast."

She glanced up at him. The coldness in his eyes sent a shiver down her spine. He downed his wine in two gulps and set his glass on the dresser. He went to the closet and pulled a hard-shell, black suitcase from its depths. He knelt in front of it on the floor.

She moved to stand beside him, looking at the suitcase. "What's that?"

"The reason I brought you here."

He flipped the locks and tossed the lid open. Aggie's eyes widened. He had all kinds of things inside, ranging from obvious paddles and candles to things she couldn't identify.

He looked at her. "You still trust me, right?"

The anxious flutter in her stomach excited her. She had no idea what he had in mind, but whatever it was, she was game. He had yet to disappoint her. "Yeah."

He began to sort through the case, arranging things in piles. She couldn't decipher any pattern in his groupings as she watched him, sipping her wine. He lit candles, setting them on the side table. He left the room and returned moments later with a bowl of ice, a bottle of chocolate syrup, and a can of mixed fruit.

"What are you doing? Preparing for nuclear winter?"

He smiled slyly. "You'll see. How's the wine?"

"Perfect."

"Do you want another glass?" He seemed ready to start his orchestrated pleasure session. Or would it be torture? She was eager to find out.

Aggie finished her wine in one long swallow and set her empty glass next to his. "No, I don't want any more wine. I want you."

"Soon." He closed the bedroom door and approached her. He undressed her slowly, caressing every inch of flesh he revealed, first with his fingertips, and then his lips. His tenderness never ceased to amaze her. He fucked her hard. Made love to her gently. "You're so beautiful," he murmured as he unhooked her bra. "I love your curves."

She had plenty of curves. She'd never possessed the athletic slenderness that Hollywood and fashion runways considered beautiful, but she was comfortable with her body and glad that Jace appreciated it. Her dancing kept her in good shape, but her feet never touched a treadmill. Her heavy breasts fell free of her bra, and he cupped them, gazing at the flesh overflowing from his hands.

He lowered his head to kiss the soft globes, his tongue sliding over her nipples. Aggie's belly tightened. She rested her hands on his shoulders as he kissed his way down the center of her belly. He removed her jeans, panties, and sandals with equal care and agonizing slowness. By the time he led her to the bed, she was more than ready for him to possess her body, and he hadn't even started using the objects from his suitcase.

They knelt in the center of the bed, facing each other. Jace pulled something from his back pocket and fastened it around Aggie's left wrist. She looked down at the thick leather cuff, lined with fleece. Her heart thudded against her ribs. Restraints? He fastened a matching leather cuff around her other wrist and attached them to each other with a length of chain.

"Why are you restraining me?" she asked.

"So you don't interfere with what I do to your body."

Her heart thudded even harder. "Are you going to hurt me?"

He stood in front of her on the bed and lifted her hands above her head, securing her wrists to the hook in the ceiling with the heavy chain. He didn't answer her question.

"Jace, I don't like to be on the receiving end of pain. Only inflict it." She supposed if she got too freaked out, she could stand on the bed and free her hands from the hook. She was well versed in self-defense, but something inside told her she could trust this man. Her intuition had never failed her in the past.

He knelt in front of her and touched her cheek gently. "I'd never hurt you, Aggie. I only like to be on the receiving end of pain. Never inflict it." He stroked her arms with the backs of his hands, and then continued down to draw them along the sides of her breasts, the indent of her waist, and the flare of her hips. "I do plan to make you beg for mercy, but from the pleasure I give your body, not pain."

Well, okay… if he insisted.

"Do I have your permission to continue?" he asked.

She bit her lip, looking into his gentle brown eyes for signs of deceit. She found none. "Yes."

"Good."

He pulled something else from his back pocket and slid a blindfold over her eyes.

"I can't see," she said breathlessly. Her heart thudded faster. She wasn't afraid, not exactly. Excited. Yes, that's what had her breath hitching, her heart racing, her core aching with emptiness.

He chuckled. "That's the idea, sweetheart. You don't need to see. Just feel. Feel me, Aggie."

"I do. I feel you."

He gathered her hair in his hand, twisted it, and clipped it to the back of her head.

"Your skin is so soft," he murmured into her ear from behind. His hands gently stroked her back... her belly... her breasts. "Smooth. Warm."

"Pale," she added with a grin.

"Perfect."

He suckled and kissed the flesh on the backs of her shoulders while his hands continued to stroke her belly, breasts and hips. His hands slid between her thighs, spreading her legs apart. She trembled. His fingers parted her swollen flesh and dipped inside her. Her head fell back against his shoulder. He rubbed her clit, slid his fingers into her pussy, rubbed her clit again. How did he know exactly how to excite her beyond her limits of tolerance?

"Jace."

He continued to stroke her until she was ready to explode, and then he moved away, leaving her trembling. Unfulfilled.

Something ice cold slid down her spine. She shuddered. It continued down the crack of her ass, over the aching opening to her pussy, and finally her clit. He stroked her there, with the ice between his fingers and her flesh, until the ice completely melted. She didn't know how it was possible for her clit to feel like it was on fire and frozen at the same time.

"Jace," she said in a pleading tone.

He slid two of his fingers into her mouth. They tasted like chocolate. She sucked the sweet treat from his digits. He withdrew them and inserted them again with more chocolate. Something cool and thick drizzled over her nipple. His hot mouth sucked at her nipple while he continued to thrust his fingers in and out of her mouth. Did he realize what he was doing to her? She ached from wanting him already. He'd likely restrained her hands above her head so she couldn't get herself off while he tortured her with pleasure. She was definitely desperate enough to do it.

He moved away again, and she heard a strange grinding sound. Her heart rate kicked up a notch until she identified it as a can opener. Hadn't he brought a can of fruit...?

Something cool and slick slid into her mouth. The gritty bite of sweet pear dissolved on her tongue. She smelled wax the instant before liquid heat burned down the center of her back. Her spine arched involuntarily. He traced either side of the hot trail with ice. His mouth moved to suck on the side of her neck. Only his mouth wasn't hot as expected. It was cold. He let the water from the melting ice trickle from his lips as he kissed his way down her throat and shoulder. Thin rivulets of water traced paths down her chest, following the contours of her body to collect between her breasts, slide down her belly, around her navel, and finally between her thighs. She shuddered when the first droplets found her shaved mound.

"Jace." She'd given up on trying to figure out what he was going to do next.

He paused to put more ice in his mouth. She heard him slurp it inside, and it clicked against his teeth. As the water dripped between her legs and found new paths along her hip bone, she squirmed with impatience. He shifted his mouth to the other side of her neck and used the flat of his hands to stroke her belly and the undersides of her breasts. He pinched her nipples unexpectedly, and she shuddered on the brink of orgasm.

"Jace, fuck me, please. I want you. I want you inside me."

He moved away abruptly. She listened to the sounds of his movement. A slice of peach entered her mouth. She sucked on it, savoring its slick sweetness. She waited for his return. It seemed like hours before his hands were on her again. They had an unusually rough texture now. He stroked the skin of her belly and breasts gently with his gloved hands while he blew soft breaths over the skin of her back.

"Oh God, Jace. You're driving me insane."

"Do you want me to stop?" The low rumble of his voice made her spine tingle.

"Yes." She gasped when he drew his hands away. "No. Don't! Don't stop."

He curled his body against her back. She felt his cock against her ass, and she rubbed up against him, arching her back in an attempt to get him to enter her. His rough gloves moved between her thighs, pressing them open so the cool air bathed her heated flesh.

"Hold still," he murmured.

She tried to hold still, but the neglected parts of her body were greedy for his touch. She twisted her hips and rubbed her mound against the hand he had stroking her inner thigh. She sucked a shuddering breath between her teeth. He slapped her ass with a loud smack. Her entire body tensed.

"No, Aggie. Hold still."

"Jace. Please. Please. I can't take any more."

He moved away again, and she choked back a sob of protest. Something tickled her shoulder blade. *A feather?* And then nothing. When she'd given up on him ever touching her again, he traced her lowest rib with the feather. She groaned. An eternity later, he stroked her hip bone. She fought her chains, her hips undulating involuntarily as she sought fulfillment.

The door opened. Two rapid inhalations came from the general vicinity of the threshold.

Jace slipped something into Aggie's mouth. It burst against her tongue, releasing sweet juice. White grape. Aggie swallowed, her ears straining for sounds that would tell her what was going on beyond her perception.

The door closed again.

"Who was that?" Aggie whispered.

"Sed and Jessica. Looks like they're back together."

"Are they in here with us?"

He chuckled. "No, baby. They left."

The mattress beside her sagged.

She leaned toward him, disappointed when she found nothing but empty space beside her. "Are you going to let me off the hook?"

He wrapped an arm around her waist and lifted her from her knees. Her hands came loose from the chain above her head.

She chuckled. "I didn't mean literally. Are you finished torturing me with pleasure then?"

He massaged her hands, returning circulation to her fingers. He kissed each fingertip, sucking gently, before massaging each knuckle with a gentle pressure. She hadn't even realized her hands were numb. Every sense was tuned to pleasure. Discomfort didn't register. "Do you want me to be done?" he asked.

That was a difficult question to answer. He played her body like a mastered instrument. Within a few minutes, she knew she'd be begging him to fuck her again. "I'm not sure. How long are you going to make me wait before you give me what I need?"

"I don't know. I've never had a woman make it this long before."

So if she held out for a while longer, that would make her special to him. Is that what he was hinting at? His lips brushed a sensitive spot below her ear. She turned her face toward him and inhaled his scent. A hint of mild aftershave. A heap of hot male.

"I'm pretty sure I can keep going for hours," he whispered. His deep voice toyed with the nerve endings in the skin along her spine. She wanted more of him—his scent, his taste, his voice. The tools he used to excite her were exceptional, but the man in charge held a far greater appeal.

"Hours?"

"If you want me to." He sucked her earlobe into his mouth, still rubbing her hands. Her fingers were tingling now.

He pushed her back down on the bed. "Put your arms over your head," he murmured, sliding his hands up her arms as she obeyed. He fastened her restraints over her head and then grabbed her hips to pull her down the bed and make the chain taut. "Lift your hips for me."

She was used to issuing orders to men, not taking them. Why was she so willing to submit to this man? Because she knew he was going to make it worth her while, that's why.

When she lifted her hips, he slid a couple of pillows under her lower back, tilting her pelvis up and lifting her butt off the bed. With one hand on each thigh, he spread her legs apart.

"If you stay like that, I won't restrain your legs."

She chuckled. "I already know I won't be able to stay like this once you get to work."

Rough beard stubble scraped her inner thigh. A smooth fabric soothed the slight sting, and then a cool tongue traced the same path. He repeated the action on the other thigh—rough, smooth, cool. It reminded her how achy she felt as it directed her attention to the emptiness between her thighs. Something hot trickled over one hip bone and then the other. She sucked a sharp breath through her teeth. Paraffin. She could smell it. The liquid heat burned a path above her mound as if he were framing her throbbing pussy with a triangle of wax. A single drop of hot wax splashed on her pubis. Jace's finger traced a path around the drop, drawing her attention to the cooling substance until it hardened, and she couldn't feel it any longer. A second drop of wax near the first—more tracing.

"Jace."

Another splash of hot wax. This time he traced the drop with ice. She gyrated, desperately fighting the urge to clamp her legs together and rub her clit between her swollen labia to get off.

"Hold still."

"I'm trying." She gasped. "This makes me want you."

She felt him move away and heard the candle being set on the table. Ice clinked, and then he moved between her legs, spreading them wide and holding them open with his shoulders. His fingers held her labia open, and the first drop of ice-cold water struck her clit. She jerked.

"Shh. Hold still." His words were garbled around the ice in his mouth. His aim was remarkable. Each drop struck her overstimulated clit, but sought a different pathway over her lips, opening, and ass. Drip. Drip. Drip. His sweet torture was too much to bear. She shifted her legs from his shoulders and clamped her thighs on his head. Digging her feet into his back, she pulled his face into her pussy.

"Ah God, lick it, Jace. Suck it."

He worked an ice cube inside her with his tongue. She shuddered.

"Fuck me, please. Please. Please. Please. Fuck me."

He pulled her legs apart to free his head.

"I guess you aren't ready for the entire sequence yet," he said. "Maybe next time."

There was more?

She heard something crinkle. A condom wrapper? Thank God he wasn't going to leave her like this. He released her from the chain above her head. She reached for her blindfold, but he flipped her onto her stomach, shoved her face into the mattress, and entered her with one deep thrust. She cried out, an orgasm shaking her core. She rocked back to meet his deep thrusts, her juices and the melting ice dripping down her thighs. She'd never needed to be fucked so badly in her life. And he was giving her exactly what she needed. Her wrists were still joined by the restraints, so she moved both hands between her thighs, rubbing her clit, while he pounded into her. She came again with a startled cry, trembling uncontrollably. Cool, slippery fingers massaged her anus, slipped inside. Again. Lubricating her ass. Oh, yes. She wanted it there too. Jace pulled out, and before she could protest, he spread her ass cheeks and plunged his huge cock into her ass.

She gasped.

He hesitated. "You okay?"

She hoped her indiscernible moans sounded like agreement. He pulled back slowly. Just before he fell free, she lunged back against him, taking him deep again. "Oh God, Jace. Fuck my ass. Yes. Fuck every inch of me."

She slid three fingers into her pussy, her restraints limiting her motions.

"My cock's not enough for you?" he asked, pulling her hair as he thrust into her ass relentlessly.

"More. Please, more."

He pulled out.

"No!" she cried desperately.

He pulled her fingers out of her pussy and replaced it with something thick, long, and cold. Some sort of phallus, with a second attachment that touched her clit. The device hummed to life, vibrating against her clit, and writhing inside her body. "Oh," she purred.

He buried his cock in her ass again. "Is that enough for you?"

She couldn't respond. She was coming too hard. And screaming.

She couldn't stop screaming. She wasn't sure how long Jace kept her like that, bucking against him, taking everything he had to give and craving more. She collapsed eventually, trembling with a mixture of fulfillment and exhaustion.

"You done?" he asked.

"Yes," she whispered breathlessly. "Yes. Yes… thank you."

He pulled out and removed the churning vibrator from her body. She rolled onto her side and watched him remove the condom. He was still hard. He hadn't followed her down the road to bliss this time. She realized it was because while he had given her what she needed, she hadn't done the same for him. He needed pain to come.

"Come here," she murmured drowsily.

He pointed toward the exit. "I'm just going to—"

"Come here," she demanded.

When he was within reach, she tugged him onto the bed. Flattening him on his back, she took his cock into her mouth, sucking him deep into her throat. As she pleasured his shaft with her mouth, she squeezed his balls rhythmically with her hand. The pain soon had him gasping with excitement.

"Aggie," he whispered, his fingers tangling in her hair. "Aggie, you're gonna make me come."

Well, *yeah*, that was the idea.

She bobbed her head faster, sucked harder, squeezed rhythmically. His unexpected, excited vocalizations started to excite her again. Two minutes ago she would have said she'd had enough orgasms in the past half hour to last her a lifetime. She was already reevaluating that analysis. Jace cried out and pulled her head away as he sputtered with release. His cum splattered over his flat belly.

She watched in confusion. "Why didn't you let me have that?"

He took a deep breath and lifted his head to look at her. "You wanted it?"

"I begged you to fuck me in the ass, Jace. That requires a fair amount of intimacy."

"You were so turned on I could have done anything I wanted to you."

She grinned and then laughed, remembering where she'd been only minutes before. "True."

She settled beside him, her head resting on his shoulder, her fingers toying with the fluids on his belly. His breathing slowed and became even.

"Jace?" she whispered.

"Hmm," he murmured drowsily.

"I think you should know that I don't take many lovers."

"Really? Why's that?"

"As a rule, I don't like men."

"You're a lesbian?"

She laughed. "That's not what I meant. I'm around men all the time and see what they're like—doesn't do much for my libido. You, on the other hand, have me set on full throttle."

"I'm… glad." He snored softly as he succumbed to his exhaustion.

Aggie slapped his belly, and he grunted awake.

"I'm having a moment here," she said.

"Sorry. What do you want me to say?"

"I don't know. What are you thinking?"

"I like this—whatever this is between us."

She grinned. "I like it too."

"Can I sleep now?"

"For a little while. I want to see if I can take your pleasure torture longer next time."

"You did pretty good the first time." He stroked her hair.

A woman's cries of sexual excitement carried from the front of the bus through the bedroom door. Aggie lifted her head.

"What was that?"

"Jessica, I presume."

A deep voice answered the higher pitched cries of ecstasy.

"And Sed. I guess they really are back together."

Aggie had completely forgotten they'd barged in earlier. They'd seen her defenseless and needy. Now that she had regained her wits, it bothered her. It was bad enough that Jace had seen her that way—so unlike herself. So powerless, she'd actually begged. "I should probably go. I have several sessions tonight." She'd feel better after she made a few submissives lick her boots.

Jace lifted his head to look at her. "Sessions?"

"Mmm-hmm." She trailed a finger down his belly between the bumps that made up his six-pack. This guy's body really was amazing in so many ways. And that sexually inventive mind of his? *Oh, my God.* "If you stop by later tonight, I'll treat you to a free session. Around midnight?"

His cock twitched and began to swell.

"Were you serious when you said you don't fuck clients?" he asked.

Why had he asked her that? "You're the first. I'm not sure what it is about you that made me break my own rules."

Jace eased from under her body and climbed to his feet. "I need to go visit Trey in the hospital now."

From the outer cabin of the bus, Jessica and Sed's vocalizing came to an abrupt end. Jace wiped the cum from his belly with a dirty shirt and slid into his jeans. He opened the door. "Is it safe to come out now?" he called down the corridor.

Why did Aggie get the feeling he was trying to escape? Typical man—getting what he wanted in the bedroom and then losing interest. She was going to whip him good for this.

Chapter 9

JACE COULDN'T BREATHE. FACE firmly lodged between some fangirl's huge tits, no amount of struggling secured his release. Had it been Aggie trying to suffocate him with her succulent breasts, he wouldn't have minded as much. He hadn't realized visiting Trey in the hospital might be life threatening.

"Oh Jace, you're sooooo cute," the young woman squealed at the top of her lungs. Sed somehow got a hand between Jace's forehead and fangirl's cleavage and pried him loose.

Jace gulped air greedily. "Thanks."

"Don't mention it," Sed said in his typical baritone growl.

This time Jace stuck close to Sed and Jessica as they pushed their way through the crowd of Trey's concerned fans and eventually made it to Trey's private room.

They found him, Eric, and their live sound engineer, Dave, sitting hip to hip in the hospital bed watching some porn video on the band's laptop. When the guys noticed Jessica had entered the room, Trey slammed the computer closed on Eric's hand. Dave sprang from the bed and was out the door within seconds. It didn't take long to figure out what had three grown men freaking out. The guys had been watching *The Video*. Granted, it would be upsetting for most chicks to see themselves getting drilled on the Internet, when they'd been unaware that someone was filming, but what did she expect? She and Sed had been having sex in public. That kind of made it fair game as free Internet porn. Eric seemed to be the only one to understand her over-the-top angst. When she stormed out of the room with tears flying, it was Eric who suggested Sed go after her.

When Sed raced out of the room in pursuit, Jace said, "I think she was upset."

"You think?" Eric said. He shook his head. "We shouldn't have watched it."

"Yeah, we should have," Trey said. "That was one of the hottest fucking things I've ever seen in my life. Jesus Christ, no wonder Sed wants her so badly. She's a sex goddess. I wouldn't mind tapping that every night for the rest of my life."

Eric shook his head slightly. "But us watching it hurt her."

Trey laughed at Eric's obvious upset. "Dude, you are such a pussy when it comes to women. That's why they walk all over you, you know."

Jace glanced at Eric. He'd never seen Eric with a woman long enough to witness him getting walked over. Eric tended to avoid anything remotely resembling a romantic relationship. Hell, he rarely engaged in sex. Usually watched and only participated if he was sure the woman wasn't truly interested in him for anything other than leftovers. The only exception was Myrna. Myrna had only wanted Brian, no matter how touchy-feely Eric had gotten. Had that been his attraction to her? Knowing she'd never really be interested in him, so it was safe to pine away for her?

Eric scowled at Jace. "What the fuck are you looking at, little man?"

Jace lowered his gaze to the floor, hiding the defiance he knew would be in his eyes. "Nothing."

"That's what I thought."

Jace shifted his gaze to Trey. "How are you feeling? Are they going to let you out of here soon?"

Trey lifted his hand and tried to make a fist. His hand didn't even close halfway. "That's how I'm feeling, Jace. Fucked up and pissed off. Whatever. I'm getting out of here tomorrow. I don't give a shit what my doctor says."

Jace nodded. He didn't want Trey in here any more than he wanted to stay.

"Don't be an idiot," Eric said. "You'll stay in the hospital until you're better."

"These places kill people." Jace bit his lip. He hadn't meant to say that, but he couldn't help but get lost in his past when confronted by such blatant reminders.

"This place saved Trey's life," Eric said, slim black brows drawing together over his piercing blue eyes. "I'm the only one who had to witness his fucking seizure. I almost had a heart attack when Trey stopped breathing and pissed himself."

"I'd appreciate it if you'd keep that 'pissed himself' part to yourself," Trey murmured.

Eric placed a hand on Trey's brow and brushed his bangs off his forehead. "That is nothing to be ashamed of, brother. I thought you were dead. It was the least of my concerns."

"I would have been dead if you hadn't called the ambulance."

"You were coming around by the time they got there. I performed CPR on you for like twenty minutes, dude."

Jace's eyes widened. He hadn't realized what Eric had done for Trey. Jace wondered if he would have gone to the same lengths to save Trey or just curled into the fetal position and hid, as he had when his mother had died.

Trey grinned crookedly. "So that's why I've been tasting tequila since I woke up. Was it really necessary to give me tongue?"

Eric laughed. "Hey, I know you like that kind of thing. I thought it might revive you."

"You gave him tongue?" Jace's nose curled. He knew Trey was bisexual, and Jace was fine with that, as long as he wasn't confronted by it. To each man his own—just keep it behind closed doors.

Eric rolled his eyes toward the ceiling and shook his head. "No, I didn't really give him tongue. Jeez, dude, do you have any sense of humor at all?"

Jace had a hard time figuring out when Eric was being serious and when he was joking. He'd probably do better if he erred on the side of joking. The guy was rarely serious.

"I knew you were joking," Jace said.

"Whatever."

"I'm bored. Let's watch Sed and Jessica's video again," Trey said.

Dave peeked in the door. "Eric, are you ready to go?" he whispered loudly.

"Sed and Jess left," Eric said, waving Dave back into the room. "It's safe."

Dave stepped into the room, glancing around cautiously. "Was Sed pissed at us for watching that?"

"Sed?" Trey asked. "Nah, I'm sure he's proud of it. Jess, on the other hand…"

"She ran out crying," Jace said. "Sed went after her."

"If she was upset, then Sed will be upset too," Dave said.

The four exchanged glances and nodded in unison.

"Fine," Trey said. "We won't watch it again." He sighed loudly.

"A shame really," Eric muttered. "Excellent jack off material. I just don't want to upset Jessica. She's a good woman."

Jace had never given Jessica much thought. She was gorgeous. No mistake about that, but he didn't know her well enough to judge her character. There must be something pretty great about her if she could keep Sed interested for two years, even while absent.

"Where have you been all day, Jace?" Dave asked. "We wanted to borrow your bike earlier, but couldn't find you."

Jace flushed, thoughts returning to Aggie. "Sorry, I was…"

Trey chuckled. "He was getting laid. Look at him blush."

Jace's already hot cheeks burned even more.

Dave nudged him with his elbow. "Good looking chick?"

"Perfect."

"How much did you pay her?" Eric chided.

Jace was pretty sure his face was about to burst into flames. "Uh… a grand."

"You *paid* for it?" Trey asked. "Dude, I can hook you up with any chick you want. Don't ever pay for pussy."

Jace's defenses rose. "Not the sex. I didn't pay her for that part."

"Then what?" Dave asked, looking puzzled.

Jace shook his head. He was unwilling to share this part of himself with the guys. They'd think he was a freak. Eric grabbed him in a headlock and pulled the back of his shirt up. Dave gasped as he took in what must have been a matrix of bruises, welts, and scratches.

Eric poked a bruise with one finger. "Just as I thought. Dude, if you want someone to hit you, just ask. I'd love to knock you around."

Trey laughed. "Careful. You'll give him a boner, Eric."

Jace's hard fist to Eric's ribs gained his release.

"Ow, *fuck*, you hit hard." Eric grabbed his side, wincing in pain.

Jace felt immediate remorse for hurting him. "Sorry."

"So you paid some guy to beat you up?" Dave asked, perplexity written in every confused line of his face.

Trey burst out laughing. "Uh no, Dave. Hanging around us, you'd think you'd come out of the shelter of your vanilla existence every now and then. He likes *women* to hit him."

Jace's eyes widened, and he diverted his gaze to his boots. "I need to leave."

"Don't leave. Tell us what she did to you," Trey insisted. "It might alleviate my boredom for a couple minutes."

"Did she piss on you?" Dave asked. He shifted to his other foot and adjusted the fly of his khakis.

"No, she didn't *piss* on me."

"But you want her to piss on *you*, don't you, Dave?" Trey said.

"Em, no," Dave said. "That's sick." He adjusted his fly again.

"You're all hard just thinking about it," Trey noted. "She'll probably piss on you for a couple bucks. What do you say, Jace? Give her a call. Ask her if she'll piss on Dave. I'll spot him a twenty."

"Don't," Dave said, flushing from the collar of his mint green polo to the line of his immaculately styled, light brown hair.

Jace scowled. He didn't know if Aggie pissed on guys for money, and he didn't *want* to know. Talking about this cheapened his experiences with her. He didn't like it. She treated him different from the rest of her customers. She'd already told him that. Part of him wanted to believe it.

"I don't think she does that kind of thing."

"Puh-lease. A chick like her will do anything for money," Eric said.

"No. She's not like that." Why did he feel the need to defend her? She did serve men for money. But it was on her terms. Wasn't it? "I've got to go."

Jace left, but he vowed he wouldn't go to see Aggie again tonight, even though he had an appointment with her in five hours and thirty-seven minutes. He could not allow himself to get any more attached.

Chapter 10

JACE STOOD ON AGGIE'S stoop, one index finger on her door buzzer, the other aimed at his temple as a mock pistol barrel. What was he doing here? He'd promised himself he wouldn't come.

The door opened to the annoyed scowl of a cranky redhead. "Aggie!" Aggie's mother turned and screamed into the house. "Another one of your *freaks* is here!"

This woman really knew how to make Jace's balls wither to the size of raisins. Aggie emerged from behind the door. She didn't say a word, but the look she gave him—like he was the vilest piece of shit on the planet—had those raisins back to full size in an instant. She opened the door wider and turned, stalking toward the sanctum, her full hips rocking side to side with each step.

Panting, Jace followed.

"Close the fucking door, Maynard! You're letting out the AC," Aggie's mother yelled. How had that woman given birth to the luscious, sensual creature that was Aggie?

Jace closed the door and followed Aggie into the sanctum. She slid the door closed, startling him. When he turned to look at her, she locked it. Her eyes were as cold as arctic steel. He didn't know if she was actually pissed at him or if it was all an act. Its source didn't matter. Her glare made his cock swell uncomfortably in his jeans.

Her gaze unwavering, Aggie backed him into a corner. She slid her riding crop under the hem of his T-shirt and lifted it a few inches. Her eyebrows rose, and she didn't have to tell him what she wanted twice. He peeled his T-shirt over his head and tossed it aside. She lashed him across the belly, and his entire body jerked. The tip of her crop disappeared into the waistband of his jeans. She slid it further down, along the entire length of his cock, and then pulled the crop free. Again she raised her eyebrows at him, but said nothing.

Shuddering, he released his fly and pulled his cock free of his pants. It stood at rigid attention between them. She didn't strike him for obeying her. Just continued to stare at him and wait. What did she want?

"Aggie?"

She shoved a ball into his mouth and fastened the gag around his head. He'd told her last night that he didn't like to be gagged. When he lifted his hands to release the gag's buckle, she turned and strode away in that prowling cat walk she'd perfected. He lowered his hands, the gag still in place, and watched her move toward the table where her whips and paddles rested from least to most vicious in a neat line. She set the riding crop down, third in line, after a small paddle and a larger wooden one, and selected her fourth tool—three whips on a short handle. She glanced over her shoulder and gave the clothes on the lower half of his body a pointed look.

Did she want him naked? Would she hit him if he did what she wanted?

He pulled off his boots and shucked his pants, kicking them aside. Wearing nothing but his socks, he waited. She smiled at him coldly and sashayed her way back in his direction. She turned him to face the wall. He felt the cool leather of the three whips slide sensually over his naked back, buttocks, between his legs to tease his balls, his asshole, up his back again to his shoulders. She lashed him once, twice, between the shoulder blades. Sweet, sweet agony. His cock twitched in anticipation. She didn't give him more though. Something cold wrapped around his neck and tightened just short of choking him. A collar? Was she really that determined to treat him like a fucking dog? She leaned against his back, the luscious globes of her breasts pressing into his flesh. She slid the tails of her whip up and down his belly. Whenever the ends of the lashes brushed his cock, he tensed. Concentrating on sensation, he relaxed. He didn't even notice the cuffs attached to his collar until she had his left wrist immobilized in one.

Jace grabbed the collar's fastening with his free hand. He'd had enough of this. She had no right to—

Her whip cracked against his ass. He went still, relishing the pain. *Oh yes.* That's what he needed. She struck him again and again until he went limp against the wall, his face pressed into the padding. That's when she secured his free hand to the other cuff attached to his collar. Now that she had both his hands trapped and useless, she grabbed him roughly by the collar and turned him to face her.

"You do not treat me with disregard," she growled.

Jace's brow furrowed with confusion. Disregard? What did she mean?

"I am in control."

Yeah, fine, she was in control. Was she going to hit him some more?

She fastened a leash to his collar and tugged him out of the corner. His first instinct was to fight. He struggled to repress that urge as she pulled him down to the floor on his knees. He stared venom at her for treating him this way.

Aggie stood over him, gazing down with confusion in her pretty blue eyes. "You really don't like this, do you? To be treated like a dog?"

He shook his head.

"Huh. I thought you were just putting on a tough guy act. It really is just the pain you want."

I tried to tell you that, he wanted to yell, but couldn't because she'd gagged him.

"Do you want me to free you?"

He nodded.

"Too bad. You need to be taught a lesson."

Why? he tried to say. It came out as a muddled sound deep in his throat.

"You made me submit to you and then the minute you finished getting off, you discarded me. You wouldn't even come in my mouth."

The tears in her eyes totally threw him for a loop. He hadn't discarded her. He couldn't think of anything but her all day. Not even when he should have been worrying about Trey's injury and recovery. And he'd just assumed she wouldn't *want* him to come in her mouth. Most women didn't like it. He had pulled out as a courtesy, not as part of some stupid dominance game. Why was she twisting everything around?

"I hate you for making me feel like this," she said.

She shoved him down on his back.

"This needy, stupid, totally mixed up weakling is not me, Jace." She glared at him. "You will come in my mouth this time. Do you understand?"

He was strangely glad she'd gagged him at that point, because he would have laughed at her demands. Silly woman. She didn't have to restrain him for that. He nodded obediently to make her happy. Or himself happy, he wasn't sure which.

Aggie lowered her head and sucked his cock into her mouth. His body jerked in response. One of her hands massaged his nuts. The other gently twisted the base of his shaft while she sucked the head of his cock into the back of her throat. She remembered their rhythm and used it relentlessly, as she swallowed him and withdrew, swallowed him and withdrew. He groaned against his gag, his hands tightening into fists in his restraints. This much pleasure couldn't be right. He closed his eyes and let the feelings consume him. The tug. The heat. The friction. Slick. Moist. Pulling at him.

Pulling. His orgasm approached within minutes. Something about her dominating him and then admitting that he made her weak pushed him to the edge of bliss quickly. His body tightened with inevitable release, and she cracked her flail hard against his lower belly. He erupted in her mouth with a strangled cry, his muscles rigid as he let go of everything for a few moments of blissful surrender. She allowed his fluids to fill her mouth before she swallowed. He lay there, trembling in the aftermath, trying to catch his breath by sucking air through his nose. She lifted her head and stared at him for a few minutes. "I have another lesson for you."

If this lesson was anything like the first, he was more than ready to learn.

Aggie went to her table and returned with a black cloth sack. She slipped it over his head. The room was tinted black as he stared through the gauzy material. He could see just fine, and he could breathe. He realized she couldn't see his face like this. Was that her purpose? So she didn't have to look at him?

"Stay," she said, before leaving him lying there on the cold floor, his leash lying loose beside him. He tilted his head and watched her walk into the second room of her sanctum. She returned a moment later with a big, muscular man on a leash. He was hooded, but otherwise unrestrained.

"Kneel, Loser," she growled at the man.

"Yes, Mistress V." He dropped to his knees, bent over her boots, and rubbed his leather-encased face over her feet and ankles with feverish reverence.

He noticed Jace lying naked-with-socks on the floor and glanced up at his dominatrix in question.

"Don't look at me directly."

He averted his gaze.

"We're going to show this misbehaving slave the proper way to respect his mistress. Do you think you can handle that?"

"Yes, Mistress V."

She ran his leash through a metal loop in the floor and pulled until his face was pressed against the ground. On his knees with his shoulders on the floor, and his ass sticking straight up in the air, Loser's balls and dick swung freely beneath him.

"Hold," she said and handed him his own leash. He held himself in that position while Aggie went to retrieve the thick rectangular paddle from the table. She returned to Loser and stepped on the back of his neck with one boot.

"How many do you want?"

"Five."

"Only five? What are you? A fucking pussy? Say it."

"I'm a pussy."

"How many do you want?"

"Six, six. Please, Mistress V."

She drew her arm back and hit his ass with a resounding crack. His flesh distorted to the shape of the paddle then settled back into place, a bright red shade. He grunted in pain. Mistress V drew her arm back again and hit the guy's ass in the exact same spot. This time he cried out hoarsely. Jace stared up at Aggie, watching her relish her power as she smacked her slave's ass a third time. A fourth. Loser, or whatever the hooded man's name was, whimpered in anguish, but did not call for mercy. And his cock had grown harder with each strike. Jace's had as well. Not from watching another man's pain. From seeing the absolute joy on Aggie's face as she gave this man exactly what he wanted. Loser didn't deserve her attention. And neither did Jace.

After the sixth strike, Aggie removed her foot from the back of Loser's head and rubbed his red ass with one hand. "Do you want more?"

"Plug me, Mistress V. Please. Please."

"I don't think you screamed loud enough to be plugged."

"I'm sorry, Mistress V." He gasped, literally in tears. "I'll do better. Three more, please."

She struck him three times in succession, and if she didn't think he screamed loud enough this time, she was in need of a hearing aid. "Good boy," she crooned. "Release."

He let go of his leash and belly-crawled to her feet. "May I?" he whispered. "May I?"

"You may."

Again he rubbed his face against her boots like an affectionate cat, crooning softly to her feet as she stood there and allowed it.

"Do you still want the plug?" she asked.

He started trembling uncontrollably and rubbed his face over her boots. "Y-yes, Mistress V. T-thank you."

She nudged him aside and disappeared into the room she'd retrieved Loser from earlier. Jace wanted to ask the guy what kind of plug, but he was still gagged. Loser was avoiding looking at him anyway. It wasn't as though Jace would recognize him if he met him on the street. His face was completely obscured by the hood. Jace's by the black bag.

Aggie stalked back into the room, her heels clicking on the cement floor. "Assume the position."

On his knees again, Loser planted his face on the floor, grabbed his ass cheeks in both hands and pulled them apart. Aggie took something thick, black, and glistening and inserted it into the guy's anus. Jace flinched when she lifted one foot, pressed it against the end of the plug, and pushed it deep into the guy's ass with a solid kick. Loser shuddered and then grabbed his dick in both hands, stroking himself in earnest. Aggie smacked his ass with the paddle again.

"No. No touching yourself until you beg for mercy."

He released his cock, breathing hard as he struggled to contain his excitement. Aggie paddled him relentlessly now. Not as hard as before, but without pause. Hitting him so the vibration would travel through that butt plug he enjoyed. Whimpering, crying, writhing on the floor,

Loser found some glorious place where pain became pleasure. After several minutes, he sputtered, "Mercy, Mistress V. Mercy."

Though she was obviously worked up by her ministrations, her arm halted in mid-swing. She relaxed her stance. "You may proceed."

Loser grabbed his cock and started jacking-off excitedly.

"If you get that on my floor, I'm going to make you lick it up," she warned him.

When he sputtered with release a few seconds later, she was a woman of her word. She unzipped the mouth of his hood and forced him to lick his own cum off the floor—except she wasn't actually forcing him. He was doing it quite willingly, eager to please his mistress. Once he'd cleaned the floor to her satisfaction, she allowed him to kiss her boots. Jace couldn't believe making out with some chick's boots could excite a man so much, but Loser was undoubtedly enjoying his privilege. He sucked them with his open mouth, his tongue rolling over their shiny black surfaces. He made delighted sounds in the back of his throat the entire time.

"Go clean up now," Aggie said. "And take your butt plug with you."

"Yes, Mistress. Thank you for your mercy."

Loser crawled into the second room.

"Don't come out of there until I tell you to."

"Yes, Mistress."

Aggie leaned over Jace and pulled the cloth from his face.

"Do you get it now?" she asked.

Jace had gotten it from the beginning, but he wasn't like most masochists. He didn't need the little show to accept his punishment. He knew he deserved it whether she thought he did or not.

He rolled onto his back, his hard cock pointing at the ceiling.

She sucked a breath through her teeth when she saw the evidence of his excitement. "Damn it, Jace. Why are you hard again? Did you like watching me make a grown man cry?"

He nodded vigorously. She knelt over him and slid the crotch of her panties to one side. Before he could even comprehend what she was about to do, her hot pussy sank down and his throbbing cock was buried inside her. "Why do I want you so much? Tell me why. I don't get it. I just don't get it."

Aggie rode him until she came, her body going rigid as she let go. She kissed his eyelids and pulled the cloth over his face again. She regained her footing and left him there, unfulfilled, bound, gagged, and flustered, with his cock hard and his balls full and heavy. She showed Loser to the door, accepting his tribute, and showed another man into the sanctum. If she thought Jace was just going to lie there on the floor all night and watch her beat other men until they begged for her mercy, she had another thing coming. At least that's what he was thinking before he watched the second guy beg for mercy after two lashes of Aggie's bullwhip to the back. God, the look on her face when they submitted to her was the most beautiful thing he'd ever seen. She was all powerful—in total control.

A goddess. A demon. An angel.

Her submissives never saw that look. They were too busy staring at the floor or had their eyes squeezed shut tightly, but Jace saw it. When the second guy left, Aggie straddled Jace's hips again and fucked him until her next client arrived.

"As punishment for making me crazy, I'm going to keep you around to entertain me between sessions for the rest of the night," she said.

Was this another lesson? Fuckin' A—she was the best teacher he'd ever had.

Aggie leaned over him and whispered into his ear. "I usually have to get myself off in the back room if I get too worked up, but this is a lot more fun."

For her, maybe. His cock protested as she moved away again. Okay, he had to admit it. He was thoroughly enjoying this for some twisted reason. Not watching the guys being submissive to his sweet demon in leather, but watching her get off on it.

Too bad he'd never be able to give her the pleasure of *his* submission.

Chapter 11

AGGIE ALMOST FELL OFF the stage when she recognized Jace sitting at a nearby table in a baseball cap and sunglasses. He should have known better than to come here. The club's bouncers had long memories and short tempers.

She hopped off the stage and slid onto his lap. "What are you doing here?" she asked, doing her typical lap dance routine to keep the bouncers from getting suspicious.

"We're leaving early in the morning," Jace said. "Going back to LA. I wanted to say good-bye."

She turned around, rubbing her ass against his crotch. "Will I get to see you again?"

"I'm sure I'll turn up every now and then. Do you do this kind of thing a lot?"

"What kind of thing?"

"This lap dance stuff."

"It's part of my job, sugar."

"Yeah, well…"

"You jealous?" she teased, turning to face him again. She didn't know how he could possibly be jealous of anything she did after he'd survived watching her punish clients for over two hours and then still managed to fuck her properly after they'd all gone home. She'd never seen a man come so hard as he'd come last night.

He ducked his head. "Nah."

"I'll be finished in a few minutes. Meet me in the alley, and I'll give you a proper good-bye."

"This isn't so bad as far as good-byes go." He chanced a glance at her, grinning crookedly.

She leaned forward to give him a good view of her breasts and traced the edge of his ear with her fingertips. "If this is enough of a good-bye for you, then—"

"I'll meet you in the alley."

She grinned at him and returned to the stage, cracking her whip at some pasty-faced businessman who was drooling all over himself and fluttering a twenty-dollar bill in her direction. The guy shuddered with a mixture of fear and excitement as the whip stirred his hair, but didn't touch his skin. She should give him her card. Invite him to her sanctum of pain. Talk him into thinking he could take thirty minutes and break him in two. Easy money. She didn't offer her services to him though. She wasn't sure why she hesitated.

She glanced at Jace as she accepted the businessman's cash between her breasts, but Jace had already left. When her set ended, she hurried to the dressing room and slid a skirt on over her costume. It didn't tone down her leather bustier and thigh-high boots much, but at least her ass was covered.

"Mel, I'm going on a break for about twenty minutes," she called to one of the blonde twins who'd just come off stage. "Cover for me, 'kay?"

"No problem, Aggie."

Aggie hurried out the back door to find Jace leaning against his motorcycle with his arms crossed over his chest. She lifted his visor when she stopped before him.

"I'm glad you came to say good-bye," she whispered.

"Do you want to go for a ride?"

She glanced back at the building, fidgeting. She shouldn't take more than a twenty-minute break this time of night, but she didn't want to miss her chance to be with Jace. What if she never saw him again? "I don't think I can be gone for long."

"We can just ride around for a while."

"I'd rather kiss you for a while," she said, tilting her head to the side so she could kiss him inside his helmet.

"Kissing will be involved."

"Yeah?"

"Among other things."

She liked the sound of that. She kissed him again and stepped away so he could mount the bike. The Harley roared to life, and he extended a hand to help her climb on behind him. She molded herself to his back, loving the scent of his body mixed with the smell of leather. He drove to a secluded area far outside of town, turned off the bike, and shifted it back onto its kickstand. Roy was going to skin her alive for taking off like this. She should already be back at work by now.

She'd give herself the pleasure of Jace's company for a minute more. Just a minute. She unzipped his jacket, her hands sliding over the T-shirt beneath the worn leather. She couldn't get enough of his hard little body. She was so stupid about this guy. Dammit. Why did he make her feel so out of control? And why did she like it? Control had always been her forte.

He removed his helmet and stuck it on the end of his handlebars.

Looking up at the sky, he said, "You can see the stars out here away from the city lights."

She tilted her head back and took in the beauty of the speckled sky. "I never take the time to look at the stars. I'm usually working." She snuggled closer to Jace. She hoped Roy didn't fire her for leaving. She could tell him she had an emergency. Knowing Jace was leaving Vegas counted as an emergency, didn't it? Her arms tightened around him. She had to admit she didn't want him to go.

"Come here," Jace murmured, sliding an arm around her waist to coax her to move around his body.

She slid so they faced each other, her back to the handlebars and her legs straddling his. Up on the main road, a car passed, but no one seemed to know their little dirt road existed.

"You said you wanted to drive out to the desert to have an orgy on my bike." His low voice sent ripples of delight through her body. "If you still want—"

Aggie kissed him, thrusting her tongue into his mouth. He remembered that offhand comment? He groaned, his hands gripping her bare thighs beneath her skirt. She tugged his T-shirt up and ran her hands over the smooth, warm flesh of his belly. Why did this man drive her so crazy? No other man ever had. Not like this. Her fingers moved to his fly, releasing his thickening cock from its confines. She stroked his length with both hands until he was fully erect.

She tugged her mouth from his. "Condom," she whispered.

"We don't have to rush," he murmured.

"Yes, we do. I want you."

He pulled a condom out of his pocket, and she took it from him. After applying it, she slid her thong to one side and shifted her hips closer to his on the bike's seat.

"Careful," he said, "the engine's still hot."

"I'll show you what's hot." She rose up, directed his cock into her body, and sank down, taking him deep. Her head fell back in wonder. Her breath released in a shuddering gasp.

"That is hot," he murmured.

"It's always hot for you." She found good footholds, having no idea what part of the bike she was using for leverage and not much caring. Rising and falling over him, she rocked her hips with each downward motion, grinding her clit against him. He held her to support her motions, his forearms running along her sides and back, palms at her shoulder blades, fingers pressing into her skin. His lips gently caressed her throat and chest.

Why did his tenderness drive her insane with need? "Jace."

He rocked with her, coaxing her into that perfect rhythm. He seemed to know her body better than she did. The rough beard stubble along his chin scraped over the sensitive flesh of her nipple as he nudged her bodice down. Her back arched, her breast offered willingly to his attention. He sucked her nipple into his mouth, rubbing the tender bud with the flat of his tongue. The rhythm of his mouth matched the rhythm of their joining. She felt the tug at her breast through her womb, her pussy, her clit.

"Oh, Jace. Oh."

Her breath caught as her body spiraled toward orgasm. She increased the tempo of their joining, rising and falling over his thick cock, faster and faster—driving it hard into her body. Deep. So deep. Seeking release.

Wanting it.

Needing it.

Now, Jace. Make me come.

But he would have none of it. His elbows clamped into her sides, and he slowed her motions into their perfect rhythm.

He released her nipple from his mouth. "Don't rush, baby. Savor it. It might be awhile before I see you again."

So he planned to see her again? She usually hated making plans for the future. Things never seemed to work out the way she intended, but as unusual as it was for her, she *wanted* to see him again. The sooner, the better.

Jace used his chin to brush the other cup of her bustier down and tugged her neglected nipple into his mouth. Again, he sucked with the same rhythm of their joining.

"Oh, Jace. Please."

He shifted forward slightly, changing the angle of penetration.

She gasped, her head falling back in wonder. "Feels so good."

He murmured in agreement around her nipple. He'd probably like her to hurt him, but she didn't want to. She wanted to be tender with him, the way he was always tender with her. Well, until he got overexcited and fucked her hard. She wondered if he could get off without pain.

Jace's tempo increased at her breast. She met it, grinding down as he rotated his hips. He pulled away from her breast, gasping in delight. "Aggie. Hurt me."

"Not this time, Jace."

It was too dark to see his expression. Was he disappointed?

He kissed her. Their bodies moved together faster. Faster. She gasped into his mouth. Ground against him. Seeking release. Seeking.

He separated their mouths and rested his forehead against her jaw. "You feel so good, baby."

"Can you come if we're gentle like this?"

"It will take awhile," he murmured.

"I've got all the ten minutes in the world. I'm so gonna get fired for taking a fuck break in the middle of my shift."

He chuckled. "If you get fired, I'll hire you as my personal dominatrix. I'll go broke in a matter of days, but—"

"I'll give you a frequent flyer discount."

He laughed, the deep, rich sound warming her insides. Why did that laugh mean so much to her? It made no sense. She cherished it. More than any of the other things she loved about this man, his laugh meant the most to her.

Their bodies continued to come together, moving in perfect synch. Her thighs trembled in exhaustion.

"You getting tired?"

"A little," she admitted.

He shifted back on the seat, pulling her with him. "Lie back for a while."

She leaned back against the tank, the gas cap between her shoulder blades, the handlebars hitting her in the back of the head. Not the most comfortable position, but he took over the motion, rocking forward to possess her body. She arched her back to get more comfortable. He gasped brokenly.

"God, baby, I'm going to miss you," he murmured.

"Los Angeles isn't that far away. Come visit me when you have a spare evening."

"Can I?"

"I want you to. I'm going to miss you too."

He slid his arms under her back and lifted her so he could kiss her passionately. His breath caught. Their bodies moved together faster. Her pleasure built. Their breaths mingled in excited hitches. He moaned, rubbing his open mouth over her throat. She cried out. They strained against each other as they flew to nirvana together. The stars in Aggie's eyes had nothing to do with those in the sky above.

Chapter 12

JACE OPENED HIS APARTMENT door and tossed his duffel bag on the floor. He set his bass guitar down gently beside it. "Hi, honey, I'm home." His voice echoed through the sparsely furnished one-bedroom apartment. He hung his keys on their hook and closed the door.

"Brroowww rrrown rrown rrrown rown." Brownie, a black tuxedo cat with white paws and a large, white inverted triangle under her chin, trotted in his direction and wrapped her sleek body around his boot. Round and round his ankle she went, still meow-purring in her unusual fashion.

He lifted her and snuggled her against his chest, her front paws resting on his shoulder. Her soft tail flicked against his arm repeatedly.

"Did you miss me?"

She rubbed her face against his jaw and batted at his small hoop earring with one paw.

"I missed you too. Tony been feeding you properly?"

"Brrroowww rrrowwwn." He carried her toward the kitchen, and she switched from her unusual meow to purr in earnest.

Jace opened a cabinet and found the cat food stash had dwindled significantly in his absence, so Tony had been feeding her regularly. And from the lack of bad odor in the room, he'd also been cleaning her litter box like he was supposed to. A good, trustworthy kid. Jace would give him a big bonus for taking care of his girl in his extended absence.

Jace set Brownie on the kitchen counter and pulled out several cans of food, reading the contents to her as he set them one at a time in a row in front of her.

"So what will it be?"

She put a definitive paw on the top of one can.

"Salmon?"

"Brrrooowww rrrowwwn."

"All right. Fish breath it is. But if you think I'm going to let you lick my chin later, you're in for a surprise."

While he opened the can, she jumped off the counter and rubbed round and round his ankle again. He set her saucer of food on the floor, gave her a good scratch behind one ear, and went to unpack.

Most of the clothes in his bag were dirty. He sorted them into piles to take to the laundry room in the basement later. Laundry wasn't his favorite chore, but unlike the rest of his bandmates, he wasn't a slob. He just pretended to be messy in order to fit in better. He also pretended that he couldn't cook and that he didn't clean. None of them knew that he had a cat or that he talked to her as if she were a person. He was very careful to disguise himself around the guys. To be who they expected him to be, not who he really was.

He removed his most treasured possession from the deep recesses of his bag and set it on the two pedestals on the center shelf of his bookcase. He ran one finger over the drumstick with a slight smile on his lips. This slender piece of wood had changed his entire life, and the man who had given it to him, completely by chance nine years before, had no idea the impact he'd had on an abused and neglected kid headed down a path of self-destruction. Jace had no doubt that Eric Sticks had saved his life. In a different way than he'd saved Trey's life, but no less important in the outcome. Jace turned on the stereo and sank into the sofa that was covered with a sheet to hide the rips and stains in the upholstery. He wasn't sure why he didn't get new furniture. It wasn't as if he couldn't afford it, but this was enough for him. He didn't need much—didn't want much. An image of Aggie's lovely face, her ruby red lips curled in a sexy smile, settled in his thoughts.

Brownie joined him on the sofa and helped herself to his lap while she licked her paws and rubbed them over her face.

"I met a girl."

Brownie paused and stared at him with amber eyes.

He chuckled. "What's that look for?" Sometimes he thought she understood what he was saying. "Don't worry. I won't let myself get too attached to her." Though he was considering calling Aggie right now. She was probably asleep. He shouldn't bother her. Maybe he should text her. She'd sent him a picture of her left nipple earlier that day and typed that she wished his tongue was on it at that moment. Oh yes. She had his full attention, even without the sexy little text messages. "I think I'll head to the gym," he told his cat. "Get in a good workout. Box a few rounds."

"Browww wwowwn." The cat looked at him morosely.

"All right, I'll work out here instead." He pulled off his shirt on his way to his tiny bedroom. He'd installed a bar in the doorway and used it now to do pull-ups.

After he'd completed a few dozen reps, Brownie lay down on the floor and batted at Jace's toes every time they came in reach. Jace slid his feet between the bar and the upper doorsill and switched to doing inverted sit-ups. Brownie wiggled her butt, leaped into the air, and attacked his head repeatedly. After one too many claws to the scalp, he caught her in midair and lifted her to look her in the eye upside down. "Will you knock it off?"

She batted his nose with one paw, careful to keep her claws concealed.

"You've been bored, haven't you? I need to get you a friend. I've been on the road too much lately."

"Browww wwowwn."

She grabbed his earring with one claw and urged him forward so she could rub her mouth over his jaw.

"Ugh. Fish breath."

He set her down, grabbed the bar, and released his feet before lowering himself to the floor.

"Let's jam." He knew what Brownie was after. His cat loved bass guitar music. For his one feline audience, Jace played Sinners' entire set list, not the way the original bassist, Jon Mallory, had written it, but the way Jace felt it should be played. He'd never let the guys in the band know he'd rewritten every bass line. They wouldn't appreciate that kind of creativity. While he played, Brownie watched him, tail flicking earnestly to the beat. Eventually, the neighbor in the apartment below started banging on the ceiling. Jace turned off the amp and put his guitar back in its case. His cell phone beeped. Another text from Aggie. Another picture. Of her pussy. *I'm imagining your cock inside this,* she'd typed. Damn. Was the woman trying to kill him?

Chapter 13

JACE SHIFTED THE CASE holding his bass guitar to his left hand and rang the doorbell. After a moment, Sed opened his front door and beckoned Jace inside. "Eric isn't here yet. He's on his way."

"Thanks for inviting me," Jace said. He'd been holed up in his apartment for almost three weeks waiting for Trey to get better so they could go back on tour. When Sed had invited him to help work on the new album, Jace had almost pissed himself with excitement.

"Why are you thanking me?" Sed said. "I'm putting your ass to work."

Which suited Jace just fine. This was only the second time Jace had been inside Sed's condo. The first had been Sed's housewarming party, probably the wildest in the history of man. Jace didn't remember most of the evening. He'd passed out on the rooftop patio in nothing but a pair of women's blue satin panties, and Eric had drawn flowers all over his back with an indelible marker. Jace didn't recollect where he'd gotten those panties.

Sed's place was huge and extravagant. Maybe it was time for Jace to buy a place of his own. His little apartment didn't get much use, but Brownie would probably like a balcony she could sun herself on. It just seemed a waste to spend all that money on something so rarely used. Normally, Jace was on the road far more often than he was at home, but since Trey was out of commission until his finger mobility improved, they'd had to cancel a bunch of tour dates.

Jace followed Sed through the huge, open living room with its twenty-foot ceiling and red, white, and black decor. The second floor of the condo had a master bedroom and an open loft equipped with everything from a wet bar to a pool table. On the first floor, there were two additional bedrooms. One served as a guest room, but the other had been converted to a recording studio. They entered the studio, and Jace set his bass behind the black leather sofa. He took his jacket off, tossed it on a chair, and went to inspect the amps and other equipment.

"Wanna beer?" Sed asked.

"Yeah."

Sed opened a minifridge in the corner, pulled out a couple of cans, and tossed one to Jace. While Jace sipped his beer, he fiddled with a soundboard. He couldn't guess what all the knobs and sliders and switches did. "Do you actually know how to use this thing?" he asked Sed.

"No fucking clue." He laughed. "I think Eric might. I dunno."

The doorbell rang.

"That's probably Eric now." Sed left to answer the door.

Suddenly nervous, Jace perched himself on the edge of the sofa. Eric would give Jace shit for being there. For intruding in his creative process and for trying to take his best friend Jon's place. Eric and Jon had composed Sinners' last three albums together. As a band, they were diving into new territory, and Eric was sure to resent Jace for not knowing what the fuck he was doing. Jace wanted to learn—wanted to help and to share his ideas—but feared he'd just get in the way and somehow make Sinners less.

Eric entered the studio, examined Sed's equipment setup, and then sat in the chair across from Jace. "Hey, little man. Been keeping busy?"

Jace rubbed his earlobe, fiddling with the ring there. "No. I'm ready to get back on the road." Or make a run to Vegas to see Aggie. So far he'd been able to resist her pull and intensify his misery, but he knew he wouldn't hold out much longer.

"Yeah, no kidding. I hope Trey gets better soon."

"He won't get better until he starts trying. Lazing around by his parents' pool all day isn't helping." Sed scowled. "I guess I'll have to go straighten him out."

Jace hoped Sed wasn't too hard on Trey. He knew Sed meant well, but he wasn't too easy on a person's feelings.

"Let's get busy," Sed said.

"This should be cool." Eagerness getting the better of him, Jace sat up straighter so he could see all the scraps of music on the coffee table. Maybe if he just stayed quiet and tried not to interfere with Eric's genius, they wouldn't make him leave.

Eric rifled through the stack of guitar music he'd brought with him. Stuff Brian had composed while fucking Myrna. Jace wasn't sure how anyone could think well enough to write music while having sex, but it seemed to work for their lead guitarist.

Eric arranged bits of guitar music and sheets of paper that contained Sed's lyrics. Jace's heart rate accelerated. Few things excited him. The talent of this band was at the very top. A set of sexy red lips smiled at him in his mind's eye. Well, and Aggie, but she excited him in an entirely different way.

Eric rearranged the sections several times and then nodded. "Okay, I've got the guitar music worked out. Now we need the bass line." He glanced at Jace. "Did you bring your guitar?"

Jace retrieved his bass from its case and looped the strap over his shoulder. Eric tapped a rhythm on the table with two pairs of drumsticks. "Match it."

Jace more than heard the beat, he felt it. He'd listened to Sinners' songs so many times that he instinctively knew what the bass line should sound like. It echoed in his mind. Complimented the beat. Filled it. Enriched it.

He plugged his bass into a small practice amp and played the series of notes running through his head.

Eric smiled. "Not bad."

That was almost a compliment. Jace couldn't help but grin. He noticed Sed watching him with an introspective look on his face.

Eric glanced at Sed. "You ready to sing?"

"I'm ready." Sed cleared his throat.

Eric related his vision of how the lyrics should sound, and Sed tried to copy him. It took several tries to figure out that Eric should sing it, and Sed should do his typical rumbling screams in accompaniment. Jace's heart thudded as he listened to the unique duet. That was it. That was the sound that would get them to the next level in their music. To grow. *Together.* Jace couldn't believe he was finally a part of this. When they stopped singing, Sed and Eric stared at each other in surprise. They knew it too. Jace's only regret was that Brian and Trey weren't there to share the moment.

"That was awesome," Jace said. "Holy shit. Do it again."

When Eric broached the possibility of using an electric violin in some songs, Sed was less accommodating to his vision.

Electric violin? Did they really need another stringed instrument? Something like a piano would be better, but Jace was too intimidated to say it. Eric obviously knew what he was doing. Jace needed to curtail his eagerness and let the man work.

"Just try it," Eric said to Sed. "I'll be trying something different. You should too."

Jace leaned forward. He couldn't help it. He wanted to participate. "Do I get to try something different?"

"No," Eric said.

Jace's hopes plummeted.

"Well, maybe," Eric amended. "You should add more embellishments to the bass lines to complement Brian. You're a better bassist than Jon was. I think you need to push your skill level on the new album. You must be bored as fuck playing that repetitive shit Jon composed before you signed on."

Better bassist than Jon was. Eric recognized that? He was probably just jerking Jace around, but hope insisted on floating back to the surface. Jace grinned until his cheeks hurt and glanced from Eric to Sed and back to Eric. "Okay."

"I'm going to call Trey," Sed said unexpectedly. "He needs to be here a lot more than I do. Lyrics last." Sed climbed to his feet. "Carry on. I'll be right back."

"Hey, I can't wait around all day. I've got shit to do," Eric said. Sed left the room.

"Like what?" Jace asked.

"None of your business," he said. "Go get me a beer."

He didn't have to be such an ass about it. And Jace was *not* going to get him a beer.

Eric stared him down for a few moments and then reached for another set of music. "Okay, little man. I've got another beat for you. Match it."

He listened to Eric's tapping on the table, and like before a complementary bass line sounded in his head. He started playing before Eric had completed his progression.

"How do you do that?" Eric asked. "Have you been writing music behind our backs?"

Jace shook his head. "I don't know. I hear your beat, and I just know what goes there. I think because we've been playing together for a couple years now."

"I guess it has been that long, hasn't it?" Eric looked nostalgically sad. "Here's the next one."

They continued that way for a while. Eric producing a beat. Jace matching it with bass lines. Eric scribbling down the notes Jace played. Sed still hadn't returned.

"I wonder where the fuck Sed went."

Jace shrugged.

Eric left the room. Jace scanned the score sheets on the table until Eric returned a few minutes later. "He's going somewhere with Jessica."

"Something wrong?"

"She looked upset, but what's new? Drama follows her like a little lost puppy. But Sed loves her, so what can we do?"

"We can keep writing while he's gone."

Eric considered him for a moment and then nodded. "Yeah, I guess so. What do you think about the electric violin idea?" Eric asked. "Brilliant, huh?"

Jace lowered his eyes. He knew Eric just wanted affirmation, but he still didn't see the point of adding yet another stringed instrument to a band that already had three of them. "Maybe a piano instead," he said quietly.

Eric stuck his finger in his ear and wriggled it around. "I swear I need a hearing aid. Too much drumming, I guess. What did you say?"

"I said, maybe we could do a song with some piano music."

"Piano?" Eric sat there for a moment. "Well, that's a swell idea, little man, but Sed doesn't play piano, and I can't play while I'm drumming."

"I play." The moment it was out of his mouth, he wished he could take it back. He'd given up piano over a decade ago when his mother had died. That had been the thing they had always done together, and he never felt right playing without her.

"You do?" Eric said, shifting forward in his seat. He had that thinking look on his face, and Sed wasn't there to talk him down.

"No, I—"

"You've been holding out on us? Are you any good?"

He was, but he sure didn't want Eric to know it. "No, I suck. Forget I mentioned it."

Eric refused to be deterred, and after much berating, pleading, and bullying, got Jace to play something on the keyboard. It wasn't a piano technically. At least that's what Jace told himself as his fingers moved over the flimsy keys.

"Well, there you go," Eric said. "You get to try something different."

"I'm not really comfortable playing the piano."

"Why not? You rock at it."

Jace lowered his eyes. "My mother—"

"Don't have one of those, so can't relate, sorry. Can you play a guitar riff on the piano?"

Jace shrugged. "I guess."

Eric had piano music embedded into a song in a matter of minutes.

"How do you do that?" Jace asked.

"Do what?"

"Put all that together so quickly."

Eric shrugged. "Don't know. The layers just mesh in my head. Where the hell did Sed go? I have this thing I need to go to."

"What kind of thing?"

"Some program to keep kids off the street. I was hoping Sed would come with. Brian used to go and give the kids guitar lessons. They loved that shit, but he's MIA—probably lost between Myrna's thighs. So I figured Sed could take his place. He's great with kids, believe it or not."

Jace didn't find that hard to believe at all. Sed kind of took a father figure role with everyone around him. Jace included.

"You wanna go?" Eric asked.

Jace's heart thudded. "Me?"

"Yeah, why not? The kids probably won't have any idea who the fuck you are, but we can still have fun with them."

"I'm not good with kids."

"It probably would be a pain in the ass to have to look up to eight-year-olds all the time."

And they were back to making fun of Jace's height. "Yeah, it does put a kink in my neck."

Eric laughed and pounded him on the back enthusiastically. "So you're coming with, right? I don't want to go by myself, and you're the only one here."

Jace was surprised he asked, even if it was because no one else was available to coerce. "Yeah, fine. Whatever. I've got nothing better to do."

"Awesome. You'll look real special in the purple dinosaur costume."

"What?"

———

Thank God for small favors; there was no dinosaur costume. Jace had a great time showing underprivileged kids how to thumb a bass groove, but he had even more fun watching Eric, the human jungle gym, make a total and complete ass of himself for their amusement. When Eric finally got around to his reason for being there, he gifted each kid with a set of drumsticks. Jace considered telling Eric about the drumstick he had treasured for the past ten years. How Eric had changed his life without even knowing it. Jace just couldn't find the words. His one-sided connection with Eric was too personal. Too stupid. Embarrassing. So he accompanied Eric's obnoxious table-drumming with an improvised bass line instead.

To keep time with Eric's beat, the kids drummed each other more than solid surfaces, but everyone was laughing and having a good time. Even Jace.

Their hour with the kids flew by. Eric had more energy than all twenty kids put together. On their way out the door, Eric pounded Jace on the shoulder. "Let's go grab a beer or two. What do you say?"

Jace smiled. Was he finally making that elusive connection with Eric? "Yeah. Sounds great."

Two beers turned into ten or twelve. Jace lost count. Being a quiet drunk, Jace stared into his magically refilling mug while Eric chattered enough for five people with everyone in shouting distance. He kept himself and half the bar entertained. Jace wasn't sure that

Eric was even aware of his presence. He wondered what Aggie was up to. Three weeks was long enough to let his pain fester. Maybe he'd drop in on her the next day. Assuming he didn't die of alcohol poisoning or asphyxiate on his own vomit in the night.

"You drunk, yet?" Eric asked near midnight.

Jace closed one eye to get rid of the three or four extra Erics in his line of sight. "Define drunk."

"Wanna go get a tattoo with me?"

Jace nodded.

"Let me pick it out. I promise it will be wicked awesome."

Jace shrugged.

"Then you're drunk enough."

Apparently, Jace was also drunk enough to get his nipple pierced, which hurt less than expected. And too drunk to stay conscious through the tattooing, despite the evil grin Eric sported as he talked to the tattoo artist who was preparing the skin on the top of Jace's foot for Eric's idea of a "wicked awesome" design.

Chapter 14

AGGIE CHECKED THE PEEPHOLE and grinned, her heart thudding with excitement. She threw the door open and tossed herself into Jace's arms with a happy squeal. She hadn't seen him in almost a month and had been starting to think she never would again.

"Sorry to just show up like this," he said. "I should have called first."

She kissed him hungrily, clutching the sides of his open leather jacket and pulling him into the house. She slammed the door closed and pressed him against its surface, still kissing him as she fumbled with the dead bolt. She eased away and gazed at him, her cheeks aching from smiling so broadly.

"I take it you aren't mad at me," he murmured.

"I missed you," she said, kissing him again. "I thought you were on tour again."

"We were, but it looks like we're going to have to cancel more tour dates."

"I thought Trey was okay now."

"Yeah, he's fine. Sed injured his throat a couple days ago. Blew a vessel in the middle of a concert. Passed out. Fuckin' blood everywhere."

"Jeez, are you all on a bad luck train, or what?"

"Eric thinks the album is cursed." He laughed and lowered his eyelids to conceal his chocolate brown eyes. "I brought you…" He flushed as he reached into a pocket inside his jacket.

Oh God, adorable.

He pulled out a single rose and presented it to her. He didn't look at her as she accepted it. What had once been a perfect blossom was now squashed from her enthusiastic hug. It was the most beautiful thing she'd ever seen. Her heart gave a little pang.

"Thank you," she whispered.

His eyes shifted to hers for a moment and then back to the floor. "Do you like it?"

She could just picture him buying it for her, embarrassed and uncertain. A flower had never meant so much to her. She touched his stubble-rough cheek, and his gaze finally met hers. "I love it, Jace."

He grinned, his eyes softening as he looked at her. She melted and leaned closer to kiss him. His firm lips commanded every sense to full attention. She moaned softly, her eyes drifting closed, her free hand curling into his chest. He was just as good as she remembered.

"Uh… Mistress V?" a hesitant voice said behind her.

Shit! She'd totally forgotten she had a client waiting in the sanctum. Reluctantly, she pulled away from Jace.

"You're busy. I'll go," Jace said. His gaze focused over her shoulder at the huge, tattooed man at her back.

Good ol' Larry. One of her few regular customers.

"I don't want you to go. Will you wait? He's my only appointment tonight. It'll only take me three minutes." She kissed him again. "Three minutes."

"I paid for twenty," Larry said gruffly.

Aggie grinned. "Three minutes," she whispered.

Jace nodded. "I'll wait."

She leaned away from him and went to punch in the code to disarm the alarm. She opened the door to her personal home and ushered Jace inside. "Make yourself at home," she said. "There's some leftover soup on the stove if you're hungry. Wine in the fridge." He stepped across the threshold, glancing around anxiously. Probably on the lookout for her mother, who was not home. Supposedly, she was at a job interview—her first in a month. Aggie drank in the sight of Jace in her home. God, he was fine. She'd forgotten how attractive he was. "Or you can get naked and wait for me in my bedroom," she whispered into his ear.

He grinned. "Go take care of your *friend*. I'll be fine."

She turned to find her customer watching her with a dark scowl. "Did I tell you that you could come out of that room, you fucking wuss?" she yelled.

"No, Mistress V." Trembling, he stumbled back into the sanctum.

"I'm going to beat your ass for disobeying me!" she added for good measure. She turned back to Jace and brought the rose to her nose, inhaling its delicate fragrance. "Will you take this to the kitchen so I can put it in water?"

He nodded, accepting the rose. She planted a tender kiss next to Jace's amused lips. "See you in a few, baby."

She closed Jace into her home and locked herself in the sound-proof room with her customer. She found these big, tough guys were always the easiest to break. Easy because they wanted to submit, but never had the opportunity to do so in their daily lives.

"Why are you still dressed?" she asked. "I told you to strip. I am not pleased."

"Forgive me, Mistress V."

"I will not! Your discipline will be strict and painful."

It took him longer to get his clothes off and the restraints on than it took her to make him cry and beg her to stop. She gave him a little time to pull himself together before she took his money and escorted him out the front door.

"Same time next week?" he asked.

"Are you going to make it the full twenty minutes next time?"

He chuckled. "Probably not, but I'll still pay for it, just in case."

She smiled and patted his cheek. Her favorite kind of customer—ones who wasted a lot of their money and little of her time. "I'll jot you down, Larry. Now go home, and fuck your wife. Consider bringing her with you next time." Aggie loved to work with couples.

He chuckled again. "Maybe I will. Our sex life has never been better. She loves it when I come see you."

"I'll bet she does."

"Maybe I'll surprise her with one of those corsets you make. Do you think she'd like that?"

"You won't be able to surprise her. She'll have to be fitted."

His face fell. "Oh."

"But we'll let her pick out the design."

He grinned. "Yeah, okay. Thanks, doll."

Aggie winked and locked the door behind him. And now, a little pleasure for herself.

She found Jace sipping reheated vegetable soup at the breakfast bar. Her magnificent, squashed rose was in a blue plastic tumbler of water on the counter beside him. She smiled at the sight. She'd love him to be in her kitchen every evening, but knew he was skittish about relationships. She didn't mind taking it slow. But, God, she'd missed him. His monosyllable phone conversations and occasional text messages weren't nearly enough.

He started in surprise when he caught sight of her. "I thought you were joking when you said three minutes."

"I think he made it all the way to four this time. He's a regular of mine."

Jace lowered his gaze, slurped another spoonful of soup into his mouth. Every line in his body strained with tension.

She'd thought he was cool with her profession—she'd shared it with him and showed him what it entailed—but apparently, she'd been wrong. Was that why he hadn't come to see her? She'd gotten tired of inviting him and getting turned down over and over. Maybe he wasn't skittish. Maybe he was embarrassed by her. She refused to put up with that bullshit. She needed to know what his intentions were. If he was only here to feel the bite of her whip, he was going to pay for it just like everyone else. She wasn't a fool. Aggie leaned on the counter across from him and ducked low until she entered his line of vision. "Does it bother you?"

"What?"

"What I do for a living?"

He shook his head.

"It doesn't bother you that I hit men the way you like to be hit?"

"No."

"That I watch the welts rise on their naked skin and listen to their cries of agony, night after night?"

"Nope."

"That I beat them until they beg for mercy because it gives me some sick sense of empowerment to make them cry?"

"Not at all."

"Really?"

He lifted his gaze and pinned her with a hard stare. "No, not really. I fuckin' hate that *they* give you joy, but that's my problem, not yours."

He was jealous. Oh my God, she loved him.

Unable to keep her hands off him any longer, she climbed over the counter and tackled him to the floor. He tumbled off the stool onto the hard tile. "Ow." Aggie landed on top, tugging his shirt up his body.

"Wimp."

He laughed. Her heart melted. She couldn't get him naked fast enough. She wanted to fill herself with him. Not just her dripping wet pussy—her hands, her mouth, her gaze.

Everything. Filled. With him. All him. Jace.

He laughed again as she worked at removing his jeans. Was this all it took to make him happy? Pouncing on him in the kitchen?

"Do you have a condom?" she asked.

He pulled an entire strip out of his pocket.

"Did you think you were going to get laid tonight?" she asked with a teasing grin.

He chuckled. "I was hoping more than once."

"You got another date later?" she asked, looking at him with a fabricated scowl.

"Just with you."

"Good," she whispered.

She bent her head to kiss his belly. A spasm wracked his entire body. She trailed open-mouthed kisses over his stomach, just above the low waistband of his jeans.

His fingers sank into her hair. "Aggie."

Well, hello there, erogenous zone.

Nibbling, licking, sucking on his lower belly, she located his most sensitive spots inside the ridges of his hip bones, indicated by his outrush of breath and the sucking of air between his teeth. When her fingers brushed the growing bulge in his pants, he shuddered and cried out. She grinned with sudden realization.

She kissed her way up his body until they were face to face. She waited for him to open his eyes and then asked, "Have you had sex since we made love on your bike?"

He stared at her forehead and shook his head.

"Me neither."

His gaze shifted to hers. His smile could have lit the heavens.

"Why haven't you come to see me sooner?" she asked.

"I didn't think... I thought it was best..." He took a deep breath. "I have no fucking clue. I wanted to."

"Do you mind if I think of you as my boyfriend?" She wasn't going to let him brush her off. If she had to do the pursuing, so be it. She'd always gone after what she wanted in life. And she wanted Jace Seymour.

He paled and moved his gaze from her eyes to her forehead again. She waited for him to find his voice. She wasn't going to give him an easy out. If he wasn't ready to commit, that was fine, but he would have to say it. She wouldn't.

"Okay," he said finally.

"*Okay?*" She grinned at him.

"I don't mind."

She cupped his cheek. "Do you think of me as your girlfriend?"

He hesitated. "I think of you. Constantly. Is that enough?"

She chuckled. "It's a start." She kissed him gently.

He looked guilty. "I'm sorry. This is new for me."

"You don't have to apologize."

He touched her face. "It was so hard to stay away. I want you to know you mean more to me than just awesome, awesome sex."

"Only two awesomes?"

His eyes rolled into the back of his head and drifted closed. "A thousand awesomes."

She slid down his body, kissing his throat. She pulled his shirt up and caught sight of the new addition to his sculpted chest. She flicked the small silver ring in his nipple with her fingertips.

"What's this?"

He laughed again. "Bonding moment with Eric."

She sucked the ring into her mouth, and his body stiffened. *Ooo, fun.* She flicked it with her tongue. "Who's Eric?"

"Our drummer."

"Anything else I should know about?"

"Hmmmm. The wicked awesome tattoo on my ass?"

She stripped his jeans and boots off and inspected his cute, little butt to find nary a mark on his perfect ass. "I don't see anything."

"Look closely."

She ran her hands over the smooth cheeks, up and down. "Nothing here."

"That's right. It wasn't on my ass, was it? I swear I got a new one somewhere. I doubt you'll find it."

She remembered he had a few on each of his upper arms, one on the left side of his chest. Problem was she wasn't sure if she could pick a new one out of his collection. She coaxed him onto his back and pulled his shirt off, leaving him naked except for his socks, and started with the tattoo on his upper arm. A skull engulfed in flames. "I remember this one."

"You sure?"

She wasn't. "Yeah." The dagger and roses beneath it looked familiar. "This one's old too."

The demon horse and the Grim Reaper on his left pec? Old. She did like playing with his new nipple ring though. She flicked it with her tongue until he squirmed. On his other arm he had a tribal pattern in red and black from shoulder to elbow. She definitely remembered that one.

"Where is it?" she asked.

"Lower."

She kissed his nipple... his ribs... his belly. "Am I getting warm yet?"

"You are getting warmer," he murmured. "It doesn't have anything to do with how close you are to finding that tattoo though."

She sucked on the skin around his belly button. He laughed, squirming sideways across the floor.

"I had no idea you were so ticklish," she murmured.

"There's a lot you don't know about me."

That was true. Was he ready to share? She looked at him. "So tell me something."

"After you find that tattoo, I'll answer any question you ask."

She searched every inch of visible skin and found nothing. Her interest was rapidly shifting to his thick shaft, which was far more fascinating than any tattoo had ever been, but she did want to ask him a question. She searched his scalp.

"Okay, I give up. Where is it?"

"Maybe you should look under my sock."

Well, of course, that's where it would be. She peeled off his socks and found it. Her eyes opened wide, and she fell on the floor laughing. An animated daisy with a smiley face in its bright yellow center decorated his skin at the base of his left big toe.

"The moral to this story is never pass out drunk when Eric Sticks is picking out your wicked awesome tattoo."

"And it's permanent?"

"Yeah, until I get it removed." He grinned. "Or maybe I'll keep it. No one will see it there. Unless I go to the beach."

She was surprised he seemed so cool with it. Shouldn't he be upset that a friend had tricked him into getting an embarrassing tattoo while he was too drunk to stop it?

"Didn't you get mad?"

"Nah. I should have known better. The last time I got that drunk with Eric, he drew flowers all over my back with black magic marker."

"Yeah, but that washed off."

"After a week."

"Great friend you have there."

Jace lowered his eyes. "Yeah."

She saw something in him at that moment that she'd never seen before. Vulnerability. Could she get him to open up? She knew if she pushed him too hard, he'd completely shut himself off.

"So what's the story with the Eric guy?" she asked.

He didn't speak for a long moment. "He's the reason I became a bassist."

"What, is he like an old guy or something?"

Jace shook his head. "Not even five years older than me."

"And he had that much influence over you?"

"I saw a Sinners show when they were just starting out. I was fourteen and in a bar with a fake ID."

"How did you pass for twenty-one when you were fourteen? You're so cute, you scarcely look twenty-one now."

His scowl told her she'd said the wrong thing. She could practically see his wall of defense rise.

"Are we gonna fuck or what?" he said.

She wasn't going to let him change the subject that easily. "So you saw Sinners when you were fourteen. Then what? How did that make you a bassist?"

More silence. She waited.

He took a deep breath. "They were amazing even then. Brian and Trey have always been completely in tune with each other—two halves of a whole. Sed's voice is unbelievable, and Eric is the best drummer on the planet. I just stood there. Stunned. I couldn't move. All I could do was listen. I could scarcely breathe. The four of them were so incredibly talented. And then there was their weak link. Jon Mallory."

"Let me guess. Their bassist?"

"The band deserved better. He's totally average. Not horrible. Just not as good as the rest of them, and I think he was high or something. He wasn't into the music. He was into himself."

"So you decided to become their bassist."

"No. I didn't know how to play bass. I've always loved music and had some talent, but it never occurred to me to make a life of it. At the end of the show, Eric tossed his drumsticks into the crowd, and I caught one. I didn't even reach for it. It sort of connected with my hand. It was a wake-up call for me. I'd spent the previous four years getting into trouble, but right then, I knew what I wanted to do with the rest of my life—what I had to do. It was fate. I had to become part of Sinners."

This was the most Jace had ever spoken to her at once. Aggie was careful not to say something that might encourage his silence again. "So how long did it take you to become their bassist?"

"Six years. And if it wasn't for Trey's brother, I'd probably be playing with another band now."

"Trey was the guitarist who was hurt, right?"

"Yeah, his brother, Dare, is the lead guitarist for Exodus End."

Exodus End? They were huge worldwide. And Sinners were pretty big too and growing. "Wow. It just occurred to me that you're famous."

He chuckled. "Not really. Brian? Maybe. Sed? Definitely. But I'm just the bassist."

"I want to see you in concert."

"You do?"

She nodded. "Yeah, just thinking about it is making me hot."

"We're supposed to have a show in San Francisco this Saturday. I could get you tickets if you want to go, assuming Sed can sing by then. Knowing Sed, he'll find a way."

"Really? I'd love to go. Count me in."

"I'll make the arrangements then."

His eyes lowered to her mouth, and he ran his tongue over his top lip before gnawing on it. She could only imagine what he was thinking. Hopefully, something sexy. She decided they could talk later.

"Let's go to my bedroom. No telling when my mom will show up, and you're sort of naked."

He glanced down at his body. "Ah, I hadn't noticed."

"Well, I have, and you look fucking hot. I can't be expected to keep my hands off you."

"Even with the smiling flower tattoo?"

She laughed. "Especially with the tattoo. You explained why it's special."

"Special?" He laughed. "Yeah, it makes me feel real *special*."

The front door opened. Jace's eyes opened wide.

"Shit, that's my mom. Put your pants on."

Aggie grabbed his pants, tossed them at him, and then scrambled to her feet. She smoothed her hair and plastered an innocent smile on her face. Her mom tossed her purse on the counter.

"Any luck?" Aggie asked.

Mom sighed. "No. It's impossible for a woman over thirty to find a job in this town."

She lit a cigarette and pointed its glowing red tip at the single rose in the tumbler of water on the counter. "What's with the crumpled up, half-dead rose?"

Aggie scowled. "My boyfriend gave it to me."

Said boyfriend climbed to his feet to stand beside her. He had managed to get his pants on, but was still shirtless.

He took a deep breath and extended a hand toward Aggie's mother. "I'm Jace."

Mom shook his hand briefly. "Tabitha," she supplied her name and then glanced at Aggie. "Since when do you have a boyfriend?"

"Since about ten minutes ago."

Mom lifted an eyebrow at Jace. "You move fast, Maynard." She nodded toward the floor at his feet. "And you seem to have dropped your condoms. All twelve."

Jace's eyes widened, and he bent to scoop up the strip of condoms. He shoved them into his pocket. He retrieved his T-shirt and tugged it on over his head. "I've got to go."

"Don't go," Aggie said, her heart sinking with disappointment. "You just got here."

"I-I've got stuff to do. I should probably check on Sed. Make sure he's okay. He just got out of the hospital."

Funny how he always showed up when one of his friends was injured. Aggie made a note to ask about it when her mother wasn't staring at him with brutal scrutiny.

"Don't mind me, Maynard," Mom said, taking a deep drag off

her cigarette. "By all means, continue to boink my daughter on the kitchen floor."

"*Mother!*"

"What?" Mom shrugged and took another drag, smoke curling toward the ceiling slowly.

"Why do you always do this to me? I really like him."

"So boink him then. This is your house. I don't care what you do. Could I get something to eat before you continue? Your boinking is blocking the fridge."

Jace picked up his socks and boots and headed for the front door. Aggie scowled at her mother and then went after him.

"You're not even going to say good-bye?" It had been a long time since a guy had hurt her feelings, but unshed tears burned her eyes and made her forehead ache. She rubbed her brow in annoyance.

He turned toward her, his eyes downcast. She'd finally gotten him to open up with her a little, and her stupid mother had to show up and ruin everything.

He nodded toward the dining room. "I forgot my jacket."

"If you don't want to stay here, we can go somewhere. And we don't have to do anything sexual if you don't want to. I'm sure my mother creeped you out and put your sex drive in park."

"More like reverse."

"That's okay. I just want to spend some time with you."

His eyes rose to meet hers. "You do?"

"Yeah. We can talk."

"I don't talk much."

He just had, but she wouldn't push him away by pointing that out. "Then I'll talk. You listen."

"I'm good at listening."

She stepped closer and wrapped her arms around him. "That's not the only thing you're good at."

Aggie slid her fingers into the hair at his nape and drew him closer for a plundering kiss. Slowly, he relaxed into her. She could feel his heart thudding in his chest against her breasts as their mouths melded.

"Agatha, where's the Tabasco sauce?" Mom called from the kitchen.

Jace stiffened and pulled away.

"I'm going to change clothes. You can wait for me outside if it makes you feel more comfortable."

He nodded appreciatively. "Bring my jacket out with you, please." Still barefoot, he let himself out of the house.

Aggie stormed into the kitchen. "I could just slap you right now," she sputtered at her mother.

"You shouldn't get messed up with your clients anyway, Agatha. They've got more baggage than a 747's cargo hold."

"I didn't ask for advice. Do you want me to end up like you? Alone and miserable and bitter. No money. No job. With a hit out on you because you're stupid enough to borrow money from the Mafia."

Mom's eyes narrowed. "I think you're the one who needs to be slapped, young lady."

Aggie shook her head in annoyance. "I'm going out, not that I need your permission. And shouldn't you be leaving?"

"Yeah, I'm leaving soon. I'd already be gone if I had a choice in the matter."

"You chose to get yourself in trouble, so I don't want to hear it."

"Isn't your boyfriend waiting for you?"

"Yeah. And don't wait up. I plan to boink him all night." Aggie fled the kitchen, feeling like an intruder in her own house. She needed to get away from her mother in a bad way.

After changing into jeans and a T-shirt, Aggie grabbed her leather jacket along with Jace's and then met him at the curb. He sat on his bike, gazing up at the sky. She touched his arm gently, and he started.

"Do you always think that hard?" she asked, handing him his jacket. He slipped into the worn leather garment.

"Mostly."

"Where do you want to go?"

"Anywhere."

So he was back to answering her questions with as few words as possible.

"Do you want to go someplace quiet where we can be alone? Or crowded where we can have a lot of fun?"

"I don't like crowds."

"Then let's just ride."

"You'd like that?"

"Yeah."

He smiled, and her heart melted. "Me too."

He took her hand and helped her climb onto the bike behind him.

"Aggie?"

"Yeah?"

"I really like you too."

She slid her arms around his waist and put her chin on his shoulder to try to see his expression under the light of the corner street lamp. "I'm glad to hear you say that, Jace, but what brought it on all of a sudden?"

"You told your mom you really liked me, and I didn't say it back."

She kissed the edge of his ear. "You were probably too uncomfortable to form words."

"Kinda."

"I know my mom is overbearing, and I'd like to say she means well, but I don't think she does. Sometimes I think she's trying to make me into her. And I don't want to be like her. I'm not her."

"I had a father like that."

"Had?"

He started the bike, and they headed out of town. He never answered her query.

They picked up some takeout Chinese food and headed to the

desert. Sitting on a huge rock in the middle of nowhere, they ate quietly, enjoying the sunset on the horizon.

"How long have you done what you do?" Jace asked.

She glanced at him, surprised he was the one to break the comfortable silence between them. "Which part?"

"All of it."

"A long time. I started hitting men in my teens and decided to apprentice under another dominatrix about eight years ago to become pro. I worked in a sex club with a few other dommes for several years and then went out on my own. But first I needed to buy a house, so I started dancing to earn extra money. I never meant for it to become a permanent career, but I do enjoy it." She chuckled. "Well, most of the time. And it does make it easier to find clients."

Jace scowled.

"I never would have met you if I wasn't dancing."

"I guess."

She pressed on. "My grandmother taught me to sew and do embroidery when I was seven. I'm sure she never thought I'd use that skill to make leather corsets. She had a stroke when I was nine and died. Then my mother took over *raising* me." If what her mother did counted as raising a child.

"You make corsets?" he asked.

She nodded, noting how he always avoided conversations about family. "It's mostly a hobby. I started out making them for myself, but people see me wearing them and ask where I buy them. When they find out I make them, they want me to make one for them. I like doing it. It's fun."

"You mean you make those corsets you wear by hand? The ones with the designs on them."

She nodded.

"Wow, babe, you're really talented. Artistic."

She felt herself flush. Or maybe it was the desert heat. "It's just a hobby."

"Don't hobbies make the best careers?"

"Yeah. My first hobby was making men cry." She leaned over and kissed his temple. "So what's your family like?"

He erected a reinforced emotional barrier between them so fast, she feared she'd suffer whiplash. "Wanna go to a hotel?" he asked.

She wanted to know more about him. She already knew he was good in bed. "I thought we were going to talk."

"How about some pillow talk?"

He stole a kiss, and she decided they could talk some other time. A month without Jace's intoxicating touch was a month too long.

Chapter 15

IT WAS ALMOST TEN when Aggie's cell phone rang. She smiled when she saw Jace's name on the caller ID. Her plane had landed safely in San Francisco a few minutes ago and was sitting on the tarmac waiting for an open gate. She couldn't wait to see Jace in concert the next night and tonight she had big plans for him in their hotel room.

"Hello."

"Aggie, I know I'm supposed to be picking you up at the airport right now."

"*Supposed* to be?"

"Could you do me a huge favor?"

"How huge?"

"Bail me and Eric out of jail."

Jail? She dropped the phone in her lap. Picked it back up. "Why are you in *jail*?"

"Because Eric is an idiot."

"How in the hell was I supposed to know that was illegal?" some guy said in the background. "How soon can she get here? That guy is looking at me again."

"Are you in Los Angeles?" Aggie asked. "That's a long way from here. I haven't even gotten off the plane in San Francisco yet."

"No, we're downtown. In San Francisco."

"I can't believe you got arrested when you're supposed to be picking me up from the airport," she grumbled. "It would serve you right if I let you rot in there."

"I know. I don't have a problem with a night in jail. Eric seems to think he's going to be raped."

"You saw the way that drunk guy keeps looking at me," the same guy, apparently Eric, said in the background.

"He's trying to figure out why your hair is green."

"Not all of it is green. Just one little section. Besides, my hair is not on my ass."

"You sure about that?"

Aggie shook her head, wondering why Jace had called her if he was going to argue with Eric the entire time. "Don't you have someone closer who will come get you? I don't even know where to pick you up. This is my first time in San Francisco."

"There's no one else. When Eric called Brian and Trey, they just laughed their asses off."

"And Sed is having the orgy of his life on a sailboat with Jessica," Eric added.

"Neither of us has any family or friends around here, and the roadies have been threatened with job loss if they bail any of us out of jail. Ever."

"So is she coming?" Eric asked.

"I dunno. Shut up."

"We should have called Jerry," Eric said.

"Jerry will string us up by our balls. You know that."

"Jace," Aggie interrupted.

"Sorry. Eric is freaking out. He's driving me crazy. He's driving the cops crazy. And he's driving six or seven pissed-off drunk guys crazy. He does this pacing-yelling thing when he's upset. If it was just me, I'd say forget it, but—"

"I'll see what I can do. Why are you in jail anyway?"

"So we could win a bet."

Well, that explained everything. Not!

"Defacing public property and disturbing the peace!" Eric called.

"Nothing worth getting raped over, I tell you that." Apparently, he was listening in on their conversation.

"Eric, will you *shut up*?"

"No, but I will kick your ass, little man. That's what I *will* do."

Jace sighed heavily. "If you can't come, Aggie, I understand. But if I beat him to death with his own shoe, it's going to be on your conscience."

She sighed with resignation. "Where do I go to get you bailed out?"

He handed the phone to a police officer who explained the process. She jotted down some notes. She could probably catch a taxi to the courthouse without a problem, but so much for the delicious night she'd planned with Jace between her thighs.

Jace got back on the phone. "Thanks, baby. I owe you one."

"You'll be making this up to me for years, *baby*."

By the time she had Jace and Eric in her custody, it was well after two a.m. "Let's get to the hotel and get some sleep." Aggie knew she had a serious crankitude, but she couldn't help it. What kind of idiots thought it was okay to ride a motorcycle down the pedestrian sidewalk on the Golden Gate Bridge and drape the national monument with enormous banners? Her boyfriend and his drummer friend apparently. It was pretty sweet of them to help Jessica propose marriage to Sed, but not smart.

"Sounds like a plan. I'm beat," Eric said. He was tall and slender—good-looking in a rugged, crazy haircut kind of way. She vaguely remembered him being the guy who'd been escorted from the club by the bouncers the night she'd met Jace. Under normal circumstances, Aggie might have appreciated Eric's graceful masculinity, but at the moment, she really wanted to kick him in the teeth.

"Uh, get your own room," Aggie grumbled.

"The hotel is booked, and he doesn't have any place to stay tonight," Jace said.

"There's a perfectly good park bench right there." Aggie

indicated a bench already hosting a sleeping, reeking man, who was snoring softly under a newspaper.

"Aggie," Jace murmured close to her ear. "Why can't he sleep in our room? It's not like you're going to let me touch you in the mood you're in."

"And why am I in this mood, Jace?" She hadn't even let him kiss her yet.

Eric grinned. "Because he was supposed to pick you up from the airport and take you out for a nice dinner before you two trashed a hotel room in a lust-crazed frenzy of sex. I'm guessing none of that's happening tonight."

No argument. Aggie collapsed into the backseat of their cab and slid to the far side. "Fine. Eric can sleep on the floor. It will make it easier to stomp on him repeatedly in the morning."

"Dude, your chick is hardcore," Eric said to Jace.

Jace slid into the cab beside Aggie with a wicked grin affixed to his gorgeous face. "I like that about her."

Eric folded his long form into the backseat. "She's also a total babe. You've been holding out on me. So how did you like his new tattoo, Agster?" Eric sniggered. "Is it wicked awesome, or what?"

"I was just glad it was you who picked it out and not him," Aggie said. "I wouldn't want to think a guy I'm fucking has the taste of a total pussy."

Eric licked the side of Jace's forehead. "He does sorta taste like pussy." Eric smacked his lips as he contemplated his palate. "A touch saltier than lady sauce, but not bad."

Aggie tried to maintain The Cranky, but it was impossible. She burst out laughing. Jace wiped Eric's spit from the side of his face, obviously annoyed. "You are paying to get my bike out of impound, jackass."

"Uh, no, I'm not."

"The whole Golden Gate Bridge thing was your idea."

"You could have said no."

Aggie took Jace's hand in the darkness and gave it a squeeze. She knew that he couldn't easily say no to Eric—what with the hero worship thing he had going on. Now that Aggie had met Eric, she understood Jace's devotion to the guy even less. She had been expecting the mentorly type, not this crazy dude with the wacky sense of humor.

"You should pay half," Jace said.

"I'll pay half. Only fair." Eric poked Jace in the side, a huge grin on his face. "At least we won the bet. What kind of tattoos should we make Brian and Trey get on their asses?"

"Smiley-faced daisies?"

"No way. That's vintage Jace Seymour. I was thinking more along the lines of kittens and unicorns."

"And rainbows?"

Eric's eyes lit up. "Yeah, definitely rainbows. Good call, man. Good call."

There were too many hands on Aggie's body. She recognized the one tangled in her hair and the one resting on her back as belonging to Jace, but the one on her ass? Nope. Not familiar. Or perhaps a bit too familiar. She lifted her head from Jace's shoulder and turned it to find Eric Sticks grinning at her.

"Good morning," he said, blue eyes sparking with mischief.

"Is there a reason why your hand is on my ass?"

He removed it and winked. "It felt right at the time."

"You're supposed to be sleeping on the floor."

"It's hard on my back, and I have a concert to perform tonight. I knew you'd understand."

"The only thing I understand is you getting out of this bed."

"Shh," Jace murmured, his arms tightening around Aggie. She'd used him as a pillow all night because Eric had insisted that he needed three pillows if he had to sleep on the floor. That left one pillow for Aggie and Jace to share. "Early…"

"We can get it on while Jace sleeps," Eric whispered. "He doesn't join the living until noon."

"I did bring Jace's favorite flail," Aggie said. "It's in my luggage. I'm sure you could use a good, hard beating."

Eric's eyes widened. "You're joking."

Aggie lifted her eyebrows. "Do I look like I'm joking?"

"Don't worry. She won't break the skin," Jace mumbled.

"I think I'll pass." Eric scooted over a few inches and flopped onto his back to stare up at the ceiling. "I'm bored."

Aggie snuggled closer to Jace. She was starting to think he could sleep through an earthquake.

"So Aggie, what do you like to do for fun?" Eric asked.

"Besides make men cry?"

He laughed uncomfortably. "Yeah, besides that."

"She sews," Jace murmured.

"Sews?"

"Yeah, sews."

"What? Like pot holders?"

"No, like leather corsets," Aggie said.

"She makes them by hand and sews designs on them," Jace said, starting to sound more alert now.

"Embroidery," Aggie clarified.

"They're works of art." Jace's hand stroked her hair lethargically. "And sexy."

"Oh," Eric said flatly. "Well, that gives me a boner. Now I'm bored *and* horny."

"And I'm wide awake," Jace said. "Time for you to leave." He reached over Aggie and shoved Eric onto the floor.

Eric climbed to his feet and stood at the side of the bed with both hands resting on his narrow hips. "Why do I have to leave?"

"Because those plans I had with Aggie last night…"

"Destroy the hotel room in a lust-fueled frenzy of sex?"

"Yeah, those plans. I'm ready to get started now. We have a lot of making up to do before the concert tonight."

Jace rose up on one elbow to stare down at Aggie with his most smoldering look. She smiled, knowing she was about to have a wonderful day. *Rock on!*

"So I'll help you," Eric offered. "I owe her too."

"Get lost, Eric," Aggie said, her body already thrumming with anticipation.

Jace lifted his gaze to Eric. "You heard the lady."

"Aw, come on, little man. I'm dying here. Just let me watch a little."

Jace shook his head. "Not this time. Now go away before I kick your ass."

"Yeah, right." But even as he said it, Eric reached for his shirt and tugged it on over his head. "I'm starving anyway. Who needs sex when you can have scrambled eggs?"

"I'll see you at the arena," Jace said.

Eric launched three pillows at them before showing himself to the door. "Don't forget we have that thing to rehearse for Jessica."

"I'll be there."

The door closed, and Jace turned his attention back to Aggie.

"What thing for Jessica?" she asked.

He smiled. "You'll see. It's a surprise. For everyone."

"Eric's a bit…" She scrunched her forehead, trying to think of the proper adjective.

"Eccentric?"

"Yeah, I guess that's the word."

"Most geniuses are."

"You think he's a genius?" Aggie stuck a thumb in the direction of the door Eric had just exited.

"I know he's a genius. I've seen him compose."

"You're the genius," she whispered and tugged his lips to hers for a kiss.

"I really am sorry you had to bail me out of jail last night." He trailed suckling kisses along her jaw.

"I'm glad you realize you can depend on me."

He froze. There she went scaring him off again.

"But I do think you need to be punished for ruining my evening," she added.

He relaxed again, took her hands in his, and drew her arms up over her head. "Later," he said. "First, I need to offer my apologies. Consider every kiss an 'I'm sorry.'"

It didn't take her long to realize how very sorry he was.

Chapter 16

AGGIE STOOD BESIDE THE stage on the stadium floor. Roadies and all five band members milled about in the darkness. It was almost time for Sinners to take the stage. She longed to grab Jace and plant a big wet kiss on his lips. He'd more than made up for that bail-me-out-of-jail incident, and she was primed to show her appreciation. After hours of apologies, she figured he'd be relaxed in her company. Just the opposite. As soon as she'd arrived at the arena, he had become withdrawn and skittered away if she even touched him. She blamed it on nerves. He didn't seem to enjoy performing live.

"Are you sure you can sing, Sed?" some dark-haired roadie, adorned with more tattoos than all five band members combined, asked. Everyone was treating the vocalist like fragile glass. Apparently, no one trusted his throat was well enough for a show.

"Yeah, my doctor said singing was not a problem. I'm supposed to limit my screaming though, hence the violin." He lifted a black, electric violin and drew a bow across the strings. It screeched in protest. "I'm still not sure how I'm supposed to hold a microphone and a violin at the same time."

Someone squeezed Aggie's shoulder. She turned to find Jessica beaming like a lighthouse beacon. "Aggie! It's been ages. How are things?"

"Great. Anything new with you?"

She thrust her left hand in Aggie's face and did an excited little dance while Aggie examined the small diamond engagement ring on her finger. "Sed and I got engaged last night."

Aggie hugged her and didn't mention bailing Jace and Eric out of jail because they'd helped make her over-the-top proposal happen. "I'm happy for you, sugar. I knew you and Sed still had a thing for each other."

Jessica released Aggie and snagged her fiancé around the waist. She kissed Sed passionately before chastising him about taking it easy while singing and screaming onstage. Sed assured her that he was fine—his doctor had cleared him to do this concert—though no one looked convinced, least of all Jessica.

Someone cued the band. Jace pecked Aggie on the cheek as he passed her. She decided that was the most affection she'd get from him until they were alone.

A bass drum thudded repeatedly. The low, rhythmic sounds of a bass guitar filled the undertones of the song. Aggie held her breath in anticipation of the stage lights coming on so she could see Jace. Now all she could see were four sets of feet in a blue light that shone across the stage floor. A guitar wailed. The crowd cheered. The carried note of an electric violin screeched through the speakers. An astonished hush fell over the crowd. Bright lights bathed the stage. When the note came to an end, Sed held the violin and bow in one hand and plucked the microphone off its stand with his other to sing. The crowd's enthusiasm increased throughout the song until Sed took to his violin again, grinding one long note against the strings, and the audience fell silent in shock. Aggie wasn't sure what was going on.

Jessica stood beside her with both hands clutched against her chest as she watched Sed muddle his way through the song, alternating his singing with violin playing. "What's going on?" Aggie asked her.

Jessica tore her gaze from her fiancé onstage. "Poor baby. I've never seen him so nervous."

Nervous? The guy was unequivocally dynamic. How could anyone think he was capable of nervousness? Jace, on the other hand, had inched so far toward the back of the stage, Aggie rarely caught a glimpse. She could hear him though. The low pitch of his bass guitar throbbed through her entire body—the sound rich and alive and incredibly sexy.

When the song came to an end, the crowd cheered and then fell silent as Sed spoke into the microphone. "I guess you noticed the violin."

Fans whispered to each other.

"Doc says I'm not allowed to scream for a while. So I'll replace some of my vocals with the violin. If you hate it, blame Eric Sticks. It was all his idea."

"I think it sounds cool!" a fan yelled.

"Yeah, cool!" someone else yelled.

The crowd broke into enthusiastic cheers.

Sed grinned. "Sinners fans are the best. You know that?"

"Oh shit," Trey said into his microphone. "I think Sed's gonna cry."

"And if Sed starts crying, you know Jace will soon follow," Brian said.

At the mention of Jace's name, Aggie's ears perked. She climbed a step at the side of the stage and craned her neck to see him. No luck.

"Better get a mop ready, Travis," Trey said.

The excessively tattooed roadie tossed a sponge onto the stage. It skittered to a stop at Sed's feet. The crowd roared with laughter. Sed picked it up and pretended to mop up tears then threw it toward the back of the stage. A discordant bass guitar note rang through the speaker and then a sponge hit Brian in the back of the head. Aggie wished she could see better.

"You shouldn't stand on the steps," the roadie, Travis, said. "You'll block traffic flow."

"But I can't see."

Travis's pierced eyebrow wrinkled in confusion. "You've got the best seat in the house."

"Jace," she clarified.

"Oh." He took her by the elbow and led her up the steps, around equipment on the edge of the stage.

When Jace came into view, her heart skipped a beat, and she smiled. Perfectly attentive to his surroundings, yet lost in his own world, he was an expert at pretending disconnection. Aggie knew better.

"Thanks," she whispered to Travis just before the next song started.

Now that she could see Jace, she couldn't take her eyes off him. His concentration was absolute, every note given equal care and precision. He was caught up in his music, as if nothing else in the world mattered. He played his instrument with the same care and attention he showed her when they made love. Her heart gave a painful lurch when she realized that music *was* his entire existence. His purpose in life. His reason for being. She would never matter to him as much as his band—these songs, this stage, any crowd. She tore her eyes from Jace and forced herself to watch the rest of the band, terrified by the direction of her thoughts. Why was she so hung up on this guy? Why did she care that she'd never be the most important thing in his life? It wasn't as if she was contemplating a future with him. She didn't contemplate her future at all. There was no point. If fate wanted to take her for a ride, it was beyond her control. Why even worry about it?

When her eyes drifted back to Jace, she found he was watching her. He offered his sexiest, gentlest smile, and she had the inexplicable urge to flee. She forced herself to stay put—to face these alien feelings swirling through her heart. To come to terms with the idea that he was important to her. It didn't matter if he reciprocated her feelings. She wanted him to be happy, to be with him in any capacity he allowed—devoted and dedicated so he could pursue his first love. Music.

Oh God, I'm a groupie. Pathetic and needy. Over a guy.

What in the world was wrong with her? The foreign idea of putting someone's needs before her own, especially a *man's*, had her head spinning. So much so that she didn't recognize the band had left the stage until an arm slid around her back and a firm pair of lips brushed her neck beneath her ear.

She shuddered and clung to Jace's T-shirt with one hand.

"Enjoying the concert?" he murmured.

"Is it over?" she asked, astonished.

He chuckled. "Are you distracted?"

That was an understatement.

"We're taking a short break, but Sed has a surprise for Jessica that we're all involved in, so I can't stay long." Jace had left her alone in the hotel for a couple hours to practice for this surprise, but he hadn't shared what it was. Not even when she'd taken her flail to him until he came.

The side of the stage where they stood was bathed in shadows. Aggie was certain that privacy was the only reason Jace claimed her mouth in a toe-curling kiss.

"I'm glad you're here," he whispered against her lips. "That I can share this part of me with you." He kissed her again, sucking at her lips gently. "Like you shared your passion for the dungeon with me."

Well, that had been sort of different. He'd watched her make grown men cry, and strangely, had been okay with her twisted nature. His passion, his music, was so much more than either of them. It touched millions of people around the world. She cupped his face, his beard stubble rough against her fingertips.

"I'm glad I'm here too." Even though it meant she had some troubling feelings to sort through.

He smiled, his even features just visible in the dim light. Jace touched his fingertips to Aggie's cheek and then returned to the stage.

Sed took Jessica by the hand and led her toward center stage.

"What are you doing?" Aggie heard Jessica's tremulous voice through Sed's microphone.

"What I planned to do before you one-upped me and proposed before I had the chance."

The band played a sweeping intro to a ballad. All three guitarists used bows on their instruments, so the music sounded more orchestral than metal. It was hauntingly romantic. When Sed started singing the tender words of a love song to Jessica, Aggie's breath caught in her throat. The pair was so lost in each other that the twelve thousand other people in the arena were forgotten. Watching them gaze at each other brought tears to Aggie's eyes. She'd never witnessed anything like it—unmistakable, unconditional love flowing between them—and she'd never thought she might have something like that. Never even wanted it—until now. She tore her eyes away from the couple at center stage and watched Jace, again caught up in his first love, his music. As scary as the idea was, she couldn't deny it. She wanted that—what Sed and Jessica had. And she wanted it with Jace.

Chapter 17

AGGIE TOSSED A PLATE of scrambled eggs in front of her mother, who was sitting on a stool at the breakfast bar. "So when are you leaving?"

"When it's safe," Mom said, sprinkling Tabasco sauce on her eggs and then digging in.

Standing, as it would take actual effort to climb onto a stool, Aggie yawned and picked at her own eggs. She'd had a rough night at the club. Some drunk dickhead had climbed on her stage and gotten fresh. Well, fresh was putting it lightly. The bouncers had to mace him to get him off her. She hated men. Well, most of them. At the moment, Jace was the only exception, and as he was touring the Northeast, she hadn't seen him for several weeks. He was always gone. They kept in contact via text message. He didn't like to talk on the phone. She missed him and worked hard not to feel bitter about his touring. Or that he was never out of her thoughts for a moment, while he was undoubtedly having the time of his life. Sinners were on their way home to LA today. Maybe she could see Jace sometime this week. She didn't handle these long stretches away from him well. "I'm tired. I'm going to bed."

"Most people sleep at night, you know." Mom waved a hand at the early morning sunshine streaming through the kitchen window.

"Most mothers don't visit their daughters for three fuckin' months, you know."

Mom pointed at her with her fork. "Watch your mouth, Agatha Christine. I'm leaving soon."

"You've been saying that every day since you moved in. The least you could do is *admit* that you're here to stay."

Mom shook her head. "I'm waiting for the all clear." She reached into the neckline of her baggy sweatshirt and pulled a necklace free. "Here, I want you to have this." She lifted the long chain over her head and handed a hideous, heart-shaped locket to Aggie. It attempted to be gold, but the paint was flaking off to reveal the white plastic beneath. Aggie had never seen it before.

"Gee thanks, Mom. Did you pick this up from Goodwill or the dumpster behind Dollar General?"

"I found it in an old shoe box the other day. Your father gave that to me."

Aggie rolled her eyes. "The deadbeat Elvis impersonator?"

"Don't disrespect your father."

"I don't think I can call a man I never met my father. He doesn't know I exist."

"Oh, he knows. I told him I was pregnant. That's why he split." Mom smiled nostalgically. "He was really handsome, doll. You look a lot like him."

"Yes, my legacy is to be the greatest female Elvis impersonator to ever live. Too bad I sound like a strangled ostrich when I sing." Aggie slipped the locket's chain over her head. It wasn't like her mother gave her things of importance on a regular basis. She did appreciate the gesture. She was just... tired. And really wanted her life back. And to be able to make love to Jace on the kitchen floor whenever the urge struck her. Not that he was around enough to appease those urges, but if he had been.

"Be proud of who you are, Agatha."

Aggie nodded and squeezed the gaudy locket in her hand. "Thanks for the necklace, Mom. It's the ugliest thing I've ever seen, but I'll treasure it."

Mom smiled one of those rare smiles that touched her tired eyes.

She'd had a hard life. It showed in every line of her face. Hard to believe the woman was only forty-seven.

Mom grabbed Aggie around the waist and pulled her next to her side. "Are you happy, baby?"

For some reason, her mother's question made an image of Jace dominate her thoughts, like it did every twenty seconds or so. Aggie smiled, examining the locket more closely. "I'm working on it. Is there a picture inside?"

"It doesn't open. Never did. It's not really a locket." Mom elbowed Aggie in the ribs affectionately. "We're okay, right?"

Aggie nodded. "We're okay."

Mom kissed Aggie's arm and patted her butt. "Go on to bed."

"I have someone coming to pick up a corset this evening," Aggie said. "I have to get it done before I even think about sleeping."

"No, you don't," Mom said with an ear to ear grin. "I finished it for you."

Aggie felt the blood drain from her face. "Please tell me you didn't."

"I did a bang-up job."

Aggie dashed into her dining room and stopped dead in her tracks. Spread across the surface of the dining room table beside her sewing machine was the corset she'd been working on before she'd headed to the club the night before. Her mother had done a bang-up job all right. If bang-up was a synonym for fucked-up. The stitching was uneven. One cup of the garment was the premeasured D, the other a lopsided A. The Forget-Me-Not embroidery pattern didn't match because Aggie's practiced stitches decorated one side, and her mother's kindergarten project disgraced the other. It wasn't like Aggie could remove the misplaced stitches and fix it. Unlike cloth, if you poked a hole in leather, it stayed there. She'd have to completely start over.

"Mother!"

"Not bad for my first try. Maybe we could go into business together."

Aggie picked up the corset and tugged at it to see if by some miracle it would straighten itself out. The ribbing was sewn in so that any woman unlucky enough to put it on would have her rib cage punctured and suffer a collapsed lung. "It's ruined."

"Don't be such a drama queen, Aggie. It's fine."

She couldn't make out her mother's expression through her tears of frustration. "It isn't fine. Nothing you touch is fine."

Her mother took a deep, shuddering breath. "You're right. I'm the biggest fuckup on the planet." And now she was crying. Great, just fucking great. She destroyed Aggie's work and then somehow managed to make her feel guilty about it.

"You need to not be near me right now, Mom," Aggie said. "I have a lot of work to do." She grabbed a seam ripper and tore the garment into sections, praying that she might be able to salvage some of the panels—especially the one she'd embroidered—and just replace those her mother had messed up.

"I'm sorry," Mom said in a shaky voice. "I thought I could help. I know how hard you're always working, and I'm a huge burden on you. I make up stories about the Mafia so you'll take me in, and I eat your food and borrow money out of your purse to buy cigarettes. I know I deserve to be kicked out, but I don't have an-anywhere else to gooooo." She was wailing now.

Aggie paused in her angry retaliation against a helpless corset. "Wait. What? You made up that story about borrowing money from the Mafia?"

Mom probably should not have revealed that while Aggie had a sharp object in her hand.

"Are-are-are-are you mad at meeeeee?"

The woman should go into acting. She was a natural.

"Un-fucking-believable. Well, at least I can stop working overtime, since I no longer have to save money to pay off your stupid loan."

"So you're not mad at me?" Mom turned off the waterworks like a plumber with a pipe wrench.

"No. Just go away. You've done enough."

"Now you're just being bitchy."

Aggie stiffened. *Bitchy?* "I need a freakin' vacation," Aggie said under her breath, shredding the ruined half of the corset with her seam ripper so she didn't attack her mother with its deadly point.

Chapter 18

SITTING IN THE STUDIO on their first day off-tour in three weeks, Jace smiled when he saw who the text message was from. Aggie. He couldn't wait to see her again. He had plans to see her in Vegas that weekend, though he hadn't shared those plans with her. As he read her words on the screen, his smile faded.

I'm in LA. Text me your address. I thought I'd stay with you for a few days. Mom is driving me insane. I had to get out of Vegas.

His place? He'd never invited her to his place for a reason. He lived in a dump in a bad neighborhood. That was sure to cause a barrage of uncomfortable questions. Jace needed to intercept her and convince her that they should spend a romantic weekend in some expensive hotel. He turned to the producer, Chris. They were sitting outside the booth where Eric was recording drum tracks for their upcoming album.

"Do you know any five-star hotels in Los Angeles?" Jace asked.

Chris lifted an eyebrow. "I dunno. That big pink one where all the celebs go. What's it called?" He snapped his fingers. "The Beverly Hills Hotel."

"Where's that?"

"Sunset Boulevard. Where else?"

Jace didn't hang around Beverly Hills. He did know Sunset Boulevard though. "Do you think I can get a reservation there?"

Chris chuckled. "If you can't, I'm sure Trey can."

Unlike Jace, Trey hung around Beverly Hills regularly. He'd

been raised there and had social connections with the rich and famous. Jace texted a message back to Aggie.

Why don't you meet me at The Beverly Hills Hotel? It's on Sunset Boulevard. We'll spend the weekend there together.

He decided to sweeten the deal.

I'll bring my suitcase and spoil you.

Waiting for her response, Jace gave Eric a thumbs-up in the booth when he came to the end of his track.

"Perfect," Chris said to Eric through the mic.

Eric shook his head. "I stumbled over a beat at around three minutes. Is Jace breaking your concentration?"

Jace's cell phone beeped with the arrival of another text.

I'd rather just stay at your place.

I'm not prepared for company, he returned.

I'm not company. I'm your girlfriend.

If you see where I live, you might change your mind.

I'm not that shallow, Jace.

Jace supposed there was one way to find out if she could handle the real him. He texted his street address.

I'll meet you there.

"I've got to go," he said to Chris.

"You'll be back later, won't you?" the producer said. "You're up next."

"I don't know. I might be back later today. Tell the guys I'm sorry, but I have unexpected company."

In the parking garage, Jace climbed onto his bike and started the engine. He headed toward home with demons on his heels. He had to beat Aggie to his place and hide his dirty laundry in his closet. Put clean sheets on his bed. Scrub the toilet. Then he'd have to take her grocery shopping. He'd just returned from touring for three weeks, and his refrigerator was empty. Maybe if he made her a nice dinner, it would make up for the fact that she had to eat it off a paper plate.

He parked his motorcycle on the street and headed up the stairs to his apartment. He was stripping the sheets off his bed when his cell phone rang.

"I'm here. Will my car be safe parked on the street?" Aggie asked. "This neighborhood looks a little shady."

Little shady? Maybe. If she considered a dense forest a little shady. He glanced around his bare-walled apartment. She would not be happy here. He was embarrassed that he even lived here. "Let's go to a hotel."

"Don't be silly. I'm already parked. Come help me with my luggage."

"I'll be right down." He kicked the dirty sheets under his bed and headed down to help her with her bags.

By the time he reached the sidewalk, a couple of men were already helping her with her bags. Or rather, trying to help themselves *to* her bags.

One tossed her suitcase into the back of a pickup. Another tugged on her purse, which she was clinging to with both hands. "Give me your purse, bitch."

"Let go, you fucking jerk." She kicked him in the shin and gave her purse a hard yank. Contents spilled across the cement, but she was unwilling to give an inch in their tug of war. Not even when the man pulled a gun.

"I'm going to shoot you if you don't let go."

"Get a job, you fucking loser," she bellowed. "This is mine. I worked hard for it."

Apparently, Jace's woman was lacking a fear gene. He knew fear though. It hadn't gotten its claws into him in years, but it did now. His blood turned cold in his veins, and all he could think was to get her away from danger.

Jace charged forward and shoved Aggie aside, sending her scrambling to maintain her balance and still keep a grip on her stupid purse. Before he could turn to confront the mugger, two successive gunshots sliced through his body. The back of his right shoulder. Through his right arm. Tires squealed. The ground tilted beneath him and rose up to meet his face. Someone screamed his name. Everything went black.

Chapter 19

AGGIE TURNED AT THE sound of gunshots. Saw the blood splatter out of Jace's arm. Watched him fall. Felt her world crumble. "Jace!"

Someone grabbed her arm and shoved a gun under her chin. "I said, give me your fucking purse. Don't make me kill you too, you stupid bitch."

She couldn't comprehend the danger she was in, could only watch the blood spread in a widening puddle from beneath the only man she'd ever loved. "Jace…"

Gritting her teeth, she dropped her purse on the cement and grabbed her left fist in her right hand. With a scream of rage, she delivered a vicious elbow to her captor's stomach.

He grunted in pain. She stomped the instep of his foot.

"Ow, bitch. What do you think—"

She punched him in the balls, taking him down to his knees. His grip on his gun slackened. She grabbed the back of his head and drove the bridge of his nose into her knee. He fell unconscious on the sidewalk, the gun tumbling from his grasp.

Aggie flew to Jace's side. "Oh my God," she gasped, too upset to do anything but hover over him. He was bleeding so much. Surely, he was dead.

She dialed 911. Before the dispatcher even answered, the sound of sirens coming from the distance sounded like a chorus of angel harps.

"What is your emergency?"

"M-my boyfriend's been shot."

"Your location?"

She didn't know. She didn't know anything.

"I'm outside. On the sidewalk."

"Can you see a street sign?"

Aggie looked up and read the names of the streets from the signs on the corner of the nearest intersection.

The dispatcher said, "Take a deep breath, honey. Someone called about a mugging in progress a few minutes ago. Police and paramedics are already on their way."

Aggie could hear the sirens growing louder by the second.

"What's your boyfriend's name?"

She covered her lips with a trembling hand and looked down at him. The puddle of blood beneath him was spreading. "J-Jace."

"Is he still breathing?" the dispatcher asked.

She stared at Jace, but her blurry eyes refused to take in anything but the blood pooling around his right arm. "I– I don't know." She glanced around, hoping someone with a lick of sense was nearby to tell her if Jace was still breathing. The streets were eerily empty. It was as if the world had deserted her. Deserted Jace. Her only lifeline was the calm woman on the other end of the line.

"What's your name, sweetie?" the woman asked.

"Aggie," she squeaked.

"Aggie, listen to his chest. See if his heart is beating. If it isn't, I'll help you start CPR."

Aggie leaned over Jace and pressed her ear to his back, listening for the sound of his heart. It still beat, sluggishly at best.

"It's still beating," she said to the dispatcher.

"Is he breathing? Feel for air coming from his nose and mouth."

She moved her hand in front of his face and felt his warm breath against her fingertips. "Yes. He's breathing."

"Then just sit tight until help arrives."

Sit tight? That was the woman's advice? Aggie dropped her cell phone on the ground. She had to do something for him, but didn't know what. Should she try to stop the bleeding? Turn him onto his back? She rubbed her forehead. "I don't know what to do," she whispered brokenly. She smoothed his leather jacket over his back, not knowing how that was supposed to help. She brushed Jace's hair from his forehead, leaving several streaks of his blood on his skin. "I don't know what to do. Jace? Jace, tell me what to do!"

The sirens continued past the corner and toward the end of the next block. Maybe they had the wrong address. She had to flag them down. For Jace's sake. As useless as she currently was, *they* would know how to help him.

"I'll be back," she promised Jace, scared to leave him, but more scared not to leave him.

She raced to the curb and waved her arms wildly at a passing cop car. Tires squealed as the officer stomped on his brakes. An ambulance did a U-turn at the end of the block and pulled up to the curb on the opposite side of the street.

An officer climbed from his cruiser, eyeing the blood on Aggie's face and hands with concern. "Ma'am. Ma'am, are you hurt? Someone called in shots fired."

"No, I'm fine. Please. You have to help Jace. He's been shot. Hurry."

She ran back to where she'd left Jace and found the mugger with the gun groaning as he struggled to regain consciousness. He took a deep, startled breath and reached for his gun. The cop beside Aggie drew his weapon and went down on one knee.

"Drop your weapon," the officer yelled.

Aggie didn't hesitate. She rushed toward the thug and kicked him in the side of the head. The gun went off, bullet flying wildly without aim.

"You son of a bitch," she growled. She kicked him in the crotch. Once. Twice. Feeling his nuts crunch against bone beneath her foot. He cried out, clutching his balls in agony, the gun forgotten beside him. She didn't know how to help Jace, but she sure as hell wasn't going to stand there while the dick who'd shot him hurt someone else.

"Are you crazy?" the cop said, toeing the gun out of the man's reach. "He had a gun, and you jump him? You're lucky you didn't get shot."

"What are you doing?" she yelled at the cop. "Help Jace. I don't know what to do for him. *Help* him!"

Two paramedics jogged across the street toward them, wheeling a gurney that carried a large first-aid kit. While the police officer wrestled the injured mugger into a pair of handcuffs, the medics worked with Jace, trying to stem the flow of blood. They removed his jacket and tossed it aside. The entire right side of his white T-shirt was saturated with blood.

Aggie scooped up his coat and cradled it against her chest, watching the EMTs do their thing.

"There's an exit wound for this one, but the second bullet is still lodged inside his shoulder."

"Keep pressure on it. We've got to get him to the hospital. He's losing a lot of blood."

Two officers escorted the gunless thug toward a cruiser. "You're dead, you fucking bitch. As soon as I make bail, you're dead!" he shouted at Aggie.

Aggie heard him, but was too worried about Jace to feel any concern for herself. The cops heard him though. "I'll be sure to file that threat in my report," one officer said as he shoved the guy into the back of the cruiser. "Bail is not an option. Where's your accomplice?"

"I don't know what you're talking about," the mugger claimed.

His accomplice had Aggie's suitcase and had sped off as soon as his buddy had shot Jace. Not that it mattered—nothing mattered but seeing Jace smile again.

"Ma'am, we need to ask you a few questions."

Aggie didn't look at the speaker. She couldn't take her eyes off Jace.

When the police officer grabbed her arm, she twisted away. "No. Get your hands off me."

The paramedics lifted Jace onto a gurney, pushing hard on the wound in his shoulder. His hand was ghostly white as the tourniquet around his upper arm stemmed the blood flow to the gunshot wound in his biceps.

"He needs oxygen."

"He needs blood is what he needs. Jesus."

"Get him in the ambulance."

In a strange state of detachment, Aggie followed the stretcher as they wheeled it toward the waiting ambulance. She stepped off the curb, oblivious to the traffic that an officer was directing around the police cruisers. Someone grabbed her arm again. This time he did not let go when she tried to twist away.

"Ma'am, we need to ask you a few questions."

She shook her head vigorously, tears blinding her.

The officer tugged her arm, trying to get her to follow him toward the police car. "What happened? Ma'am, tell me what happened."

"They took my suitcase. Wanted my purse too. I should have just given it to them. Jace!" she yelled. "Jace!"

"We're taking him to County," a paramedic said. Aggie didn't understand what they meant. County? What county? Jace's gurney was lifted into the back of the ambulance, and the paramedics climbed inside. Someone closed the door and slapped the back of the vehicle. It took off down the street, lights flashing, sirens blaring.

"Was there more than one?" the officer asked.

Aggie nodded and burst into quaking sobs, her face buried in Jace's ruined leather jacket.

Chapter 20

JACE GROANED, TRYING TO force his eyes open. He felt like an elephant was standing on his right shoulder. Someone touched his cheek gently.

"Hey there, open your eyes, cutie," a soft voice said.

"Aggie?" he whispered.

"My name is Karen. I'm your nurse."

Nurse? What? Memories flooded his mind, one on top of the other, converging into an indecipherable mess. He could only make sense of two things. He'd been shot, and the guy with the gun had Aggie.

"Aggie!"

He sat bolt upright in the hospital bed. The nurse tried to coax him back down. "We couldn't find identification on you. Do you know your name?"

"Where's Aggie? We have to send someone to help her. We have to…"

"I don't know who Aggie is. She's not here. You came in by yourself. Does she know where you are? We could call her."

He pushed the nurse aside and tried to climb from the bed. Pain stabbed through his shoulder and his arm, but he could tolerate that pain. Not knowing where Aggie was, knowing he'd failed to keep her safe—*that* he could not tolerate.

"You have to stay in bed. You just got out of surgery and are in no condition to go anywhere." The nurse pushed the call button for help. "I'll give you another sedative and something for the pain."

Jace shook his head vigorously. "That guy is going to kill her," he said, slumping sideways in the bed as a wave of dizziness took him.

He tried to get up again, but his body refused to cooperate. *Get up, Jace. You have to get up.* The nurse tucked him back in bed. "No. I can't stay here," he murmured.

His right arm felt funny and not because he'd been shot in it. The thick leather cuff he usually wore on his wrist was missing. He covered the scars there with his left hand. "Where's my bracelet?"

Karen opened a drawer and handed it to him. He hurriedly secured it around his wrist, not releasing his breath until his shame was covered again.

The nurse watched him with compassion. "We didn't know who to notify of your condition. Do you have any family?"

He shook his head. He couldn't catch his breath. Who cared if he didn't have any family? Aggie might still be in danger. He'd taken a bullet for her—*two*—but still had no idea if she was safe, injured, or dead. "No, no family. Please," he said. "You don't understand. Send someone to help Aggie. Send. Please. Someone."

"Jace?" Aggie's sweet voice came from across the room. He had to be hearing things. Delusional from his meds.

And then she was beside him. He didn't know by what miracle she was there. Not dead. Apparently unharmed. She fell against him, sobbing against his neck, clinging to him. The pain she caused reminded him he was alive. And more important, that she was alive.

Ah God, hurt me, Aggie.

"I'm sorry it took me so long to get here. Those stupid cops wouldn't let me leave. Those two guys that mugged me have been in a rash of burglaries, and I'm the only one who's seen the other guy's face. They made me go look through mug shots and file a report. I just wanted to be with you." She looked up at the nurse. "Is he going to be okay?"

"Not if you keep squeezing him like that," the nurse said disapprovingly.

Jace chuckled. "Squeeze me as hard as you like. How did you get away from that guy? Did the cops rescue you?"

She winced. "Not exactly. After he shot you, I went crazy and kicked his ass." She flushed. "Mostly his nuts actually."

Jace chuckled. "He had it coming. Wish I'd have thought of that."

"He shot you in the back, the coward. I wasn't going to let him get away with that." She kissed his lips gently, her eyes watery with tears. "I should have just given him my purse. Then you wouldn't have been hurt."

Jace concentrated on lifting his uninjured arm and stroked her hair from her face tenderly. "All I care about is that you're safe."

"I'm so glad you're okay. So glad." She kissed him again. "I love you so much. If anything happened to you, I wouldn't want to go on living."

He touched her cheek. "Don't say things like that," he murmured. He kissed her gently. "I'm not going anywhere."

She sniffed and stared down into his eyes. He'd never seen an ounce of weakness in this woman, and her tears tore at his heart. "Promise?" she whispered. When he didn't answer her immediately, she grabbed two handfuls of hair and gave him a hard shake. "Promise me, Jace."

"I promise." As weak as he felt at the moment, he feared it was a promise he might have to break.

Chapter 21

AGGIE WATCHED JACE SLEEP for over an hour before she thought about informing anyone else about his injury. He never talked about his family, so she didn't know how to contact them, but she did have Jessica's number. As Sed's fiancée, Jessica had to know how to get in touch with the guys in Jace's band. They needed to know what was going on. She was sure they would want to know, and they would know who else to inform. Aggie stepped into the hall so she didn't disturb Jace's sleep. He tried to pretend he wasn't hurt too bad, but Aggie saw through the tough guy act. He needed his rest, and she was going to make sure he got it.

"Aggie!" Jessica answered the phone. "How are you? Sorry I bailed on you after the show in San Francisco. Sed thought we needed to do more celebrating."

"Don't worry about it. Speaking of Sed, is he around?"

"Why?"

Aggie almost laughed at the jealous edge to Jessica's tone. "Jace has been shot. I wasn't sure who needed to be informed."

"Shot?"

"Yeah, shot."

"What do you mean Jace has been shot?"

"I mean some dickhead shot him with a gun."

"Shot him?"

"Yes, shot him. Can I just talk to Sed?"

"He's not here. He went to the studio. Eric said Jace bailed on recording this afternoon, so Sed's working on vocal tracks."

Aggie realized if she wouldn't have surprised Jace with a visit, he'd still be safely in the recording studio and not lying in some hospital bed. "Will you let Sed know what happened? Jace will be in here overnight. Probably longer."

"Which hospital are you at?"

"County."

"I'll round up the guys, and we'll come see him. How'd he manage to get shot?" Jessica asked.

"Some guy tried to grab my purse, and I refused to give it to him. He pulled a gun, and Jace shoved me out of the way. He took two bullets for me—all because I was stupid. I should have just given that bastard my fucking purse." Aggie rubbed the center of her chest, her heart aching.

"Don't blame yourself, Aggie. Blame the guy with the gun. We'll be there as soon as possible."

"Thanks, Jess."

Aggie returned to the room, sat in the chair beside the bed, and took Jace's hand. She kissed his knuckles—pressed them to her cheek. She really did love him. She couldn't deny it. Did he feel the same? He'd never said much about his feelings, but she knew he felt something for her. He always spoke far more in actions than he did in words. Of course, it could be simple sexual attraction on his end. She wasn't sure if that was enough for her. It had once been, but now... now she wasn't sure about anything.

Over an hour of worry later, she heard a commotion near the end of the hall. "Yes, we're his family. Get the fuck out of my way." Was that Sed? Had to be. That deep baritone was highly distinctive. "Jace," Aggie whispered, shaking him slightly. "They're here."

He groaned, but didn't open his eyes.

"Jace!"

"Tired," he murmured. At least she was pretty sure that's what he said. She was completely sure he was still asleep.

Within minutes the room was packed wall to wall with people.

The entire band had come to visit him? Aggie knew that would mean a lot to Jace, had he been conscious.

"Thanks for coming. I didn't know who else to call," Aggie said, glancing from one rock star to the next.

"The band isn't complete without little man," Eric said.

Sed stood at the side of the bed, staring at Jace as if to heal him with the power of his will. "He's in bad shape," Sed murmured. "He looks like shit."

"He's not going to die on us, is he?" Trey asked.

"His doctor said his surgery went well," Aggie said. "They got the bullet out. The wound is clean. It just needs to heal."

"Should have known something like this would happen," Eric said, looking at Jace anxiously. "He was supposed to record in the studio this afternoon, and pow—he gets shot. This fuckin' album is cursed, I tell you."

"You recorded drum tracks this afternoon, and nothing happened to you," Trey reminded him.

"Yet," Eric said, glancing over his shoulder as if searching for the curse cloud now following him.

"Any idea how long he'll be out of commission?" Sed asked.

"A few weeks."

"We leave for Canada in three days," Brian said.

"You're leaving again already?" Aggie hated to be the needy girlfriend, but she never got to see him, and Jace had no business touring the continent while he was injured.

"Supposed to," Sed said. "Can't really perform without our bassist though."

"How did he get shot?" Eric asked.

"Protecting me."

Eric grinned at her crookedly. "You'd never know it from looking at him, but the dude is badass."

"I'm sure he'd like you to tell him that," Aggie said.

"No can do. We don't need another egomaniac in the band. Sed's got that persona covered." Eric winced when Sed slapped him on the back of the head.

"What do you need us to do for you, Aggie?" Jessica asked, putting an arm around Aggie and rubbing the middle of her back.

Aggie's brow wrinkled in confusion. "Me?" She shook her head. "I wasn't hurt."

"That's not what I meant. It must've been horrible to witness someone you..." Jessica's eyebrows arched in question. "*Care* about?"

Aggie nodded. She'd admit that she cared about Jace. Even in front of all these guys that meant so much to him and whom she didn't know very well.

"It must've been horrible to witness someone you care about get shot. I thought I'd stroke out when Sed blew out his throat onstage last month."

Sed kissed his fiancée's temple. "It wasn't as bad as it looked, baby."

"How would you like to watch helplessly while I lay unconscious in a puddle of blood?"

Sed jerked Jessica into his arms and rubbed his lips over her silky, strawberry blonde hair. "Don't even put that vision in my head." He offered Aggie a pat on the shoulder. "If you need anything, anything at all, just ask. We'll help."

"I'm fine. And I think Jace mostly needs to rest. I don't know what he'll want to do about the upcoming tour." Aggie could guess that he wouldn't want to let his bandmates down, but she didn't want to speak for him.

"Actually, I might have a solution," Eric said. "I'll need to make some phone calls."

"*You* have a solution?" Brian asked.

"What? You don't trust me to solve our problems?" Eric asked.

Sed, Brian, and Trey shook their heads in unison. For the first time since Aggie had stepped out of her car in Los Angeles, she smiled.

Chapter 22

JACE MOANED IN HIS sleep.

The gurney followed him. He ran down an endless corridor. White tiles, white walls, blinding white light from above. Antiseptic smells. Jason was too afraid to look behind him. He could hear the squeak of the wheels, so he knew the gurney was still there. Still following him.

Kiss your mother good-bye, son.

Jason stopped. The squeaky wheels stopped right behind him.

Kiss your mother good-bye, son. Kiss your mother—

He covered his ears to drown out his father's voice. *No. I can't. Don't make me.*

This might be the last time you see her. Don't you love her? Don't you care?

That's not her. It's not her.

He didn't want to look at her, with her face smashed, swollen, and bruised.

Unrecognizable. Not human. Her body twisted. Contorted. That *thing* on the gurney was not his mother.

The gurney bumped into his shoulder blades. His heart lurched. He ran. Ran faster than he'd ever run before.

Don't step on a crack. He tried to jump over them, but they moved beneath his feet, and he couldn't avoid them all.

He stepped on one. He'd heard her body crunch when the approaching headlights disappeared. Over the sounds of the rending metal and shattering glass, he'd heard it from the backseat.

Her back is broken, son. If she lives, she'll never walk again.

But she'll still be able to play the piano, won't she, Father?

I don't think so.

For that, Jason grieved.

Don't cry, boy. Men don't cry. Not ever.

He didn't cry. He ran. Ran until he couldn't run anymore. No breath left in him. No energy. If he couldn't run, he had to hide. Hide from it. If it found him, it would get him. The thing on the gurney pretending to be his mother would get him.

An old shed became his salvation. He crammed his body into a small space. A dark place. Musty like an old attic. The air stale and stifling. But he was alone here. He liked being alone. Alone was safe. He listened for the squeak of wheels. They never came, but after a long time his father did.

Everyone has been looking for you all day. I don't have the patience for this bullshit right now, Jason. Your mother is dead. Do you understand? She's dead! You're alive—not a fucking scratch on you—but she's dead.

Jason was too stunned to feel the first blow.

Dead? What did it mean to be dead? Was it like sleeping? A long sleep with no more pain?

Too confused to feel the second blow.

Don't you ever hide from me again, you piece of shit. Not ever.

Jason heard the squeak of the gurney's wheels outside the shed door.

Too afraid to feel the third blow. The fourth. Fifth. The pain washed over him like a comforting blanket. He deserved this. *Hurt me, Father. Hurt me.*

Jace's eyes flipped open, his heart thumping with terror. His gaze darted around the sterile white walls. The IV bag hanging beside the bed. The heart rate monitor. The curtain rod above his bed. Instead of receding, fear rose up his neck until it strangled him. An instinctual need to run gripped him. Jace reached for the IV needle in the back of his hand, but before he could jerk it out, someone grabbed his wrist.

"Jace," Aggie said. "It's okay. Do you remember what happened? You're in the hospital."

He knew he was in the fucking hospital, and he needed to get out. Immediately. Years ago, a counselor had told him that he had post-traumatic stress disorder, but somehow, putting a name to it didn't make it easier to deal with when it caught him off guard and sent him into a panic. It had been a long time since he'd dreamed of his mother's death. A long time since the traumas of his youth had controlled his reactions to the outside world. He'd thought he'd moved beyond this bullshit—apparently not.

"Aggie," he said, grabbing her with both arms and pulling her against him on the bed. He hugged her as tight as he could, which didn't seem nearly tight enough. "Aggie, you have to get me out of here."

"Sweetheart, you're hurt. You can't leave." Her voice was muffled against his shoulder, which he vaguely recognized as throbbing dully in pain.

"I have to leave. Right now."

"Let go. You're going to damage your shoulder."

He had no idea what she meant. "Aggie, please."

"I'll talk to your doctor."

"They can't keep me here against my will." He released her reluctantly, and she stared into his eyes. She cupped his cheek and offered him a sad smile.

"It's okay, baby," she said. "I'll take it away." She kissed his lips tenderly. "Take it."

Chapter 23

JACE OPENED HIS EYES to absolute darkness. His body was on fire. His throat drier than a saltine in the Mojave Desert. What had woken him? His bladder protested its fullness. Oh. The glow of the streetlight outside his apartment and the comforting purr of Brownie near his pillow sank into his addled thoughts. He was home? How had he gotten home? A warm hand rested on his belly. Oh yeah. Aggie.

God, he had to pee. He felt for the edge of the bed, rolled to his feet, and immediately hit the floor with a loud thud. Pain radiated through his shoulder and arm. Fuck, getting shot hurt, and not with that sweet, stinging agony he so enjoyed.

"Jace?" Aggie's concerned voice came from the bed above him. She switched on a lamp and peered over the edge of the mattress. "Are you okay?"

He lay on the floor, simultaneously breathing through his pain and trying not to laugh so he didn't piss himself. "Can you help me up? I need to get to the bathroom."

So much for rescuing his damsel in distress. She'd done most of the rescuing, and now she was going to have to help him take a piss. *Some hero I am.*

Aggie climbed from the bed and hefted him to his feet. He clutched the chest of his hospital gown with one hand and held on to Aggie with the other. Apparently, those wonderful pain meds they'd dripped into him in the hospital had worn off.

"You're burning up, baby," Aggie said.

"I'm freezing."

"We've got to get you back to the hospital," she said. "If you get an infection—"

"No, I don't need a hospital. I need a toilet."

He leaned heavily on her as she helped him out of the bedroom and to the bathroom next door. He tried to get his balance, but decided without her support, he'd soon find himself on the floor again. He'd never felt so woozy.

"I can't stay on my feet without you," he whispered.

"Just go," she insisted. "It won't bother me."

She helped him keep the hospital gown out of the way as he mostly hit the toilet. He couldn't help but sigh with relief as he drained his bladder. His eyes rolled into his head in bliss. Aggie chuckled. When he'd finished, she helped him back to the bedroom and tucked him into bed.

"Thirsty," he murmured, almost asleep again. Just the walk to the bathroom had sapped his energy.

She shook him awake and pressed a bottle to his lips. "Jace, you have to drink."

When had he fallen asleep again?

"Jace? Please drink, baby."

"Aggie?"

"Yeah, it's me. Take a drink. Come on."

The first swallow hurt going down, but then he couldn't get enough. He chugged the icy sports drink until the bottle was empty, and then shivered uncontrollably. Why was he so cold? Aggie stood and started to leave him alone.

"Stay," Jace whispered.

"I was going to get you another blanket."

"Stay."

She sat beside him, her fingers stroking his cheek. He could feel himself drifting back into oblivion, but wanted to keep his eyes open—wanted to look at her. He missed looking at her when they were apart, and they'd been apart far too long while he'd been touring last month. Aggie sniffed. A lone tear slipped down her cheek and dripped off the edge of her jaw.

"Don't cry," he murmured.

"This is my fault. If you'd never met me, this wouldn't have happened."

"If I'd never met you, I would have never gotten to hold you. I'll take the bullet."

He hadn't meant to make her cry harder. She wrapped her arms around him and pressed her face into his shoulder. Her body quaked with sobs as she clung to him. "Don't die on me, Jace, please."

"Not planning to."

He wanted to hold her, comfort her, but his exhaustion had reached absolute, and he had no choice but to succumb to it.

Chapter 24

THE NEXT TIME JACE opened his eyes, a bright light was shining in his face. "Ah good, you're awake." A blurry face came into focus. At first he thought it was Trey, but the man was older and lacked Trey's long bangs and face piercings.

"Doctor Mills?"

"I don't usually do house calls."

Well, of course not. He was a frickin' plastic surgeon. What in the hell was he doing here anyway?

"Your friends think you're on death's door, but you're just healing. No signs of infection. You are anemic and dehydrated, but you'll recover."

"I feel like shit."

"Not that any of you kids ever listen to me, but you really need a blood transfusion and a month of uninterrupted bed rest. Preferably in a hospital, in case there are complications with your recovery."

"Can Aggie take care of my complications?" He chuckled.

"This is no joking matter," Aggie said from the opposite side of the room. He might have watched what he said if he'd known she was there. "He will stay in bed and rest, Doctor. You have my guarantee. I know fifteen ways to tie a man."

Doctor Mills chuckled. "I bet you do."

"I can't spend a month in bed. We have three shows next week. In Canada."

"Then you'll be playing your bass from your bed," Aggie said.

"Don't worry," Eric said. "I've got the perfect solution."

Eric? Just how many people were in the room?

Jace lifted his head, his eyes scanning the room. Aggie, Brian, Trey, Sed, Eric, and Doctor Mills. Okay, all the guys were there witnessing firsthand how pathetic and helpless he was. Jace lowered his head to the pillow with a groan.

"What kind of perfect solution?" Sed asked.

"I asked Jon to stand in for Jace for a few shows," Eric said cheerfully. "He said it wouldn't be a problem."

Jon? Jon Mallory? Sinners' previous bassist, the sun rises and sets over his fingers, the only bassist who could ever properly fill Eric's drum progressions, Jon Mallory?

"Yeah, that'll work," Sed said. "Good thinking, Eric."

Fuckin' A. Shoot me now.

Jace lifted a hand to cover his eyes. A burst of pain stabbed the back of his shoulder and snaked down his right arm, reminding him he'd already been shot.

Well then… shoot me again.

"You rest up, and we'll see how you are when we get back from Canada," Sed said.

"Fuck that. I'm coming with you," Jace said. There was no way in hell he was letting Jon Mallory tour in his place without him there.

"Are you sure you're up for it, little man?" Eric said.

Aggie took his hand and gave it a squeeze. "He'll have me to take care of him until he gets better. If he's going, then I'm going."

Chapter 25

Despite Doctor Mills's assessment of Jace's condition, Aggie made him go to a hospital for a more thorough examination while the band and crew prepared for the next, extended leg of their tour. A blood test, MRI, and IV of enriched fluids later, Aggie seemed satisfied that Jace was okay to travel. He wasn't used to having a woman as a fixture in his life. Wasn't sure how to react to her constant hovering and concern. He hoped he healed quickly so she'd knock it off already. And she'd made him go shopping. Sure, her suitcase had been stolen, and she needed clothes and other necessities, but shopping? Jace hated shopping. Almost as much as he hated that pitying look she kept giving him.

"Maybe you should just stay at my place while I'm gone," Jace said, leaning heavily on the shopping cart as they ambled through the aisles. She'd tried to get him to use one of those electric scooters when they'd first entered the store. Next, she'd ask him to hand over his balls on a plate. "I promise I'll take it easy."

"You don't want me to go on tour with you?"

He trod carefully into loaded-question territory. "It's not that I don't want you to go with me." *The guys are going to rip on me constantly if I bring a smothering chick on tour.* And this whole go on tour "thing" had been her idea, not his. He didn't get why she insisted on it so vehemently. He knew she needed a break from her mother, but she didn't have to ride on the tour bus to get away from her. "I just think you'd be more comfortable at my place. You'd still be away from your mother, and Brownie would love the company." He rubbed his jaw on his shoulder to catch sight of her expression. Was she buying it? That would be a negative. She stared at the shampoo display with her pretty face twisted in a harsh scowl.

"I see," she said in a clipped tone. "I might as well go back to Vegas."

"No, I didn't mean…"

She tossed shampoo and conditioner in the cart.

"It's gonna suck for you to be trapped on a bus with five…" And Jon made six. "Uh, six guys for a month. I think you'd be better off—"

"This has nothing to do with my mother. Don't you get it? I'm worried about you. I feel responsible for you getting hurt."

He understood what that guilt felt like. He shouldn't have been so worried about what the guys would think. He wrapped his good arm around her, his injured one trapped in a newly acquired sling, and held her close, stroking her silky hair with one hand.

"Okay. If it makes you feel better to go on tour with us—"

She stiffened and pulled away with a frustrated sigh. While he tried to figure out what was wrong with what he'd said, she tossed toothpaste, mouthwash, and a toothbrush in the cart, yanked the cart from his grasp, and zoomed off to a different aisle.

Jace struggled to catch up, a stitch in his side. He needed to lie down again. He found her several aisles over selecting cosmetics. He smiled when she added a tube of glossy, cherry-red lipstick to the cart. She looked incredibly hot in red. And leather. He missed her leather.

"I don't want to force myself into your life, Jace," she said. "If you don't want me around, then just say it."

Why would she think that? He thought the world of her. He just didn't want any of his bandmates to know it. "I do want you in my life, Aggie. I'm not used to… the hovering. I… my mother died when I was nine, and my father never remarried, so women…

confuse me. Why are you mad at me?" And why did asking that question make his heart thud so hard?

"I'm not mad at you," she said.

She wasn't?

"I'm sorry about your mom." She slid her hand into his hair and kissed his forehead. "Why don't you tell me about her?"

"No. I didn't bring her up to make you feel sorry for me. I want to know what I said that made you mad."

She smiled and hugged him. "You're fucking adorable. Do you know that?" She kissed the tip of his nose.

Scowling, he wiped at the wet spot with the back of his hand.

"The reason I'm mad—though I'm not exactly mad, just a little hurt—is that you make me feel like you don't want me on tour with you."

Well, he kind of didn't. He wanted to see her, yes, but having her on tour? No, thanks.

"I was hoping that you'd be happy to spend time with me, Jace. Show some enthusiasm. Not look at me like, oh fuck, now I'm going to be stuck with this stupid bitch for a month."

"I never said that. Never even thought it."

"It's the vibe you're giving off."

He was supposed to keep track of his vibes now too? Fuck, he couldn't win. At least he understood what she wanted.

"I can't *wait* to be stuck with you for a month," he said earnestly.

She laughed and hugged his arm. "Oh, you. What am I going to do with you?"

He kissed her deeply, lust flooding his loins. "I can think of a few things."

Chapter 26

JACE CARRIED A FEW of Aggie's lighter shopping bags up the tour bus steps. He paused when he noticed Eric and Jon sitting on the sofa laughing hysterically. Eric was wearing what Jace suspected was a Kevlar vest. He didn't bother asking why. The seven horseshoes nailed to the wall above the sofa were new—undoubtedly Mr. We R. Cursed's idea.

"Ah, here's little man now," Eric said, wiping tears from his eyes with the back of his wrists. "Need help carrying that stuff? I wouldn't want you to hurt yourself."

"I've got it," he said, hurrying toward the bedroom.

He'd thought he and Eric were starting to get along. Now, with the return of Jon the Magnificent, they were back to square one.

"Baby, slow down," Aggie called after him. "You've got to take it easy."

Great. Just what he needed. Aggie in smother mode in front of Eric. And worse. Jon.

Jace tossed the bags into the back bedroom, brushed past Aggie on his way back down the hall, and opened the fridge. "Now that Myrna's out of here, we need to get some fuckin' alcohol on this bus," he growled. He grabbed a bottle of orange juice from the refrigerator and slammed the door shut. He gripped the bottle with his wounded arm and attempted to unscrew the top with no success.

"Yeah, we finally get rid of Myrna and Jessica, and *someone* brings another chick on tour with us," Eric said.

"She can tour me any time she wants," Jon said. "What a babe."

Eric laughed. "She's too hot for little man, that's for sure."

Jace didn't have the patience to deal with their bullshit right now. He tossed the unopened juice bottle into the kitchen sink and returned to the bedroom to find Aggie sorting through her purchases. She smiled, and his pissy attitude lightened. "Where do I put my stuff? I don't want to infringe on anyone's territory," she said.

"We sort of throw all our shit together wherever it fits."

She lifted her hand to touch his face. "Sweetie, you look pale. You should lie down for a while."

"I'm fine."

"The faster you get better, the faster you can get that jackass, Jon, out of here," she whispered and turned those pretty blue eyes of hers in the direction of the common area.

She had a point. He kissed her tenderly. "I could use a nap."

"And I could use a shower and a change of clothes." She kissed the tip of his nose. "Get into bed."

"Are you going to join me?" he murmured, his hands moving to slide over her luscious ass.

"After my shower."

"Hurry."

"Are you planning to get me all sweaty again?"

"Yeah. You'll have to do all the work. I'm just going to lie there and take it."

She smiled. "I think we'd be better off cuddling. You really do need your rest."

Geez, woman, I'm feeling inadequate enough here. He shrugged his arm out of his sling and peeled his shirt over his head. She traced the stark white tape holding his bandages in place. He needed to heal quickly for more than one reason. This new pity attitude of Aggie's grated on his last nerve. He removed the rest of his clothes and moved out of reach.

"Come join me after your shower. Don't bother putting on clothes."

She grinned. "If you insist."

"Towels are under the sink." He climbed into bed and admitted that he did need rest. He was almost unconscious the moment his head touched the pillow. He heard her close the bathroom door. A moment later, the water started flowing. He considered joining her as he drifted toward oblivion. Next time.

Aggie's scream woke him. "Get out of here, you fucking pervert!"

The bathroom door closed. "I told you she'd go Brazilian, Eric. You owe me twenty bucks."

Jon.

"How do I know you're not just saying that?" Eric said.

"Have a look." The bathroom door opened again. There was a loud thud. "Hey, baby, don't throw stuff. We're just settling a bet."

Jace leaped from the bed and stalked down the hall. He grabbed Jon by the arm and spun him around. Jace's left-handed uppercut to Jon's chin sent him flying. Jon landed on his back at Eric's feet. Eric stared at Jace in astonishment.

"Do you want a piece?" Jace asked Eric.

"We were just having a little fun. Chillax, little man."

"If you disrespect my woman like that again, I'll kick your fuckin' ass. You won't get back up."

Jon rose up on one elbow, rubbing his jaw. "Jesus Christ, that hurt, dude."

Aggie opened the bathroom door, a towel wrapped around her curvy body. "Jace, you should have let me punch him. You'll tear out your stitches."

He shrugged. It would have been worth it.

She turned to Eric. "Your perverted friend owes you twenty bucks, Eric. I'll have you know, I do *not* go Brazilian. I shave it in the shape of a butterfly."

Jace chuckled, glad she had a sense of humor about the situation.

She wouldn't last long on a bus with six guys if she didn't. "A butterfly?" Jace said. "I don't recall that. You'd better show me."

Jace coaxed her toward the bedroom. The faster he got away from Jon, the better.

"Why do you call him little man, Eric? The guy is hung like a whale," Jon said as he picked himself up off the floor.

"It's an optical illusion. It just looks big. Even at three inches, it's half his height."

"I guess that explains what she sees in him. Shape of a butterfly, my ass."

Jace closed the bedroom door, shaking his head in disgust. Aggie's towel snapped against his ass. His entire body tensed in response, and his cock stirred with excitement. He turned to look at her. She traced a butterfly shape on her clean-shaven mound.

"You don't see the butterfly?" she asked.

"No, I don't."

She climbed onto the bed, rolled onto her back, and spread her legs wide. She traced the shape again. "See it now?"

Oh, he saw it all right. Not a butterfly. Everything she had to offer between her thighs. He grew light-headed as his cock thickened.

"Maybe if I come closer," he murmured.

"I think you should."

He settled on his stomach, resting on his elbows between her legs. His injured shoulder protested the weight he put on it, so he shifted to his left side. "I still don't see it. Are you sure it's there?"

"Maybe if you touch it, you'll feel it."

He stroked the smooth skin of her outer lips and mound until she shuddered. Her scent intensified as she grew excited. Wet. Her inner folds swelled. Reddened. Invited him in. He resisted though, touching only her clean-shaven areas.

"Do you feel it yet?" she asked breathlessly.

"I feel plenty," he said, "but no butterfly."

"Maybe your mouth can find it."

He grinned. "I think I'm being manipulated here."

He licked her smooth flesh. Suckled it. Inhaled her intoxicating scent but purposely avoided tasting her fluids. He could feel her heat against his face—see how swollen and wet she was. His cock protested its neglect.

"Maybe I was wrong," she said. "Maybe Jon won that bet after all."

"Don't say his name in our bed."

He slid up her body and thrust into her delightfully warm pussy. Ah God, why did she feel so good? Her silky flesh gripped him, stimulating every pleasure sensor in his cock with each forward thrust and withdraw. It had never felt this good before. He couldn't get enough. Couldn't think of anything but the feel of her around him. He possessed her faster, unable to believe the pleasure could intensify, but it did. It built so quickly, he couldn't contain it. He was scarcely aware of her body convulsing with release beneath him. Her pussy tightened as she came, pulling at him, encouraging him to join her in ecstasy.

"Jace, Jace, pull out," she said frantically.

Pull out? What?

He couldn't. It felt so good to be buried in her silky depths. Why did it feel so good?

No condom.

Fuck.

His body stiffened as he forced himself to withdraw completely. He slid his cock up her slit, rubbing his length against her clit. He shuddered violently as his seed spurted over her lower belly, the muscles at the base of his cock contracting involuntarily.

"Aggie," he groaned, wishing he was spurting inside her, wanting her to accept his offering into her body, needing her tight warmth around him as he let go of everything.

Spent, Jace collapsed on top of her, feeling drained—sexually, emotionally, physically. He wanted to give her more, but didn't have anything left to offer.

Aggie kissed his forehead, drawing his body closer in an embrace. "Maybe it's time for me to get on the pill so you can come inside me," she murmured. "Would you like that?"

"Yeah." Something warm dripped down his arm from beneath his bandage. He didn't have time to decipher what it was before he passed out.

Jace didn't move, much less wake, as Aggie replaced his blood-soaked bandage. She couldn't encourage him to get worked up like that again. Not until his wounds healed. The bleeding had stopped for now, but the hole in his flesh looked jagged and uneven. She supposed gunshot wounds always looked like that. He'd have a horrible scar because of her. Could have died if the paramedics hadn't been so close.

Aggie kissed Jace's back and covered him with a blanket.

Someone knocked on the door. Jace stirred but didn't wake. "Just a minute," Aggie called. She was still naked. She used her discarded towel to wipe traces of Jace's cum from her belly and reached for her sack of new clothes. As soon as she was covered, she opened the door to find the lead guitarist waiting calmly in the corridor. Brian. The gorgeous one (or was he the sensitive one?) was also the married one, she reminded herself, but my lord, he had a face that belonged on a rocker version of *GQ* and a raw sensuality that could not be ignored.

"We're heading out in a couple minutes. Did you get all your stuff on the bus?"

Since her suitcase hadn't been recovered, she didn't really have stuff. Just the things she bought at the discount store earlier. "Yeah."

"How's Jace?"

"He's sleeping."

Brian grinned, his intense brown eyes softening. "You wore him out already?"

She flushed under his attention. Why was she flushing? Brian was married. And she liked Jace a lot—loved him even. She just wasn't used to being around men who weren't customers. That had to be it. "He's wounded. Doesn't take much to wear him out."

"Well, make yourself at home, Aggie. If you need anything, let me know."

"Thanks." What a totally nice guy. No wonder he was married.

The sexy one (or was he the ornery one?), Trey, nudged Brian aside with his huge duffel bag. He tossed it into the back bedroom with a loud thud. "Shhh," Brian said. "Jace is sleeping."

Trey rolled his eyes. "You are such a drag since you traded your balls for a wedding band. Thank God, Myrna's not here. You might act like something other than a pussy for a change."

Brian grabbed Trey in a headlock and rubbed his knuckles over his scalp vigorously. Trey pretended to protest, but Aggie saw the pleased look on his face that he hid from Brian. Trey placed his palm flat on Brian's belly and halfheartedly tried to escape his torment. Aggie decided that these two had a thing. Well, Trey definitely had a thing. She wasn't sure about Brian.

When Brian released Trey, Trey said, "It's such a relief to not have any stuffy chicks on tour with us this time."

Aggie cleared her throat.

Trey looked at her. "Fuck, you're a stuffy chick? I took you as the kick-ass party girl type. You know. Fun."

"Myrna's fun," Brian protested.

Trey's eyebrows lifted. "Yeah. Whatever you say, dude."

The hunky one (or was he the cocky one?), Sed, entered the bus and carried several brown paper bags to the kitchenette. He set the bags on the counter and started stocking the refrigerator with beer.

"See, Brian, we get our beer back when your stuffy wife isn't around," Trey said.

"Myrna is *not* stuffy," he insisted.

"Uh, yeah, she is," Sed said. "But we love her anyway."

"I miss her," Brian said miserably.

"Which means you need beer," Trey said, grabbing a bottle out of Sed's grip, twisting the top off, and pressing it into Brian's hand. "Get nice and drunk so I can molest you in your sleep."

"Ha. Ha. Very funny," Brian said, tossing back his beer and swallowing half in several gulps.

Aggie got the feeling that Trey wasn't joking. Watching those two go at each other would be sexy as hell.

Eric entered the bus with the pervert-jerk, Jon, on his heels. "Everybody ready?" Eric asked.

"Let's get this show on the road!" Jon said.

"Who's driving?" Sed asked, crumpling a brown paper sack and tossing it on the floor.

The most ordinary guy on the planet leaned around Jon. While every male on the tour wore leather pants or jeans and a black T-shirt, this guy was dressed in khakis and a green polo shirt. His light brown hair was neatly trimmed and swept off his forehead with a light application of gel. One word described him perfectly: *normal.* "That would be me." His blue-eyed gaze fell on Aggie. "I'm Dave," he said with a wave. "Live audio engineer and designated driver."

She placed a hand on her chest. "Aggie."

"Jace's girl," Eric clarified.

"Nice to meet you," Dave said. "All right, we're heading out. Did everyone go potty?"

"Brian didn't go," Trey said in a singsong whine.

"You're such a tattletale." Brian belched and tossed his empty brown bottle in the sink. He grabbed Trey in another headlock, but this time he backed Trey through the open bathroom door. Trey stumbled over the rim of the stall and into the shower. "Say you're sorry, or you get soaked."

"If you'd go potty when Dave tells you to—"

Brian turned on the water.

"Ah, cold!"

Trey grabbed Brian's shirt and hauled him into the shower. They wrestled and hit each other beneath the flow of water as Brian tried to escape, and Trey tried to get his hands on as much of Brian's wet skin as possible. If they started making out, Aggie swore she'd rip off her clothes and join them. Jace would just have to get over it.

Sed nudged Aggie in the ribs with his elbow. "Those two should just fuck each other and get it out of their system, don't you think?"

"Oh yeah. Can I watch?" Aggie murmured.

Sed laughed. "Just what they need. A witness."

Brian tumbled out of the shower, landing on his face between the toilet and the sink. A puddle of water spread beneath him, flooding the white linoleum floor. He scrambled toward the door, laughing so hard, he was gasping. Trey grabbed his ankle with both hands, pulling him back into the bathroom.

"If you two want to shower together, you should get undressed first," Sed said. "Myrna will kick your ass for making a mess." Sed glanced at Aggie. "Or maybe Aggie will."

Aggie shook her head, grinning. She was enjoying the show immensely. The two sexy-as-hell guitarists could flood the bathroom all they wanted.

The bus eased forward, and Trey slipped on the wet floor, hitting the back of his head on the wall. "Ow, fuck!"

"It's all fun and games until someone gets hurt," Aggie said.

"And then it's hilarious," Eric said. He peeked into the bathroom and shook his head at his two drenched bandmates. "We don't need more injuries in this band." He pulled a bright green rabbit's foot out of a pocket and rubbed it between his thumbs. "No more injuries."

Brian's demeanor changed the instant he saw Trey holding the back of his head and wincing. Brian reached up and shut off the water. Kneeling before him, he took Trey's arms in both hands. "Did you hit your head? Are you okay?"

"I think I might have another concussion. Are my pupils the same size?"

Brian leaned closer, looking into Trey's eyes. "I can't tell."

"Closer."

Brian moved in. Trey grabbed him around the neck and kissed him on the mouth.

Brian punched him in the ribs. Hard. "You ass! What in the hell did you do that for?"

"Totally worth it," Trey murmured, lying in the bottom of the shower rubbing his ribs with a blissful grin on his face. Brian climbed to his feet and shoved everyone out of his way on his way to the bedroom.

"Trey's getting desperate," Eric said.

"He's wound up tighter than your snare, Eric," Jon said. "That boy needs some pussy. Why don't you help him out, Aggie?"

Aggie did not like this guy. It had nothing to do with how Jace felt about him either. Jon Mallory was slimy. She knew an eel when she saw one. "Why don't you? I think he likes guys anyway."

Eric shook his head. "Trey likes both."

Both? Now that had possibilities.

Chapter 27

LOUD VOICES WOKE JACE from a deep sleep. Someone was certainly having a good time. From the feminine pitch of one of the voices, it seemed one of those someones was Aggie. He rubbed his face with both hands, scrubbing the sleep from his eyes, and searched the darkened room for some clothes. He stumbled as the bus rounded a corner and grabbed the edge of the dresser to prevent himself from falling.

A pair of shorts in place, he opened the bedroom door and headed for the bathroom. He could hear Aggie's animated voice through the thin wall as he relieved himself.

"I mean this guy was huge, even bigger than Sed. I just snapped my whip at him, didn't even touch him, and he came down his leg. Then he started crying that his father sold his teddy bear at a garage sale when he was eleven."

The guys laughed uproariously.

"Is that what Jace does when you whip him?" Eric asked.

"Jace is on the opposite end of the spectrum. I beat the crap out of him, and he doesn't even flinch."

Now why did she have to go and tell them that? He exited the bathroom and moved to stand by her shoulder at the dining table. Across the table, Trey offered an uncomfortable wave. Aggie glanced at him, her eyes glassy and face slack. He supposed that explained why she was running off at the mouth.

"Jace!" she said, excitedly. "Did you have a good sleep?"

"Who can sleep with all this racket?"

"Oh, poor baby." She climbed from the booth and hugged him enthusiastically, putting most of her weight on him as she stumbled. Her lips smacked loudly against his jaw.

Jace stiffened. *Not in front of the guys, baby.*

"Aren't you going to kiss me?" she said.

"Maybe later."

"Oh poo, you're no fun."

"You're drunk."

"Jus' a little." She pinched her fingers together and laughed, clinging to his neck with one arm for balance.

"She already drank Brian under the table," Sed said. "I think I'm next."

At the sound of his name, Brian lifted his head from the back of the booth. "Myrna?"

Trey chuckled. "No, stud, she's still in Kansas City. Go back to your wet dream."

Brian's body went slack again, this time his head resting against Trey's shoulder. Trey grinned like the Cheshire cat on Prozac.

"Sit," Aggie insisted.

She shoved Jace into the booth.

And then...

She sat on his lap.

Jace chanced a glance at Trey, but he was too interested in Brian to tease him about Aggie's attention. Trey didn't comment when Aggie toyed with Jace's hair affectionately.

Jace brushed her hand aside. "Don't."

She shrugged, dropped her hand, and snuggled closer, her breath tickling his neck. "You smell good."

"Do we need to leave you two alone?" Sed asked.

Jace's face warmed instantly. "No."

He nudged Aggie off his lap and went to the refrigerator. "I'm starving. What's there to eat?" He looked back at the table, hoping he'd missed the feast sitting there waiting for consumption. Nope. Just empties and half empties and mostly fulls. So they were back to living on a diet of beer. Wonderful.

"Whatever you cook," Trey said. "Unless Aggie—"

"I'm female, so I get cooking duty? Fuck that."

"Not because you're female," Trey amended. "I've tasted the cooking of these guys, and let's just say it isn't good."

"You're the worst cook of us all," Brian murmured. He lifted his head from Trey's shoulder, a concerned look on his face. "Trey?"

"Yeah, buddy?"

"Is that your hand or mine?"

"I think it's yours."

"M'kay." Brian's head hit the table with a loud *thunk*. He grunted in pain. Trey helped him upright, settling Brian's head against his shoulder again. Brian had a spreading red spot in the center of his forehead now.

"I think Brian needs another beer," Trey said, holding his hand toward Jace.

Jace pulled a brown bottle from the refrigerator.

"Brian's done." Sed shook his head at Trey. "We all know what you're trying to do, Trey."

Brian poked Trey in the back of the hand repeatedly. "What are you try… hic… What are you trying to do, Trey?"

"I'm just making sure you're having a good time."

"I'm having a verygoodfuckingtime, my friend, thankyouvery-much." His head hit the table again.

Jace returned the beer to the fridge. He searched for something edible that took minimum preparatory effort. He settled for a stale toaster pastry, leaning against the stove while he munched it. Aggie watched him, looking confused. And a little hurt. He avoided her gaze. He really was just hungry. And craving meat. Steak preferably. Bloody rare. He moved to the front of the bus to talk to Dave.

"Any chance we can stop somewhere for food? I'm fuckin' starving to death."

"I'll keep an eye out for a place to stop."

Jace's stomach rumbled.

Dave took his eyes off the road to glance at him. "Soon. Go sit down. You look like shit."

"I feel like shit."

Jace sat in one of the captain's chairs across from the sofa where Jon and Eric were involved in a competitive card game. Jon selected one of Eric's cards, and Eric sniggered.

"Shit. I don't want your old maid, Sticks. Take it back."

Jon tried to return the card to Eric's fan, but Eric held his cards securely to his chest.

"Eh, no. That old bitch is yours now."

Old Maid? You've got to be fucking kidding me. And why was Eric wearing a motorcycle helmet on the bus?

Eric glanced at Jace and did a double take. "You okay, little man? You—"

"Look like shit. Yeah, I know. I'll live."

"Or not," Jon said. "Whatev."

Eric rolled his eyes and shook his head. "Dickhead much, Mallory?"

Eric was sticking up for him?

Aggie pressed a sports drink in Jace's hand. "Drink this, sweetie. The doctor said you need fluids."

"Yeah, sweetie," Eric said. "Drink your fluids like a good little man."

Well, that was to be expected. Jace climbed to his feet. "Come get me when we stop for food."

He took his drink to the bedroom and closed the door. He sat on the edge of the bed, staring into the darkness. He wasn't sure what to do about the band. He'd been with them for almost three years, and they felt like strangers. The door opened. He knew it was Aggie without looking up. He wasn't sure what to do about her either. He liked her, but he didn't want a solid commitment. He couldn't give her what she needed, and he knew that wasn't fair. She deserved better.

She switched on the light and sat next to him on the bed, her soft hand resting on his lower back. She kissed his shoulder. He didn't mind her affection now that they were alone—liked it pretty well actually.

"You okay?" she asked.

"Why does everyone keep asking me that?"

"I don't think you are. Not really."

"I'll live."

"I didn't ask if you'd live. Talk to me, Jace. You're so quiet around the guys. Why is that?"

"I—" He shook his head. He wasn't about to spill his guts. He needed to keep them inside. Festering. Where they belonged. "You seem to get along with them just fine."

"I get guys. Well, most guys. I don't get you. I want to though."

He wasn't afraid of much, but she scared the hell out of him. Not the whip-wielding dominatrix. That part of her was enough for him. This open, caring, wonderful woman was too much. He didn't deserve her. And he knew it.

"Why do you crave pain?"

"Why?" She wanted a reason? His throat closed off. "You shouldn't ask me things like that."

"You can tell me anything, Jace. It won't change how I feel about you."

"Are you sure?"

She shifted closer, her arm brushing his. "I'm sure. Whatever it is, you can tell me."

"Why don't you tell me why you like to hit men?" he countered.

She shrugged. "That's easy. My mom pawned me off on neighbors while she went out of town chasing some stupid dream or some stupider man. One of the neighbor men, who I now know is a pervert, liked to spank me. He'd sneak around and try to catch me doing something wrong so he could drag me into his garage, pull my pants down, and spank me. I hated that bastard. One day, I got tired of taking it. I waited until he dragged me into the garage, and then I took a belt to him. I expected him to beat me for it, even thought it would be worth it, but instead he let me hit him. He cried at my feet and begged me to forgive him for all the times he'd spanked me. I'll never forget the rush I felt when I wailed on that pervert's ass for the first time. There were many times after that. He started buying me gifts—made it worth my while." She laughed. "That's when I realized how easy it is to have complete power over men. I was eleven at the time."

Jace shook his head in disbelief. How could she be so matter-of-fact? "Fuckin' sick bastard. Didn't anyone try to stop him?"

"I didn't need anyone to stop him. *I* stopped him." She patted his cheek. "Trust me, it was better that way. Now you have to tell me why you think you need pain."

He sat in silence for several minutes. If he told her, she would no longer be able to accept him. She'd be like all the others who thought he was a freak.

But she sat there in silent support, and he felt his wall of protection crumble.

"Nine years ago…" He stared at his clasped hands, his stomach roiling. He shouldn't tell her. He closed his eyes and whispered, "I killed my father."

Chapter 28

AGGIE TOOK A DEEP breath, her mind unable to comprehend what Jace had told her. He'd killed his father? As in *murdered* him?

The bus shuddered and sputtered as it drew to a halt. "Food!" someone yelled. A clamor of voices and footsteps moved toward the bus exit.

"Are you ready to go eat?" he said.

"I… You're just going to leave it at that? You aren't going to explain why or how or—"

"Aggie, I can't change what I did. I can't take it back. I can't make amends. All I can do is cope—the only way I know how."

Her heart ached for him. Whatever he'd done in his past, she didn't care. She knew he was a good man. She took his hand and squeezed. "I want to help you. How can I help?"

His gaze drifted to the ceiling, the pain in his eyes so absolute, she felt it deep in her chest, in her throat, and behind her eyes.

"Hurt me, Aggie. Just hurt me."

She wrapped her arms around him, hugging him, wanting to reach him, but he remained stiff in her embrace. If he would just submit to her and admit what he really needed, they could make progress, but until he opened up and accepted the love she could give him, they'd go nowhere.

She kissed his cheek and stood. "Get some clothes on. Let's get you something to eat."

He stared at his hands again, a muscle flexing repeatedly in his jaw as he worked at burying his pain. After a moment, he nodded, slipped into some clothes, and headed for the door.

As they walked toward the exit, Aggie took his left hand in hers and refused to let go as he tried to shake it off.

"I won't make you hold my hand in front of the guys, but when they're not around, you're holding it." She poked him in the ribs. "Got it?"

He chuckled. God, she loved it when he laughed. She wanted him to laugh hard and often. She hoped she could give him that.

"Got it." He wrapped his left arm around her shoulders and linked the fingers of his other hand with hers inside his sling. She turned her head to grin at him, and he surprised her by kissing her.

What started as an affectionate brush of his lips soon deepened into something that made her ache. She leaned on him for support, blaming the alcohol she'd consumed earlier for the sudden weakness in her legs.

"Isn't that the sweetest thing you've ever seen, Jon?" Eric said from just inside the door. He took off his motorcycle helmet and set it down on the driver's seat. "Little man has a girlfriend."

"If by sweetest you mean the most nauseating, then I'd have to agree," Jon, acting as Eric's shadow, said.

Aggie extended an arm in their direction and gave them the finger.

"Did you see that, Eric? She propositioned us," Jon said.

"All right!" Eric clapped his hands. "You bang her. I'll watch."

Jace eased away, his eyes drifting open slowly. "Did you hear something, Aggie? Sounded like a couple of pussies crying for something they'll never have."

"Or be able to handle." She slapped Jace's ass hard and then squeezed until his breath caught with excitement. "There's a paddle in the bedroom with your name on it, sugar."

"She scares the hell out of me," Jon whispered.

"Me too," Eric agreed.

"What do you have to be scared of? My favorite whip was stolen, you wimps."

Jace squeezed Aggie's shoulder consolingly. "Don't worry, baby, we'll get you a new one."

Her eyes widened with eagerness. "With a thorn?"

Jace grinned. "Oh yeah. Definitely one with a thorn."

They continued past Eric and Jon on their way out of the bus.

"And can I get a new crop? And a flail?"

"Anything you want, as long as you promise to break them all in on me."

"Aww, can't I hit them?" She nodded over her shoulder at Eric and Jon. "Just a little bit? I'll clean off their blood when I'm finished. I wouldn't want to spread their diseases."

"I'll think about it." As soon as they exited the bus, Jace burst into laughter. "Did you see their faces?"

Not really. She'd been too busy looking at the smile on his.

Chapter 29

Jace's eyes flipped open, his heart still thumping with terror. He hadn't had that nightmare about his mother's death in years. Now it haunted him regularly.

A hand stroked his belly in the darkness. "You okay?" Aggie murmured groggily.

"Yeah."

"You've been moaning in your sleep."

"Nightmares. I probably shouldn't eat a twelve-ounce steak right before bed."

She cuddled closer and rested her head on his shoulder. Pain snaked through his chest as the weight of her head disturbed one of his slowly healing wounds. He kept all protest to himself. He wanted her there to remind him that he deserved it. The pain.

"Tell me about it."

"You don't want to hear it."

"Was it about killing your father?"

He hesitated. He should have never told her about his father in the first place. "No, it was about my mother's death."

"How old were you?"

"Nine."

"That's the same age I was when Grams passed away. How did your mother die?"

"We were in a head-on car accident. I was in the backseat when it happened. Wasn't injured. She lived for a day. Broken back. Multiple internal injuries. Her face was pulverized."

"I'm sorry, baby."

Thinking about it made his stomach clench with disgust. Not with his mother. With himself. "I was afraid of her—afraid of my own mother. Just because of the way she looked. So I never said good-bye. My father never forgave me for surviving the crash."

She took his hand and squeezed it. "That's horrible. No wonder you have nightmares about it."

"I haven't for a long time though. I thought I'd finally buried it for good. It must've been that hospital stay that brought it all back." *Or you.* He pulled his hand from hers and rolled onto his side, dislodging her from his shoulder.

She snuggled against his back, her arm stealing around his waist. "Thank you for sharing yourself with me. I know it's hard for you."

He snorted. "Are you this caring and understanding with everyone?"

"No. As a rule, I hate men." She chuckled. "You're just lucky I latched onto you, I guess."

"Enjoying your little pity party?"

Her breath caught. "Wow, Jace. That was hurtful."

He didn't like the breathless quality of her voice. He didn't want to hurt her. He wanted her to hurt him. He turned to face her and cupped her cheek in the darkness, feeling the wetness of her tears against his fingertips. His heart squeezed. He'd made her cry?

"Do you really think the reason I'm here is because I pity you?" she asked.

Of course that was why she was there. Why else would she be? "Don't you?"

Her hand covered his upon her cheek. "I sympathize, Jace. I want to take your pain and replace it with laughter, but that's not pity."

"I don't want you to take my pain, Aggie. I need it."

"Why? Because you feel guilty about your mom? About whatever you did to your father?"

"I do feel guilty, but that's not why I need it."

"Then why? Help me understand, Jace. You know I'll hurt you physically as long as you need it, but I want to know why."

"It's what I deserve. And sometimes I think even pain is too good for me."

She kissed him tenderly. "You're wrong. You don't *deserve* pain. You deserve to be happy."

"I'm happy enough. I have my music."

"Yes, I'm glad you have something important to you. And you have..." She hesitated. "...me."

His heart skipped a beat. "I'm not sure what to do about that actually."

"Do you like me?"

"Very much."

"Then just go with it."

"Go with it?" This conversation was getting entirely too serious and high-pressure. He took a deep breath. "Does going with it involve you tying me up and doing things to me against my will?"

"Maybe."

He pushed her onto her back and covered her body with his. "Awesome."

Before he could kiss her, she asked, "Will you tell me about your father?"

"Sorry, I can't, but you can tell me about yours."

She hesitated.

He kissed her chin, her jaw.

"I never met him," she whispered, as if the words frightened her.

"Never?"

"No. He seduced my mom, knocked her up. As soon as he found out she was pregnant, he split."

Jace released a huff of air. "Lucky you."

"You didn't have a good relationship with your father? Is that why you killed him?"

He kissed her gently, hoping to distract her. He didn't like to think about his father, much less talk about him. As his lips caressed her jaw and throat, she melted beneath him. So receptive. So wonderful. So understanding and accepting. He knew he'd never find another woman like her. Knew she'd be gone as soon as she figured out what kind of man she'd mixed herself up with. He wished he was worthy of her. He also wished he wasn't so physically weak and tired. The spirit was willing. The body wanted to curl into the fetal position and pass out from exhaustion.

"You're tired," she murmured.

"I'm sorry I haven't been a good lover to you lately."

"Not true."

He yawned. "I'll make it up to you when I'm back on my feet."

"I have no doubt that you will."

"Anything you want to do, I'm game. I promise."

His body sank into hers as his strength waned.

She chuckled. Just before he drifted back to sleep, he heard her murmur, "You don't want to promise that, sugar. I have some pretty unusual tastes."

Chapter 30

AGGIE SEARCHED THE MEDICINE cabinet for some aspirin. She needed to remember that drinking wasn't a contest. Especially when in competition with big guys like Sedric Lionheart.

"Will you hurry up in there?" Jon said from the corridor.

She swallowed several painkillers and slid the bathroom door open. "All yours."

"About time. Tell me something, Aggie, why do you and your little boyfriend get the bed while I'm stuck sleeping on the hard sofa?"

"Jace is injured. He needs a comfortable place to recover."

"You two should have stayed in LA. I don't even know why he's here. Doesn't he get it? I'm back. There's no way in hell I'll ever let him take my place again."

Aggie crossed her arms over her chest. "I thought you were the spare."

"You thought wrong. I'm the original. He's a bad copy. A fake. A wannabe."

Aggie was certain Jace's position in the band was secure. At least she hoped it was. If he lost his music because he'd gotten himself shot trying to protect her, she'd never forgive herself.

"Where did you get this hideous necklace?" Jon lifted the heart-shaped pendant from between her breasts. "Did Jace pick it out for you?"

"My mother gave it to me," she said, snatching it out of his hand. "Don't touch things that don't belong to you."

"I'll touch anything I damn well please."

She didn't expect him to grab her. Kiss her. Ugh! Arms pinned to her sides, she struggled for release. Why was he so strong? A hand appeared from the top curtained bunk behind Jon and grabbed him by the collar. "Let go of her, dipshit," Eric said.

As soon as Jon released her arms, she slapped him across the face.

Jon covered the red handprint on his cheek with one hand. "You fuckin' bitch." He lunged toward her.

Eric jerked Jon's collar, and he stumbled backward. "You deserved that. Leave her alone."

"What? Do you need to protect your new best friend's little whore?"

Eric shoved him, and he stumbled into Aggie. "I should have never suggested you stand in for Jace. Why don't you just go home?"

Damn, Jace needed to hear this. He probably wouldn't believe her if she told him.

Jon burst into laughter. "Good one, Eric." He swaggered into the bathroom and slid the door shut with more force than necessary.

Eric muttered under his breath, punched his pillow a couple of times, and turned to face the wall in his bunk. Aggie approached him and poked him in the back.

"Trying to sleep here," he grumbled.

"Thank you," she whispered loudly.

He peeked at her over his shoulder and grinned. "No problem." He scooted over in his bunk. "Room for you up here, if you'd like to offer a more personal thank you."

"Hmm," she murmured. "As soon as I get a new whip, I'll be sure to show you my gratitude."

He chuckled. "If you didn't scare the shit out of me, I might take you up on that offer, gorgeous." He turned back to face the wall and pulled his covers up to his chin.

She drank a large glass of water from the kitchen sink. Her head throbbed like Eric's bass drum. Jon exited the bathroom. As he passed her, he lifted his fist as if to hit her and then laughed when she flinched.

"You ain't so tough."

If he didn't quit fucking with her, she was going to show him tough. "Would you like me to kick your ass in front of your friends? I'd be more than happy to oblige."

"Whatever." He wandered back to the couch, and when he laid down made a big, pissy show of its lack of comfort.

She hoped Jace recovered soon so they could get rid of this ass, if for no other reason. She liked the other guys in the band and was even growing attached to Eric, who she hadn't understood at first. Jon? She wondered whether anyone would care if she accidently threw him out of the bus and over a bridge.

Even crossing the Canadian border was an adventure with Sinners. Aggie couldn't remember the last time she'd laughed so hard.

Eric marched up and down the bus aisle like a British soldier, using a drumstick as a baton as he sang at the top of his lungs. "O Canada! O Canada! How friggin' cold are thee!"

"Sit down, Eric," Sed demanded.

"O Canada! O Canada! A population of twenty-three!"

"Eric! I said sit."

Aggie clutched her abdomen to keep her spleen from rupturing in her hysterics.

"O Canada! O Canada! At least you have some trees!"

"Eric!" Sed tackled him into a captain's chair. "Wait until we're across the border. Do you want us to get searched again?"

"Trey always enjoys the body cavity search," Eric said.

Aggie tumbled off the couch, still laughing. She lay on the floor on her back, holding her midsection with both hands as she tried to catch her breath. "Stop. Stop, I'm gonna throw up."

"Now look what you did to Aggie, Eric," Brian said with a grin. "She's damaged goods."

"She looks healthy to me," Trey murmured, looking down at her from his perch on the arm of the sofa. "Mmmmm, incredibly healthy. Of course, I could be mistaken. We could go play doctor for a couple hours. I'll examine you thoroughly to make sure."

"Help me up." She extended her hand in the air, and Jace knocked Trey's hand out of the way to help her to her feet. She forced herself not to hug him when she noticed the twinges of jealousy sparking in his deep brown eyes just before he lowered his gaze to the floor. She knew he didn't like public displays of affection, but it was so hard to keep her hands to herself. The guys always seemed to be around. "Do you need your bandages changed?" she asked hopefully. If she got him alone in the bedroom, she could smother him with affection without repercussions.

"Not right now."

"And…" Dave called from the driver's seat. "They want to search us. Everyone get your passports and step off the bus."

"Shit," Sed grumbled and slapped Eric on the back of the head.

"You don't really think they want to search the bus because I was making fun of their national anthem, do you?"

"No, I just like to hit you. They want to search the bus because they assume if we're rock musicians, we must be on illegal drugs."

"I fuckin' love Canada," Eric said. "I can't wait until they reinstate the draft so I have a legitimate reason to move here."

"Border patrol," a uniformed officer announced as he stepped on the bus. "Anything to declare?"

"I declare that this sucks," Trey said, shuffling past him.

"Hey," Eric said to the officer and pointed at Trey. "I saw that guy shove something up his ass."

Sed slapped Eric again. "He's joking, sir. Just joking."

"I did see him shove something up his ass. Another guy's cock." He snorted with laughter.

Sed pushed Eric toward the exit. "Just ignore him, officer. He has no concept of when a joke is inappropriate."

"That was funny though, right?"

"Oh yes, hilarious, Eric. We won't tell the nice officer about what you shoved up your ass."

"I didn't—"

Sed covered his mouth. "Just ignore him. He gets jittery when he comes down off the crack. That was another joke, by the way. This bus is clean. I guarantee it."

A second officer entered the bus with a German shepherd, which was fighting its leash and barking excitedly. The man waited with the dog in the driver's area while everyone exited.

"Are you sure it's clean?" Aggie whispered to Sed.

"Unless you brought something with you."

Aggie shook her head. "No, I gave up drugs after high school. Almost OD'd a couple times."

"Well, there you go. You have something in common with Jon."

Aggie's lip curled with displeasure. Now there was something to be proud of. She glanced at Jon, who was staring venom at Jace as usual. Aggie huddled against Jace to block the cool breeze. She wasn't expecting it to be this chilly in September and hadn't put on a jacket. After around fifteen minutes, the border patrol came off the bus.

"Can we take a look underneath?"

"Do you have a legal right to?" Sed asked.

"Yes."

"Then why bother asking?"

Dave opened the doors to the storage compartments under the bus. The dog sniffed around and pawed someone's jacket. The officer set it on the ground. After a second sniff, the dog lost interest.

For no apparent reason, Jon careened into Jace, knocking him into Aggie. At Jace's gasp of pain, Aggie turned to scowl at Jon. "What did you do that for?"

She saw him shove something into Jace's pants pocket and then his empty hand retreated.

"You two just looked like you needed to cuddle a little closer," Jon said with a chuckle. "There was at least a quarter of an inch between you."

Aggie stuck her hand in Jace's pocket. Felt the small bag full of dried leaves inside. Knew what the bastard had done. Before she could return Jon's bag of pot to him, the dog caught scent of it and charged toward them.

"Where is it, boy?" the officer asked.

Huge paws landed in the center of Jace's chest. Jace winced and turned an alarming shade of puce.

"Wait!" Aggie grabbed Jace's good arm, but the second officer wrenched him from her grasp and slammed him onto the asphalt. Having his arm trapped in a sling, he had no way to catch his fall.

"Easy. He's severely injured," Sed said, grabbing the officer by the shoulder.

The dog located the bag in Jace's pocket. "Good boy," the man said to his dog. "What do we have here?"

"It's not mine," Jace said, gasping through his pain.

"Sure, it's not."

"He's telling the truth. Someone planted it on him." Aggie glanced at Jon, who was doing a poor job at feigning innocence by inspecting the clouds.

The patrol man lifted the bag from Jace's pocket and examined it. Got a strange look on his face.

Jon busted out laughing.

"What the fuck are you laughing at?" Sed grumbled in his deep baritone.

The officer opened the bag, crunching the green leaves with his fingertips, and gave it a hesitant sniff. Dipped a wet finger inside and touched a leaf to his tongue. "This isn't cannabis."

Jon laughed harder. "It's just oregano. Best practical joke ever, huh, guys?"

No one was laughing.

"Then what tipped the dog off?" the officer asked. "He wouldn't go after oregano." He shook the bag at the dog, which pawed its nose and whined.

Jon shrugged. He leaned over Jace. "You okay down there, buddy?"

Aggie helped Jace to his feet. He staggered as he regained his balance. Blood had seeped through the bandage on his shoulder and through his white T-shirt in several spots. He lunged at Jon, murder in his eyes. Aggie wrapped herself around him and widened her stance to hold him back. "Not here, sugar," she whispered, nodding toward the officers. "Get him back later."

"Need your girlfriend to hold you up, little man?" Jon said, sneering.

"That was so uncool," Eric said. He touched Jace's shoulder. "You okay? You're bleeding."

Jace nodded slightly, breathing hard as he worked to bury his anger. He had every right to be angry, and if there hadn't been two cops standing right there, Aggie would have beat the shit out of Jon herself.

"Officer, can I take him on the bus and redress his wounds?" Aggie asked.

"He looks like he's in pretty bad shape," the patrolman said. "Maybe you should take him to a hospital."

"I'll be okay," Jace murmured. He stumbled against Aggie. She grabbed him to keep him on his feet.

"Can I take him inside?" she asked again.

"Yeah, we're done here. You're free to go." The officer pointed at Jon. "You better watch it, buddy. That wasn't funny at all. Your friend had no business being slammed on the ground. It appears he's hurt badly."

"Sorry, sir." Jon grinned cruelly. "It won't happen again."

The group made their way toward the bus, walking slowly behind Jace, who leaned heavily on Aggie. She wasn't sure how he was still on his feet. She was going to kick the shit out of Jon.

"Let me help him," Brian offered.

Brian took Jace's arm and eased his weight off Aggie.

"I'm fine," Jace said.

"You're not fine," Brian said. "And we're taking you to a hospital. We're not going to let you do a Trey and talk us out of getting you medical attention."

"Hooray for socialized medicine," Eric cheered.

"You have to be a Canadian citizen to get that benefit, idiot," Sed said.

"I told you I was moving here."

"Dave, ask that cop where the nearest hospital is," Trey said to Dave as Brian helped Jace climb the steps. Aggie followed one step behind, prepared to catch Jace should he fall backward. He was scarcely able to lift his leg high enough to get up the steep steps.

"I'm not going to the hospital," Jace said, his breathing labored. "It just knocked the wind out of me."

"You're bleeding all over the fucking place," Trey said, one step behind Aggie. "Aren't you already low on blood?"

"A couple pints," Jace said. "I'll be okay. Just need to lie down for a minute."

And he did lie down—on the floor at the top of the steps.

Chapter 31

"Go on without us," Aggie said. "I'll get a car somewhere, and we'll catch up in a few days. He won't be able to perform anyway. Isn't that the whole reason you brought AssHat Jon with you?"

"I'm not sure bringing AssHat was the brightest idea," Sed murmured. "I know he played that whole drug bust like it was a practical joke, but if I know Jon, he was taking the focus off himself because he had something to hide."

"He's clean now, Sed," Eric said. "He knows the band doesn't tolerate illegal drugs on tour. We told him that before we asked him to come."

Sed slapped Eric on the back of the head. "Get a fuckin' brain, dude. Do you think he'd be honest about it? He wants to be onstage again more than anything. Why do you think he's mean to Jace?"

"Jace is an easy target."

Sed rolled his eyes and turned his attention back to Aggie. "We have a show tomorrow night here in Vancouver. We can probably stay another night if we need to and still make it to our next gig in Edmonton. We'll see if Jace is feeling better by then. If not, you two can catch up later."

Aggie nodded. She supposed there was a reason that Sed led the band. He was a natural.

"It's best to keep him in the hospital for as long as possible," Sed said.

Eric chuckled. "A day, if you're lucky. The doctor said all he needed was bed rest."

"And no roughhousing," Sed added.

Aggie's eyes narrowed. "That was all Jon's fault."

"I'll deal with Jon," Sed said.

"Let Jace deal with Jon when he feels better."

Sed looked down at her. For a minute she thought he was going to yell at her, but he nodded. "I'll give him that."

Aggie smiled.

"Unfortunately, we've got to rehearse right now. Jon's a bit rusty."

"Like a hundred-year-old iron gate in a bayou," Eric muttered.

"Thanks, guys. I'll give you my number in case you need to call," Aggie said.

After they left, Aggie sank into the chair beside Jace's bed. She watched him sleep for a while. She hoped he voluntarily agreed to stay in the hospital for a few days. She knew the stress of being around Jon was getting to him. Yawning, she decided to go for a cup of coffee and walked to the vending machine at the end of the hallway. Her phone rang. Thinking it was one of the band, she answered immediately.

"Are you talking to me now?" her mom asked.

"No."

"Are you coming home soon?"

"No."

"A regular customer of yours stopped by last night. Said he'd been trying to reach you at the club, but they said you'd taken an extended vacation."

Probably a permanent one. Roy had been furious when she'd called and told him she wasn't sure when she'd be back to work. Aggie set her coffee on the counter and leaned against a wall. Her mother always prefaced big revelations with noncommittal statements. "And you told him I was out of town, right?"

"He likes me."

"Who?"

"Gary."

Loser Gary? "You didn't take him into the sanctum, did you?"

"Maybe."

Aggie squeezed the bridge of her nose between her thumb and index finger. "Mom, if you don't know what you're doing, you can really hurt someone."

She laughed. "Isn't that the whole point?"

"No. I trained under a professional domme for two years before I did any sessions on my own."

"You could train me." She sounded excited—for now. Aggie knew once she got into the actual *work*, it would hold her attention for about three hours.

"Aren't you ashamed of what I do?" Aggie said.

"Ashamed? No, baby, I could never be ashamed of you. You're only twenty-six, and look at all you've accomplished. You own a nice home. Have a well-paying job. Run two businesses. Have a man who loves you enough to take two bullets for you. You command respect. What do I have, Aggie? What have I done with my life? Nothing. You're the one who should be ashamed. Not of yourself. Of me."

Aggie clutched the gold-painted plastic heart between her breasts and blinked back tears. "I had no idea you felt that way, Mom," she said, her voice hitching. "You're always saying how much you want to get me out of the club. I thought…" *I thought you hated me.*

"So will you train me to hit men?"

Aggie laughed. "Not a chance."

"Why not?"

"I've specialized. If you really want to do this, you need to be trained by someone who's good at everything."

"Sounds hard."

"It is hard."

"Speaking of hard. You should have seen how hard Gary got when—"

"Don't say it!" Aggie felt her face flush. She didn't know she was still capable of blushing.

A gray-haired woman entered the room and fixed herself a cup of coffee. She smiled sweetly at Aggie, who returned her smile and turned to face the other direction.

"I can't talk about this right now, Mom. I'm at the hospital with Jace."

"I thought he was out of the hospital."

"He's back in. I can't get him to rest."

"Is that why you fell for him? He doesn't do what you say?" Aggie could hear the amusement in her voice.

It was more complicated than that, but she didn't want to discuss Jace with her mother. "I don't know. Maybe. I've got to go. Promise you'll behave."

"I don't make promises I can't keep."

Aggie could practically see the woman's mischievous smile. "Mom."

"Be careful. Thanks for talking to me." She hung up.

The elderly lady, who was adding sugar to her coffee, grinned at Aggie. "Challenging mother?"

Aggie snorted. "That's an understatement."

"I had one of those. You'll miss her when she's gone."

If she ever left. Aggie smiled at the woman, collected her coffee, and returned to Jace's room. He was fully dressed, including his leather boots, sitting on the edge of the bed waiting for her.

"Are you ready to go?" he asked, tugging on the IV line in his hand. "I feel fine now."

She sighed and sat beside him, knowing he would not be deterred. "Just let me finish my coffee."

He nodded and stared at his knees while she took tiny sips from her coffee cup. If her mother didn't give her a stress-induced heart attack, her boyfriend surely would.

Chapter 32

JACE PACED THE AISLE as he and Aggie waited for the concert to end and the band to return to the bus. She sat on the kitchen counter watching him pass back and forth in front of her. She hadn't let him out of her sight all day, but at least she'd gotten him out of the fuckin' hospital. He owed her another one.

"Why don't you go watch the show?" Aggie asked. "You aren't getting any rest."

"I can't watch." Just the thought of Jon onstage, playing his music, was making him insane. Except it wasn't Jace's music. Not really. Jon had composed every bass line in their current set list. The new album? Yes, Jace had something to do with those compositions—they had his stamp on them—but their previous three albums were all Jon.

"Why don't you tell me what's bothering you?" Aggie snagged him around the waist as he paced past her and wrapped her long legs around his hips to keep him from escaping.

He stared at the cheap heart-shaped locket nestled between her breasts. "Why do you always wear this thing?" he asked, lifting the light, peeling piece of jewelry from its resting place.

"Uh-uh," she said. "No."

He glanced at her in question.

"You aren't changing the subject. I'm not going to let you."

He lowered his eyes again and shrugged. She drew him closer, her arms stealing around his neck.

"Tell me, Jace. No one's here but me."

He stroked the plastic and gold-foiled heart with his fingertips as he struggled to find words. It wasn't that he didn't want to tell her. Saying his feelings out loud made his palms sweat and his heart race.

Aggie ran her fingers over the edge of his ear. "Do you miss being onstage that much?"

He shook his head slightly. He loved playing live, but not for the glory like Sed, or the excitement like Brian, or the fun like Trey, but to share the music, his soul... like Eric. That wasn't what was bothering him though.

"Is it because Jon is out there trying his damnedest to replace you?"

He nodded.

Her fingers slid down his jaw under his chin. "Look at me."

He took a deep breath and forced his eyes to hers. He expected her pitying look, but found her expression sincere and so caring that his heart rose to his throat, stealing his air.

"He won't. Don't worry. There's only one Jace. You are one hundred percent irreplaceable." She hugged him close, her cheek pressing against his. "Irreplaceable," she whispered.

He shrugged out of his sling and wrapped both arms around her body, drawing her closer still. He leaned against her, holding her. No, she was holding him, comforting him. It felt good to lean on her and at the same time terrifying. He wanted to let her in. Let her see everything he was, but what if something happened to her? What if she left him? What if she died? What if she saw what was really inside him and she hated him? The way his mother had hated him... and his father... and Kara. Every person he'd ever loved had hated him before dying.

Jace jerked out of her grasp, turned away, and pressed on his temples with the heels of his hands. He had to force those memories from his thoughts. He couldn't deal with them. Not now. Not ever.

Being with Aggie kept bringing them to the surface. Things he'd thought he'd buried years ago. He didn't know how much longer he could let her stay—for the sake of his sanity.

She hopped off the counter, leaned against his back, and wrapped her arms around his waist. "You okay?"

He twisted away, unable to stand her tenderness.

"I see," she murmured. "Do you want to talk about it?"

"No, I don't want to fuckin' talk about it." He lifted a hand, his palm in her face. "Just give me a minute to myself."

She grabbed him by the front of his T-shirt and pulled him toward the bedroom.

"I said I didn't want to talk about it."

She glared at him over her shoulder. "I'm done talking, Jace. It's time for your punishment."

The hard, cold look on her face had him instantly aroused. Punishment. That's exactly what he needed. But how could she hurt him effectively? She didn't have her tools of torture. She shoved him into the room and slammed the door. Her hands moved to the waist of his jeans. She unfastened his belt and yanked it free of the loops.

"Turn around," she demanded.

Even without the leather and thigh-high boots, she turned him on. Her commanding demeanor was enough to get his blood pumping.

"Hit me."

"I'll hit you when I think you've earned it. You owe me an apology."

His brow knitted with confusion. "For what?"

"Disrespect. Dismissing my concern by putting your hand in my face."

Had he done that? He hadn't been thinking clearly. Never did when his past intruded on his thoughts. "I'm sorry."

"I'm sorry, Mistress V," she said, reminding him to address her with respect.

"I'm sorry, Aggie. I just…" He turned his unfocused gaze to the floor.

"I know, baby," she whispered. "Turn around."

He turned.

When the leather snapped hard against his ass, his body shuddered. She hit him in the exact same spot again. Again. Each time the pain intensified, and his cock grew harder. He knew there was something wrong with him. This connection between sexual excitement and physical pain. But he couldn't help it. And Aggie gave him exactly what he needed without criticizing. She understood.

Understood him. He didn't know how. Wasn't sure he wanted her to.

She kept all her stinging blows to his ass. He wanted to feel the bite of the leather against his bare flesh, but she hadn't told him to remove his clothes.

"Is your cock hard, Jace?"

"Yes." He sucked the word between his teeth.

"Show me. Unfasten your pants and pull it out for me to see."

He did what she said, growing even harder as he released his cock from its confines.

"Very nice," she murmured. "Do you want me to strike your bare ass?"

"Please."

"Lower your pants to your knees."

Trembling with anticipation, he eased his jeans down his hips and thighs.

"Your skin is already really red. Are you sure about this?"

"Ah God, Aggie. Hurt me. Please, hurt me."

"Well, since you pleaded so nicely."

The belt cracked as it struck the sensitized skin of his ass. His body jerked, and he gasped. He focused on the pain, needing it as a cover, needing it to blot out the vivid pain that stained his soul black.

With each lash, the white hot sensation pressed the darkness deeper, where he could pretend it didn't exist.

After twenty or thirty strikes, Aggie moved her body against his back. She caressed his stinging, heated ass with her free hand. Cool and soothing. He shuddered with excitement as she continued to stroke him.

"Touch yourself," she whispered in his ear.

He opened his eyes and caught her gaze in the mirror over the dresser. She was gazing at his reflection, her attention riveted to his hard cock.

"Touch myself?"

"Wrap your hand around that big cock of yours and stroke it." She bit his ear. He shuddered again, but didn't obey. He couldn't bring himself pleasure. Never had before. Didn't plan on starting now. "Do it," she insisted.

"No."

She backed away. "Are you disobeying your mistress?"

"I can't, Aggie."

"Bullshit."

She went to the side table and pulled out the drawer where Brian kept his toys. Jace watched her warily. What was she planning on doing to him?

She pulled a bottle of oil from the drawer and squirted some into his hand. He resisted as she attempted to direct his hand to his cock.

"Aggie, don't."

"You seem to think the only reason you crave pain is because you deserve it."

"I *do* deserve it."

She shook her head at him. "You like it. It wouldn't make you hard if you didn't like it."

"No. That's not why," he insisted.

"Baby, it's okay to like it."

"It's weird." He knew that it was. That's why he tried to fool himself into thinking he needed the pain for a reason. Not because he liked it. He deserved it.

She closed their combined hands and drew his oiled hand up the length of his cock, pausing at its swollen head. Jace gasped as pleasure coursed through his body, already beyond excited by the throbbing sting in his ass.

"Maybe some people think it's weird," she said, "but I don't. I like that you like it. It makes me hot to see you like this."

"It does?" She pulled his hand down his shaft toward its base. The pleasure wasn't nearly as intense as it had been when the pain had been fresh. It was already dissipating.

"Yeah. Tell me what you want, Jace."

"I want…" He hesitated. "I want pain."

"And what else?"

She slid their combined hands up his cock again. He shuddered. "And pleasure."

"That wasn't so hard to admit, was it?"

Yeah, it kind of was, actually. He had never wanted to admit it even to himself.

"The faster you stroke yourself the harder I hit," she said. "Do you want me to hit you hard?"

"Yes." Their combined hands moved faster over his oil-slicked cock. Pumping it. Faster. "Hit me hard, Aggie. Hurt me."

She released his hand and took a step back. He waited for the next blow, but it never came. He glanced over his shoulder. "Are you finished?" he asked.

"You've stopped moving your hand."

He bit his lip and closed his eyes, rubbing his palm from the throbbing head of his cock down to its base. The belt tapped his ass. He stroked faster. She hit harder.

Faster. Pumping it hard. Relishing her response. His pleasure built. His excitement intensified. He worked the sensitive head with his oiled hand, the grooves between his fingers bumping over the rim. She was striking him so hard now his flesh tingled in protest, but he wanted more.

"Ah God, Aggie." He stroked his shaft even faster, massaged its head until pain and pleasure converged. "Wait. Stop. I'm gonna come. Wait." He released his cock. The belt fell still. "No. Keep hitting me, please."

"You stopped touching yourself."

"Yes, I know. I don't want to come. I don't... I don't deserve it."

"You need that release, Jace. It's the fifteen seconds out of the day that you actually let go of everything. I want that for you."

"I need the pain more."

"I don't believe you. Besides, watching you jack off is really turning me on."

He glanced at her over his shoulder again, his brows lifted. "It is?"

"Oh yeah." She peeled her red T-shirt off and then tossed her bra aside. "I want you to come on my tits, baby. Do you see how hard my nipples are?"

He saw them, all right—wanted those taut tips against his tongue. She tapped his ass with the belt again.

"Keep going. Stroke it until you come."

He kept going. Mostly because she wanted him to, but a part of him liked the pleasure blended with the pain, liked that it made her hot—couldn't get enough. He wondered why it had never occurred to him to jack off while someone hit him. Stroking himself as vigorously as he was, it didn't take him long to find his peak. When he shuddered and gasped, Aggie turned him around, dropped to her knees in front of him, and offered him her breasts. He slid his cock between the luscious globes and pressed them together. His breath hitched as spasms gripped the base of his cock, and he spurted his cum between her breasts, over her chest, and up her throat. When his body stilled, Aggie tipped him onto the bed.

"Oh my God, I'm so turned on right now," she said.

"You should have told me that before I wasted my load."

"That was no waste." She lifted her large breast toward her mouth and licked at what fluids she could reach with her tongue.

"You keep that up, and I'll be hard again in no time."

She stood, took off the rest of her clothes, and crawled beside him on the bed. "Suck them, Jace."

He didn't hesitate in drawing one hard nipple into his mouth. He tasted his own cum on them. Loved how it mingled with the taste of her skin.

She shuddered. "God, I'm hot."

Fuck yeah, she was. He watched her hand move down her belly and settle between her thighs. When her fingers disappeared from view, he lifted his head and moved down her body for a better view. She slid two fingers in and out of her swollen, dripping wet pussy. Her other hand rubbed at her clit.

"Oh," she gasped. "Don't stop yet, Jace. Suck my nipples. Please."

He was torn between giving her what she wanted and watching her pleasure herself. He couldn't do both at the same time. Aggie shuddered and cried out. The door burst open.

Jon stood on the threshold, looking mildly amused. "You two done? I've got four easy chicks and a raging hard-on. None of them are willing to wait a minute longer."

"Get the fuck out of here," Jace yelled.

Jace stood and pulled his pants up, hurriedly fastening them. He headed for the door with a balled fist. "I've had enough of your bullshit, Jon."

"Is it my fault you didn't lock the door?"

Aggie grabbed Jace by the arm, but he shrugged her off.

"There's no lock on the door, jackass. And it is your fault that you didn't knock," Jace said.

Jon's eyes moved to Aggie, who stood beside Jace trying to get his attention. Jace glanced at her. Beautiful, as usual, and entirely naked. "Go put on some fucking clothes!"

"Don't yell at me," she growled.

"My God, Aggie, you're a bombshell." Jon jerked a thumb in Jace's direction. "What do you see in this lame ass?"

Jace had taken enough abuse from this prick. He still hadn't paid him back for planting fake drugs on him at the border. Jace placed both hands on Jon's chest and shoved. Jon stumbled backwards into the young girls who'd accompanied him on the bus. And by young, Jace meant young—still in high school probably. Jace would be surprised if any were of age. What was this guy thinking?

"Get off the bus," Jace said.

"You get off the bus. I'm not even sure what you're still doing here. Thanks for taking up my slack while I was gone, but I'm back. The band doesn't need you anymore."

"That doesn't mean much, coming from you," Jace said.

"What about the fans? What they want? When's the last time they chanted *your* name?"

Well, never, to be honest, but that didn't matter. Sed, Brian, and Trey kept the crowd entertained. Jace just did his job and put every bit of his tattered heart and lacerated soul into his playing. He didn't need the spotlight. The guys tried to get him to interact with the crowd more, but...

Shit, maybe Jon was right. Maybe Jon *was* better for the band. Not musically. Jace knew he was a better bass player than Jon, but as an entertainer, Jon had the more outgoing personality. Jon engaged the crowd and had a good time onstage. Maybe that's what really mattered to the fans. Maybe the music wasn't so important after all.

Jon grinned. "That shut you up, didn't it? Now get the fuck

out of my way. I need to get laid. And my chicks won't have to get themselves off, unlike yours." He glanced at Aggie, who was still naked. "Aggie, if you need to get boned, my pants are always open."

Jace didn't really gauge the punch. His training, his boxing instincts, had total control. He didn't even feel his fist connect. Jon crumpled to the ground. Jace took less satisfaction from knocking him out than he thought. His right arm and shoulder protested the force he'd put behind the punch, but even that pain didn't make him feel better.

"I told him never to disrespect my woman again," Jace muttered, before swinging himself up into the upper curtained bunk to rest like he was supposed to. The fastest way to get rid of Jon was to get better. Enjoying Aggie and getting into fistfights wasn't exactly conducive to healing.

—◊—

Aggie tripped over Jon's prone body and stepped on the bottom bunk to peer at Jace, who was "resting" on the top bunk. He was breathing so hard, she feared he would hyperventilate. "You okay?"

He plumped his pillow, but didn't turn to look at her. "Why do you keep asking me that? I'm fine. I just need sleep."

She rubbed his lower back, feeling the tension in his body. She'd just worked some of that out of him and then… Jon appeared.

"If you're hungry, I could make you some eggs or something."

"Maybe later."

She planted a kiss on the nape of his neck and climbed down to the floor.

Two of the girls Jon had brought on the bus had fled. The other two were bent over Jon, trying to revive him.

"How old are you two?" Aggie asked.

"Eighteen," they gushed in unison.

"Yeah, and I'm a black man with giant, hairy balls." Their eyes drifted down her naked body. To check for giant, hairy balls, she supposed. "I think you two should go. I'll take care of him." Aggie took each girl by the arm and led them to the exit.

"Don't make us go. We want to meet Trey."

"Trey? Then why are you here with Jon?"

"He was the only one interested."

Aggie grinned. "I see. That makes more sense. Maybe if you wait outside the bus for a while, Trey will show up and give you an autograph or something." She hated to put Trey on the spot, but she didn't want the guys to get in trouble for having underage girls on the bus, even if the pervert who'd planned to abuse them was out cold on the floor.

"That's probably for the best." The girl glanced down the aisle at Jon, who was still lying unmoving on the floor. She giggled. "Jace really knocked him out."

"You know who Jace is?"

"Of course I know who Jace is. He's the best bassist on the planet. I'm so sorry I didn't get to see him onstage. He's such a doll. So shy and cute. And cuuuute. And oh m' God cute, eh." She grinned and hugged herself. "Sed said he was sick, so Jon was filling in."

Aggie averted her gaze. "Something like that."

"Tell Jace I hope he gets over his explosive diarrhea quickly."

Aggie's eyes widened, and then she burst out laughing. "Is that what Sed told everyone?"

"Was he teasing us?"

Aggie wiped her eyes with the back of her hand. "Yeah, Sed was teasing you. Jace's right arm is injured, but I'm sure he will be back onstage in no time."

The girl gave Jon one last disappointed look and then hopped down the bus steps.

Eric paused outside the door, looking the young girl over with confusion. "I thought you were with Jon tonight."

"Jon isn't with anyone tonight," Aggie said. "Except the floor."

"Jace knocked him out cold," the girl added and then giggled.

"No shit?" Eric climbed the steps and stood at the end of the aisle. "Is he still breathing?" He wrapped an arm around Aggie, his hand skimming over the bare skin of her hip. Aggie shrugged out of his grasp.

"I didn't check," Aggie admitted. She honestly didn't much care.

"And where's Jace?"

"He's resting in his bunk. I wouldn't bother him. He's a teensy bit cranky."

Eric moved down the corridor and worked at reviving Jon. Aggie slipped past them to find some clothes. When she returned, she paused to watch Eric slap Jon's cheeks.

"Fuck!" Jon complained as he concentrated on opening his eyes.

"I told you not to mess with Jace," Eric said.

"*You* mess with Jace."

"That's different. He likes me. He hates your fucking guts."

Jon rubbed his bruised jaw. "That's obvious. Geez, I can't even joke around with him."

"You weren't joking around with him." Aggie crossed her arms over her chest. "You were being an asshole, and he called you on it."

"Whatever." Jon took Eric's offered hand and pulled himself to his feet. He glanced around the bus. "Where'd my girls go?"

"Hopefully back to their parents. I think it's past their bedtime," Aggie said.

Jon's eyes narrowed. "What's that supposed to mean?"

"They couldn't have been much over sixteen."

"So?"

Aggie wrinkled her nose in disgust. "Pig."

"Cow."

"Will you all shut the fuck up?" Jace bellowed. "I'm trying to sleep."

"You might as well take the bedroom," Jon grumbled. "You completely messed up my plans for the evening."

Jace hopped out of his bunk and headed to the back bedroom.

"You messed up my plans for the evening as well, little man," Eric said.

Jace glanced over his shoulder at Eric. "You didn't really want to watch him violate four young girls."

Eric grinned. "Let me watch you do Aggie next time, and I'll forgive you."

"I don't think you'll be able to handle it."

Aggie scratched her head. What were these guys talking about?

"Try me," Eric challenged.

"That's up to Aggie," Jace said and entered the bedroom. He removed his clothes and climbed into bed.

Eric clasped his hands together in front of his chest. "Please let me watch, Aggie. I'll stay out of the way."

"Watch? Watch what?"

He wrapped an arm around her shoulders. "Watch you and Jace have sex, what else?"

"He's in no condition for sex tonight," she said.

Eric's breath caught. "You didn't say no."

"I didn't say yes either." Something about the hungry look in Eric's bright blue eyes had Aggie's juices flowing again.

Chapter 33

AGGIE OPENED HER EYES to Eric's inquisitive gaze. "Are you awake?"

She started and covered her eyes with a pillow. "Jeez, how can I sleep with you staring at me like that?"

"You didn't have a problem for the past hour."

"You've been watching me sleep for an hour?"

"Uh huh."

"Eric, you have a problem."

"I am well aware of that. I'm ready."

"For what?"

"To watch."

"This kind of takes the spontaneity and romance out of the act, you know?"

Eric leaned back and sat on the floor with his back against the wall. "Just pretend I'm not here."

"Yeah, like that's possible."

Jace spooned up against her back. "It's early," he murmured.

She turned her head to look at him. His lips curled into a gentle smile, but he kept his eyes closed.

"Sorry. Did I wake you?" she asked.

"Yes. You know I'm not a morning person."

His hands moved to cup her breasts. Apparently, he wasn't aware of Eric's presence. She wasn't sure why the thought of Eric watching had her hot and bothered. She'd had some wild times in sex parlors in her youth, but she hadn't done it in front of an audience for years. She'd gotten a certain level of excitement back in the day, knowing other people could see her performing sexual acts and having acts performed on her. Those had been strangers though. This was different. She'd have to look Eric in the eye after this was over.

"You don't mind him watching?" Jace asked.

"You knew he was there?"

"I'm not *that* groggy in the morning." His grin widened, and his hand slipped down her belly.

"I think it will be sexy. I want him to watch."

"Me too," he murmured.

She rolled over in his arms and brushed her fingers through his hair. He hadn't been putting gel in it recently, and she loved its silky texture beneath her palms and between her thighs.

She kissed him and directed his hand between her legs. "I never got to come last night," she whispered. "I want your mouth right here." She squeezed his hand against her mound.

"I think I can handle that."

He slipped her panties from her body. He surprised her by rolling onto his back. When she crinkled her brow at him in confusion, he grinned and said, "Come up here, baby. Sit on my face."

She climbed from the covers and moved up his body to straddle his face. He wrapped his arms around her thighs and lifted his head to suckle her clit.

"Wow," she gasped.

He suckled every bit of slick flesh between her thighs and then plunged his tongue inside her. She shuddered. "Jace."

His rough beard stubble scraped against her sensitive flesh as he made out with her pussy. Kissing, sucking, and licking her until she couldn't take any more. She shifted backward with the intention of sliding down his body. He wrapped both arms around her thighs and wouldn't let her move. After a long moment, Jace turned his head, gasping for air. Aggie sat back on his chest to let him catch his breath.

"Eric, can you see?" Jace asked.

"Not really."

"Come on up here with us."

Eric launched himself onto the bed.

"Do you want him to participate?" Jace nodded in Eric's direction.

"What do you mean?" Aggie asked.

"Can he touch you?"

Aggie's eyes widened in surprise. "I thought he was just going to watch."

"Here's the thing with Eric. He starts out watching, but sometimes he gets carried away. If you don't want him to touch you, I won't let him, but if you don't mind, he can help me bring you pleasure."

She laughed. "I can't handle how much pleasure you give me on your own. How do you think I'll handle even more?"

Jace slipped her tank top over her head. Eric half growled, half moaned as her breasts were revealed.

"I think you can handle it," Jace murmured, his fingers brushing over one taut nipple.

She glanced at Eric. She didn't have a problem with him participating. She found it a little disheartening that Jace had no qualms about another man putting his hands on her. Or seeing her naked. Yes, she went topless onstage, but this was different. This was far more personal. Or maybe it wasn't. It didn't have to be.

"He can touch me. Lick me. Suck me. Fuck me. Whatever."

"Yes," Eric said, making a victory fist.

"No," Jace said. "He's not going to fuck you. Only I fuck you."

Aggie smiled to herself. Okay, that made her feel better. She wasn't sure why. It wasn't much of a boundary, but it was something.

"But I can come on her, right?" Eric asked.

Jace shrugged. "That's up to her."

"We'll see."

Jace eased her off his chest to sit in the center of the bed and moved to kneel beside her. He brushed her hair aside and planted a gentle kiss on her shoulder. "Isn't she beautiful?" he asked Eric.

"Yeah. Gorgeous," Eric agreed. He extended a hand toward her breast, but hesitated with millimeters between their skin. Her nipple hardened, straining toward his fingertips. He took a deep, shaky breath and lowered his hand to rest in a tight fist on his thigh.

Jace grinned crookedly. He was in a strange mood this morning. Calmer than usual. Kind of cocky. She decided it was because Eric was there, and he knew he was the top man on the totem pole.

Jace took Aggie's chin and turned her head in his direction. He kissed her tenderly and stroked her hair from her face. He whispered into her ear so Eric couldn't hear. "This is just sex, Aggie, okay? Don't attach yourself to it emotionally."

She nodded, understanding what he meant. This would lack their usual emotional connection. Fine with her, as long as she got to see inside his heart when they were alone together. "I know the difference. I'd have said 'no' if I had issues with this. Don't worry about my feelings."

He kissed her deeply and then pulled away. When he looked at her, she got the feeling he wasn't seeing her as Aggie, but a stranger to experiment with. She'd try to forget her feelings for him this morning, but she knew it wouldn't be easy. She loved him. She didn't think he had the same feelings for her, but hopefully, someday he would.

On his knees, Jace moved in front of her body and lowered his head to rub the flat of his tongue over her nipple. Eric, still fully clothed, spooned up against her back, his lips against her shoulder as he watched Jace tug her nipple into his mouth.

She shuddered. Eric lightly stroked the bare skin of her upper arms with his fingertips, drawing goose bumps to the surface of her skin. She leaned back against his solid chest, concentrating on not lifting her hands and clinging to Jace's hair as he suckled. She wanted to practice self-control for as long as possible. A test of her willpower. The tugging feeling at her breast spread down her belly and between her thighs, tightening her womb with gentle spasms, making her lips swell and grow wet with desire. When Jace moved his mouth to her other breast, Eric kissed a trail along the top of her back and settled against her other shoulder so he could watch Jace drive her mad with need.

Aggie clenched her hands into fists, letting Jace have his way with her, when every instinct urged her to hold on to him.

Jace's hands slid over the skin of her lower back. Eric's moved to circle her waist. They held her in a double embrace. Her heart thudded in anticipation.

"Shift her onto her back," Jace instructed.

Eric moved from behind her and eased her down on her back. Jace pulled her legs out straight and returned to suckling her left nipple. Aggie gasped brokenly when Eric shifted to lie against her right side and sucked her other nipple into his mouth. She lifted her arms above her head and glanced down at the two of them. Their techniques were totally different. Jace sucked and stroked with his tongue. Eric nibbled and soothed with his lips. She closed her eyes, her head tilting back in ecstasy. Jace slid a hand down her side and belly. She spread her legs, wanting him to put her out of her aching misery. Eric's hand mirrored Jace's movements a few seconds after.

Aggie moaned when their fingers moved between her thighs in unison. They stroked her flesh until she couldn't take it anymore. A pair of fingers slid inside her. She'd lost track of who belonged to which hand, which mouth sucked her left nipple, flicked her right. Another pair of fingers slid into her pussy. They spread her wide, plunging into her and withdrawing, as they worked against each other.

"Oh, that feels good."

A third hand stroked at her clit.

Eric released her breast from his mouth and slid down to watch the action between her thighs.

"Make her come, Jace. She's close. Look how swollen she is."

"Don't talk, Sticks."

"Sorry."

She felt Eric's warm breath against her mound and then his tongue flicked over her clit, joining the fingers still stroking it. She'd never felt anything like it—fingers and lips and tongues. Here. There. She rocked her hips impatiently, mewing in the back of her throat.

Her pleasure built quickly and within seconds she was shuddering with release. Eric rested his head on her lower belly, his fingers still inside her. Jace released her nipple from his mouth, removed his hands from her body, and slid off the end of the bed.

Eric's fingers slid free a moment later, leaving her completely empty.

"Are you going to fuck her now?" Eric asked excitedly.

"Not yet."

Jace grabbed her by the hips and pulled her to the end of the bed. He knelt on the floor and plunged his tongue into her body. Her back arched, and she shuddered. She opened her eyes when she heard a zipper release. Eric was on his hands and knees, peering between her legs upside down, watching Jace eat her out. Eric grabbed his long, hard cock in one hand, stroking himself with Jace's rhythm.

"Does she taste good, Jace?"

"Mmm," he murmured in agreement.

Aggie couldn't take her eyes off Eric's hand as he stroked himself slowly. She shuddered when Jace sucked her clit into his mouth. He plunged his fingers in and out of her, bringing her to orgasm so quickly she lifted off the mattress. "Jace!"

He didn't give her time to recover—kept sucking and plunging into her.

"Yeah," Eric whispered, still watching and stroking his cock. Aggie extended one hand in Eric's direction and ran her fingers over his scrotum.

His mouth fell open, and his eyes drifted closed.

"Jace. Look at him. He's about to come all over himself. Put your cock inside me," Aggie said, watching Eric's reaction as she barely touched him. If watching Jace eat her out excited Eric that much, she could only imagine how excited he'd be when Jace's massive cock stretched her to her limits.

Jace stood and spread her legs wider. He grabbed his cock and pressed it into her, sliding in and out to wet himself with her juices.

"Oh God, that's hot," Eric gasped. He shifted further down the mattress to improve his vantage.

Jace held onto Aggie's hips as he buried himself inside her.

"Jace," she gasped. Goose bumps rose to the surface of her flesh. Could Eric tell how perfectly they fit together? She wanted him to recognize it.

"You feel amazing," he whispered.

He withdrew. His eyes were on the connection between their bodies. When scarcely an inch of him remained inside her, he lunged forward. She cried out as their bodies collided. He picked up his tempo, quickly finding their familiar rhythm. Aggie watched Eric stroke his cock with the same tempo.

"God, I'm about to come already," Eric gasped. "This rhythm is insane."

"Perfect," Aggie said. "He's perfect. His rhythm... perfect."

"Yeah, if your goal is to come. Jesus, dude. I can hear how wet that makes her. What does it feel like?"

"Silky," Jace murmured. "Slick. Hot."

Eric whimpered.

"Tight. Soft."

Eric loosened his hold on his cock, skimming its surface more gently as he continued to stroke himself in time with Jace's deep thrusts. "Aggie, what does it feel like to have Jace inside you?"

"Full. Hard. Warm. Thick. Hard. Full. Full. Oh, God."

Jace continued the same relentless tempo for a long while. Aggie lifted her head to look at Jace and found him watching her. He smiled gently, and her heart melted. It seemed strange that by allowing Eric to join them, the bond between them was strengthened. It was as if having a witness and sharing this made it more profound, not less. She hadn't expected that when she'd agreed to this arrangement. She'd expected Eric's presence to cheapen the experience.

Eric cried out, drawing Aggie's attention. He spurted cum over her lower belly, trembling uncontrollably as he let go. "Damn," he gasped.

"Done already?" Jace murmured, still maintaining the rhythm that held Aggie suspended on the brink of orgasm.

"Already? How long do you plan on continuing?"

"Oh, an hour, though without a condom I might not last that long. Aggie's body is heaven."

"I bet."

Eric lowered his head and sucked Aggie's clit into his mouth. Her back arched as ripples of pleasure radiated out from her core, clenching hard on Jace's cock. She screamed with unexpected release.

"Oh God, don't stop. Don't stop," she pleaded. They didn't stop. Jace pounded against her, filling her as only he could, and Eric sucked her long after her first orgasm subsided.

"I'm gonna come again," she cried. "Oh. Oh."

Eric squeezed her breast, pinching her nipple as she came a second time.

The pleasure was so intense that she was in tears.

Jace pulled out.

"Please don't stop," she gasped.

"Eric," Jace said to get his attention.

Eric stopped sucking on Aggie's clit, and she groaned with torment.

"My turn?" he asked.

"No, I'm changing position."

Eric moved away while Jace eased Aggie onto her hands and knees.

"Oh hell, yeah," Eric said.

Jace climbed onto the mattress, knelt behind her, and spread her knees apart.

"Wait," Eric said. "Don't put it in yet."

Jace chuckled. He seemed to be enjoying this. Another thing Aggie hadn't expected.

Eric slid on his back beneath Aggie until his head was between her knees, and he was looking up where the action was about to take place. His hips were between her hands on the mattress, and when she looked down, his cock was in her field of view.

"Okay, ready when you are," Eric said.

Aggie laughed. She felt the head of Jace's cock touch the rim of her pussy, and her laugh became a groan of torment.

"Slow," Eric coaxed. "Slide it in real slow."

Jace slid it in real slow. Aggie watched Eric's cock jerk excitedly in response.

"God, look at it stretch and swallow you. And she smells so good."

Eric lifted his hands to rub his fingers up and down her belly. Aggie shuddered.

"Deep, Jace. Take her deep."

Jace was already fully inserted, but he ground against her to drive himself deeper.

"Give her pleasure, Eric, or you're leaving," Jace said.

Eric's fingers found her nipples and stroked them persistently.

"Does that feel good, Aggie?" Jace asked.

"Y-yes," she gasped, grinding her hips to stimulate herself on Jace's cock. She pulled forward and then rocked back to bury him deep again.

"I think she wants you to fuck her, Jace."

"Yes." She groaned. "I want it."

Eric's cock lengthened and thickened as Jace began to move. Jace's finger slid into her ass, and her legs buckled. "Yeah, Jace, that's good. Tease my ass. Eric, rub my clit. Rub it."

Eric rubbed her clit with one hand, and his other went to his hard-on. She loved watching Eric stroke himself while Jace filled her and dipped his fingertips into her ass. A single bead of precum glistened at the head of Eric's dick. Unable to resist his offering, she lowered her head and licked it. Salty. Sweet.

"Oh sweet heaven," Eric gasped.

Encouraged, she sucked the head of his cock into her mouth. His entire body convulsed. Jace picked up his tempo, his thrusts deep and steady. He buried two fingers in her ass and curled them down to stimulate the head of his cock as he thrust into her. Aggie cried out, gasping brokenly on the wet head of Eric's cock. Eric stroked her clit faster—himself twice as fast. Jace vocalized his pleasure louder with each thrust.

"Make her come, Eric. Make her come."

Eric wasn't making her come, Jace was. His thickness. Filling her. Rubbing her. His fingers filling her further.

While her body convulsed with release, Jace slowly slid his fingers from her ass.

She lost track of the number of times she came. She sucked Eric's cock when she thought of it, but most of the time she was too delirious to pay any attention to what he was doing beneath her. Jace's tempo increased, his breath hitching in the back of his throat. He pulled out at the last moment and came on Aggie's back with a startled, sputtering cry of release.

"Did I just miss the money shot?" Eric asked. "Ah, fuck."

Jace collapsed onto the bed beside her, still breathing hard. "Let me catch my breath, and we'll start over. I'll do better next time. I didn't mean to come that fast."

"Better? That was amazing," Aggie said, still trembling in the aftermath of multiple orgasms. "Amazing."

Jace lay beside her, unmoving, his eyes closed.

"Okay, okay." Eric shuddered, spurting all over his belly. He groaned as he pumped his fluids out with a tight fist. "God, I needed that."

When Eric went still, breaths still coming in trembling gasps, Jace forced his eyes open. He smiled gently at Aggie and tried to get up. He managed to lift himself on one arm before crumpling to the bed.

"What's wrong?" Aggie asked.

"I think I need some breakfast."

He'd overdone it again. "No more sex until you're fully healed," Aggie insisted.

"I'll be okay. I'm just hungry."

"I'll go make some scrambled eggs," Eric said. He wiped the cum off his belly and stuffed his softening cock into his blue boxer briefs before heading for the door in his underwear. Eric should always walk around in his underwear. Dear lord, that long, lean body was some serious eye candy.

"Wait!" Jace called desperately.

Eric paused at the door and looked over his shoulder in question. "What?"

"Don't get creative with the spices this time—salt and pepper only."

"What's the fun in that?" Eric grinned and left the bedroom, closing the door behind him.

"Aggie, you have to stop him," Jace whispered as if Eric were on a murder mission. "Last time he mixed cayenne, cinnamon, garlic, and basil."

Aggie's nose wrinkled. "In eggs?"

"And I'm starving. I need to eat."

Aggie kissed his lips and rose from the bed. "I've got you, baby. You rest." She reached for her clothes.

While Eric pretended to be the Swedish Chef from the Muppet Show, Aggie monitored his progress and cooked the bacon. Whenever he reached for a spice to sprinkle in the huge pan of eggs, Aggie smacked it out of his hand. Eric cooked like he did everything else: to the beat of a different drummer with all the heart and enthusiasm he could muster. And while she expected things to be weird between them now (she'd just washed his cum off her belly, after all), he didn't act differently around her at all. If anything, he seemed more relaxed and friendlier than before.

Aggie spread strips of bacon over a paper towel to collect the grease and dumped frozen hash browns into the bacon pan. She put a lid on the top to stop the grease from spattering.

"Why don't you make some toast? The bread's in that cabinet there." He pointed with his spatula.

While she was occupied with opening the bread wrapper, Eric reached for the allspice.

"No," she said, grabbing the bottle from his hand.

"It's called *all*spice," he said. "Doesn't that mean it should be used to spice all?"

"Eric, add that crap to your own eggs after everyone gets their safe serving."

"Safe? Boring, you mean."

"Eggs are supposed to be boring."

Jace opened the bedroom door and hobbled to the table. Wearing nothing but jeans and his sling (which he'd been using less, so its appearance must mean his shoulder was bothering him), he slid into the booth. Resting his left elbow on the table, he propped his forehead up with his hand.

"You wore his ass out, Aggie. Look at him."

Oh, she was looking at him, all right.

"Shut up, Sticks," Jace murmured.

The toast popped, and Aggie buttered a slice. She handed it to Jace. "Eat this while you wait for your eggs."

Jace lifted his head from his hand, patted her butt affectionately, and accepted the piece. "Thanks."

"I smell food," Brian said, leaning out of his bunk. "Smells good. Who's cooking?" He blinked his eyes in the light of the cabin until they focused on Eric at the stove. "Sticks? Never mind. I'll starve." He closed his curtain again.

"Good," Jace called, his mouth full of toast. "Leaves more for me."

"Aggie's got him under control," Trey said, hopping out of his bunk and stealing bacon from the counter.

Trey sat across from Jace and handed him a piece of his bacon. "You okay, man?"

"Yeah."

Sed climbed out of his bunk and slid next to Trey, his big body taking up more than its share of the booth. "I'm in," he said. When he tried to help himself to Trey's bacon, he got his hand slapped.

Brian hopped down from his bunk. "I guess if the rest of you die of food poisoning, there's no reason for me to go on alone."

"Think of Myrna," Trey said.

"I'm mostly thinking of my stomach." Brian scooted in next to Jace. "Man, you sure you should be out of the hospital? You look like death warmed over."

Now Aggie felt guilty. She exchanged glances with Eric. "We should have let him sleep in this morning," she whispered as she turned the hash browns.

"He usually doesn't get out of bed until noon. He always looks like shit in the morning."

Aggie went to the refrigerator and shoved the beer aside until she found a bottle of orange juice. She unscrewed the top and set it in front of Jace. "Here, baby, drink this."

He blushed at her sentiment, and it did not go unnoticed by the other guys. "Yeah, baby, dwink your juice all up," Trey said. "Be a good widdle man."

Brian pinched Jace's cheek. "Such a cute widdle baby, isn't he? He needs to dwink his juice from his sippy cup."

Scowling, Jace slapped Brian's hand away.

Aggie grinned. The guys loved him. That's why they teased him relentlessly. He was like their adored little brother. Why couldn't Jace see that? Maybe Aggie needed to help him see what was already there.

Chapter 34

JACE STOOD BEHIND THE stage watching the roadies set up for the concert in Edmonton. He could hang out here until they were done. Then he'd have to leave because Jon would start rehearsing with the band for their show. He couldn't force himself to watch that.

The next night there'd be a symphony playing in this venue, and the orchestra's instruments had already been delivered. They were lined up along the back wall behind the stage area which made it challenging for the roadies to maneuver their stage sections into place. Feeling woozy from looking at the rigging, Jace meandered to the bench in front of the symphony's grand piano. He sat heavily and took a deep breath. Maybe he should check himself into a hospital. He couldn't regain his strength. That probably had to do with keeping Aggie satisfied. It was impossible to keep his hands off her. He didn't bother trying.

Jace leaned against the keyboard of the piano, and it *pinged* discordantly. Someone had forgotten to cover the keys. He turned on the bench, tossed back the heavy canvas covering the instrument, and reached for the little knob connected to the wooden lid. His wrist hit the keys. He paused, instantly transported back in time. He could almost feel his mother sitting beside him, her arm pressed against his shoulder, her leg against his. During those times, he pretended she cared about him.

Jace shrugged his sling aside and allowed his fingers to settle on the keys, his feet on the pedals. He definitely felt Mother as his fingers found a familiar melody. He could hear her, speaking in that barely perceptible whisper of hers. *Don't play the music, Jason. Let the music play you. Give yourself over to it. Let it inside. It's alive. Do you feel it?*

Music *was* alive. He did feel it. He always had. It was more real than his own existence.

Jace let the melody take him, giving his fingers free rein. The keys beside him, where his mother's fingers should have rested, remained still, but he heard her playing with him as surely as if she'd been sitting beside him. When he reached the end of the song, the final note rang and his mother faded away.

"I didn't know you played piano," Aggie said. "That was beautiful." She slid onto the bench beside him. "Play something else."

He shook his head and pulled the cover forward to hide the keyboard. He hurriedly slipped his arm back in his sling so she didn't harass him about playing. Aggie took his left hand and squeezed. How did she always know when he was feeling most vulnerable? She sensed it like a vulture senses carrion, and circled overhead, waiting for the perfect opportunity to swoop down and rip his heart out.

"Where did you learn to play?" She brushed his hair behind his ear with her free hand. It was getting too long to spike, and he needed to bleach his roots, but since he wasn't performing, he didn't bother.

The shiny black cover that hid the keyboard blurred out of focus. "My mother taught me."

"She must have been talented."

"Yeah. Music was the only thing she really loved."

Aggie's hand slid over his lower back, and she leaned against him. "And you. She loved you."

He shook his head slightly. "No. She never wanted me."

"I don't believe that."

He found the anger—found it and clung to it. "I don't give a fuck what you believe."

He shoved her away and tried to stand, but she grasped him around the waist and pulled him back on the bench.

"I don't believe that either. Talk." She slid a hand up his face and turned his head. He couldn't meet her eyes, so he stared at her chin. "Talk to me, Jace."

He didn't want to talk. He wanted to fester. Why wouldn't she leave him alone?

"Tell me why you think your mother didn't want you."

The ache in his chest spread up his throat, stealing his air. "Because…" He took a deep shaky breath. "Because she told me. Every day she told me."

He fought the stinging ache behind his eyes. *Men don't cry, son.* Yes, Father. I know. I know. It's her fault. Aggie's. She won't leave me alone. She keeps pushing. And pushing.

"What did she say exactly, Jace?" Aggie asked. "Maybe you misunderstood."

He laughed bitterly. "Yeah, I was just a dumb kid. I must have misunderstood." He peeled her off his body and stood. He'd lock himself in the men's room for a while until he got himself under control. Surely she wouldn't follow him there.

Aggie shoved him back down on the bench. His back hit the fall board covering the piano keys, and pain snaked through the healing wound in his shoulder. She straddled his lap, facing him, and grabbed his chin in one hand. She had that cold, dominatrix look in her eyes. It effectively got his attention.

"You're not going to get out of this that easily. You can pretend to be mad at me, but it won't get me off your case."

"Who's pretending?"

"You are. Tell me what your mother said that hurt you so deeply."

"I'm not hurt."

"You are hurt, you dummy, and that pain won't ever go away unless you let it go. I want to help you, but I don't know what I'm up against, Jace. Talk to me. Tell me."

"Maybe I don't want it to go away. Maybe I like it. You're the one who made me admit I like pain."

She hit him in the chest with both palms. "This isn't a game anymore, dammit. Don't you get it?" She hugged him unexpectedly, pressing her nose into his neck. Her warm breath brushed his skin beneath his ear. "I'm sorry I hit you. I'm so frustrated. What did she say to you, sweetheart? What did she say? Go away? Give me a minute to myself? Go play in your room for a while, Mommy's busy right now? What? Just tell me."

Jace snorted. If Mother had only been so kind. He repeated his mother's mantra to Aggie in the same low whisper she'd always used. Mother had always whispered it close to his ear, as if she wasn't *really* saying those hurtful words, if she said them quietly enough, if no one heard them but him. "If it weren't for you, Jason, I could have had my dream. If it weren't for you, Jason, I wouldn't have had to marry your father. Why did I get pregnant? I should have given you up for adoption. I never wanted you. You're the reason I live like this. In this hovel. With that man. I could have been a concert pianist. I could have been somebody. And now, you know what I am? I'm just your mother. That's all I am. *His* wife. *Your* mother. I am no one. I don't want to be your mother, Jason. I never did. I'll give you away. Give you to someone who can stand to look at you."

His hands gripped Aggie's waist as old fears found their way into his heart. "She left me places, Aggie. She pretended she was happy to see me when the cops brought me home. 'He's always wandering off by himself,' she'd tell them and then give them coffee and cookies while she told them stories about my wandering ways. They'd laugh about how cute I was. 'He's adorable. You're lucky no one took him,' they'd say. I was afraid to leave the house with her. I never knew where she'd leave me. When we were out, I didn't dare go to the bathroom or turn my back or let her out of my sight, because if I did, she'd be gone. I could never find her. I'd look for her and call for her, but she'd be gone. She didn't want me, Aggie. She never wanted me. But when we played piano together, I felt something—some closeness to her. I don't know what it was." Something hot and wet slipped down his cheek. "She loved that fucking piano, but she never loved me." He dashed a tear away angrily. "Do you see why I don't want to talk about this? Now I'm fuckin' crying like a little girl."

Aggie crushed his face into her chest, her body shaking with sobs. What was she crying about? She'd wanted him to tell her, so he had. And now she was crying? *Women.* He didn't understand them.

Aggie kissed the top of his head, rubbing her face against his hair. Getting it wet with tears. Messing it up. Making him feel like a total ass. What if one of the guys saw them like this? He'd never hear the end of it.

"She's gone, Jace. She can't hurt you anymore."

She *was* gone. His mother. And before she died, he never got to tell her it didn't matter that she didn't love him. He loved her. And that fucking piano of hers? He loved it too. A week after she'd been buried, his father had donated her piano to some school—gotten rid of it because it reminded him of her. That had been worse for Jace, somehow, than her actual death. Father wanted no reminders of her in his house. The woman had been everything to him. Not just his wife. *His life.* He'd changed after she'd died. He became crueler than Jace's mother had ever thought of being, because Dad needed someone to blame for the love of his life's premature death, and Jace had been the only one available to hold responsible.

Jace closed his eyes tightly, blocking thoughts of his father from his mind.

Aggie kissed his temple tenderly. "I think she did love you, Jace, but it doesn't matter. She's gone, and I'm here. I love you. I do. I love you."

Fear paralyzed him. He couldn't move when every instinct told him to run. "Don't," he whispered.

"Shhh," Aggie murmured. "It's okay. I know you don't know how to respond. I understand. I won't ever abandon you. I'll be here whenever you need me."

And that was far more terrifying than being six years old and left alone in the reptile house at the zoo. At least there, the things that frightened him were in cages. They couldn't get to him. But Aggie got to him. And it scared the hell out of him. "Will you hurt me?" he asked. "I need it." The pain was too raw. He needed help burying it again.

She cupped his face in both hands—kissed his eyelids, the tip of his nose, his lips. "Yes. I'll hurt you. I know what to do now."

Panic flooded his chest. She knew what to do? What did she mean by that?

"We need someplace private," she murmured. "Do you think the guys would be willing to install a soundproof room on the tour bus?"

Jace laughed. "You know, they might. We wouldn't be the only ones to benefit from that."

She kissed him again, smiling down at him. "Let's go."

―――

Aggie approached Sed, who sat slouched on the couch watching television in a trancelike state next to Eric. Jace headed straight for the bedroom.

Sed glanced at her. "What's up?"

"Do you think you could get everyone to stay off this bus for about an hour? Jace and I need a little privacy. Well, a lot of privacy."

"It's just me and Eric here. Don't mind us. We've heard it all before."

"Can I watch?" Eric asked eagerly.

"No, this is different. He won't let me in if he thinks you guys can hear him." She leaned close to the guys and whispered so Jace couldn't overhear. "He always worries about what you guys think of him—that you won't accept him for who he is. We'll work on that eventually, but right now, I need to help him bury his mother."

"His mother died?" Sed asked, looking stunned. "When?"

"Around fifteen years ago. You didn't know?"

Sed shook his head. Both he and Eric glanced down the corridor at Jace, who was trying to play it cool by leaning against the door frame. He looked ready to leap out of his skin.

"He never talks about himself," Sed said. "He has this wall thing he does."

Aggie knew exactly what Sed meant. Jace's wall. He hid behind it often, and once he put it up, it was nearly impossible to tear it down. "I'm working on that too," Aggie said. "So, do you think you could get lost for an hour?"

Sed climbed to his feet. "Yep. I could use a workout anyway."

"And keep everyone off the bus?" Aggie added.

Eric pulled a drumstick from the inner pocket of his leather vest and held it across his chest like a sword. "I shall guard this dwelling, m'lady, and vanquish all who dare attempt to trespass." He took a stab at Sed with his improvised weapon. "Back, foul beast."

"With this guy as your knight, you'd better be sure to lock the door." Sed slipped into his jacket and headed down the bus steps.

Eric winked at her and loped after Sed. Aggie closed the bus door and secured it. She took a deep breath and let Mistress V come to the surface. As much as Aggie would have loved to help Jace by talking, listening, and showering him with love, she knew she wouldn't get through to him that way. But Mistress V could. Mistress V could break him. Mistress V *would* break him.

She stalked down the hall. "Get in there," she demanded, shoving him toward the bedroom. He stumbled sideways through the open doorway.

"Why did Sed and Eric leave?"

"Do you want them to hear you beg?"

"I won't."

She lifted her eyebrows. "Wanna bet?"

He chuckled. "Yeah, actually—"

"Take off your clothes." She went to the closet and lugged his big suitcase out. There had to be something in there she could use.

She found the chain and the cuffs on top of his tools of pleasure and climbed on the bed to suspend them from the ceiling.

"Aggie, what—"

She hopped off the bed and grabbed him by the ear. "Mistress V," she corrected.

"Mistress V," he said breathlessly.

"I told you to strip. Take off the sling too." She released him and returned to the suitcase. She found a paddle, slapped it against her thigh, and set it aside.

Jace made short work of his clothes and moved to stand over her shoulder, peering into the suitcase. "I think there's a riding crop in there somewhere."

"Did I say you could speak? Go tip the mattress and box spring against the wall."

"Why?"

"Don't question me."

He did as she asked and revealed a wooden platform under the mattresses. Perfect.

"Stand there," she pointed to the center of the platform, right beneath the restraints.

"I don't like to be restrained."

"No one asked what you like."

"But—"

"We do this my way or not at all."

He glanced at the restraints and then down at her. He nodded. Gave up his power, except his willpower. But she planned to take that too and give him more in return.

She climbed onto the platform and took his left hand. She lifted his arm above his head, and he held still while she fastened the cuff around his wrist. Before she could secure his other hand, he sank his fingers into her hair and pulled her mouth to his, stealing her thoughts with a deep kiss. She might have him chained to the ceiling, but she was the one ensnared, and she knew it.

When he pulled away, she stared into his eyes. "Don't hate me for this, okay?"

"I don't think it's possible to hate you."

"I wouldn't be so sure." She carefully lifted his injured right arm, watching for signs of distress. The only distress he showed was when she tried to remove the leather cuff on that wrist. "No, don't take that off."

"Why?"

"I don't want you to."

She shrugged and secured his other wrist over his head by fastening the restraint over his studded bracelet. "Is your shoulder okay in that position?"

He nodded. She got to work.

She paddled him until he trembled with excitement and then set the implement aside. She moved to stand behind him and gently ran her hands over his chest and belly while she trailed gentle kisses along his shoulders and back. As she figured he would, he fought his restraints. She continued her tender caresses until he twisted out of her grasp.

"Not gentle, Aggie. Please, I can't stand it."

"Mistress V," she reminded him.

"Hit me, Mistress V. Now."

"I don't think I will," she whispered, spooning against him and running her hands over his belly and his most sensitive places inside the ridges of his hip bones.

He chuckled. "Ah, tickles."

That laugh. It made her heart ache with longing. She almost didn't have the stomach to continue.

"Your mother's failure wasn't your fault, Jace," she said.

He went still.

"She still could have been a concert pianist. You weren't standing in her way. She was standing in her own way. She did it to herself and used you as her excuse."

"Don't tell me about my mother. You don't know anything about her."

She should have expected his anger to surface first, but it wasn't the reaction she was looking for. She had to push harder—dig deeper. God, she hoped he didn't hate her after this. She didn't know if she'd be able to handle his hatred, even if she did this for his own good. "She was a selfish bitch, Jace. Why are you defending her? What kind of mother blames an innocent child for her own failure?"

"Don't say bad things about my mother, Aggie."

"Why not?"

"She was my mother."

"Yes, she was, but she was also a person. A person who hurt you. I don't like it when people hurt those I love."

"Need to inflict all the pain yourself? Is that it?"

She slapped his ass with the paddle, and he groaned, his head tilting back.

"I don't hurt you the way she did," Aggie said.

"But you're trying to."

"No, I—"

"Do you think I'm stupid, Aggie? That I don't know what you're trying to do? You think I'm broken. You think you can *fix* me. All that 'I love you' bullshit doesn't mean a damned thing, does it? You don't love me. Not the real me. You love who you think you can make me."

"That's not true."

"Yeah, it is. Unfasten the cuffs. I'm done."

So that was his game. She wasn't going to release him—no matter how unaffected he pretended to be.

"I'm not. Not even close to done." She tossed the paddle aside and caressed his skin with her hands and her lips. Touched him. Kissed him with the same tenderness he frequently showed her.

After several minutes, he pulled away, yanking on his restraints. "Okay, you win. Let me go. My shoulder hurts."

"What do you mean, I win? Do you think this is a game?"

"Yeah."

"Do you blame yourself for your mother's death?" she asked. "Or just for her failures in life?"

"Shut up."

"Do you think she would have been more successful if you'd never been born?"

"I said, shut up, Aggie! I'm not in the mood for games."

"Do you wish you would have died in that car accident instead of her? Do you think she would have been happy if you'd died? Do you—"

"Shut up, Aggie." He yanked on his chains hard now, trying to pull the hook from the ceiling. "Just shut up. You don't know a goddamned thing about how I feel."

"Because you won't talk to me. If I'm wrong, then tell me how you really feel."

"You're not wrong," he shouted. "Okay? I do wish I'd died instead of her. I did ruin her life." He took a deep shuddering breath. "Just... just let me go. Take the cuffs off."

"Then you'll run. You'll hide."

"That's all I know how to do. It's all I can do. Hide from it. If I don't, it will find me. Hurt me. Until I feel like I've been eviscerated. Until death would be a blessing."

She touched his face, and he looked into her eyes. She'd never seen his pain this close to the surface. It tore at her heart.

"I love you," she whispered.

His gaze drifted to her forehead.

"Look at me, Jace. I want you to believe what I say. I want you to see it in my eyes."

After a long moment, his eyes settled on hers.

"I love you," she said.

"Why?"

"I need a reason?"

He squeezed his eyes shut. She was losing him again. And she had plenty of reasons. She wasn't sure which one would get through to him.

"I love the way you make love to me, so tenderly, and with such care, that I feel like the only woman in the world."

"That's just sex, Aggie."

She caressed the crease in his forehead gently. "It's more than that to me. It's a way to connect with you. I love your smile, your laugh, your ticklish spots."

His eyes opened.

"I love how you put everything you are into your music."

He smiled slightly.

"I love when you confide in me. I know you don't do that with many people. It makes me feel like you trust me, and somewhere in there, you know I love you, even if you don't think you're worthy."

"I'm not worthy."

"You are. I'm not such a great person, Jace. I have a dark past too—things I wish I could take back, change, but I realized long ago that you can't change the past. You have to let it go. Move on."

"I can't forget, Aggie. I've tried."

She shook her head. "You'll never forget. You *shouldn't* forget, but you have to forgive yourself. And there's nothing to forgive as far as your mother is concerned. Being born is not something that needs to be forgiven."

He stared at her, his defenses crumbling. "I never told her good-bye, Aggie. I was too afraid."

"Why were you afraid? Tell me."

He didn't lower his gaze as he spoke. "She looked like a monster. The accident twisted her body, smashed her face. Every inch of her was swollen and broken and bloody and bruised. I couldn't stand to look at her. My father told me I'd better tell her good-bye before it was too late, but I ran away and hid. I hid for hours until my father found me. He beat me so badly that I couldn't get out of bed. I missed her funeral. I couldn't stop him from getting rid of her piano. I was too weak. And too scared." His eyes brimmed with tears. "There was nothing left of her for me to hold on to. Nothing." He took a deep shuddering breath. "I should have said good-bye. I wasn't strong enough. I wasn't…" Tears dripped from both eyes, and he squeezed them shut.

"Of course, you were afraid. You were a child, Jace. You shouldn't have been forced to be strong. It's okay. You have to forgive yourself. You have to."

He bit his lip and shook his head.

She reached up and released his hands from the restraints. When he tried to turn away, she wrapped her arms around his waist and held him. He didn't pull away as she expected, but instead, burrowed his face in her neck and trembled with emotions. She didn't push him. She let him fall apart or pull himself together, whichever he needed.

Slowly, his ragged breathing returned to normal. Sometime in the long moments that he held her, she realized she needed this as much as he did. He gave her something no one else ever had. He gave her a reason to live—a future to look forward to and someone to love. With everything she was or dared hope to be.

"Let's go watch the show," he murmured.

She leaned away to look at him. "Huh?"

"The concert. I want to watch it tonight."

"Even with Jon onstage?"

"Yeah."

"Do I get to be your date?"

He flushed and grinned. "Will you?"

"Of course. Will you tell me about your father?"

His smile faded into a scowl. "Haven't you already pushed me enough about my past?"

She watched his fortified emotional wall slip into place.

"When you're ready, baby," she amended. "I'll wait. I want you to know you can tell me anything."

"Can I tell you that you're too nosy?"

She chuckled. "Yeah."

"Can I tell you that even though you always rip my heart out, you really do make me feel better?"

"I do?"

He nodded. "Not sure why you stick around."

"I already told you why. I love you. You'll get it eventually." She kissed him tenderly. "Get dressed. We have a concert to attend."

<hr>

Jace took a seat in the folding chair at the edge of the darkened stage. Aggie stood behind him and rested her hands on his shoulders. He knew she was staking her claim—could practically feel the *my man* vibes coming off her—but he didn't mind. He was getting used to the idea that he belonged to her. He concentrated on the noise of the crowd and not the sound of Jon thumbing his bass guitar behind them as he warmed up.

"When are you going to start playing shows again?" Aggie asked.

"As soon as Jon leaves."

"Are you well enough to play now?"

"I think so."

"Then why don't you say something to the guys?"

Jace shrugged. He didn't want to sound like a complainer. Jon was doing them a favor by taking up his slack. Besides, Eric preferred Jon. The rest of the band probably did too. And the fans. He knew they'd rather watch Jon perform.

Aggie leaned over and kissed Jace's temple. He glanced at her, and his heart swelled with emotion. These feelings he had for this woman were foreign. He wasn't sure what they meant.

"You should play at least one song for the fans tonight," she pressed. "They miss you."

"Nah."

"One song for *me* then. I want to hear you play. Go say something to Sed."

"Say what to Sed?" Sed asked from the dark space near Jace's right elbow.

Jace turned his attention to the empty stage. "Forget it."

"Does your woman need to speak for you?"

Jace sighed. "She wants me to play a song onstage tonight."

"How about 'Twisted' in the encore?" Brian said.

"Yeah, that would be sweet," Trey said.

Had anyone *not* overheard their conversation?

"Yeah, good idea," Sed said. "I'll go tell Dave." He trotted down the steps to the floor beside the stage where all the mixing equipment had been set up. He picked up a headset with a mic and started talking to Dave, who was manning the soundboard and controls in the middle of the audience.

Jace supposed he had to play now. He wondered how Jon would react. And wasn't sure why he cared.

As soon as Sed returned, a blue light flooded the stage from ground level. Eric tapped the first beats of "Gates of Hell," and Trey and Brian dashed across the stage to take their places. Jon followed several steps behind, careening into Jace's chair on his way past. Jace planted his feet firmly on the floor to keep from toppling over. Aggie's hands tightened on his shoulders.

"Whoops, didn't see you there, little man," Jon said, before joining the band onstage.

"He did that on purpose. He's a fucking asshole," Aggie said between clenched teeth.

Sed entered with his signature battle cry, having abandoned using the violin in several songs now. The stage lights came on from above, and the crowd went wild. Sed lifted his hand to the audience, increasing their excitement with his attention. The guy had been born to be a star. Jace was used to seeing the back of Sed's head while onstage, so watching his facial expressions as he sang his heart out held a strange fascination. As did Jon's blatant attempts to upstage him. Jon moved from leaning against Trey, who was laughing his ass off, to standing on the center ego-riser in front of Sed and banging his head to his bass riff.

"Am I the only one who thinks he looks like an idiot?" Aggie mumbled.

Apparently. The crowd ate up every minute, especially when Sed elbowed Jon out of his way, and Jon did a backwards somersault off the riser.

During Brian's guitar solo, Jon played his riff lying on his back at Brian's feet. Trey entered the solo midway through, to play the dueling segment of the insanely fast progression. He leaned against Brian's back, the synchrony between the guitarists intimate in its perfection. Trey placed his foot in the center of Jon's chest as he played. The three of them—a unit. Jace tore his gaze from the scene, the ache in his chest acute, and focused on the pair of drumsticks flailing behind the drum kit. He wasn't sure why it bothered him that Jon was having such a good time being part of the group. Jace had known all along that he had never fit in with Sinners. Not completely.

Jace started to get out of his chair, but Aggie leaned against him, her hands firmly on his shoulders. "He's too busy showing off to realize he sounds like crap."

He glanced at her. She smiled with that damnable pitying look in her eyes. He brushed her hands away and climbed to his feet.

The song ended, and Sed talked to the crowd. "How we doing tonight, Edmonton?"

The roar was deafening.

"We've got a special treat at the end of the show, so don't go anywhere." Sed glanced to the side of the stage where Jace stood. "As you might have heard, our bassist, Jace, has been a little under the weather. Some might remember Jon Mallory from our earlier days. He's filling in until Jace gets over a case of explosive diarrhea."

Jace's eyes widened. *What?*

Sed grinned like a shark and glanced offstage at Jace again.

"He needs to quit eating those expired burritos," Trey said into his microphone.

That is what they'd been telling the fans? Jace laughed and shook his head. God, these guys were too much.

"I've got a backstage pass for the first fan who offers up a can of industrial strength air freshener," Brian said into his microphone on the far side of the stage. "The ventilation on our tour bus sucks."

Jace crossed his arms over his chest, his grin broadening.

"Eh, we're just fuckin' with you," Sed said to the crowd. "Jace, come out here. There are rumors spreading that you're dead."

Jace glanced at Aggie, who was wiping tears of mirth from her eyes, and then headed across the stage. The crowd cheered as he approached center stage. Sed wrapped an arm around Jace's shoulders and spoke into his microphone. "He looks pretty good for a dead man, don't you think?" He paused while the crowd responded with excited screams and yells. "Say hello to the fans." Sed held the microphone to Jace's mouth.

His heart thudded, and heat flooded his face. "Hello to the fans."

Sed chuckled. "Do you think you can muster the strength to play something later in the show?"

"I think that can be arranged."

Jace was stunned by the crowd's enthusiasm.

"Did you really get shot, Jace?" an excessively loud fan yelled from behind the barrier fence in front of the stage.

Sed promptly spun Jace around and pulled his shirt up to reveal the large bandage on his right shoulder. "He got shot fuckin' twice, dude. Brutal, huh? He doesn't look it, but he's a tough little shit. If it were me, I'd be flat on my back."

"Kinda like that time you took a whole week off after you burst a blood vessel in your throat?" Trey asked.

Sed scratched his head and grinned sheepishly. "Uh, yeah, just like that." Sed flattened his palm over the side of Jace's head and kissed him on the opposite temple. Jace was too stunned to respond. He'd seen Sed do that to Brian more than once. It was his mark of friendship, but why had he extended it to Jace?

Jace took a deep breath. Sed's attention was probably just a show for the fans. Jace didn't mean anything to him. He knew he didn't.

"Are we going to rub our noses in Jace's asshole all night, or are we going to play some music for these people?" Jon's annoyed voice came over the sound system.

"Go get some rest, buddy. We'll see you near the end of the show."

Jace lifted a hand at the crowd as he returned to the side stage area. Aggie hugged him as soon as he was within reach.

"They loved you out there," she said.

"Nah."

"You honestly don't see how people feel about you, do you?"

He met her eyes. "What do you mean?"

"There's so much love in your life, but you don't recognize it. You won't let it in. That's why you feel so lonely, baby. Don't you get it? It's not them. They care about you. It's you. You don't see it."

He scowled and watched the band play the next song while he contemplated Aggie's words. What did love look like anyway? What did it feel like? He'd thought he'd experienced it a few times. His parents. The first girl he'd ever fallen for. His band. And his more recent feelings for Aggie. Was any of it really love? Was all of it love in different forms? He didn't know. He had nothing to judge by. But he was lonely—always lonely. Even in a crowd. But not when Aggie was near.

He turned to look at her and found her dancing to the music. He grinned. "Having a good time?"

"Yeah, this song is great. I have to get a copy of your CD."

"I could probably get you one for free."

"Will you autograph it for me?"

"Maybe."

He watched her sensual movements as she danced with her arms extended over her head. She was definitely a professional dancer. She used her body like a piece of moving art. He wondered if she missed her job. Her home. Her life. Was her mother really that horrible? He supposed he wasn't the only one with family issues. And yes, his father had been cruel, but at least he'd known him. Aggie had never met her father.

Aggie shrieked in surprise when Jace wrapped an arm around her waist and pulled her into his lap.

"You're distracting the roadies from their work," he said close to her ear.

She glanced around. "I don't think anyone is watching."

"Maybe I wanted an excuse to hold you."

Her smile melted the cold lump in his chest that he was starting to recognize as his heart. She wrapped both arms around his neck and hugged him.

"Are you worried about leaving your mother in charge of your house?" he asked.

"She's probably burned it to the ground by now. I try not to think about it. No sense in worrying myself sick over things I have no control over."

He really wished he could live life by her model. "True."

"And I have great insurance, so I can just build a new house."

"But we have great memories in that dungeon."

She slid her fingers into his hair and kissed him. "We can make some new memories in this chair."

"You do owe me a lap dance."

He hadn't expected her to take him seriously. The band had just begun to play their one and only ballad, "Good-bye Is Not Forever." It had a deep, sultry beat. He loved playing this song live. Jon didn't do it justice, but Jace was trying very hard to ignore every lost opportunity to enrich the bass line, add body to it, subtly support the guitars and the drums without drawing attention to the fill. Truth be told, Jace was trying very fucking hard to ignore Jon entirely. The lighting was always kept dim for this song, so the side of the stage was bathed in darkness. Jace wished he could see Aggie better as she used his body for her prop throughout her sensual dance. Her hands and body brushed over him as she moved around him, behind him, over him, on him. His eyes drifted closed, and he concentrated on the sensation. The woman. He knew he had to get his shit together, or she'd get tired of him shutting her out. He hadn't been afraid of being alone for a long time—not since he'd been a kid. But now? He couldn't imagine a day spent without Aggie. He didn't want to.

When she slid into his lap backwards, he wrapped both arms around her waist and held her close. She tried to get up, but he tightened his hold.

She hesitated briefly and then relaxed. He pressed his face against her shoulder and inhaled her scent.

"You okay?" she asked after a moment.

He knew he was trembling, but he couldn't stop. "Yeah," he whispered.

She covered his hand with hers and squeezed reassuringly.

"Why are you so good to me?" he asked. "All I do is push you away."

"You're not pushing me away now."

That was true. Even though he knew he should, he couldn't let go. And though her body was pressed against his from shoulder to shin, he wanted her closer. Physically. And emotionally. Did that mean he loved her? His heart rate picked up. "Are you going to leave me after you fix me?"

Why had he asked her that? He didn't want to know. He needed to hang on to the moment. Stop worrying about the past. Stop fretting over the future. That's what she gave him. She gave him *now*. That's all that should be important to him, but it wasn't.

"Why would I do that?"

"Sometimes I think I'm your current pet project, and as soon as it's over, we'll be over."

"That's hurtful, Jace."

Hurtful? His brow crinkled with confusion. "Why?"

"Because you think I have some ulterior motive. It's not enough for me to let you know I care. You question it. Cheapen it."

"I don't mean to. I just…" He took a deep breath.

"Just what?"

"I just don't want you to leave." After he said it, he felt so blatantly exposed, he wished he could take it back.

She lifted his hand and kissed his knuckles. "No chance. You are stuck with this crazy bitch whether you like it or not."

He laughed, the tension draining from his body, and squeezed her tightly. "I like it."

She relaxed against him and let him hold her while they watched the concert. Halfway through the set, Brian was left alone onstage to entertain the crowd with his guitar solos. The rest of the band filtered offstage and surrounded Jace's chair.

"Did you see that super-fine chick in the front row?" Jon said excitedly. "She couldn't take her eyes off me. I've got to get me some of that tonight."

"I'm sure she was looking at Sed," Trey said, lifting the neck strap of his guitar over his head and handing the instrument to a roadie. He chugged half a beer and chased it with a bottle of water.

"Yeah, she was looking at me, Jon-boy," Sed said, chomping on red licorice to keep his vocal cords lubricated, "but I'm on the wagon. No pussy for me until we get back to LA."

"Five weeks with no pussy?" Jon burst out laughing. "You? Sure, Sed. That's possible."

Sed crossed his arms over his chest resolutely. "That's right. Three more weeks. It's already been almost two."

Trey laughed and pounded Sed on the back. "Jessica will never walk again." Trey sat on Aggie's lap, squirming to crush her into Jace. "This chair is so fuckin' lumpy."

Aggie chuckled and wrapped her arms around Trey's waist.

He glanced over his shoulder. "Oh, sorry, Aggie. Didn't see you there." Trey leaned back and crossed his legs at the ankle.

Crushed beneath them, Jace couldn't draw a decent breath. "Damn, Aggie, have you gained weight?" His quip earned him an elbow in the ribs.

Eric came to stand with the group. He pulled his sweat-drenched shirt off and tossed it in Trey's face.

Trey swatted it to the floor. "For that, I suggest you don't go to sleep tonight, Sticks."

Eric took a long drink of water and then upended the bottle over his head. He shook his head like a wet dog, sending droplets of water and sweat flying in all directions. "What? You gonna hurt me?"

"You should be so lucky," Trey said.

Eric continued his public shower and then patted himself dry with a hand towel before donning a clean shirt.

Trey was now watching Brian onstage. "He gets better and better, doesn't he?"

"Dude, my legs are falling asleep," Jace complained, trying to dislodge Trey from the top of the pile by squirming. "Get off."

"You hear something, Aggie?" Trey asked.

"Nope. I'm too fat to hear anything."

Jace's heart stuttered. Had he hurt her feelings? She was perfect. How could she possibly think he had been serious when he'd asked her if she'd gained weight? He slid his hands between Trey's back and Aggie's stomach, pulling her securely against his chest.

"You're not fat," he whispered into her ear. "I meant Trey was heavy."

"That's not what you said."

"But that's what I meant. It was a joke."

"Since when do you joke around, Jace?"

Since I started to believe that I can be myself when I'm with you. But he couldn't say that. Not with Trey sitting right there. His jaw clenched as emotion threatened to bubble to the surface. "Whatever."

"If you two are gonna argue, I'm going to join Brian onstage." Trey removed himself from Aggie's lap and settled his red electric guitar in place. He was crossing the stage before Jace could take a decent breath.

Aggie didn't try to remove herself from his lap, but her body was stiff and unyielding.

He kissed her shoulder, not knowing what to do to make her forgive him for his offhand comment. He thought she was perfect. And even if she were fat, he wouldn't have cared. He would love her no matter what she looked like. Should he tell her things like that? That he *loved* her no matter what? His throat closed off. He was panting again. He couldn't get a grip on himself. Not since he'd told her about his mother. Told her things he'd never told anyone. Things he'd never admitted even to himself.

"I love you," he whispered.

He figured he'd said it too quietly for her to hear over Brian and Trey's guitar duel, but her body relaxed into his, and she squeezed his hand. "I'm glad," she said.

They watched in silence as the band returned to the stage and continued the concert. She must have sensed his turmoil at expressing his feelings aloud. She was supportive, but didn't push him. He knew if she had, he would have slipped back into denial. He'd never figure out how she could understand him so completely. No one understood him. He didn't even understand himself. He gently rubbed his left hand over her forearm, needing the tactile sensation of her bare flesh against his fingertips.

When it came time for the band's encore, Aggie climbed off his lap and offered him a hand. He looked at her and found her cheeks wet with tears. His heart stumbled over several beats.

He climbed to his feet and took her shoulder in his free hand. "Aggie. What's wrong?"

She shook her head, closed her eyes, and swallowed. "I'm glad." She hugged him unexpectedly, rubbing her tear-damp face against his neck.

"I'm glad," she whispered.

A roadie, Jake, poked Jace in the back. "You'd better get ready to go onstage."

Jace released Aggie, and his favorite, solid black bass was pushed into his good hand. He settled the familiar strap around his shoulder, wincing slightly when the full weight of the instrument settled over his trapezius muscle and collarbone. Maybe he had overestimated his ability to play. He slid his arm out of its sling and tested the mobility of his fingers. A bit stiff, but he could play. He was sure.

The crowd was chanting. "Sinners, Sinners, Sinners." The arena's overhead lights were still off, so even though the stage was dark and empty, they knew the show wasn't over.

"Break a leg," Jon growled into Jace's ear as he handed him his earpiece. "Or better yet, your fucking neck."

With no time to tell Jon to fuck off, Jace stuck the earpiece in his ear so he could hear the music and directions given by Dave. He then trotted after Brian and Trey onto the stage. There was a soft glow of blue lights at the level of their feet, and when their shadows crossed the stage, the crowd cheered. Jace's heart rate kicked up a few notches. He really hoped he didn't screw up.

Eric tapped a cymbal, starting the intro to "Twisted," and Jace entered with his bass progression. There was stiffness in his knuckles, and the pain in his right shoulder was agonizingly sharp as he strummed, but the thick strings between his fingertips and the solid fret board were comforting. He'd missed this. Standing next to the drums, he closed his eyes and let the rhythm carry him, head-banging in time with Eric's bass drum.

Sed entered the song with a long note on his violin. The lights flashed so bright Jace could see them through his closed eyelids. A heavy arm wrapped around his shoulders and urged him forward. Sed apparently didn't want him hiding by the drum kit this evening. Jace hoped he didn't expect him to writhe around on the floor the way Jon did. Sed grinned between lyrics and gave him a little wink. He nodded toward the crowd.

Yeah, Jace got it. He should play this up. Make his brief stage appearance special for the fans. He wandered out of Sed's hold toward the front of the stage. He drew to a halt at its edge and leaned forward to play the steady bass riff at shin level. He head-banged while he played, adrenaline flowing through his body, his shoulder protesting each movement of his fingers. Brian moved to stand beside him, placing one foot on a speaker at the front of the stage while he played the insanely fast guitar riff. Jace stood upright and leaned against the guitarist. Brian beamed and pressed his arm firmly against Jace's shoulder. Sed paced the front of the stage now, lifting his hand up and down to get the crowd to participate, and thrusting the microphone toward the audience during the chorus so they'd sing along. They especially loved to sing the part that went, "Twisted, crazy hell-born bitch." Probably because that was the only part they could easily understand. Sed screamed the rest of the chorus in his signature baritone growl, which was fucking awesome.

Trey moved to Brian's other side during his guitar solo. Jace had to concentrate on the sound of Eric's drums to continue his low, repetitive bass riff. It was admittedly hard to maintain with Brian wailing away beside him. The man was fucking gifted on that guitar. Jace wanted to stand there and gawk at him in awe. The fans screamed their appreciation of Brian's skill when he lifted his guitar over his head to carry the final note of his solo.

Jace wasn't sure what possessed him to add a mini bass solo of his own right before the final chorus. Trey and Brian glanced at him in surprise. The crowd cheered unexpectedly. Jace felt the heat of embarrassment rise up his neck and face until his ears were burning. He returned to the repetitive bass riff that carried the undertones of the entire song. Sed punched him in his good shoulder affectionately.

When the song ended, the crowd cheered. Sed got carried away and lifted Jace off the floor with one heavily muscled arm. "Jace Seymour, ladies and gentlemen."

And they cheered. "Jace, Jace, Jace."

For him.

Jace smiled until his cheeks hurt. He couldn't help himself. Sed set him on his feet. Jace moved to the front of the stage and tossed his pick into the audience. The crowd sank in a circle in search of the prize. Jace lifted his bass off his shoulder and carried it offstage with his good arm. He was actually looking forward to getting his right arm back in its sling. As much as he hated the damned thing, it did take the weight off his shoulder and made it feel a thousand times better.

"Man, that was fuckin' awesome," Trey said. "When did you write that bass solo? And why have you been holding out on us?"

Jace hadn't exactly written that solo. It had come to him spontaneously onstage. Before he could explain that to Trey, a curvy, warm body pressed against him.

"My God, baby, that was amazing," Aggie said. She captured his face between her hands and kissed him passionately.

Someone took his bass out of his hand, and Jace wrapped his arms around her—both arms. He returned her kiss, his lips sucking on hers gently. Someone squeezed his shoulder, and he drew away from Aggie to find Eric grinning at him.

"Great show, man."

Jace found himself smiling again. "Thanks. You too."

Sed hugged Aggie and Jace in one giant embrace. "The crowd loved that. You have to play the encore every night until you're better, dude. And hurry up and get better, will you? The show isn't the same without you."

Did he really mean that?

Jace glanced around. "Where's Jon?"

"He stalked off sulking right after you started playing," Aggie said. "Jealous of your superior skill, I'm sure." She kissed him again. "God, I want you. You're so sexy when you play onstage." She released a breathless gasp as she gazed at him.

"I am?"

"Oh yeah." She offered him her come-hither smile. Was his sudden urge to shove hundred-dollar bills down her shirt wrong? Probably.

Sed released the pair. "Take it easy there, stud. You need to concentrate on healing."

Aggie's hand cupped his crotch over his jeans. His cock stirred against her palm. "How about some sexual healing?"

"I'm game."

He eased his arm back into its sling and let her lead him down the steps by his belt buckle.

Jace had kept Aggie suspended at the brink of orgasm for a good thirty minutes now. She was moaning and writhing in tormented bliss, but she hadn't asked him to stop once. His cock was so hard, his balls so full, he almost wanted her to beg so he could fuck her already, but until she broke, he'd continue to pleasure her. He pulled the clothespin from her nipple. The device plucked her nipple hard as it came free.

"Ah," she gasped.

Her rosy nipple flushed red from overstimulation. Jace lowered his head to soothe the tender bud with his lips. The instant he touched her there, she shuddered, the chains that suspended her arms above her head rattling with her jerky motions. While he kissed her nipple with the slightest suction he could manage, he lowered the clothespin, careful not to touch her sweat-slick thighs and alert her to what he was going to do, and clamped it on her clit.

"Oh," she moaned, her hips undulating in torment.

He flicked the clothespin, which tugged on her clit.

"Jace!"

Come on, baby, beg for it.

But she didn't. She took deep shaky breaths, trying to curb her excitement as she had been for the past two hours. He kept flicking that damn clothespin and kissing that tender nipple until her excitement built to the pinnacle. As soon as her body shook with the first ripple of release, he pulled the clothespin off her clit and moved away, leaving her there unfulfilled.

Surely now she would beg him. How many times did he have to make her almost come before she couldn't stand it anymore? She whimpered. Her entire body—slick with sweat and sticky with syrup—trembled.

Jace was running out of ways to excite her. He'd used every object in his suitcase, in every way he'd imagined, yet she still hadn't submitted to the pleasure. She let him give her more. He stared at her, bound and blindfolded, and wondered how to proceed. He was out of ideas. Jace reached for a wet cloth and rubbed it over her anus. He trickled chocolate syrup over the area and lowered his head to lick it off. He pressed the tip of his tongue inside her.

"Mmmm," she murmured, spreading her legs farther, so he could press his tongue deeper with less resistance. He sucked and moved his tongue in chaotic circles. Gasping, she wriggled her hips in excitement.

"I like that."

He slid two fingers into her sopping wet cunt and pleasured her ass until her internal muscles convulsed. He moved away again, watching her writhe with unfulfilled desire, tears dripping from beneath her blindfold, fluids dripping down the inside of her thighs.

He couldn't stand it anymore. Maybe she could go all night without coming, but he couldn't. He climbed from the bed and grabbed some oil from the nightstand. He poured it into his hand and rubbed it over his cock. His head fell back, and he gasped brokenly.

"Jace?"

He should make her watch this. He climbed in front of her, kneeling on the bed, and pushed her blindfold up. She blinked, her eyes adjusting to the light. Her gaze eventually lowered to his straining cock. She gasped, her hips thrusting forward involuntarily. So she did want it. He wasn't going to give it to her until she begged.

He closed his eyes, trying to ignore her little pained whimpers as he stroked his cock with both hands.

"Jace!"

He stroked himself faster. As soon as he came, he could pleasure her again. He'd start his routine from the beginning.

"Don't you dare fucking come before me, you asshole!" Aggie yelled, jerking on her restraints.

He opened his eyes to look at her. Her attention was riveted to his cock, her hips undulating with his motion as he pumped it vigorously.

"You want this?" he murmured.

"No," she growled.

He stroked himself slowly, in the rhythm he knew she responded to best. Her hips churned. "No?" He shrugged, closed his eyes, and massaged the head of his cock with his palm. He didn't really want to come this way anymore, but he'd keep pleasuring himself to drive her crazy. He absolutely loved her response.

He moved his free hand to his nuts. Massaged those too. "My balls are so heavy, I'll probably spurt like ten minutes once I get going."

Aggie sobbed.

"Where do you want it? On your mound?"

She shook her head vigorously.

"On your tits?"

"N-no."

"Your face? Tell me, Aggie. Where do you want it?"

"Inside. Put it inside. Please, please." She shook her head, hair flying in all directions "Fuck me, Jace. I can't take it anymore."

Jace breathed a sigh of relief. "Finally," he gasped and released her ankles from the cuffs keeping her in a kneeling position on the bed.

"What do you mean, *finally*? I've been trying to give you what you want for hours."

"What do you think I want, Aggie?"

"A woman who can take all your pleasure torture until you're finished."

Jace grinned. "Not even close, sweetheart."

"What?"

"I just want to fuck you when you want it. For you to tell me when you need it."

"I needed it two hours ago."

"Then why didn't you say so?"

He moved around her and knelt. Slowly, he slid his hands up her arms toward her restraints, thinking he'd like to tease her just a little longer. Gritting her teeth, she wrapped her legs around his waist and pulled him against her. His cock slid against her hot slit. He shuddered.

"Put it in, damn you," she growled.

He moved a hand between their bodies and redirected his cock into her body. Her back arched, and she sank over him. They cried out together. She shifted her feet to the bed behind his hips and pushed, drawing him out of her hot, slick pussy before driving her body against him and taking him deep again. He inched forward to give her more play in her chains and rotated his hips as she controlled the joining of their bodies.

"Oh, oh, oh," she cried. Her body convulsed in orgasm. Her pussy clenched over him, trying to coax him to follow her in bliss. He fought it, wanting to give her as many orgasms as he'd withheld earlier. It would probably take him all night. He hoped she'd had Wheaties for breakfast.

Aggie collapsed against his chest, breathing hard.

"Ah, God, I needed that," she panted.

He grinned and unfastened her restraints. When her arms came free, she wrapped them around him and then rotated her hips, grinding his hard cock inside her. He tipped her onto her back and followed her onto the bed, driving himself deep. He then pulled out halfway and rocked into her repetitively, relentlessly, until they were both gasping and she was screaming, "Deeper, deeper."

He thrust into her once and then backed off, pumping into her fast, but shallow. One deep thrust and then fast and shallow again. She clung to his shoulders as another orgasm gripped her. He pulled out until she stopped shuddering and then slipped inside her again.

"Ahhhhh," she cried as a second orgasm converged with the first.

He thrust into her slowly then, concentrating on not letting himself come—tried to think of anything but her hot, slick body against him, around him. No use. Oh dear God, she felt good. He thrust faster. Pushed deeper. Gave himself over to the pleasure. It built and built. Consumed him until he had no choice but to let go. Jace shuddered uncontrollably as his seed pumped into her. Almost unbearable in intensity, his climax stole his breath. His lungs stung, protesting his lack of air, but the pulsations of pleasure in his groin made it impossible to concentrate on anything as unnecessary as breathing. He drew back slightly and lunged forward again, still shuddering with release. Aggie held him, with her arms and legs and pussy, as he came. She murmured sweet words of love against his throat. When his body collapsed against hers, she drew him closer still. He sucked air desperately, trying to recover.

"Are you too tired to continue?" she asked several minutes later.

He chuckled. Apparently, he had come a lot harder than she had. He'd help her with that as soon as he could move again. "Not yet."

Aggie wriggled out from beneath him and urged him onto his back. When she reached for the piece of satin on the bed, the one he'd used to drive her to distraction earlier, he wasn't sure how long he'd last before begging her to fuck him. He was more than ready to find out.

Jace knew he was dreaming and didn't want to wake up. He liked this part of the dream. He wished it could go on forever. He'd gladly give up the good though, if he could avoid reliving what he knew would come at the end.

Young, dumb, and full of cum, Jason ducked into the passenger side of the yellow Ford Mustang waiting in the parking lot.

"Did you get it?" Kara asked, her intense brown eyes wide with excitement.

Jason opened his leather jacket and showed her the bottle of whiskey tucked inside. "Let's get out of here. I think the clerk was suspicious."

Kara slammed the gearshift into reverse and backed out, before shifting into first and speeding through the parking lot with her tires squealing. So much for being inconspicuous and making a quiet getaway.

"Open it, Jason. I need a drink."

He pulled the bottle out of his jacket and unscrewed the lid. He passed it to her, and she took a long swallow, blowing through a stop sign without a moment's hesitation. Kara Sinclair was undoubtedly the most beautiful girl Jason had ever seen. She was already making a name for herself in the world of fashion modeling. But that wasn't what had him under her spell. She was wild. Reckless. He'd pursued her because she was Brian Sinclair's little sister, and he'd originally hoped she'd introduce him to Brian's band, Sinners. Five minutes with her had convinced him none of that mattered. He was in love with her.

Kara passed him the bottle of whiskey, and he took a drink. It burned his throat and made his eyes water. Jason winced, wishing he'd stolen something of higher quality. She deserved the best, and he had absolutely nothing to offer. She pulled into the long driveway of a Beverly Hills estate. Why had she brought him to her house?

She parked in the driveway and took the whiskey from him, taking a long draw from the bottle. "I like this," she said. "Thanks for getting it."

"It was nothing."

"Did you really just walk in there and steal it right in front of the clerk?"

Jason shrugged. "I guess."

"You're so bad." She leaned closer, and he caught the sweet fragrance of her expensive perfume mingling with alcohol. The bangle bracelets on her wrists rattled. "I like bad boys."

He could be bad. As bad as she wanted him to be.

Her breath tickled his ear. "Do you want to kiss me?"

His heart stuttered and then raced. She leaned away to stare into his eyes, and the next thing he knew, they were kissing. Her soft lips tasted of whiskey. His cock was instantly hard, straining against his jeans. He could think of nothing but her. Possessing her. He lifted a trembling hand to her breast. He wasn't sure what he'd expected a boob to feel like. Not this soft. It yielded to his touch as he squeezed.

Her brutal slap to his cheek caused him to jerk his hand away.

"I didn't say you could feel me up," she said, glaring at him in the dim interior of the car.

He didn't know how to respond. Her slap had only managed to excite him more, and he wasn't sure how to deal with that unexpected reality, so he kissed her again. He was careful to keep his hands to himself as he suckled her lips. Licked them. Nibbled them. Caressed her lips with his.

"Jason," she gasped into his mouth.

Kara launched herself across the car so that she was straddling his lap, facing him. She rubbed her crotch against his, mewing in the back of her throat. He could feel the heat between her legs against his cock. Only layers of fabric separated him from sinking into her body. What would it feel like to bury himself in her moist heat? In her... pussy. Oh God, he was going to explode.

"Touch it," he murmured against her lips. That's all he needed—her fingers against his bare skin. He could make do with that. "Please, Kara."

"Tomorrow," she whispered. "I think I want my first time to be with you. If I show up at your house tomorrow night, you'll know for sure."

Kara Sinclair was a virgin? He wasn't sure why that surprised him. Maybe because she seemed so worldly. He'd expected her to be far more experienced than he was. He would undoubtedly disappoint her with his lack of skill in the sack. It didn't stop him from wanting to try it, however.

Kara slid off his lap into the driver's seat, pressing her fingers to her cheeks.

"Get out," she said.

Was she mad at him now? "Kara?"

"I need to think about this. So you need to go now. Maybe I'll see you tomorrow. Maybe not."

He walked over seven miles to get home. He had a huge case of blue balls, but the agonizing ache was bittersweet. Would Kara show up tomorrow? He was kind of glad she'd put him off for at least a day. He had plans to make. He wanted to satisfy her. Make this special for her. Let it be more about her and less about him.

His father laid into him the moment he stepped through the door. "Where the fuck have you been, you worthless piece of shit?"

"None of your business."

Dad grabbed him by the front his jacket. "You smell like whiskey. Have you been drinking?"

"Maybe."

Dad cuffed him on the ear. Jason cried out in pain, covering his ear with one hand. He'd become accustomed to the belt years ago, so his father had started using his fists, and when that no longer made Jason beg for mercy, he'd started boxing him on the ears. Jason never got used to that pain. "Your mother is looking down on you from heaven, weeping over what you've become. Weeping that her son is no better than a delinquent, a criminal, a useless, no good pile of shit. You'll never amount to anything."

Jason sneered, pretending the words didn't affect him, but even though he'd heard them a thousand times, they still stung, and he believed them a little more every day. "Are you finished?"

Dad boxed him on the other ear. "Get your ass up to your room, boy. You're grounded."

Jason had both ears covered with his hands now. "For what?"

"Drinking. And whatever other trouble you got yourself into tonight."

"Get your hands off me." Jason shoved his father, who stumbled back against the wall. "I'm leaving, and I'm never coming back."

He turned to go, wondering where he could stay, wishing he could get his bass guitar out of his room, but knowing he had to get out immediately.

Jason should have learned by now that his father wasn't afraid to beat him unconscious to make him obey. He wasn't sure why he never fought back. He probably could have taken the old man if he really wanted to. But somewhere inside, he knew he deserved this. This pain.

When Jason regained consciousness on his bedroom floor, it was mid-afternoon the next day. His door had been secured with a padlock from the outside, and his windows had been intentionally painted shut long ago. There was no escaping this room.

He went into the tiny connecting half-bathroom and washed up in the sink. A dark bruise marred his cheek, but it was the only visible evidence. The rest of his injuries were under his clothes. He had a hard time taking a deep breath and figured he had another fractured rib. He fingered his rib cage, looking for evidence of protruding bones. At least, he had no complete breaks this time. Nothing bleeding. He was sore, but he'd live.

As expected, his father had confiscated his bass guitar again. With nothing to do, Jason sat on his bed, leaned against the wall, and dreamed of better days. Days of freedom and playing his bass guitar onstage with his favorite band, Sinners. Nights of making love to the most beautiful girl on the planet, Kara Sinclair.

He'd spaced out like that for hours. When he couldn't stand the ache in his heart anymore, he cranked up his space heater until the coils glowed bright orange. He'd removed the protective grate months ago. As he'd done numerous times, he pressed his right wrist against the hot coils until his flesh seared and blistered. Eventually, the pain became too much, and he pulled away from the punishing heat. Breathing hard, he tightened his leather wrist cuff around the blistered flesh to keep the pain constant. He needed something to hurt him more than the hurt inside. The hurt he couldn't dig out, no matter how hard he tried.

Someone knocked on his door, and he kicked the heater against the wall in case his father came in and saw what he was doing. He didn't want him to know. Didn't want anyone to know that he hurt himself when no one was looking.

"You want dinner?" his dad called.

"No."

"Suit yourself." His footsteps faded down the hall.

Sometime later, Jason heard a car with a big engine pull to a stop outside his house. He went to the window to gaze into the darkness. Across the street, Kara had parked. She honked her horn and sat there, waiting for him with the engine idling. She would think he stood her up. That he didn't want her.

He fought with the window for several minutes, knowing it wouldn't budge. Desperate for freedom, he grabbed a boxing trophy from his bookshelf and smashed it against the corner of the window. The sound of breaking glass was louder than he expected it would be. The pieces rained down on the porch roof. He paused, waiting for his father to come charging up the stairs to permanently put him out of his misery, but he never came. He must've fallen asleep in front of the TV.

Jason threw his blanket over the broken glass in the window frame. His stepped on his space heater to help himself over the windowsill. He dropped onto the roof, paused to make sure his father wasn't coming to kill him, and then shimmied down the porch post and into the bushes. He fled across the yard and raced toward Kara's car. Before he could climb inside, she sped off.

Jason watched her retreating lights—heart simultaneously thudding and sinking.

Her taillights brightened, and then her reverse lights came on. She almost ran him over as she backed up the car at a high rate of speed. She stopped, not looking at him. She stared out the windshield and wiggled in her seat. Jace climbed in beside her, and she sped off into the night.

"I thought you weren't coming," she said breathlessly. "At first, I was mad, and then a little relieved. When I saw you climbing down from your porch, I got scared. Sorry I took off."

"It's okay. If you're not ready…"

"I am ready," she said. She reached across the car and squeezed his hand. Her hand was damp, but he didn't mind. He was pretty nervous himself. "My parents will be at a party until late. I thought… I thought we could… in the pool house."

He lifted her hand to his lips. "Whatever makes you happy."

She smiled, looking timid and shy. He'd never seen her this way. He liked this side of her. Maybe even more than the reckless and wild side. He wasn't sure.

When they reached her house, she took his hand and led him to the pool house. His heart thudded with a mixture of anticipation and anxiety. She opened the door, turned on a light, and they entered an open seating area flanked by two doors, one labeled ladies, the other labeled gents. There was a sofa and two chairs in the common area, but no bed. Not exactly what Jason had envisioned for their first encounter, but he could improvise.

She looked at him, and her eyes widened. "What happened to your face?" She touched the bruise on his cheekbone with her fingertips. "Did you get into a fight?"

"Something like that."

She smiled, her nose wrinkling as she gazed into his eyes happily. "Oh, Jason, you are *so* bad. Kiss me."

He drew her against his body, and she wrapped her arms around him. Pain snaked through his bruised body as she clung to him. He gasped slightly, and when she looked at him in question, he kissed her. She stiffened in his embrace, so he kept on kissing her until her body finally relaxed.

"Can I touch you?" he asked. He wouldn't really mind if she slapped him again, but he didn't want to push her if she wasn't ready.

"You can touch me anywhere you want."

His breath caught. "Anywhere?"

"Anywhere."

"And can I kiss you anywhere?"

She shuddered against him. "Yes."

He cupped her cheek and shifted his lips to her jaw, her throat, her ear. She sighed, submitting to his questing mouth. Her fingertips dug into his chest, finding bruises he didn't know he had, sending him to a strange place between pain and pleasure. When his hand found her breast, she inhaled and then drew away. She surprised him by tugging her T-shirt over her head and then unfastening her bra at her back. She looked at him. He could see her pulse thrumming fast and hard in her neck. Blushing, she let the undergarment fall free, leaving her perfect breasts naked to his eager gaze. She was the most beautiful thing he'd ever seen. He traced one pink nipple with his fingertip, fascinated by the response of her flesh as her nipple grew harder with each stroke.

"Jason."

He lowered his head and flicked his tongue over the pebbled peak. She shuddered and buried her fingers in his hair. She managed to find a bruise on the back of his head, but the pain she unknowingly inflicted fueled his fire.

He eased her toward the sofa. When she tried to remove his shirt, he pulled away and shook his head. "This is for you," he said, but in reality, he didn't want her to see his body and the ugly black and blue marks.

"Jason?" she whispered uncertainly.

"It's okay. I want to make you feel good." He didn't care about his own enjoyment. He wanted to show her how strongly he felt about her by pleasuring her body. He'd have to show her, because he knew he couldn't say it. He caressed, kissed, and suckled every inch of her silky skin above the waist, paying close attention to her reactions, seeking the spots that brought her the most pleasure. When she tugged at his shirt, he moved out of her reach and removed her jeans and sandals. Her body grew stiff with anxiety, so he left her panties in place, giving her time to grow accustomed to his touch. He found kissing the insides of her legs made her moan and writhe in delight. He caressed the backs of her knees while he suckled the flesh of her inner thighs.

"Jason, please."

Please what? Was she ready for him to remove her panties? He covered her mound with his mouth and blew a hot breath through her last scrap of clothing.

"Ah God," she gasped and grabbed his right wrist, squeezing the studded bracelet in a solid grip.

He almost lost control when the pain she inflicted on his burns registered. He grabbed her wrist and forced her to release her hold on him before he made a mess in his jeans.

"Are you ready?" he asked.

"Yes. I'm so hot and achy I can't stand it."

Her black lace panties joined the rest of her clothes on the floor. Jason knew the names of her female parts, knew what they did, how they looked from pictures. Nothing had prepared him for her scent, however. He inhaled deeply, his eyes drifting closed. His cock protested its neglect, his balls ached. He wanted to bury his face between her legs and breathe her essence, but he didn't think she was quite ready for that, so he stroked the slick, swollen flesh of her inner folds with two fingertips. The texture of her exposed flesh fascinated him. It was smoother than regular skin. Slippery. Hot. He watched her swell and redden and moisten beneath his persistent touch. Her hips rocked, and she called to him in her excitement. He sought her clit, having heard that a woman's greatest pleasure was centered in that tiny spot. He found it hard to believe until his fingers brushed the small, swollen bit of flesh, and Kara cried out in delight. Her back arched off the sofa.

"Oh yes, Jason. Right there."

He hesitated and then lowered his head to suck her clit into his mouth. She screamed, startling him as her body convulsed unexpectedly. Had she had an orgasm? He wasn't sure, but he loved knowing that he was drawing this response from her body. That he could give her pleasure. That he could do this for her. He didn't have money or his own car or anything else to offer, but he could bring her pleasure. He flicked her clit with his tongue while he sucked it. Her motions grew exaggerated, needy. His fingers stroked the slick, hot flesh of her inner lips.

"Oh God. Put your fingers inside me, Jason. Please don't tease me anymore."

She thought he was teasing her? He shifted his hand and slowly inserted one finger into her tight, little pussy. She was so small inside. How would her body accommodate his cock? He wasn't one of those guys teased in the locker room. He needed to open her so he would fit inside. He rotated his finger in a wide circle, stretching her until he could slide a second finger inside.

Her breath caught. "Put it in, Jason. I'm ready. Put it in now."

It? He went still and leaned back slightly, releasing her clit from his mouth.

He swallowed hard. "Now?"

"Yes, yes. Now."

His trembling hand moved to his fly. He wanted her. Wanted to shove his throbbing cock into that hot pussy, but what if he embarrassed himself? What if he came as soon as he put it in?

"Hurry, Jason."

He released his fly, and his cock sprang free. He was overexcited, and he knew it. She fumbled under the sofa pillow and pulled out a condom.

"Put this on first."

He pushed his pants down his thighs and fumbled to get the condom in place.

"Oh God, you're huge," Kara said as she watched him. "Go slow, okay?"

"Okay."

As soon as he had the condom in place, he climbed on top of her and settled between her thighs. He used his hand to guide the head of his cock into her body.

Oh God, it felt so good. He sank deeper. Her body struggled to accept him. He pushed forward. She sucked a pained breath through her teeth.

"Wait," she gasped. "It hurts."

How could it hurt? He'd never felt anything so wonderful in his life. He pushed deeper. Her flesh resisted him.

"Ow."

He was trying to go as slow as he could, but her snug little cunt was pure bliss, and all rational thought left his mind. Unable to control the urge to bury himself deeply, he surged forward. Her flesh tore, finally yielding to his, and she cried out in pain. He gave her no time to recover, but pulled back and thrust into her body again.

"Not so hard," she complained.

He couldn't think, could only feel. His urgency building, he fucked her harder. Harder. Faster. Oh God, harder. *Take it, Kara.* He scarcely comprehended that she was crying. He just needed to possess her. That's all. He didn't mean to cause her pain. She hit him in the shoulder with her fist.

"Jason, you're hurting me. Stop doing it so hard."

But her second blow only excited him more. "Hit me again, Kara. Hurt me."

"What?"

"Hit me." He looked down, finding her cheeks damp with tears. He pounded his cock into her body. "Please, Kara, hurt me. I need… pain."

By the look on her face, he knew he'd said something wrong, something weird, but he wanted her to hurt him, needed her to do it. This much pleasure couldn't be right. He wasn't used to pleasure. Pain he understood.

"You sick bastard, get off me."

Her elbow hit him in his fractured ribs, and his body convulsed as he came unexpectedly. He stopped moving, his body pumping his seed into her, pooling at the tip of the condom. He reveled in the pain radiating through his side almost as much as the pleasure spasms gripping the base of his cock.

"What's wrong with you?" she asked, struggling beneath him to get him off her body.

"I don't know." He pressed his forehead into her shoulder, fighting tears. "I'm sorry. I didn't mean to hurt you. Are you okay?"

"No, I'm not okay. Get off me!"

He pulled out, and she squirmed out from under him, landing on the floor.

"Kara."

"Don't come near me," she said, grabbing her clothes and heading for the door.

He saw blood on her thighs, on his cock, on the sofa cushion. It made him nauseous. Oh God, he really *had* hurt her. "Wait, don't leave. I'm sorry."

"There's something wrong with you. Just stay away from me. I never want to see you again." She yanked the door open and darted out of the pool house.

His heart twisted. "But I love you."

He didn't know if she heard him say it. The whole building shuddered as she slammed the door.

"Don't leave." But she was already gone.

The trip home was the longest seven miles he'd ever walked. He wished he could take it all back. Well, not all of it. Just from the moment he'd started taking his pleasure. That's when everything had taken a turn for the worse. And now Kara hated him, never wanted to see him again. The pain his father inflicted didn't come close to this crippling agony in his heart. He squeezed his right wrist beneath his cuff bracelet, needing the pain to take another step toward home.

As he drew closer to his house and his sure-to-be-livid father, Jason noticed something bright on the horizon. Smoke billowed into the night sky. Fire. A fire truck blared as it rounded a corner and headed up the street. An ambulance followed a moment later.

It looked like the fire was near Jason's house. The closer he got to its source, the faster his heart thudded, until he couldn't deny the reality. The fire was *at* his house. He ran the last two blocks. Firefighters were racing down the street, hooking up a fire hose to the nearest hydrant. Neighbors were coming out of their houses in their pajamas, holding each other, watching the destruction in awe. Jason stared at his burning house in disbelief, walking into the yard in a trance. Huge flames were licking from his broken bedroom window. He could hear his father in the house screaming his name. "Jason! Son, where are you?"

"Dad, I'm here!"

There was a loud splintering sound, and the roof over his room collapsed in a spray of sparks. The first jets of water from the hoses blasted into the flames, hissing as water evaporated into steam.

"Dad!"

He darted toward the house and made it as far as the porch before someone grabbed him around the waist. "Let me go," he demanded, struggling with all his strength. "He's still inside. My dad. I think he's upstairs. I heard him calling for me. But…"

A pair of firemen busted down the front door. He could hear them yelling to each other inside the house. "Give me a hand. Someone's trapped under this beam." Eventually one of them emerged, carrying a limp body over one shoulder. "Medic! We need a medic over here."

The charred body he laid on the ground was Jason's father. "My son," he murmured, clinging to the firefighter's boot. Coherent sentences were garbled with indistinguishable syllables. "Save my son. I locked him in his room. I couldn't get to the door. The roof collapsed." He coughed, his eyes glazed with pain. "He's still in there." If it weren't for his familiar voice, Jason wouldn't have recognized him. His skin was so severely burned he was unidentifiable.

Jason stood over him, trembling. "I'm here, Dad. I'm okay."

"Chopper's on its way," a paramedic said. "We'll get him to the burn center as soon as we can."

"How did you get out?" his father murmured. "Did you set the house on fire? Did you? I wouldn't put it past you, you little punk. You did, didn't you? To get back at me for grounding you. For tossing your stupid bass guitar in the garbage."

Jason shook his head. "No. I didn't do it." He glanced up at his room. There was no doubt that the fire had started there. It's where the damage was centered. As Jason watched, the tattered remains of a blanket fluttered from the porch roof as a blast of water unsettled it from its perch. He recognized his bedspread, half burnt. The bedspread he'd placed over the broken glass in the windowsill. And his space heater. The heater he'd forgotten to turn off after he'd burnt his wrist.

Then he realized. He *had* started the fire.

Jason gripped his right wrist with punishing strength, pressing the leather bracelet into his blistered flesh until his vision tunneled.

They let Jason ride in the helicopter when they learned he had no other way to the hospital. No other family. No one who cared about him. Jason couldn't stand their looks of pity. Or his father's nonsensical jabbering. Dad was delirious with pain and kept repeating, "It's all your fault. All your fault."

Jason huddled in the corner, his hands over his ears, no longer a young man of fifteen, but a scared little boy. With nothing. No one. He was alone. Alone. With no one to hurt him. Hurt him when he needed it.

They'd taken his father into the treatment center as soon as the helicopter landed. Asked Jason if he wanted to be with him. Warned him that his dad probably wouldn't make it through the night. "You might want to say good-bye to him, son," some doctor had said at one point.

But he hadn't. He'd been too afraid, just like with his mother. His last memory of his father was lidless eyes staring at him blankly as they wheeled the gurney into the treatment center.

Jace started awake, his heart thudding in his chest, the image of his hideously burned father circulating in his mind. The room was entirely dark, but he could hear her breathing, feel the gentle motion of the bus. Both brought him comfort. He loved being on the road. And he loved her. His Aggie.

His hand sought Aggie's under the covers. He clung to her fingers, feeling stupid for needing her so much, for seeking her support, while she slept unaware of his turmoil. It wasn't as if she could do anything about the ghosts that haunted him. About the pain of his father's memory. The guilt Jace felt. The fear.

Or maybe she could. She'd helped him deal with the pain of losing his mother. Her memory was still in the shadows, but no longer threatening. He'd found solace. Aggie had given that to him. She managed to give him everything he needed. Even things he hadn't realized were important. When the sun came up, he watched her sleep, wondering how he'd survive if he lost her too.

———

Aggie opened her eyes to find Jace staring at her. She smiled, stretching lethargically.

"Good morning, sweetheart," she murmured. "What are you doing awake so early?"

"I'm ready," he said.

She grinned, wrapped an arm around his neck, and shifted closer to his warm body. "I figured after last night you'd be satisfied for a couple days at least."

"That's not what I meant," he said seriously. "I'm ready to tell you."

Her heart skipped a beat, and her smile faded. "About your dad?"

"Yeah."

She wasn't sure if she wanted him to tell her. He'd said that he'd killed him. What if he had done something truly unforgivable? Would her feelings for him change? She didn't want that. She was incredibly happy with Jace. She'd never felt this way about a man for long, and she wasn't ready for this to end. She knew he was taking a huge step in confiding in her, however, so it wasn't as if she could refuse to listen. She had to be strong. She knew his burden was too great for one set of shoulders.

Aggie struggled to free her arm from the tangled sheet then lifted her hand to stroke his brow tenderly. "I'm listening."

He closed his eyes. "Where do I start?"

She didn't think he was really addressing the question to her, so she waited for him to proceed.

"I wasn't an easy teenager. I got into a lot of trouble. At home. At school. With the law. The more Dad tried to straighten me out, the more I acted out. Yelling at me didn't work. Physical punishment didn't work. Grounding. Taking away my possessions. Nothing worked. At the time I hated him, but not nearly as much as he hated me. For five years we lived like that—in constant opposition."

"Rebellion isn't unusual, baby. Many teenagers grow that way," Aggie said and touched his face. "Did he beat you?"

Jace shrugged. "I preferred that to the yelling. The bruises faded, but the words, they're still with me."

He ducked his head, his eyes closed. She waited for him to get himself together. After a moment, he looked into her eyes. "The day he died." He took a deep breath. "The day I *killed* him, I was supposed to be grounded in my room. I snuck out to be with a girl. Kara Sinclair."

"Sinclair?"

"Brian's little sister."

"I didn't know you knew the guys back then. How old were you?"

"Fifteen. I knew the band, but they didn't know me. I dated Kara to get close to them, but... and then a few months later, she..." He shook his head. "That's a story for a different day. While I was out..." His eyes drifted to her forehead. "Losing my virginity actually." When he flushed, she couldn't help but grin. He looked sort of sick to his stomach for a few seconds, but it passed. "While I was out with Kara, the house caught fire. It started in my room. Dad thought I was locked inside, so he went upstairs to get me. I wasn't there. He'd grounded me, locked me in my room. I was supposed to be there, but I wasn't, Aggie. If I hadn't disobeyed... if I hadn't broken a window and snuck out to have a good time... if I hadn't turned that heater on, or remembered to turn it off." He unfastened the cuff he always wore on his right wrist and showed her the skin beneath—burn scars too numerous to count. "I turned the heater on to do this to myself, and later I put the blanket over it without thinking. That started the fire. The curtains caught. Then the furniture. If I'd listened to him, my Dad would never have gotten trapped in the flames. He wouldn't have suffered third-degree burns on ninety percent of his body. He wouldn't have died hours later." He stared into her eyes, daring her to deny his involvement. The pain he worked so hard to conceal was right there on the surface, so tangible she believed she could touch it. "It should have been me. I should have been the one to die. I killed him, Aggie. I might as well have shot him in the head."

She knew he must feel that way, and she wasn't sure how to make him see that his father's death was a horrible, tragic accident, but it wasn't his fault. His father shouldn't have locked him in the room. And Jace hadn't purposely set the fire. He'd been a careless kid. In so much pain.

"It's in the past, baby. I love you today. Right now," she murmured, touching his face. "That's what's important." He gazed at her in the dim light filtering through the blinds. He looked miserable to the depths of his soul.

"You still love me?" he said breathlessly.

"I do."

"Even knowing…" He swallowed.

"I told you that you can tell me anything. It makes me sad that you're hurting, and I'm sorry you don't have any close family. At least you have your band—and me. We're your family."

"Nice sentiment, Aggie, but I'm not really that close to the guys. They tolerate me—"

Aggie covered his mouth. "Okay, I said you could tell me anything, but that doesn't mean you can lie. You are close to the guys. They adore you and would do anything for you. You just won't let them in. You've let me in. It's not so bad, is it?"

"It's different with you, Aggie. You've proven to me time after time that you accept me for who I am. The guys? They don't even know who I am."

"You could let them get to know you. You can trust them. They won't hurt you."

"Maybe." He didn't look convinced.

"What are you afraid of?"

"Nothing."

"Do you think if they saw behind your wall that they'd replace you in the band?"

He hesitated and then nodded slightly.

"You obviously have a pretty low opinion of your bandmates."

A spark of anger touched his eyes. "What do you mean? I think the world of them. I'd give my life for any one of them."

"Yet you won't even let them see the real you. Do you think they have any idea how you feel about them?"

"Do they need to know? I idolize them. It's embarrassing."

He'd never learned to show affection as a child. No one had ever shown him any, so he didn't know how and didn't recognize it. That's why he didn't understand that the guys were showing him affection when they teased him. Maybe the guys would help her. She wasn't sure how she could get them to cooperate. But she wanted that for Jace. He needed to recognize the love in his life. She could have been selfish and kept him all to herself. He might even be happy with only her to confide in, but he needed a bigger support network. Latching on too hard to one person could be devastating when things didn't work out as planned or circumstances tore people apart. Jace needed supportive people in his life. He'd been alone for far too long. Perhaps he'd let his bandmates in one at a time.

"I'm glad you told me what happened to your father." She needed to shift the focus away from the dead. Help him concentrate on the living. "What happened to you after he passed on? Did you live with relatives?"

He shook his head. "I don't have any living relatives who claim me. My mother's family disowned her when she ran away from Croatia to come to America. She left some local villager at the altar or something. I remember her bringing that up when she argued with Dad. Dad's parents worked hard and died young." Jace rolled onto his back and stared at the ceiling. "So I stayed in a group home until I turned eighteen, and then I was out on my own."

She cuddled against his side and kissed his shoulder. "The first time I saw you, I knew you'd been forced to grow up too fast."

She watched the emotions play across his face. He obviously had more demons to exorcise.

"What was the group home like?" she asked.

He shrugged. "Fight or die. I decided to fight."

"Didn't you make any friends there?"

He shook his head. "There was a reason we were the unwanted. I had my bass guitar. I dug it out of the trash. It was the only thing that survived the fire. And it was enough."

Aggie wondered how he hadn't ended up a mass murderer. How many traumatic experiences could one kid bear? And now here she was getting him shot and messing up what he'd worked so hard to achieve.

"You're not unwanted. I want you, Jace."

He closed his eyes and took a deep breath. He took her hand and squeezed it, but said nothing. She lay there, thinking of a way to get him closer to his bandmates. He seemed to identify most with Eric. Probably because neither had parents. Or maybe Jace and Brian could connect over Kara.

"Does Brian know you dated his sister?"

"God, I hope not. He thinks she was a perfect angel. I wouldn't want to taint his memory."

"His memory?"

"Kara died in a car accident. I never saw her again after our night together. I got too rough with her. Hurt her. Scared her. She called me a freak and told me she never wanted to see me again." He caught her eye. "I'll shut up now. Nothing worse than discussing old relationships with your girlfriend."

"I'm sorry she died. She must have been so young."

"Sixteen."

Too young. "Did you love her?"

"Yeah."

"And she made you happy?"

"For a little while."

Aggie smiled sadly. "Then I'm grateful to her for that. But you are not a freak. I happen to like it when you're rough."

"That's 'cause you're a freak too."

She laughed and nudged him in the ribs with her elbow. "Hey."

"I think we belong together, Aggie."

"I don't think so."

His body stiffened. She placed a hand on his chest and lifted her body to look him in the eyes.

"I know so," she said. He smiled, and she melted. They stared into each other's eyes until his cheeks went pink, and he looked away.

She decided that connecting Jace with Brian, using Kara as common ground, wasn't the best idea. She shifted to plan B. "You know who's a lot like you?"

His brows drew together as he contemplated her question.

"Eric."

"Eric?" Jace laughed. "I was forced to grow up too fast. He never grew up at all."

"He's living his childhood now, since he didn't have one as a kid. He's coping with some of the same stuff you've been through in an entirely different way."

"Aggie, you should have been a shrink. How do you know all this?"

She smiled and lowered her head to flick her tongue across his nipple ring. "I think they'd take my license away as soon as I took my whip to a client. But I suppose I do help men with certain components of their psychology—in an unconventional way."

"And I'm your magnum opus, I presume."

She shook her head. "You're my heart, baby."

He wrapped his good arm around her and drew her onto his chest. His heart thudded against her shoulder as he kissed her forehead tenderly. "I don't deserve you."

"I think I should be the judge of that."

Aggie's hand slid down his flat stomach, finding all his ticklish spots with ease. She wanted to hear him laugh. Maybe someday he'd manage it without her resorting to tickling.

The door opened, and Eric poked his head in. "Sounds like someone is having fun."

Jace's laughter died, and he grabbed Aggie's wrists to cease her tickling. He picked his cuff off the mattress and hurried to secure it around his scarred wrist. Aggie offered him a sad smile and fastened it for him.

Wearing nothing but his black boxer briefs, Eric entered the room and closed the door behind him. "Can I come in?"

"Aren't you already in?" Aggie asked.

"I meant in the covers."

"We aren't doing anything," Jace said. "Just talking."

"You? Talking? I didn't know you knew how." He crossed the room and dove across the bed beside them. "I'm so bored. Entertain me."

"You? Bored?" Jace said. "I didn't know you knew how."

Eric laughed and punched him in the shoulder. "It's all Sed's fault. Since he and Jessica got engaged, the only action he's been getting is between his ear and his hand."

Aggie cocked a brow at him. "His ear?"

"You're lucky you've been allowed to use the bedroom this

whole leg of the tour. You don't have to listen to him whispering into his phone all hours of the night and jerking off."

"Ah, phone sex. I would like to listen to that actually," Aggie said with a grin. "I bet he really gets into it."

"Actually, he tries to be quiet, but we all know what he's doing." Eric rolled his eyes. "Like Jessica would know if he fucked a groupie or two."

"She'd know." Jace chuckled. "Sed can never hide a guilty conscious."

"This is true," Eric said.

"You guys really don't have any privacy on this bus, do you?" Aggie asked.

"Nope. It's been the downfall of many bands. It's good we tolerate each other so well," Eric said. "I really miss Sed's performances though. And I don't mean his vocals. But I guess you two will have to do. Get busy." He propped his head on one hand and lifted his eyebrows.

"We really weren't doing anything but talking," Aggie said.

"What were you talking about?"

Her opening with Eric presented itself, so she took it. "Jace's father. How he died."

Eric glanced at Jace. "How?"

"I don't like to talk about it," Jace said.

"Do you have any other family?"

"Nope. No parents. No family."

Jace wriggled to get up, but Aggie sprawled her body over his and rested her head on his shoulder. She lay there like a dead weight to keep him from avoiding this conversation.

"Did you go into foster care?" Eric asked.

"I was fifteen with a criminal record. No one wanted to open their home to a derelict. I stayed in a group home for almost three years."

"Did you serve jail time?"

"Juvenile hall for a few months. For a couple of shoplifting charges—nothing too exciting."

"The key to being a good shoplifter is not to get caught."

"You shoplifted?"

"I was a holy terror as a kid," Eric said.

Jace snorted and stopped trying to weasel out from beneath Aggie. "Nothing's changed."

Eric chuckled. "Maybe, but I don't steal anymore. I've found other ways to get attention."

"So you never got caught?"

"I didn't say I was a good shoplifter. I got caught more than once. One of the many reasons I was shuffled from foster home to foster home. Never had to stay in a group home though. I hear those places are pretty rough."

Jace shrugged. "I lived."

"So how'd your dad die?"

"None of your bus—"

Aggie covered Jace's mouth with her hand. "He died in a fire," she said.

"Oh man, that would be a horrible way to go. Really sorry you lost him."

Jace tore Aggie's hand from his mouth. "Why? He was an abusive son of a bitch."

"Maybe. But he was your father. I'm sure you didn't want him to die."

"You would be wrong."

No, not the tough guy, Jace. Let your heart show, baby.

"Well, whatever. Are you two going to get down to business now, or do I have to go watch boring Internet porn?"

And now she'd lost Eric too. This was going to be more challenging than Aggie realized. She had to lower Jace's defenses and raise Eric's sensitivity. No problem. Yeah, right. Maybe some sexual intimacy would work—at least for getting Jace to relax. When she kissed him, his entire body stiffened. Well, except for the part she wanted to stiffen.

She lifted her head to look at him and found him glaring at her. "What's wrong?"

He glanced at Eric and then back at her. "Maybe I don't appreciate you telling people about my personal business."

"Don't know what the big deal is, little man. It's cool," Eric said. "I'm sure your past isn't half as depressing as mine was, but who gives a fuck? It's over, and you can't change it, so forget about it. Don't take it out on Aggie."

She looked at Eric. "No, Jace is right. If I crossed the line, then he has the right to call me on it." Her gaze shifted to Jace, who looked stunned by her words. "I apologize for interfering." But that didn't mean she was going to stop.

"It's okay," he said quietly, his eyes downcast.

This time when she kissed him, he responded with enthusiasm. He was so forgiving of everyone else. Why couldn't he forgive himself? She kissed her way to his ear. The one on the opposite side of where Eric was lounging, so Eric didn't overhear.

"I love you." She felt Jace's face grow warm against her cheek as he blushed. Ah God, he was so damn cute. She sucked his earlobe in her mouth, flicking his small hoop earring with her tongue. His cock stirred against her hip. She brushed her nose against his face as she whispered, "Do you want Eric to leave us alone? I'll kick him out."

"He can stay."

"Booyah!" Eric climbed from the bed and started removing things from the side table drawer. "I'm so fucking horny, I can hardly stand it."

Aggie chuckled and lifted her head to peer into the drawer. "Anything cherry-flavored in there?"

"If you use all of Trey's cherry-flavored oil, he'll never forgive you."

"I'll risk it."

Eric placed a tube in her outstretched hand.

She tossed the covers aside and slid down Jace's body. "Your turn, baby. I owe you some pleasure after last night."

"Did I miss something good?" Eric asked.

She drizzled cherry flavoring down Jace's hardening cock. "You missed something phenomenal, but I wouldn't have wanted you there anyway. The only one who gets to see me beg is Jace."

She loved the self-satisfied grin that crossed Jace's face. "I got plenty of pleasure out of the experience," he murmured. "You don't owe me—"

Jace gasped as she drew his cock into her mouth. He was rock hard in an instant.

"Hey, wait for me," Eric complained. He settled on the bed beside them, his head even with Jace's hip as he observed Aggie's motions. Aggie watched Eric out of the corner of her eye. He squirted oil in his palm and grabbed his cock, then stroked it with the same rhythm Aggie had found to pleasure Jace. She closed her eyes, focusing her attention on bringing Jace the most pleasure. She ran her hands over his narrow hips, drawing her thumbs over the ridges of his hip bones beneath his skin. He shuddered and grabbed her hair. She sucked him harder. His ragged breathing told her he was close. She pulled away and blew cool breaths over the head of his cock. Jace twitched uncontrollably for several moments until he regained control. Aggie held the base of his cock, rubbing her thumb up and down the underside. She drew the head into her mouth, working it between her tongue and the roof of her mouth, applying a light suction. She listened to his breathing as his excitement built again, waiting until he was close to letting go before drawing away. She eased his legs apart, dribbled cherry-flavored oil over his balls, then sucked and licked it off until he was writhing his hips in torment.

"What do you want, baby?" she murmured, licking the crease between his balls and continuing up the underside of his cock. "Tell me."

"Pussy," he gasped.

She grinned. "Mine?"

"Yes, yes. Please."

She moved up his body and straddled his hips. He grabbed his cock and directed it into her wet opening. He arched his back and thrust upward. She didn't drop down to meet him, but held her body suspended over his and watched him lift his hips to fuck her deeply.

She touched his face. "Settle down, baby. I've got you."

"Ah, Aggie, I can't take it."

He relaxed into the mattress after a moment. She sank down to take him deep. Her head fell back in ecstasy. She had wanted him to receive all the pleasure this morning, but there was no way not to take some for herself when he was buried inside her.

Eric shifted and rested his head on Jace's abdomen.

Jace tensed. "What are you doing?"

"I can see better from here," he said.

"Get off me."

"Don't deny me this, buddy. Please. I'm dying here."

Jace stuffed the sheet under Eric's head so his bare cheek wasn't touching Jace's naked belly. He made no further protest.

Aggie began to move. She couldn't decide which was sexier, Jace's face as she took him deep into her body, or Eric's as he watched and stroked his cock enthusiastically.

"You know why porn is so boring?" Eric asked. "There's no smell." He shifted his face closer to Aggie's pussy and inhaled. His eyes drifted closed. "Even more than the sights and sounds, it's the fucking scent that I can't get enough of. Or the taste." His tongue brushed against Aggie's clit, and she shuddered.

Jace grabbed a handful of Eric's hair and yanked him backward. "You're supposed to watch, not participate."

"I can't taste if I don't participate."

"Too bad."

Aggie was a little disappointed that Jace had stopped Eric. Her clit throbbed with excitement. She began to rise and fall faster over Jace's thick cock, rotating her hips to rub herself against his pubic bone with each downward motion. Eric had stopped stroking his cock. His oil-slick hand slid over Aggie's hip to her ass. Aggie's eyes met Eric's, and he smiled at her knowingly. Her gaze shifted to Jace. He had his eyes closed and was completely unaware that Eric was touching her, sliding his fingertips down the crack of her ass, slipping the tip of one long finger into her ass. She groaned and rocked backward. His finger slid deeper. Aggie's eyes drifted closed.

"What are you doing?" Jace asked.

"Her ass is lonely, Jace. Look at her. She likes it. She wants it."

She did, but only if Jace was okay with it. Eric slid a second finger into her ass, and she shuddered.

"Do you like that?" Jace asked.

She bit her lip and nodded slightly.

"Okay, then."

Eric shifted, and his fingers slid deeper.

"Oh God," Aggie groaned, grinding against Eric's hand and Jace's cock.

"I'm on it," Eric said.

He pulled his fingers out and moved to sit behind her. He straddled Jace's legs, sliding right up against Aggie's back. Eric took a moment to apply a condom and then she felt his cock against her ass. Slippery fingers lubricated her passage, and then he pressed the head of his cock inside her back entrance. She sucked a breath through her teeth. Eric grabbed her hips and pulled her downward. Her body strained to accept two cocks deep inside her. Full. Oh *God*, so full. She couldn't breathe.

Jace sat up, and she sank lower. She cried out, shuddering uncontrollably.

"What the fuck do you think you're doing?" Jace growled at Eric over her shoulder.

"Sharing?" Eric tried.

Aggie lifted her hips a bit, and their cocks slid out slightly. Even that little friction had her completely overwhelmed. "Oh God. Oh God. Oh God."

"She is totally getting off," Eric said. "Just go with it."

"Your balls are touching mine," Jace said between clenched teeth.

"What's a little sac connection between friends?"

Jace hesitated. "Aggie?"

"Too much," she gasped.

"You heard her, Eric. Pull out."

"You guys are killing me," Eric said.

"Deal with it."

Eric huffed, but backed out. Aggie exhaled in relief. Jace's thick girth was more than enough for her, but she had enjoyed Eric's long, thin fingers.

"What do you need to get off, baby?" Jace asked her.

"Honestly, Jace, I just need you," she whispered, "but his fingers felt amazing."

Jace and Eric exchanged glances over her shoulder. A few seconds later, fingers massaged her back opening in a firm circular motion. She groaned and ground her hips, hoping to coax one of those fingers inside. She held Jace's face between her breasts and kissed the top of his head, love welling up into her chest, her throat, her eyes. Her feelings for him were so strong that she thought they might suffocate her. Her Jace. So selfless. So giving. Oh, how she loved him.

When she released her hold, Jace dropped back on the bed and shifted his hips so she could ride him. She rose and fell over him, driving him deep and watching his face as they shared pleasure. Eyes closed, he bit his lip and gave her total control. Aggie's gaze moved to the cuff on his wrist. She unsnapped the wide bracelet and lifted his bare wrist to her lips, kissing the scars there. His eyes flipped open. *I love you*, she mouthed as she continued to kiss his wrist. He watched her as if fascinated. His slight smile brightened with each stroke of her lips.

"I'm getting bored back here," Eric said.

Jace stiffened as if he'd forgotten Eric was still present. Aggie chuckled.

"Then maybe you should leave," Jace said.

"If Aggie would just lean forward a bit, I could see better." Eric placed a hand on the center of her back and pushed until he was satisfied with her position. "That's better." Eric's fingers slipped inside her ass and pressed deep.

"Oh!" Her eyelids fluttered as attainment of release became her goal. Jace moved both hands to hold her breasts as she rode him harder and faster. He plucked at her nipples until she thought she'd go mad.

"That's it," Eric said. "Fuck him, Aggie."

She could hear Eric stroking himself behind her. She found herself moving to match his rhythm. Jace's back arched unexpectedly, lifting his hips off the bed and driving himself deep into Aggie's body. His eyes squeezed shut as he called out in bliss.

"Jace lost," Eric said. "He came first." He sucked a breath through his teeth. "I'm about to join him."

"If you come on me, I will kill you," Jace said to Eric.

He didn't come on Jace. He came on Aggie's ass. She felt his fluids hit her skin—warm and thick. "God, that's hot," Eric groaned and rubbed the head of his cock in his cum to spread it over her skin.

"You really need to find yourself a woman," she said. "Preferably a porn star."

"I'd rather share you with little man."

"Not sure why we let you participate," Jace grumbled. "I satisfy her better on my own."

Eric flopped down on the bed beside Jace. "Because I'm your best buddy, and you don't want me to die from a giant case of blue balls?"

"I don't think that's fatal," Aggie said.

"Have you ever had blue balls?" Eric asked.

She grinned and flipped her gaze to the ceiling. "Well…"

"They're not just for Smurfs."

Jace laughed and reached up to tug Aggie down against his chest to cuddle her against him. "Wouldn't that be a constant condition for them?"

"Poor little guys," Eric said with a troubled scowl.

"That probably has more to do with them only having one female in their species, more than their skin color," Jace said.

Eric laughed.

"I bet Smurfette gets a lot of UTIs," Aggie said.

Eric guffawed until Aggie thought he was going to pass out from lack of air. After several minutes, he wiped the tears from his eyes, still chuckling sporadically. "You guys kill me."

Aggie snuggled closer to Jace's chest. Did he see it now? How much he meant to Eric?

Eric stretched his arms over his head and yawned. "I could go for a nap. Are you going to finish her on your own? I don't have the energy. Haven't been getting enough sleep."

Jace rolled his eyes and shook his head. "You're worthless."

"Maybe," Eric said, "but at least I don't have a daisy tattooed on the top of my foot."

"Ass." Jace punched him in the arm and received a retaliating blow in return.

Aggie just grinned. Watching Jace's walls crumble was the greatest gift he could give her.

Chapter 35

JACE REMOVED HIS SLING and stretched his injured arm above his head. There was barely any pain now, but his strength had diminished significantly since he'd been wearing the damned thing. It was time to become proactive in his recovery so he could get back in the show. Screw Jon. This was Jace's band now. He was fucking sick of taking the backseat, not pursuing what he wanted, worrying about how everyone else felt. Jace left the tour bus and went to find Sed in the back of the equipment truck. Sed could usually be found there lifting weights, especially when he was sexually frustrated. Since he hadn't seen his fiancée in almost a month, he was bulking up like a Mr. Olympian contestant.

Jace climbed into the back of the truck. Though it was chilly outside, the air inside was stifling, thick, and moist. It smelled like an unwashed gym sock. Sed was bench-pressing twice Jace's weight, his bulging muscles straining against his skin.

Jace moved to stand at Sed's head and peered down at his red, sweaty face. "Need a spotter?"

Sed lifted an eyebrow, but instead of pointing out that Jace would make a piss-poor spotter, he nodded. "Sure."

Jace watched Sed do a couple of reps, hoping to God he never actually needed a spotter. With one useless arm, there was no way Jace could possibly hold that much weight, much less lift it off Sed's chest.

"Did you come in here for a reason?" Sed asked.

Jace shrugged.

"Hiding from your chick or something?"

"Nah, she's an angel."

"Eric?"

"Nope. We're cool." For once.

Sed grunted and lifted the metal bar to rest on the bench's stand. The truck rocked slightly with the shift in weight. Sed sat up and wiped his face on a towel. "Got a problem?"

"Kinda. I need to build up the strength in my arm. It's about healed, but…" He shrugged.

"Aren't you supposed to wear that sling for two more weeks?" Sed acted more like his father than Jace's actual father ever had. Jace had always found it comforting. He never wanted to let this guy down.

Jace ducked his head, disappointment sinking low in his chest. "Yeah."

Jace turned to leave the truck, but Sed caught him by the back of his shirt. "Let's see it."

He hesitated and then pulled his shirt off his arms and let it hang around his neck. The puckered skin of the scar on his upper arm looked a little less angry every day. He needed a mirror to see the one on the back of his shoulder, but it had healed shut as well. They no longer required bandages. The problem wasn't the wounds though. It was the loss of muscle mass from wearing that sling so long. Jace could see the difference in the size of his two arms, and apparently, so could Sed. He poked Jace's right biceps.

"You should start out pretty light and build up to heavier stuff. We'll get you evened out, but I don't want you to hurt yourself by rushing this. We've got Jon until you're better."

Jace pulled his shirt back in place, embarrassed by his puny arm in the company of ripped-beyond-belief Sed. "That's why I'm ready to get stronger. Now." Jace lifted his head, forcing his gaze not to waver. "I don't want Jon to take my place anymore."

Sed smiled, which always made him look less tough and reminded Jace that Sed really was a nice guy and genuinely cared about people. "I guess it would be boring to be stuck on the tour bus for a month and not get to be onstage. We'll get you back out there soon."

"I *never* wanted Jon to take my place," Jace clarified.

Sed scratched his head, looking perplexed. "But you wouldn't have been able to play a month ago. We would have had to cancel tour dates."

Jace's heart thudded. He knew his next words would make his feelings perfectly clear, and he had no idea how Sed would respond. Jace expected him to tell him to get lost. Permanently. "You did it for Trey."

"But there was no one readily available to take Trey's place like there was with you." A look of realization crossed Sed's face. "Oh." Sed blushed. Jace didn't know that Sed was capable of blushing. "If you felt that way, dipshit, why didn't you say something sooner?"

Jace rubbed the hoop in his earlobe. "It's selfish of me to feel that way."

"So what. We're not going to know how you feel about stuff unless you tell us. It doesn't mean it will change our decisions, but at least we'll understand where you're coming from. You're part of this band, too, you know?"

Sed hadn't told him to get lost. He had sort of chastised him though. Jace soaked it up like a sponge.

"I want back onstage as soon as I can get my strength up," Jace said, "but I don't want to suck. I want to play properly. I know I'm not ready for a full show yet. Maybe I can play half of the next show. A few songs at least."

"Whatever you think you can handle." Sed went to a rack of hand weights and lifted a set of fifteen-pounders. He handed them to Jace and selected forty-pound weights for himself. "Let's get busy then."

Sed put him through the ringer with repetition after repetition. The weight was far too light for Jace's left arm, but he struggled to lift even fifteen pounds with his right. He'd never let Sed know that though. He worked until his muscles refused to contract.

"You're done," Sed said.

Sed set his weights on the rack and took Jace's. Good thing. Jace probably would have dropped it on his foot. Sed set the weights down and then cuffed Jace on the side of his head. "Go rest for a while. We can work out again tomorrow."

"How about later tonight?" Jace should have recovered enough to move by then.

"You shouldn't overdo it, Jace."

Jace lowered his gaze. He preferred to work out with Sed. The guy was a body builder. Sed knew what he was doing, but Jace could do this on his own if necessary.

Sed chuckled. "You're really determined to get stronger, aren't you?"

Jace met his eyes. "Yeah."

"Then it's a date."

"A date?" a feminine voice said from the end of the truck bed. "Sorry, Jace, but I'm the only one he's dating for the next forty-eight hours."

Sed gasped, his eyes widening with shock as they located their guest. "Jessica."

"Hey, baby," she said, with a beautiful smile on her face. She climbed into the truck and dusted her hands off on her frilly white dress. The woman was amazingly sexy. No wonder Sed was already racing toward her. "Did you miss—"

Her words were cut off by Sed's enthusiastic kiss. He was hugging her so close Jace wouldn't be surprised if he broke her ribs. After a long moment, Sed pulled away and looked at her as if unable to believe she was really there. He touched her face, her long, strawberry blonde hair, and then settled both hands on her shoulders, tilting her back slightly so that her belly brushed against his sweaty, naked torso. "How did you get here?"

She laughed and cupped the side of his face. "Brian sent me a plane ticket. He told me to ditch school and get my ass to Canada before you spontaneously combusted. I'd have been here sooner, but I needed a passport."

"Brian did?"

"You're welcome," Brian said from the ground at the end of the truck. He had his arms crossed over his chest and looked pleased with himself. Jon stood beside him grinning, but when he noticed Jace, he scowled and slinked away.

"You two better make good use of that bedroom tonight," Brian added, "because Myrna will be here tomorrow, and we won't be leaving that room for two days."

Jace wasn't sure if Sed and Jessica even heard him. They were lost in each other's eyes. "You're all sweaty, baby," she murmured. "And damn, you're ripped. What have you been doing with yourself?" Her hands stroked his bulging biceps with obvious appreciation.

Sed's hold loosened. "Sorry, I didn't mean to get my stink all over you."

Jessica leaned closer and licked the sweat off his collarbone. Sed's body tensed. "I want all of you, Sed. All over me." Her hand disappeared between their bodies, and Sed gasped brokenly when she found her target. "Inside me."

Sed growled and claimed Jessica's mouth again. He turned, pressed her against the steel wall, and slid a hand under the hem of her skirt. He grabbed her thigh and lifted it to his hip, before grinding himself against her.

Jace doubted these two were going to make it to the bedroom.

He grinned. Sed was so in love with Jessica. It was wonderful to see. It was even more wonderful to experience it himself with Aggie. Yeah, he loved her. He wondered what she was up to. He hopped out of the truck, landing next to Brian, and left Sed and Jessica to get reacquainted in semiprivate.

"Put it in, Sed," Jace heard Jessica cry against Sed's lips as they walked away. "I can't wait…"

"That was a nice thing you did," Jace said to Brian.

Brian chuckled, and they made their way back to the bus. "I knew Sed was too damn stubborn to tell her how much he needed her here. And Myrna's too damn stubborn to come here no matter how much I tell her I need her."

"So how did you convince Myrna?"

"I made it seem like it was her idea. I think I've finally figured out how to get what I want. She's a psychologist, so she usually sees my manipulative methods coming from a mile away." Brian laughed.

Jace smiled, holding Brian's gaze. His intense, brown eyes were so much like Kara's it stole Jace's breath. And apparently, his ability to reason. "I probably shouldn't tell you this."

Brian paused. "Tell me what?"

"I dated your sister." He wasn't sure why he wanted to own up to it all of a sudden.

"Not possible. My sister has been dead for ten years."

Jace nodded. "Yeah. We were teenagers. We broke it off a few weeks before she…"

Brian's eyes narrowed suddenly. "*You're* Jason?"

Jace's heart skipped a beat. "Huh?"

"Are you the asshole who took her virginity and then never called afterward?"

Brian *knew*? How could he know? He'd never told anyone— with the exception of Aggie.

"I-I guess so."

Brian took a swing at him. Jace ducked instinctively.

"You fucking jerk," Brian growled. "She cried for weeks over you."

"She did?"

Brian's next swing hit home. Jace gladly took it in the chin.

"I thought she hated me," Jace murmured.

"No, *she* loved you. *I* hated you."

"I'm sorry, Brian. I had no idea. I never meant to hurt her."

"Well, you did." Brian considered him for a long moment. Jace wished he'd just hit him again and get it over with. Brian relaxed his stance instead. He cracked his knuckles. "God, that felt good. Do you know how long I've wanted to punch this Jason jerk in the face?"

"Ten years?" Jace guessed.

Brian laughed. "Yeah." He thumbed the bruise forming on Jace's chin. "You okay?"

"Yeah. I'm glad you hit me. I feel better now. That secret has been eating me alive."

"We'll never speak of this again. Got it?"

Jace nodded. "Got it."

They started toward the bus. "So are you and Aggie going to tie the knot?" Brian asked unexpectedly.

Tie the knot. As in *marriage*? Jace was so stunned by the idea he stopped walking in mid-stride. He stumbled, bumping against Brian's shoulder. Marriage had never crossed his mind. Not once. But wasn't that what a couple did when they were in love?

"No?" Brian squeezed Jace's shoulder. "I guess you're still pretty young. No need to rush it."

"Do you think she would?" Jace sputtered. "Marry. Me?" Why did his voice sound like he'd reentered puberty?

"You'll have to ask her."

Jace's brow crinkled. "Yeah. Maybe I will."

Aggie grinned when Jace came up behind her and wrapped both arms around her waist.

"I'm starving," he murmured. "Whatcha cooking?"

"Spaghetti. We have a guest." She covered his entwined hands with hers. "Jessica's here," she told him. "Brian just brought her in from the airport."

"Yeah, I saw her."

"Where've you been anyway? You were gone when I woke up." When she'd opened her eyes, Eric had been cuddled up against her naked body. She hadn't been comfortable being left alone with him and had been a little put off that Jace had abandoned her and not made Eric leave.

"I was working out with Sed."

"Is your body up to that?"

"It's up to fucking you a couple times a day. I think I can handle lifting fifteen pounds."

What had him out of sorts? "What's the matter, baby?" She reached behind her to run a hand through his soft hair. It was getting long, and his brown roots were showing again. She was glad he hadn't spiked it with gel today. It felt like silk against her fingertips.

"How do you feel about marriage?" he asked.

Her heart skipped a beat. "Marriage?" she sputtered breathlessly.

He stood there silently for a long moment. When she didn't say anything, he released her and backed away. "That's what I thought." He disappeared into the bathroom and shut the door before she could get a handle on what had just happened.

Did Jace want to *marry* her? Her? A trashy dominatrix from Vegas. As a doting wife? Surely he was just asking what she thought about marriage in general.

The stove hissed as her pot of spaghetti boiled over. She grabbed the handles and sloshed the excess water in the sink before returning the pot to the burner.

Marriage?

Where had that come from?

In all their time together, marriage had never crossed her mind.

She felt kind of guilty about that. How long had he been thinking about this? She walked down the hall and stood outside the bath-room door with her knuckles raised to knock. The sound of the shower being turned on made her pause. She didn't want to leave him to fester. She knew how he internalized the things that hurt him, but she needed time to think about this. She didn't think she'd ever get married. It hadn't been on her life's to-do list. But she loved Jace. Adored him. She didn't want to lose him. But marry him? She wasn't sure if that was best for either of them.

Eric leaned against the wall next to her. "What did he do now?"

Aggie glanced up at Eric's twinkling, blue eyes. "Who?"

"Jace."

"Nothing." She spun away from the door and returned to the stove to stir the spaghetti sauce. She checked the meatballs in the oven. Glanced over her shoulder at the bathroom door. Stirred the sauce. Checked the meatballs. Glanced at the bathroom door.

Eric hopped up to sit on the kitchen counter between the stove and the sink. "He did something," Eric insisted. "I've never seen you this upset."

"I'm *not* upset."

"Are too."

"Not."

"You can tell me," Eric said. "I'll help you straighten him out."

"He doesn't need straightening out."

Eric clung to the edge of the counter and swung his long legs, his heels bumping against the lower cabinet repetitively.

"Stop fidgeting," Aggie demanded. "You're driving me insane."

"Someone is cranky." Eric hopped off the counter and stood behind her to massage her shoulders. "Chillax. Everything will be okay."

As his strong hands worked her muscles, Aggie tensed further. She twisted away and brandished her spaghetti spoon at him. "Just go over there and sit down."

"Jace and I can work all that aggression out of you, sexy. Let's start without him."

When his mouth descended on the side of her neck, she tensed. Exactly what kind of claim did Eric think he had on her? He cupped her breasts and pulled her back against his hard body. She jerked away, spun around, and shoved him with both hands.

"I didn't say you could touch me, Eric."

His brow knitted. "I need permission?"

"Not only mine. Jace's too."

Eric grinned. "I'm sure Jace won't mind."

Aggie lowered her gaze. Eric was probably right. And why was that exactly? Shouldn't Jace be at least a little jealous of Eric touching her? Kissing her? Coming on to her? She knew if it ever came down to Jace choosing between her and his band, the band would win, hands down. Not that she would make him choose—but if he had to. He said he loved her. Most of the time, he acted like he did. But sometimes, she wasn't sure. She was so confused she felt like crying. Her lower lip trembled.

She squared her shoulders, turned her back on Eric, and returned to the stove. Forcing her turbulent thoughts from her mind, she drained the spaghetti and added it to the sauce. The meatballs went in next. She turned off the burner, grabbed the nearest jacket, and headed for the bus exit. "Dinner's ready," she mumbled to Trey and Brian as she passed the sofa. They watched her pass, and then exchanged troubled glances.

"Eric, what the fuck did you say?" Trey asked as Aggie stepped off the bottom step.

"Nothing, I swear! Let's eat."

Aggie slipped into the jean jacket she'd borrowed and headed toward the woods past the bus. She needed a moment away from the guys to collect her thoughts. She wasn't running away. She wasn't.

She entered the woods, autumn leaves crunching beneath her

feet. She circled behind the nearest thick tree and leaned against it, staring up at the darkening sky. What was she going to do? She never liked to think about the future. It never did what she expected— what she planned. She had to live in the now. She didn't know if she had a future with Jace. She was afraid to dwell on it too much in case things didn't work out with him. Why did he have to bring up that possibility now? Leaves crunched beside her. She wasn't ready to talk to him yet.

He stopped next to her.

"That's my jacket."

Not Jace. Jon.

She leaned away from the tree and started to remove the jacket, but Jon caught her arm. "It's okay. I don't mind if you borrow it."

She felt like she was wearing the opposing team's game jersey, but if she took it off, she knew she'd have to go back to the bus immediately. The temperature was dropping rapidly as the sun sank behind the horizon.

"What are you doing out here by yourself?" he asked.

"Getting some fresh air."

He leaned back against the tree beside her. "Stifling in there sometimes, isn't it?"

She nodded slightly.

"I know you don't like me."

It was that obvious, was it?

"I'm not always an obnoxious jackass. That's just what the guys expect. Can't let them down."

"I think they've grown up since you were with them originally."

Jon pulled a hand through his collar-length, wavy black hair. "I guess. I don't have much to offer. I know that."

He huffed a breath and stared at the few leaves still clinging to the barren branches above.

"Your guy," he said. "He has a lot of talent."

Aggie glanced at him, wondering what he was getting at.

"The band isn't ever going to take me back, are they? Not for real."

Aggie felt no need to protect this guy's feelings. "Probably not."

"Not unless something happened to Jace."

Aggie's heart thudded. "Is that some kind of threat?"

He rolled his smoky gray eyes and shook his head. "If it was a threat, would I have told you?"

His words didn't make her feel better. She needed to tell Jace what Jon had just said. Warn him that he needed to watch his back.

"I'm going inside," she said. "It's chilly out here." She headed around the tree and almost ran into Jace.

"What are you doing out here with Jon?" Jace asked from the near darkness.

She didn't know why she felt like she'd been caught cheating. Probably because she knew how much Jace disliked Jon.

"Nothing important."

"Why are you sneaking around in the dark? Tell me that."

Wait. Was Jace jealous? Of Jon? Aggie chuckled.

"Why are you laughing?"

"Don't you trust me, Jace?"

He hesitated. "Yeah, I trust you. But why were you out here alone with Jon? And isn't this his jacket?"

"I didn't know it was his when I grabbed it. Let's go talk inside. I'm cold."

"The *guys* are inside."

Aggie grinned at her sweet, predictable, tough angel. "Are you afraid I'll embarrass you?"

"Well, won't you?"

"Yeah, probably." She looped her arm through his. They had a lot to talk about, whether she was ready to face the future or not. That was what had her so freaked out. Mentioning marriage suggested Jace was thinking of the future in a big way. "I suppose Sed and Jessica are occupying the bedroom."

"Obviously."

"Where should we go so we can talk and I don't embarrass you in front of the guys?"

"We don't have to talk."

"Yeah, we do. You brought up marriage."

"It was a question, Aggie. I just wondered what you thought about marriage. I didn't mean—"

She found his lips in the moonlight and covered them with her fingertips. "We still need to talk. It makes me nervous too."

"It does?" he murmured against her fingertips.

"You're trapped by your past. I'm afraid of my future."

"Afraid?"

"Terrified."

She suddenly found herself in his arms, his lips against her forehead. "Don't be afraid, baby. I've got you."

But would he always? She snuggled closer. She actually found herself hoping—for a future. With this guy. Her heart thudded faster as her mind raced through possibilities, the good and the bad.

"Maybe both of us should concentrate on *now*," she suggested. "Forget the past. Don't worry about the future. Just *be*."

"If that's what you want."

"I'm not sure it's what I want, but I think it's all I can handle."

"Okay."

"But we still need to talk."

"Tomorrow?"

"Tomorrow," she agreed. "Let's go eat, and then you can take me to your bunk and have your way with me."

"The guys will hear us."

Aggie chuckled. "Like they don't hear us when we're in the bedroom."

"Just don't call me anything embarrassing like Sweet'ums McSugar Bear."

"I'd never called you that. What if I call you Huge Cock Master Pussy Delighter? Would that be okay?"

He laughed, and her heart warmed at the sound. "I guess I could live with that."

They entered the bus. Aggie took off Jon's jacket and tossed it on the sofa on her way toward the kitchen. The rest of the band was squashed together in the small booths surrounding the square table eating spaghetti. Jessica was sitting on Sed's knee. His hand rested against her lower back. He might as well have been growling *mine, mine, mine* under his breath. Aggie smiled, happy to see Jessica, but more happy to see her glowing. She'd always been a beauty, but with Sed beside her, she was radiant. Sed fed Jessica from his plate while she talked animatedly to Trey.

"I can't really talk about it, but Dean Taylor is still denying all fourteen counts of sexual harassment. If he was smart, he'd plea bargain. We have an incredible case against him." She accepted half a meatball into her mouth, chewing slowly.

"Do you think you're going to get through that class you had to retake then?" Trey asked.

Jessica swallowed and nodded. "Ellington and I had a long talk. She's transferred her hatred to the appropriate party. We get along okay now." She turned and rubbed her nose against Sed's. He grinned, showing a pair of dimples Aggie had never realized existed. He poked the other half of the meatball in her mouth.

"Eat faster," he whispered and glanced eagerly at the bedroom door. She chewed and swallowed.

"I'm glad everything is working out," Brian said, looking ill as he watched Jessica steal Sed's lips for a tender kiss. "I can't wait until tomorrow," he grumbled under his breath.

Jace handed Aggie a plate full of spaghetti and meatballs. She smiled with gratitude. "Thanks."

Jessica glanced up at the sound of Aggie's voice. "There you are," she said, with a bright smile. "I wondered where you'd disappeared to. Trey said Eric pissed you off."

"Not really." Aggie shrugged. But she needed to talk to him too. About their nonexistent relationship.

She looked at Eric, who sat in the booth lodged between Sed's big body and the wall. He concentrated on his meal and didn't acknowledge his name had been spoken. His dark brows were drawn together, his thin lips set in a harsh line as he chewed. Aggie had never seen Eric upset. He shrugged everything off as if life was some big joke. She hoped she hadn't hurt his feelings, because if she had that meant he *had* feelings for her, and she didn't want to deal with that. And she sure didn't want to become a rift between Eric and Jace.

As there was no room at the table, Aggie leaned against the counter, balanced her plate on her chest with one hand, and used her other to eat. With one arm trapped in a sling, Jace stood beside her and stared at his plate as if hoping his food would jump into his mouth.

"I'm full," Jessica declared.

"Finally." Sed rose from the table, tossed a giggling Jessica over one shoulder and rushed to the bedroom.

Brian shifted to the opposite side of the table so Aggie and Jace could sit next to each other and Jace could actually eat. They were halfway through their meal before Aggie noticed that Eric wasn't really eating. He was repeatedly stabbing one of his meatballs with his fork.

"What's wrong, Eric?" Aggie asked.

"He got his period," Trey said.

"Fuck you," Eric grumbled.

"Are you still moping, Eric?" Brian asked. "Trey didn't mean to hurt your feelings, bro."

"I was just fucking with you, dude," Trey said. "Some lucky girl will eventually fall for you. Marry you. Give birth to your ugly kids. You'll live happily ever after and all that shit."

"*You'll* probably find someone serious before I do," Eric grumbled.

"Party boy?" Brian jabbed a thumb in Trey's direction and laughed. "I don't think so. Who'd be crazy enough to get serious with him? He's about as monogamous as a salmon."

"A *salmon?*" Trey burst out laughing. Aggie chuckled with him and shook her head.

"I mean, even Jace is getting married," Eric complained.

Jace stiffened. Aggie's laughter died. They exchanged nervous glances.

"I *am?*" Jace said, his voice uncharacteristically squeaky.

"Since when?" Aggie demanded.

"I heard him ask you, Aggie," Eric said, looking annoyed by her obvious stupidity.

"He wasn't asking me to marry him." At least that's what he'd tried to tell her outside. Aggie's eyes widened with realization. Maybe he had been. Jace wasn't good at expressing himself verbally. She was well aware of that fact. Aggie's head swiveled so she could look at Jace. His face was the color of cranberries as he examined his plate with uncommon interest. "You weren't, were you?"

"*What?*" He glanced at the wall. "No. I already told you. I just wanted to know…" He squirmed against her, trying to push Aggie out of the booth. "Let me out. I need to go to the bathroom."

Trey laughed. "He was. Oh my God, Jace, how did you manage to fuck *that* up so spectacularly? She didn't even know you were asking her."

"Shut up, Trey. I wasn't." He surprised Aggie by lifting her hand to his lips. He kissed her knuckles gently. "If I was asking her, she'd know it."

She smiled, her heart melting. She leaned closer to kiss him, but hesitated when she realized it would embarrass him in front of the guys. He closed the distance, his lips stroking hers with incomparable tenderness. Her toes curled in bliss.

"Ha!" Brian said. "You owe me twenty bucks, Mills."

"Damn it." Trey pulled out his wallet and handed over a twenty.

Brian kissed it and slid it into his pocket.

Aggie leaned away from Jace and turned to scowl at the two guitarists. "What exactly did you two bet?"

Brian winked. "That Jace would never get mushy with you in front of us."

Wincing, Trey ducked to avoid Jace's gaze. "Sorry, Jace."

Jace laughed. "Why would you bet that?"

"He thought it was a sure win," Brian said. "But Trey's never been in love, so he doesn't know how it changes a man."

"I have *too* been in love."

Brian lifted his brows. "With who?"

Trey flushed and lowered his eyes. "No one you know."

"That's what I thought," Brian said.

Was Brian really that dumb? It was obvious who Trey was in love with. The only one who didn't recognize it was Brian. Aggie watched Trey hide his feelings behind a mischievous smile.

"Do you think Myrna will be in the mood for another one of our famous threesomes?" Trey winked at Brian.

Aggie's eyebrows shot up in surprise. From offhand remarks, she'd always assumed Myrna was straightlaced and prudish. Apparently not.

"Don't get your hopes up, Mills. I don't plan on sharing her with anyone this weekend," Brian said. "Besides, she's off birth control now. I don't want you guys naked within a hundred yards of her."

"Uh, how are we supposed to shower?" Trey asked.

Brian rolled his eyes in annoyance. "You can shower, dumbass. Just make sure you wear a condom."

Jace's lips brushed the back of Aggie's ear. Her amused grin faded, and she shuddered, goose bumps rising along her neck and shoulder.

"Let's go to bed," he whispered.

Oh, hell yeah.

Aggie took Jace's hand and tugged him out of the booth behind her.

"You kids keep it down in there," Trey said. "I don't think Brian can handle the sounds of two couples getting laid when he gets none."

"Abstinence is so not my thing," Brian grumbled.

"I told you I'd help you with that."

Brian shook his head. "I can help myself just fine, thankyouverymuch."

Aggie kicked off her shoes in the aisle near the sleeping area. "Which bunk is yours?" she asked Jace.

"Depends on who is in the bedroom. Since it's Sed, that would be the bottom bunk next to the bathroom."

She hesitated. "You don't have your own bunk?"

He shook his head. "There are only four, and we take turns in the bedroom, so I sleep wherever there's an open bunk."

She didn't know why that made her sad, but it did. That familiar need to hug him gripped her.

Before she could embarrass him by locking him in an affectionate stranglehold, he grinned. "Since you've been here, I've been getting way more than my fair share of the comfortable bed."

"I'll say," Trey said. "You dudes with the steady girlfriends always hog the bedroom."

At the mention of the bedroom, Aggie's attention focused on the sounds filtering through the door. Sed and Jessica were not shy about anyone hearing them, that was obvious. Jessica was particularly loud and enthusiastic, but it was Sed's low growls of appreciation that had heat flooding Aggie's loins.

Eric pushed Brian out of the booth. He threw his plate into the sink before storming out of the bus.

"What's eating him?" Brian asked.

"He likes Aggie. And what's not to like." Trey winked at her.

"Yeah, and he liked Myrna too," Brian said, "but he never got so bent out of shape about it."

"I'll go talk to him," Jace said.

Jace was going to talk to him? But what about…? She glanced longingly at the bottom bunk.

"I'll just be a few minutes," he murmured into her ear. "Will you wait?"

"I don't know," she whispered. "I'm pretty turned on right now. I might start without you."

She'd been teasing, but his little growl of torment set her systems to go. "I'll hurry."

He kissed her and headed out of the bus after Eric.

Aggie climbed into the bunk and tugged the curtain shut. She struggled out of her pants and tossed them onto the floor. Her shirt next.

She heard Brian curse under his breath. Poor guy. She couldn't resist making it worse for him. She slid out of her panties, and after twirling them around outside the curtain, dropped them on her growing pile of discarded clothes.

"Ah God, I can't take this anymore," Brian groaned.

When she dropped her bra on the floor, someone ran into the bathroom and shut the door.

"Brian, you should save that for Myrna," Trey called down the aisle. "Or me," he added too quietly for Brian to hear, but Aggie heard it.

―᎗―

Jace stood outside the bus, allowing his eyes to adjust to the darkness. This roadside park really was in the middle of nowhere. If it were a little warmer, he'd have asked Aggie to lie out under the stars. The brilliant flecks of white stood in stark contrast against the dark sky. A sliver of moon gave shadowy forms to the surrounding trees.

The gravel beside him crunched.

"Eric?"

"Not quite," Jon muttered and pushed past him to get on the bus.

Jace noticed a strange scent around Jon, but couldn't identify it. Not marijuana—something more chemical. Maybe he'd been cleaning a toilet.

Jace caught movement out of the corner of his eye. Eric stood leaning against the side of the bus sipping from his flask. The slim, silver container glinted in the limited moonlight.

Jace leaned beside him against the bus. The chill of metal at his back seeped through his T-shirt. He shivered. He missed his leather jacket. "You okay, man?"

"Why wouldn't I be?" Eric took a long swallow from his flask and gasped when he drew it away.

"I didn't think you'd get attached to Aggie. I just thought…" What had he thought? "She'd get more pleasure if you participated. I wanted her to enjoy really great sex. It wasn't supposed to mean anything."

"I'm not in love with her, if that's what you think."

Then what was his problem? Jace tugged on the earring in his right earlobe.

"It's…" Eric took another long drink. "I want what you have. What Sed has. What Brian has. No one has ever loved me. Not really."

Jace loved him—in a platonic way. He just wasn't drunk enough to say it.

"My mother abandoned me when I was four. She gave birth to me, and even she didn't love me." Eric scoffed. "You'd think at least her love would be guaranteed."

Jace considered telling Eric about his mother—how she hadn't loved her son much either—but he couldn't find the words. "The guys care about you." They were family. The only family Jace had. Didn't Eric see them that way too?

"It's not the same. I don't really matter—to anyone." Eric took a deep breath. "I appreciate that you came out here to cheer me up and shit, but I'll get over it. Tequila fixes everything." He attempted a sip, tipping his head way back, and then upended the flask over the ground. "Figures I'd run out of numbing juice this far from civilization."

"Wanna beer?"

"Nah. I need a few minutes to get my head on straight. Go back to Aggie." He attempted another sip from his empty flask, sighed, and then tucked it into the inner pocket of his leather vest. "Go on. You're bothering me."

Jace hesitated, wanting to make Eric feel better. He knew it was stupid to feel that way, but he didn't like Eric to be upset. "There's something you should know about me."

"I already know that you're short." Eric chuckled halfheartedly.

Jace took a deep breath. Everything was a joke with this guy. Jace pushed forward with what he had to say, even though he knew Eric would use it to make fun of him in the future. "You are the reason I am who I am today. *You,* Eric. You turned my life around. So if you think you don't matter to anyone, you're wrong. You matter to me."

Jace pushed off the side of the bus and walked back to the entrance. He blew into his hands and clenched them into fists for warmth. The tips of his ears tingled, and his butt was numb from the cold. There was a warm and willing woman waiting for him inside. He wondered why he'd stayed in the chill for this long.

"Wait. Jace?" Eric called after him. "What do you mean I turned your life around?"

Jace had already said too much. He lifted a hand in farewell and climbed the steps to enter the bus. He was looking forward to crawling into bed with Aggie. Or he had been, until he saw Jon sitting on the floor outside her bunk with his back pressed against the wall. He was talking quietly through the curtain and toying with her discarded panties with one finger.

Jace didn't need this shit right now. He didn't want to fight Jon anymore. He wanted him to go away—for things to go back to the way they used to be before he got shot—before he met Aggie. Everything had been a hell of a lot easier to deal with back then. He just had to regress inside himself, and everyone left him alone. Back when he'd played with the band, but not as one of them. Yeah, easier.

But lonely.

He sighed. He didn't want to go back to that place. Things weren't easier now, but they were better.

Jon noticed Jace standing at the top of the steps. He said something to Aggie, stood, and brushed past Jace on his way outside. Jace wondered what kind of lie Aggie would fabricate to explain herself. The traitor.

She pushed the curtain back and peeked into the aisle. When she spotted him, she smiled and beckoned him closer with a wave. Like everything was fine. Everything was *not* fine. She knew how much Jace fucking hated that guy.

On his way down the aisle, Jace passed Trey watching his *Greatest Moments in Baseball* DVD. Jace could hear the quiet rumble of Brian's voice from his bunk as he talked quietly on his cell phone. Sed and Jessica had fallen silent in the bedroom, which meant everyone would hear him when he confronted Aggie about Jon.

"What are you doing?" he asked.

"Waiting for you."

"With Jon?"

She covered her lips with one finger. "Get in here," she whispered. She shoved the curtain back, giving him a glimpse of her curvy, naked body. His thoughts grew thick with lust, but not so thick that she'd get off the hook that easily.

"I want a straight answer, Aggie."

"And you'll get one. Get in here with me."

He sat on the edge of the bunk, slumped forward so he didn't hit his head. "Why were you talking to him?"

"Take your boots off."

"Aggie," he said impatiently.

She sat up and leaned close to his ear. "Just get in here, and I'll explain."

He kicked off his boots and climbed into the bunk. It was a tight fit for two people, so after scooting and rearranging he ended up on his back, with Aggie on her side next to him, her back to the wall, her warm breath against his ear.

"I didn't really want to talk to him, Jace," she whispered. "I knew you wouldn't like it, but I was trapped in here naked. He wants to ask you something, but he's too afraid, so he wants me to ask you."

"He's afraid? Of what?"

"Probably that you'll punch him in the face again."

"Smart dude. So what is it?"

"Eric told him you were playing piano on the new album."

"A couple songs. So?"

"So if you're playing piano, who's going to play bass?"

"I'll record the two tracks separately, and then they'll mix them."

"But who will play it live?"

Jace's brow furrowed. He hadn't thought of that. "I don't know. The album isn't even done yet. Why is he asking about this now?"

"He doesn't want to lose the band. Not entirely."

"So I'm supposed to extend a hand of welcome?"

"That's up to you. He said he didn't want to go to the rest of the guys. He wants you to make the decision."

"That's weird," Jace said. "Why should this be my decision?"

"You're the bassist. He said after he heard you play live that he knew he was grasping at straws. He was hoping you might give him one last straw to cling to."

"I'll bring it up with the guys," Jace promised.

Aggie snuggled against him. "I love you."

Jace wasn't sure why throwing Jon a bone had her all sentimental, but he'd take it. He touched her soft breast with his fingertips.

She yelped. "Your hands are freezing!"

"Then warm them up."

"I'll warm *you* up," she said in a threatening tone.

He chuckled. "That's the idea."

Apparently, his idea of the best way to create warmth and her idea weren't quite the same. She tickled him until he laughed and squirmed himself off the bed. He hit the floor with a thud. Still laughing, he rolled over to climb to his feet. Unexpectedly, he found himself airborne as someone lifted him off the floor and tossed him back into the bunk.

"You lost something, Aggie," Eric said with a grin.

"Thanks, Eric. I wouldn't want him to get away."

"Keep him on a shorter leash."

Aggie's devious smile instantly had Jace warm and his pants tight. "Now there's an idea," she murmured.

He was glad she was already naked. It made it easier to fill his hands and mouth with warm, inviting flesh.

"I guess there's no room in there for me," Eric said and drew the curtain closed.

"Is Eric going to be okay?" Aggie whispered.

Jace released her nipple and slid up her body to look her in the eye. The light in the closed bunk was limited, and he couldn't gauge her expression. "He'll have to be. Call me selfish, but I'm not sharing you anymore. I'll have to be enough to feed your insatiable sexual appetite."

Aggie grinned, buried her fingers in his hair, and kissed him hungrily. When he tried to pull back to ask her about her lustful enthusiasm, she held him fast, her lips sucking on his, fingers digging into his scalp, mound gyrating feverishly against his rock hard cock. All rational thought escaped him. He immersed himself in the delight of Aggie's curves. Well, as best he could with the fucking sling pinning his arm against his body.

Her hands moved down his back to tug at his shirt impatiently. When she found her progress impeded by his sling, her hands slipped between their bodies and unfastened his pants. Both hands thrust into his open fly and pulled his cock free. She stroked him up and down vigorously between her palms, her fingertips dancing against his flesh. Jesus, he liked it rough like that. His breath caught in the back of his throat.

"God, baby, don't make me wait. Take me," she pleaded, squirming beneath him.

Why was she so eager? He didn't get it. He understood when she got this way after he spent hours teasing her body, but he'd barely had time to touch her. Hell, he was fully clothed. Was her excitement due to the guys being outside the curtain and able to hear her? Or because Brian was talking dirty to Myrna, jerking it, and groaning quietly in the bunk across the way? Or because Sed and Jessica had begun round two of their "who can vocalize the loudest" contest?

"Aggie? What's goin…"

He lost his train of thought as she slipped his cock into her warm, slick core and arched her back to drive him deep. He sucked a breath between his teeth. She bucked her hips against him, urging him into a deep, hard rhythm. The bunk had little room to maneuver, but it turned out to be a blessing in disguise. He planted his feet against one wall, and she lifted her arms above her head to hold herself stable against the other as he plowed into her with increasingly hard thrusts. He growled as instinct took over. All he could think about was claiming her, making her feel him. Taking her and all that she gave him, which was so much more than this. But God, this was what he wanted—to be inside her—part of her body. It couldn't get better than this. She lifted both legs and planted her feet on the bunk overhead, tilting her pelvis to increase the friction on the head of his cock. Wow. God, he'd been so wrong. It could get better. He thrust into her harder. Faster. His nuts were heavy, full to bursting, but he didn't want it to end. He wanted to fuck her like this forever.

She rotated her hips, rubbing her swollen clit against him, her hands somehow finding their way around his body to his ass and encouraging him to pump into her harder. She came with a startled cry, her entire body going rigid as her pussy clenched around him in hard spasms. *Yeah, baby, come for me. Come.* He almost followed her, but that would mean this would end, and he wasn't ready to stop.

"Jace," she called to him desperately. "Jace. Oh God, I love you. I love you."

And he didn't care that everyone on the bus could hear. He wanted them to. Wanted them to know that he'd somehow won this sensational woman's affection even though he knew he'd never done anything to deserve it.

Her hands moved from his ass to cup his face, and she kissed him passionately, still grinding her hips against him as he thrust into her.

"I'm sorry," she whispered. "I got carried away. The guys probably heard that."

"I don't mind," he assured her.

She paused. "You don't?"

He shook his head and nibbled on her chin while he continued to thrust into her body. "You know what I do mind though?"

"What's that?"

"That you stopped doing that thing with your hips. Feels real good."

She gyrated, squeezing his cock, releasing, squeezing, as her pussy muscles clenched with her motion. "Like this?"

His breath caught. "Ah God, Aggie."

"What about this?" She tilted her pelvis up and down, which changed the friction on the head of his cock from one pleasure point to another.

"Yeah, feels good too."

She worked her hips against him, the pleasure so intense, he knew he wasn't going to last much longer, but he was ready now. He wanted to let go and fill her with his seed. Find the release only she could offer. Not just the physical release, but the emotional one he'd never found with anyone but her. With Aggie. His Aggie. Sweet, tough Aggie.

"I'm coming again," she gasped. "Oh Jace. Jace. Jace!"

When her body went rigid this time, he thrust deep and let go. Muscles at the base of his cock contracted with rhythmic pulses of pleasure, bathing her insides with his fluids. His good arm gave out, and he collapsed on top of her. She wrapped both arms and legs around him and held him tightly as he trembled in the aftermath.

"I love you, Aggie," he whispered.

"What was that? I didn't hear you."

"I love you."

"Again. Louder."

"I love you!"

"Did you hear that guys? He loves me," she called.

"Oh, we heard that, and a whole lot more," Trey said from somewhere near the dining table.

"My balls hurt so bad," Eric moaned. "You realize there isn't any available pussy around for miles."

"I do realize that," Jace murmured. He brushed Aggie's hair from her cheeks and slid his slackening cock in and out of her a couple times. "Because this is mine."

"Fuck, yeah, it is," she murmured and kissed him.

"Will everyone shut up?" Brian called miserably from his bunk. "I can't do this with all that yammering."

Chapter 36

JACE SHIFTED THE BARBELL off its pegs and struggled to keep the bar even. His weak arm trembled immediately. Sed stood over his head as his spotter.

"I wonder when Brian will get back to the bus with Myrna," Sed said. "I hope nothing happened. They should have been here by now. We're going to be late for our show if we don't get on the road soon."

"They're probably screwing somewhere. You know how those two are. Even married, they can't keep their hands off each other." Jace lowered the bar to his chest and pushed up. Keeping the bar even was damned near impossible, but whenever it tilted, Sed pressed on the high end as a gentle reminder to work harder on the low end.

Jace tried to ease the dumbbell back on its stand, but Sed nudged it forward. "Three more."

Jace had already broken out in a sweat. The enclosed space in the back of the equipment truck made the air hot and heavy. Even with the back doors wide open, the circulation was minimal. Within minutes, Jace's entire body was drenched. His arm was so tired, he doubted he could lift a paper clip, but he lowered the bar, confident that Sed wouldn't let him crush his chest if he got into trouble. Jace gritted his teeth and pushed the bar up.

"Two more."

Again.

"One more."

His weak arm shook uncontrollably. He felt the weight slipping. Sed's hand hovered near the bar, but he didn't grab it.

"Focus, Jace. You can do this."

Jace couldn't explain the feeling Sed gave him. Always gave him. It was as if he wanted Sed to be proud—such a strange ambition. It did give Jace the fortitude to lift the bar one last time as he drew on strength he didn't know he possessed. Sed grabbed the bar at once and shifted it onto the stand. "That's it."

Jace forced himself to sit up.

"How did that feel?"

"Exhausting, but great. I'm getting stronger already. Thanks for your help."

"No problem." Sed added weights to the bar. "Spot me?"

Jace tried not to grin too widely at being asked, but he couldn't help it. No one else worked out with Sed. Just him. "Yeah, of course."

"Jessica can't keep her hands off me. I think it's the extra muscle. Must make sure I maintain it."

Jace figured it was her undying love, not Sed's impressive bulk, that kept her hands on him, but Jace didn't want to sound like a wuss, so he kept those words locked inside.

Eric hauled himself into the back of the truck. "Whatcha guys doing out here?"

"What does it look like?" Sed asked.

Eric's vivid blue eyes moved from Jace to Sed and back to Jace. "Having a 'who can sweat the most' contest? I think Jace is winning."

"He's working on getting the strength back in his shoulder and arm," Sed explained.

Jace braced himself for the dis that was sure to erupt from Eric's mouth.

"Good. Then we can send Jon home."

Jace was smiling like a dipshit now. When had things changed? When had these guys, who he'd always admired, even idolized, started to include him as one of them? Maybe they were just jerking him. He couldn't let his guard down too much. Jace remembered he was supposed to ask about Jon playing bass live in those songs Jace would play piano.

"We might need to keep Jon around," Jace said.

Eric and Sed stared in disbelief.

"For the songs on the new album where I play piano. Maybe he could play bass when we do those songs live."

"No," Sed said without hesitation.

"Why not?" Eric said.

"I caught him sharing a crack pipe with one of our temporary roadies yesterday," Sed said. "I fired the roadie on the spot. Jon's had his one and only warning. We can't get rid of him fast enough."

"Maybe if he has something to look forward to, he can quit the drugs," Jace said.

Eric nodded. "I agree."

Sed lay back on the weight bench and wrapped his large hands around the bar, flexing his fingers to find a good grip. "Doubtful."

"Think about it," Eric urged.

"I know he's your best friend, Eric, but the guy is bad news," Sed growled, lifting the weighted bar up and down as if he was at war with it.

Eric's brow furrowed. "He's not my best friend. He uses me. I know that. Jace is my best friend."

Jace's heart thudded until he realized Eric was teasing him again. The stupid follow-up joke never came.

Sed made a sound of exertion, and Jace helped him lift the weight bar onto its stand. Sed sat up and wiped his sweaty face on a towel.

"I don't know. We'll see what Brian and Trey think. As far as I'm concerned, Jon doesn't deserve another chance."

"I need to talk to him," Eric said. He hopped out the back of the truck.

Sed stood and picked up a twenty-five-pound dumbbell. He handed it to Jace. "Get to work. We need you back. Soon."

Loud arguing on the opposite side of the tour bus drew Aggie from her thoughts. She climbed from the log where she'd been sitting and watching a squirrel bury nuts beneath the leaf litter. She brushed her hands off on her jeans and went to investigate. Eric had Jon cornered against the bus.

"How could you do something so stupid again?"

"I don't know what you're talking about," Jon said.

"Sed told me about the crack pipe, Jon. You promised me. You begged and begged me to give you a second chance with the band. Said no more drugs. Reminded me how much I owed you, until I finally relented and promised the first time an opening presented itself, I'd get you in. How the hell was I supposed to know Jace would get himself shot, and I'd have to keep that promise?"

"Why are you jumping my ass? Chill. Sed won't catch me using again. I'll be more careful."

Eric growled in frustration. "You just don't get it. I promised Sed you were clean. I vouched for you, knowing Sed would hold me accountable for every stupid thing you do. I even alienated Jace to get you here, and you do this?" Eric shoved Jon against the bus with both hands.

Jon shoved him back. "Don't act all holier than thou, Eric. Do you really think this temporary stint makes us square? You still owe me."

"You think I don't realize that?"

"Then get the fuck off my case."

"How did you get Jace to ask us to keep you on? Did you threaten him?"

Jon laughed. "Do you really think I could threaten Jace? He

doesn't take shit from anyone but the four of you. I had Aggie ask. I knew he couldn't say no to her. She has him wrapped around her finger."

Aggie took a hesitant step forward. Gravel crunched beneath her shoes. Both men turned to look at her. "That nice guy routine last night was all an act, wasn't it?" she said.

"Just shut up," Jon said.

Eric cuffed him on the side of the head. "You know what? Just get the fuck away from me. I can't stand to look at you."

A taxi turned into the roadside. It drew to a stop beside them. Brian opened the door and tugged a beautiful thirty-something woman from the backseat as he climbed from the car. She wore a classy, plum-colored skirt suit and matching stilettos. What had probably been a neat, twist hairstyle was all mussed up as if *someone* had been raking his fingers through it. The woman couldn't keep her eyes, mouth, or hands off the lead guitarist, and he couldn't stop smiling.

"Myrna," Brian said breathlessly, "this is Jace's girlfriend, Aggie, and that guy is Jon. You've heard a bit about him."

Her pretty hazel gaze touched briefly on Aggie and Jon before returning to the reason she'd flown to Canada. "Nice to meet you both," she said. "I hate to be rude, but if I don't ride The Beast in the next five minutes, I'm going to die."

Brian laughed and tugged her toward the bus steps. "Now we wouldn't want that, sweetheart. Eric, would you mind paying the driver and getting Myrna's luggage from the trunk?" He said this without taking his eyes off his wife.

"I suppose," Eric said with a knowing grin.

The couple disappeared into the bus.

"Hi, Myrna!" Jessica said inside the bus. "How have you been?"

"We'll catch up later, Jess."

A moment later Jessica stumbled down the stairs, a blush staining her cheeks. "They made it as far as the sofa," she murmured.

"Oh hell yes," Eric said and entered the bus with Myrna's suitcase in hand. He didn't return. No doubt, he found a new couple to watch.

"So what do we do now?" Aggie asked.

"Looks like we've been banished to the pigsty bus." Jessica shuddered and rubbed her hands over her bare arms. Southern California girls did not have wardrobes suitable for Canadian autumns.

Sed and Jace came around the equipment truck, their bodies slick with sweat. Both looked entirely fuckable. Aggie wasn't the only one to notice. Jessica produced a sound somewhere between a growl and a purr.

"Why are you two standing out here by yourselves?" Sed asked, drawing Jessica against his body and doing something to her ear that made her shiver with something other than cold.

Aggie glanced around. They were by themselves. Jon had apparently slinked off somewhere again. Someone slammed the back door of the equipment truck. "We'll see you in Montreal," the roadie, Travis, called before climbing in the cab and pulling out of the roadside stop. A moment later, the pigsty bus followed, leaving them to stand there in the chill.

"Brian and Myrna have commandeered the living area of the bus," Jessica said. She traced a bead of sweat down the side of Sed's neck with one finger until it disappeared into the low neckline of his white tank top.

"Does that mean the bedroom is available?" Sed said in a low growl.

Eric poked his head out of the open bus door. "Aggie, Brian wants to see you."

Aggie's brow knitted with confusion. She touched a hand to the center of her chest. "Me?"

"I think you've been volunteered for one of Myrna's sexual exploration experiments."

Chapter 37

AGGIE CLIMBED THE BUS steps and found Brian and Myrna breathless on the sofa, still fully clothed, looking simultaneously hungry and satisfied. Myrna was straddling Brian's lap, her skirt hiked up around her waist, his cock buried inside her. He was whispering, "I love you," into her ear repeatedly.

"Eric said you wanted to see me," Aggie said.

"Do you do couples?" Myrna asked.

Aggie's hackles rose. "Do I *do* couples?"

"She doesn't mean it like that," Brian said, dropping a tender kiss on his wife's temple. "She means do you instruct couples on the proper way to, you know… do what you do?"

Oh!

Oh, yeah…

Every nerve in Aggie's body shifted into high alert as Mistress V clamored to be set free. She loved working with couples. Teaching them. Helping them explore their dark sensuality together. It was her favorite thing to do in the dungeon. Unfortunately, it wasn't possible here. "There really isn't the space to do this properly, especially when the bus is in motion," she said. "When we get back home, I'll invite you over for some couple's *therapy*."

"And us too?" Sed asked from the front of the bus. Jessica's head snapped up to stare at him in surprise. He wrapped an arm around her as the bus started forward and eased onto the highway.

"Sure," Aggie said. "I love to see big, tough guys beg for mercy."

"And I get to watch, right?" Eric said.

"And they'll all practice their techniques on me, right?" Jace murmured.

Aggie chuckled. "You'd like that, wouldn't you?"

Jace nodded eagerly.

"We should go into business together, sweetheart. We'd have quite the partnership. I'd get to boss a bunch of dommes around, which is so much more fun than watching men crawl around at my boots. You'd get all the pain you could ever want. We'd be in seventh heaven."

He stroked her hair from her cheek tenderly. "I'm already there."

"Hey guys!" Dave shouted from the driver's seat. "It's snowing."

Aggie had never seen snow fall.

She rushed to the front of the bus to stare at the gray sky. Large, fluffy snowflakes flew toward the wide windshield, accumulating on the wipers and slowly painting the desolate landscape white.

"It's beautiful!" she said, watching the flakes zoom toward them. "It looks like we're traveling in space at warp speed."

"Are we going to make it to Montreal on time, Dave?" Sed asked as his brow furrowed with concern.

Coming to stand behind her, Jace wrapped both arms around Aggie's waist and rested his chin on her shoulder to watch the snow through the windshield. She covered his hands with hers and relaxed against him. A few weeks ago, he never would have embraced her in front of *the guys*. He'd grown so much since she'd forced her way into his life, but not half as much as she had.

Dave's attention drifted to his speedometer. "We should. Do you want me to push the pedal to the metal?"

"Are the roads slick?"

"Not yet," Dave said.

"Better safe than sorry," Eric called from the dining area. He leaned against the counter and pulled his lucky rabbit's foot out of his pocket to rub it with his thumbs. He kissed it seven times for good measure.

"What the fuck is that?" Myrna yelled.

Aggie could hear her even through the closed bedroom door, where she and her husband had disappeared to continue catching up. Brian said something in response to his wife that Aggie couldn't make out, but he sounded apologetic.

The bedroom door burst open. "Eric Sticks, I'm going to fucking *kick your ass*," Myrna bellowed. She had lost her jacket and blouse but didn't seem to care that everyone on the bus could see her bra.

Eric grabbed Jessica, who had been kneeling in a captain's chair snow-gazing along the side of the bus. Eric used her as his human shield. "What did I do, Myrna?"

"How *could* you? On his ass, Eric. Brian has a fucking kitten riding on a unicorn permanently etched on his *ass!*"

Huh? Aggie glanced from one band member to the next, having no idea what they were laughing about.

"Hey, the rainbow background was Jace's idea," Eric said.

Myrna went after Eric with a paddle. She struck him twice before he managed to escape.

"I have one too," Trey said.

He shucked his jeans and presented his bare ass to the bus occupants. A vibrantly bright and colorful tattoo of a fluffy calico kitten riding a galloping, majestic unicorn adorned a third of Trey's left ass cheek. A rainbow and wispy, white clouds surrounded the mythical creature. Little girls would be ashamed to have that feminine monstrosity on their lunch boxes. Why would a guy have that tattooed on his ass? Correction—two guys.

Aggie joined the laughter. Clutching his abdomen with both arms, tears pouring from his eyes, Sed was lying on the floor, rolling back and forth in the aisle as he laughed. Myrna paused and ran a hand over Trey's flank as she inspected the "artwork" that matched her husband's.

"Son of a bitch! You inflicted Trey with that grotesque thing too? I'm going to kick your ass twice, Eric Sticks."

"It's not my fault. They lost the bet," Eric shouted. Trapped in the corner between the bathroom and bedroom, he tried to catch the end of Myrna's paddle as she struck his thigh.

"You can hit me if you want, Myrna," Jace said, grinning. "I did suggest the rainbow background."

"I'm not going to hit you, Jace Seymour," Myrna growled. "You'd *like* it."

"If I wasn't so scared of you right now, I'd tell you how hot you look in your bra, Myrna," Eric said. "You're giving me such a boner."

She hit him harder.

The interior of the bus dimmed as it entered a tunnel. Aggie squinted out the windshield. Ahead, she could see daylight and something flashing red. Hazard lights?

"Dave? I think someone is stopped up there," she told the driver.

"I see him," he said and eased off the accelerator. When they emerged from the tunnel, they came upon a truck parked halfway in the road. Its owner was putting chains on the tires. With no time to stop, Dave veered left to avoid the truck. The bus skidded toward a guardrail on the opposite side of the road. Slamming on the brakes, Dave veered right and narrowly missed the truck.

A patch of ice sent the bus spinning sideways around a hairpin corner. The vehicle tipped onto two wheels. Aggie reached for the back of his seat for balance. A loud horn—like that of a semitruck—sounded a warning.

"Oh fuck!" Dave yelled as headlights approached at high-speed.

Someone grabbed Aggie around the waist just as the semi clipped the right side of the bus and sent it spinning in an uncorrectable circle. The back of the bus hit the guardrail, sending everyone tumbling to the floor. The sounds of shattering glass, rending metal, and her own scream ricocheted through Aggie's mind. The bus flipped on its side.

Jace held onto Aggie as they tumbled through the interior, banging against hard surfaces and sharp edges as the bus rolled side over side. It slid sideways across the pavement—metal grinding—and finally, lurched to a sudden stop as it crashed into something solid.

—⁓—

Jace took a shuddering breath, holding Aggie's head against his pounding heart. Completely limp, she lay sprawled over his body. *She's dead*, he thought. *Aggie's dead.* Just like every other person he'd ever loved. Aggie was dead. Crippling anguish washed over him. Sharp talons pulled his heart and soul apart in every direction. He drew her nearer, wanting to follow her in death, rather than face life without her.

After a moment, she stirred. Moaned.

"Aggie?" His voice cracked.

"Jace," she whispered.

His arms tightened around her. He opened his eyes, but everything was blurred by the tears. "Are you okay?" he said hoarsely. "Aggie?"

"I think so." She tried to move away, but he was incapable of releasing her from his hold. "Let go, Jace."

"I can't." He kissed the top of her head. "I can't let you go. Not ever."

"We need to get out of here now. You can hold me forever *later*."

She was right. They did need to get out of the bus and make sure everyone else was all right. He forced himself to release her and recognized they were lying on the sofa's back—except it wasn't in the appropriate orientation. The side window Jessica had been looking out of not five minutes ago was broken out and facing skyward. The bus was resting on its driver side. Someone helped Aggie climb from Jace's body.

Sed. He had a gash on his temple and blood running down the side of his face, but had never looked more solid. Aggie took a step toward the back of the bus, glass crunching beneath her feet. "You can't get out that way," Sed said. "There's a cliff."

"Where are the others?"

Looking physically ill, he shook his head. "I don't know."

Sed boosted Aggie out of the broken window above. She scrambled from the bus.

An acidic smell filled Jace's nose and burned his eyes. The bus filled with smoke. Sed helped him to his feet. "We have to get out of here," Sed said.

"Is everyone okay?"

Sed didn't answer, but looked anxiously over his shoulder. Jace followed his gaze. The back half of the bus was missing, and beyond the torn edge lay open space—an endless chasm beyond a cliff.

Chapter 38

AGGIE STOOD ON THE side of the bus that now faced skyward and looked at the debris littering the road. The back of the bus had not plummeted over the edge of the cliff as she had first suspected. It was yards away at the entrance of the tunnel buried under an avalanche of enormous logs. The semitrailer that had been carrying the timber was on its side against a rocky embankment. The truck that they'd swerved to avoid sat untouched near the end of the tunnel. Its owner was yelling into a cell phone—hopefully calling for help. Jessica was sitting in the middle of the road, clutching her head in both hands and screaming Sed's name. Aggie was too stunned to tell her Sed was okay. Her brain and body operated in slow motion. She watched Brian pull Myrna from the wreckage. Trey wriggled out next. Aggie waited for the one person unaccounted for, her heart thudding as if it were stuck in a time warp.

"Eric?" Brian called into the wreckage.

No answer.

"Eric!" Trey yelled.

Still no answer.

Sed scrambled over the side of the bus and ran toward Jessica. He drew her into his arms, and they clung to each other, oblivious to the chaos. A hand settled on the small of Aggie's back. She turned to look at Jace. He had little bleeding cuts all over his face from being pelted with broken glass, and grime blackened his skin, but she could honestly say he'd never looked better.

"They're all okay then?" he asked breathlessly.

"Eric," she whispered.

His face fell. He climbed down the undercarriage of the bus and helped her to the pavement. Aggie's ankle protested when she put weight on it, but she ignored it. They ran and limped, hand-in-hand toward the back of the bus. "Where's Eric?" Jace asked a bewildered Trey.

"I think he's still inside."

"Did you see him in there?" Jace asked Trey, trying to crawl between two logs that were arranged like a giant game of pick-up sticks around what was left of the bus. "Did you see Eric?"

"How are we alive?" Trey murmured, his green eyes distant and glazed over. "How are we alive? We should all be dead."

"Eric!" Jace called, pushing a log with his shoulder. It refused to budge. "Eric!"

"Li-little man?" Eric's barely detectable voice came from deep inside the bus.

"He's alive," Jace said breathlessly.

He thrust an arm into the open space between two logs. "Grab my hand, Eric. We'll get you out."

Inside the bus, Eric gasped in agony. "Can't move. My leg is trapped."

Jace squirmed to extend his reach. "Try, Eric. Grab my hand."

"I guess I don't have to wonder when the new album's curse is going to get me anymore." Eric chuckled.

Count on Eric to make a joke at the least appropriate time. Aggie couldn't help but grin and roll her eyes.

"I need a few more inches, and I can get in there," Jace said as he attempted to squeeze between the logs.

"Wait for the emergency crew," Brian suggested.

"We're miles and miles away from emergency services," Jace said. "It will take too long for them to get here."

Aggie knew Jace wouldn't be able to stand there and wait while Eric was trapped. She squatted next to Jace to see if there was a way to help.

"Sed," Jace called over his shoulder. "Do you think you can move this log?"

Sed kissed Jessica's cheeks and released her. When he moved away, she made a sound like a wounded animal. "It's okay," he promised. "I'll be right back." He approached the bus. "Where are you, Eric? I don't want to crush you with one of these logs."

Eric laughed. "I'm in the fucking bathroom. My foot is stuck behind the toilet. I can't get it loose."

"But you're okay?"

"I think so. I-I smell gas though."

"The bathroom always smells like that," Sed said.

Eric laughed. "True."

Sed grabbed the log blocking Jace's entry and growled with exertion, his muscles bulging as he lifted it several inches. Jace scrambled into the wreckage, trapping himself voluntarily to help a friend. Aggie's chest swelled with pride. "You're so brave, baby," she said, tears streaming down her cheeks. "So selfless. I love you so much."

Sed released the log, and it settled back in place.

She could see a bit of Jace's white T-shirt in the interior darkness, but nothing else. "Be careful."

Aggie heard debris scatter as Jace picked his way through the bus to the bathroom.

"It's a good thing you're so little, man," Eric said. "No one else could have squeezed in here and saved me. Ow, fuck, dude, my leg doesn't bend that way."

"It does now," Jace said. "Why are you wet?"

"Uh, toilet water. Hello."

"I hope the last person to use it remembered to flush."

"Thanks for adding to my list of concerns, little man."

Jace chuckled.

After several minutes of grunting, Eric cried, "I'm free!"

"Now, how do we get out of here?" Jace asked.

"No idea."

"How did you guys get out?" Sed asked Jessica, who was clinging to his waist. He touched her hair.

"U-under the dining table," Jessica managed to say.

"Try under the dining table," Sed yelled.

After a moment, Jace and Eric found the route out. "Thanks, tripod," Eric said, holding his weight off his left leg, while hugging Jace so hard his feet lifted off the ground.

"Tripod?" Jace asked.

"As hung as you are, you practically have three legs."

Jace laughed and patted Eric on the back enthusiastically. "I don't care if you call me little man. I'm okay with it."

"Don't lie. I know you hate it. I'm calling you tripod from now on."

Beneath the grime and sweat, Jace blushed. He glanced at Aggie out of the corner of his eye. His brilliant smile made her heart sing.

"I'm glad everyone is accounted for," Brian said, his arms around Myrna, who was impossibly calm in her half-naked state. "I think I shit my pants. What a ride!"

"We are the luckiest motherfuckers on the planet," Sed said, and wrapped his arms around Jace and Eric, squishing Jessica between them. Brian drew Myrna and Trey into the circle against Eric's back.

"You don't think I'm stupid for hanging seven horseshoes on the wall now, do you?" Eric said.

"We still think you're stupid, Eric," Brian said.

"But we're glad you aren't dead," Trey added.

Someone's arm snaked around Aggie's waist, and she soon found herself trapped in the middle of a group hug. These guys. Family.

No other word described them. She was glad to be part of what they shared. And doubly glad that Jace had them in his life.

Jace suddenly jerked away from the group. "Where's Dave?"

Chapter 39

Jace turned his gaze toward the front of the bus. Smoke billowed, thick and black, from the broken window that he, Aggie, and Sed had escaped through not fifteen minutes ago. Flames licked the opening. He was running in that direction before his mind could grasp the severity of the situation.

Jace headed to the front of the bus and peered through the windshield. Dave's unconscious form was suspended from the driver's seat by a seat belt. The interior behind the driver's compartment glowed an ominous orange. *Fire.* Jace's heart froze. The person he saw in peril was not Dave. He saw his father surrounded by the flames.

"Father!"

Jace pounded on the window, trying to rouse him. "Wake up!" He fisted both hands, and using his one-hit-knockout punch, struck the glass. It broke. A hole burst through the middle of a spiderweb patterned crack. He hit it again, widening the hole. Jace grabbed his father by his pale yellow polo shirt. "Father! Don't die. Don't be dead. I'm sorry. I didn't mean to. It was an accident. I…"

Someone broke out more glass from the windshield. Hands struggled to release the seat belt. The heat of the flames brought Jace back to the moment. Dave, not his father, came free from the seat. Jace took a stuttering breath and followed Sed, who was carrying Dave from the burning wreckage. A safe distance away, Sed laid Dave's limp body on the pavement. There was something unnatural about the angle of Dave's neck.

Eric listened to his chest. "He's not breathing." He started CPR while everyone looked on anxiously.

Jace shook so hard his legs gave out. He dropped to his knees on the asphalt. Aggie appeared before him. His demon in black. No, his angel. His salvation.

Her fingers stroked his hair so tenderly it made his heart swell. He didn't understand it. What had he ever done to deserve this wonderful woman? He wrapped both arms around her waist, buried his face against her belly, and sobbed.

"I've got you, baby," she whispered.

The pain inside was unbearable—worse than anything in his experience. He couldn't breathe. "It hurts," he gasped. "God, it hurts. Mercy," he begged her, rubbing his face against her belly. "Mercy, Aggie. Mercy."

"Let it go now." Aggie's fingers tightened in his hair. "Just... let go, Jace."

Let it go?

Yeah. Let go.

Oblivious to anything but the pain searing his soul, Jace cried. He released fifteen years of torment in a flood of tears and snot and sweat and blood at the feet of the woman he knew he could not live without.

Chapter 40

AGGIE TRIED TO PICTURE everything Jace was showing her, but it just looked like a huge, empty basement to her.

"You can build at least two soundproof rooms for your dungeon down here," he said. "And a sewing room. A storage room. Whatever else you want. It's yours to do with as you please."

"Are you sure, Jace? It will be incredibly expensive to have everything done."

"You know it's really for me, don't you?" He kissed her lips and tugged her against his chest. "Besides, my lady needs her slaves."

"I don't know a man who would pay to have the basement in his brand new house converted into a dungeon for his girlfriend." She hadn't expected this when he'd asked her to move to LA and live with him. She figured she was going to have to redefine herself and give up most of the things she loved so she could make a new life with him. She'd been willing to try, but Jace didn't want her to change. He loved her for who she was and supported her in whatever she wanted to do. He never ceased to surprise her. And she'd never stop loving him for it.

Jace lifted her left hand and slid something onto her ring finger. "But he'd do it for his wife, wouldn't he?"

Aggie's eyes widened as she stared at the sparkling marquise-cut diamond on her finger. "Um…"

"Are you actually going to make me ask you?" he murmured into her ear. She could feel the heat of his blush against her cheek.

She forced her eyes to his before they returned to the ring. Whoa. It was gorgeous. And huge. And sparkly. And… and… Jace had given… Did this mean… Was he asking her to… *Really?* Her thoughts scattered like dandelion seed. "Um…"

"Okay, I'll ask you properly, but do I have to do it on my knees? You've got men begging on their knees all the time. It seems stupid to propose that way."

"Um…"

When he started to kneel, she caught him around the neck, crushed his face into her chest, and squealed. "Oh my God." Aggie had always imagined herself being cool, calm, and collected *if* someone got up the nerve to propose marriage to her. She'd also prepared a speech on how to refuse the little worm audacious enough to ask. As with her every interaction with Jace Seymour, things didn't go as planned. "Yes. Yes. Yes. Yes!" she cried, tears flying. She kissed every inch of his face as he laughed at her enthusiasm.

He caught her mouth with his and kissed her tenderly until her toes curled, and she clung to him in need.

"Let's go upstairs," she said huskily. "Break in that new bed of yours."

"You mean that new bed of *ours.*"

"Yeah." She couldn't stop smiling. Lord, the man made her happy.

The doorbell rang. Jace's cat, Brownie, sat at the top of the basement stairs and meowed down at them.

"We have a guest," Jace said.

"One of the guys?" she asked, eager to see any of them. She missed not being on tour with them, but they'd cut the Canadian leg of the tour short until they could get a new bus. And find a replacement for their live audio engineer.

"Eric's supposed to stop by so we can visit Dave later. He's being moved home from the hospital today. Do you want to come with us?"

"Of course."

Doctors had told Dave that he'd be paralyzed for life, but apparently, the guy didn't think much of their opinions. Six weeks into his recovery, he wasn't walking *yet*, but a man with that much determination would not be kept down for long. "So that must be Eric then."

The doorbell rang again. "You know Eric never bothers to ring the doorbell," Jace said. "I think it's probably someone else." He released a nervous laugh and ran a hand over his bleached-blond spikes.

Someone else?

Jace led Aggie to the front door, pressing kisses to the knuckles of her left hand. It made her acutely aware of the ring he'd put on her finger. "You are not allowed to hate me for this," he said.

"I could never hate you."

He opened the door.

On the front step, beneath the sweeping portico, stood Aggie's mother.

"You told her where we *live*?" Aggie screeched. She'd purposely not told her mother her new address, hoping that would deter her from moving in with her. Mom had not been pleased when Aggie had put her house in Vegas on the market.

Mom scowled and reached into her purse for a cigarette.

"No smoking in the house," Jace said. "Come in."

Mom took a deep breath and removed her hand from her purse. "I can't stay long."

Aggie rolled her eyes. She'd heard that before.

Jace offered Mom a sad little smile. "Could you stay here for a minute?" he asked Mom. "I need to speak to Aggie alone."

He took Aggie by both arms and led her into the living room off the foyer. Aggie's eyes landed on the beaten-up piano in the corner. It had belonged to Jace's mother. Using what little Jace knew about its whereabouts, Aggie had searched for weeks and finally found it stored in the basement of the school Jace's father had donated it to years ago. Aggie would never forget the look on Jace's face the first time he'd played it for her. Contentment. Acceptance. Love.

Jace pressed Aggie onto their new leather sofa and sat on the marble-topped coffee table in front of her. Both stylish pieces clashed horribly with the battered piano, but Jace had wanted the instrument close. He played it every evening he was home. His silly cat always batted his feet as he worked the pedals.

"I know you're mad at her," he said.

"Mad? No. She makes me crazy. She's intrusive."

"She has something important to tell you. Listen to what she has to say." He took her hand and kissed her knuckles. "For me."

"For *you*?"

"I wish I'd had the chance to make amends with my parents before they went. It would have saved me years of gut-wrenching agony. You have to take this opportunity to set things straight. Not for her. And not really for me. For you."

Aggie cupped his cheek, knowing how hard it had been for him to let go of his past and forgive himself. He wanted to save her that life-crippling regret. She'd never figure out what she'd done to deserve this wonderful, caring, understanding, selfless, brave, loving man, but she'd be forever grateful that she'd found him. That he was hers. Aggie nodded, unable to refuse his simple request. "Okay. I'll hear her out, but if she claims the spare bedroom, I'm tossing her out on her fanny."

He squeezed her knee. "Do you want me to stay while you talk to her?"

She hesitated and then nodded. The man gave her strength, and she was pretty sure she would need it to stand up to her mother and tell her no. Jace stood, kissed her gently, and went to retrieve the woman from the foyer. Aggie was surprised she wasn't puffing on a cigarette when she entered the room. Jace directed Mom to the deep blue, semicircular chair, and then sat beside Aggie on the sofa. He took her hand in his, offering nothing but infallible support.

"Is Maynard listening in?" Mom asked, nodding at Jace.

"His name is Jace."

"I know what his name is."

"He will soon be my husband," Aggie said. Saying it for the first time made her heart flutter with happiness. "Anything you have to say, you can say in front of him."

"Oh," Mom gasped quietly. Her eyes sought the ring on Aggie's finger. "Marriage? *Really?* Well, congratulations... I guess."

Aggie rolled her eyes. Was it possible for her to say anything that *didn't* make Aggie want to slap her?

"Thank you," Jace said, blushing crimson under his beard stubble. Aggie's heart did that warm, melty, fluttery thing it did every time she looked at him. She grinned, and he lowered his lashes over his chocolate brown eyes.

"Gary is waiting for me at the hotel. I can't stay long."

Aggie gaped at her. "Gary? Loser Gary?"

"He's not a loser. We got married a few weeks ago. He's taking me on a honeymoon. To Hawaii."

"You got married?" Aggie sputtered. "How come this is the first I've heard of it?"

"I didn't think you'd approve," she said quietly.

"Congratulations," Jace said and squeezed Aggie's knee. *Hard.*

She glanced at him in question, and when she met his eyes, he gave her mother a pointed look.

Aggie sighed. "Congratulations, Mom. I hope you have a long and healthy relationship with Loser. He was one of my most well-behaved slaves."

Jace choked.

Mom lifted her gaze to Aggie's. Aggie was surprised to see tears on Mom's clumpy lashes. "I know I don't make good decisions." Mom sighed, looking defeated. "I do love you, Aggie. You must know that. I'm sorry I wasn't a better mother."

Aggie stared at her. At least she was admitting she hadn't been a good mother. Never the mother Aggie had wanted or needed. It was a start. Aggie took a deep breath and clung to Jace's hand. "Apology accepted."

Mom took a shuddering breath. "All things considered, you're doing okay, kid." She glanced from Aggie to Jace and back again, a slight smile on her thin lips. "You have a great guy at your side who loves you. You know who you are and what you want out of life. That's more than anyone can say about me."

Mom climbed to her feet and kissed Jace on the forehead. "Thanks for looking after my baby girl. Welcome to the family, Jace." She kissed Aggie's forehead next. "We okay?"

Aggie nodded. Yes, the woman drove her insane, but she loved the crazy broad. What could she do? "We're okay."

"I don't know when I'll be in touch. When we get back from Hawaii, Gary wants to buy an RV and see the country. I'll try to make it to your wedding." Her blue eyes darted from Aggie to Jace apprehensively. "I'm invited, aren't I?"

"Of course," Jace said.

Mom hesitated, looking as if she'd been struck by lightning. "Wait a minute. You two aren't planning on having kids, are you?"

"Someday," Jace said without hesitation.

Aggie's heart stuttered over a beat. *Kids?* She glanced at him. Again with the warm, melting, fluttery heart thing. A baby Jace to shower with affection. What could possibly be more wonderful than that? "Yeah, someday," Aggie agreed.

Mom's nose crinkled. "Hold off on that for a couple decades, if you would, please. I am in no way ready to be a grandmother. I'm a newlywed."

Aggie rolled her eyes. "You know, not everything is about you, Mom."

The front door opened. "You guys home?" Eric called from the foyer.

"We're in the living room," Jace yelled.

"I'm going now," Mom said. "Gary is waiting, and I have the only key to his cock cage." She twirled a key ring on the end of one finger.

Aggie's eyes widened. "Too much information, Mom!"

Mom chuckled and kissed Aggie on the top of the head, before taking her chin in one bony hand and staring her hard in the eyes. "I love you, baby girl."

"I love you too, Mom."

Mom cuffed her cheek with one knuckle and smiled warmly before turning to go. She passed Eric as she left the room.

"Yo, Aggie's mom," Eric said, and saluted her with two fingers.

Mom looked at his strange haircut and pursed her lips together. "Yo, freak."

Aggie heard the door close behind Mom a moment later. Aggie figured the next time she saw the woman, she'd be in trouble again. She hoped she was wrong, but some things never changed. They just had to be accepted.

"I don't think she likes me much," Eric said as he entered the room. "You two ready to go see Dave?"

"Yeah, we'll follow you over on the Harley." Jace stood.

"You guys go," Aggie said. "I'm going to stay here."

"Are you okay?" Jace asked. "She begged me to tell you about her getting married, but I thought it was something she should tell you yourself. That's why I asked her to stop by. Are you upset?"

"Not really. I'm glad you had her come over. I just need a little time to adjust to the idea that I used to kick butt plugs up my step-father's ass."

Jace bit his lip and stroked her hair behind her ear. "If you need me to stay home—"

"What's this?" Eric said, lifting a drumstick off a pair of hangers on the wall. He inspected it closely.

Jace's eyes widened, and he strode across the room to snatch his treasured drumstick out of Eric's hand. "It's nothing."

"Why do you have an old nicked-up drumstick hanging on your wall?" Eric asked. "Do you play drums too, tripod?"

"No, I don't play drums. It's something I caught at a live show." Jace carefully set the drumstick back on the pegs he'd installed to display his most prized possession.

"Did your favorite drummer throw it to you or something?"

Jace smiled. "Yeah, something like that."

Aggie could not resist the opportunity to meddle. "That's *your* drumstick, Eric."

Eric glanced at Jace, who was doing his best impression of a cranberry again. "Mine? Why did you steal one of my drumsticks?"

"I didn't *steal* it. You threw it at the end of a show, and I caught it."

Eric's dark brows drew together. "How did you manage to catch a drumstick while on stage?"

"No, dumb ass. It happened ten years ago. I was in the audience."

"Oh." Eric grinned. "So does this mean what I think it means?"

"What do you think it means?" Jace asked.

"That *I'm* your favorite drummer." Eric picked up the drumstick again and twirled it in his right hand.

Jace rolled his eyes. "Uh, no. You're a dipshit." Jace grabbed the drumstick in mid-twirl and placed it back on the wall.

"You don't keep a dipshit's drumstick for ten years and then hang it on your wall like it's a Grammy award or a platinum record."

Jace bit his lip.

"Tell him the story, Jace," Aggie prodded.

After a bit of hesitation, Jace told him. About seeing Sinners for the first time. How he didn't think Jon was good enough. How he caught the drumstick and knew he was destined to be a part of the band. How he'd become a bassist to join Sinners. Eric's smile widened with each revelation.

"So *I'm* responsible for inspiring the creation of the best bassist on the planet," Eric said. "Is that what you're telling me?"

"The best bassist on the planet…" Jace mumbled. "Well, I don't know about that. You inspired *me*."

"Yeah, that's what I said." Eric beamed with pride. "Holy shit. I can't wait to tell the guys that you wanted to join Sinners because of me."

"I didn't tell you that story so you could get all gloaty."

"I'll get all gloaty if I want, tripod. I don't have much to gloat about, you know." Eric appraised the empty wall above the drumstick. "You know what you need? You need a giant, autographed poster of me to hang over your drumstick. I'll sign it, *To Tripod, My biggest-slash-shortest, secretly obsessed, mega-fanboy*."

Jace rolled his eyes and shook his head. "You know what you need?"

"A smaller head?"

"No, an embarrassing, smiley-faced daisy tattoo on the top of your foot."

Eric grinned and nodded. "Only fair."

Jace smiled and laughed. He gave Eric a one-armed, tough-guy hug and pounded him on the back. He was happy. And well loved. Just how Aggie wanted him. Always.

Read on for an excerpt from Trey's book in
the Sinners on Tour series

Double Time
by Olivia Cunning

Available now from Sourcebooks Casablanca

"TREY." THE SOUND OF Brian's deep voice tugged at Trey's heart.
His soul. His will. Brian comprised Trey's hopes. His dreams.
Embodied his love. His desire. Represented his past. His present.
His future. Everything Trey had ever been or ever could be, he
associated with the man. Trey knew Brian would never love
him. Not with the same all-encompassing, soul-wrenching pos-
sessiveness with which Trey loved him, but they maintained a
close friendship. It wasn't nearly enough for Trey, but was better
than nothing.

"Trey?" Brian whispered against his ear, his bare chest pressed
against Trey's naked back. "I want you."

The flood of lust that coursed through Trey's body was punctu-
ated with an inrush of breath. *Yes...* "Now?"

"Shh," Brian breathed. "Quiet. Or someone will hear us."

Trey was naked. Had he gone to bed naked? He didn't remember. It didn't matter. In the darkness, Brian pressed him facedown
on the mattress of his bunk on Sinners' tour bus. Trey felt Brian's
weight over his back. His warmth seeped into his skin. The scent of
leather, Brian's sweet aftershave, and male surrounded him. Trey
closed his eyes and relished the sensations. The texture of Brian's
skin. The raspy quality of his breath.

Emotion washed over Trey. His only regret was that they
weren't face to face, so he couldn't stare into Brian's intense brown

eyes, bury his hands in his messy, shoulder-length hair, and kiss his firm lips as he took him. Whenever Brian visited him, it was always like this. Face down. Total surrender.

Trey felt Brian's cock against his throbbing ass. He relaxed, opening himself to possession. Brian surged forward, filling him with one deep thrust.

"Ah," Trey gasped brokenly as a mix of pain and pleasure pulsed through the core of his body. He loved that Brian's cock was huge. That it stretched him to his limits. Loved how Brian clasped his hands on either side of his head to pin him down. It made Trey feel helpless. Fucked. Used. Exactly how he needed to feel, because he knew this wasn't right. Brian loved another.

Trey lifted his hips slightly in an attempt to get his own attentive cock into a more pleasurable position.

"Don't move," Brian growled. "Take it."

Trey took it. No pain now. Just intense, pulsating pleasure. Brian fucked him harder. Harder. Until Trey wanted to scream *I love you, I love you, I love you* at the top of his lungs. He didn't dare. He knew Brian would disappear the moment he said anything that remotely stupid.

Trey bit his lip and struggled to lift his hips off the bed. He wanted Brian's hands on his cock as he fucked him. Stroking him from base to tip. Giving him pleasure. Making him come. Come by his hand. In his hands. The hands that created the guitar music that was as much a part of Trey as it was of Brian.

"Brian?" he whispered. "Please."

"No."

Trey groaned and rocked his hips, rubbing his cock against the mattress. He needed to come so bad. *Oh, please. I need it. Need you.*

"Hold still, Trey. You know how this works."

Trey stopped moving. Brian had been visiting him like this more and more frequently. Especially since Brian had gotten his wife, Myrna, pregnant. It was pretty much a nightly occurrence at this point. Trey wanted him. Not just in bed. In his life. Each moment, he felt Brian slipping further away and Trey didn't know how to hold on to him.

Brian. Stay with me. Please.

"Trey?" A hand grabbed Trey's shoulder and gave him a hard shake. "Trey! Wake up. It's time."

Trey opened his eyes. The Brian of his dreams vanished and was replaced by the real Brian. This one was *not* fucking him good, hard, and selfishly up the ass. This one was fully clothed and grinning at him from just outside the curtain of Trey's bunk. Trey's balls tightened unexpectedly and he reached down to pull off his sock. He buried his cock in the soft, warm cotton. His belly clenched. Muscles at the base of his cock gave a hard spasm. He came with a tortured gasp.

Goddammit. He ruined more socks that way.

"Sorry to interrupt your wet dreams, dude," Brian said, "but we've got to catch a plane. Like immediately. Get dressed."

Still disoriented, still trembling with the aftereffects of his unexpected orgasm (while Brian watched—he'd undoubtedly relive that in his fantasies for weeks), Trey forced himself to sit up on his bunk. Feet dangling over the edge, he bent his back at an uncomfortable angle so he didn't whack his head on the tour bus' ceiling. "What time is it?" Trey rubbed his eyes and blinked in the overly bright cabin lights.

"Three."

"In the morning? What the hell, Brian? I need sleep."

"Myrna's in labor."

Trey's heart twisted unpleasantly. "She's not due for..."

"Two weeks. I know. It's the real deal though. She's already at the hospital." Brian grabbed Trey's arm and jerked him out of his bunk to the floor. "Hurry up. I will not miss the birth of my first child."

"I don't understand why I have to go," Trey said.

Brian looked a little hurt and Trey immediately wanted to take that comment back.

"You have to go because I need you there," Brian said.

"Fine. I'll go. Whatever," Trey said as if his heart wasn't singing with delight. Brian needed him? There was a first time for everything, he supposed.

Trey rearranged his boxer shorts and located his jeans on the floor next to their new soundboard operator's empty bunk. Rebekah's bunk didn't get much use. She and the band's drummer, Eric Sticks, spent most nights in the back bedroom claiming they were still on their honeymoon. Seven months of honeymooning was a bit much by anyone's standards. Even Trey's. Trey hopped into his pants, tugged a T-shirt over his head, and began his search for a spare sock.

Brian chuckled at him when he tossed his ruined sock in the garbage. "That must've been some dream. What was it about?"

Trey raked a hand through his long bangs. "These three really hot chicks," he lied without missing a beat. "I had three cocks and each of them was sucking one."

Brian quirked an eyebrow at him and Trey's heart skipped a beat. The man was so fucking gorgeous, it was a sin. "Weird."

But not as weird as having homoerotic dreams about your best friend. Your married best friend who was about to become a father.

"Did you get plane tickets already?" Trey asked.

"Your brother's jet is meeting us at the airstrip. It's already on its way. Should be landing by the time we get there."

"So Dare's coming with?"

"Nope. Just you and me."

Alone on a private jet. Trey was pretty sure they wouldn't be initiating each other into the mile high club. Bummer.

By the time they reached the hospital four hours later, Brian was in a panic. When Trey hesitated on the threshold of Myrna's delivery and recovery room, Brian grabbed his arm and hauled him inside.

"I didn't miss it, did I?" Brian asked the doctor who was between Myrna's legs with his bloody surgical gloves trying to ease a black-haired head out of something Trey wished he had never ever seen. Oh fuck. That had to hurt.

Trey's eyelids fluttered, the floor disappeared from beneath him, and everything went black.

The squall of a baby and the declaration, "It's a boy!" flittered around Trey's semiconscious mind. That and some strange ammonia smell just beneath his nose.

"Come on, gorgeous," a soft feminine voice said nearby. "Open your eyes for me. The messy part is all over now."

Trey regained full consciousness with a sudden intake of breath. He instinctively knocked the offensive smelling salts from beneath his nose and sat up.

"There, he's back with us," someone said from the opposite side of the room. The doctor maybe? Trey couldn't get his eyes to focus.

"Did I pass out?" Trey asked.

"Out like a light, buddy," Brian said from beside Myrna's bed. He chuckled much too gleefully.

"You can*not* tell anyone about this," Trey said, struggling to climb to his feet. He leaned his back against a wall to steady himself. He hated hospitals. He'd spent far too many hours in them as a child, including one entire summer when his father had been serving his residency and his mother had decided to ride a bicycle across the country. Just the smell of a hospital made his skin crawl.

"Yeah right," Brian said. "I'm having T-shirts made. I wanted to wait to cut the cord, but you refused to wake up in time to watch."

Trey's stomach did a summersault. *Cut the cord?* Yuck. "Sorry I missed it." Not.

"That's okay. I got it on film."

"Great…" Trey ducked his head to hide his crinkled nose.

A stunning brunette dressed in pink scrubs bent down to enter

Trey's field of vision. She stroked his hair out of his face. The slim brows over her striking blue eyes drew together in concern. "Feeling better now?"

He grinned at her and she flushed. "I think I'll live," he said.

Her hand slid to the back of his head. "You bumped your head." Her fingers found the scar that ran beneath his hair in a wide arch over his left ear. She traced the ridge with her index finger. "What's this?"

Trey captured her hand in his and pulled it away from his scalp. "Old war injury." If getting hit in the back of the head with a baseball bat during a bar fight could be considered war. That little incident had landed him in a hospital for days. Not one of his better memories. "You have really pretty eyes," he told the nurse, still holding her hand.

Her breath caught, pupils dilated slightly as she focused on his interested gaze. "Thank you," she whispered, lowering her lashes to hide her deep blue eyes.

Trey released her hand and she sagged against the wall. He turned his attention to the bed, glad a blue drape cloth concealed whatever the doctor was doing between Myrna's legs. Trey was pretty sure the doc was giving Myrna stitches and he did *not* want to know why that was necessary.

"So where's this baby we've been waiting to see for nine months now?" Trey asked.

Brian waved him over to the bed. Trey approached cautiously. Myrna looked exhausted, and he knew better than to tick her off. He was prepared to make a run for it, if necessary. Brian wrapped an arm around Trey's shoulders and they gazed down at the bundle in Myrna's arms. A miniature, red-faced Brian jabbed his fist in his mouth and sucked earnestly. Trey's heart skipped a beat before melting inside his chest. Brian's son was the most perfect thing Trey had ever seen in his entire life.

Brian scooped up the baby and handed him to Trey. Trey drew his little body against his chest and stared down at him in breathless awe.

"We named him Malcolm Trey," Myrna said. "After Brian's father. And, well, *you.*"

Trey tore his gaze from the small wonder to gape at Myrna. "Me? Why would you name him after me?"

She smiled. "It seemed appropriate to name him after the two most important men in Brian's life."

"We want you to be his godfather," Brian said.

"I..." Trey was honored, but he wasn't an appropriate godfather. He was scarcely responsible enough to take care of himself. How could they ever expect him to be responsible enough to care for their child? "I don't think..."

The baby in his arms gurgled, and Trey looked down to find him staring up at him with unfocused brown eyes. His father's eyes. Brian's eyes. Brian had made this. This perfect, beautiful little person.

Brian was a father.

Trey glanced at Brian and the enormity of it all stole his breath. Brian didn't notice Trey. He only had eyes for his son. His pride in the little guy was tangible.

Trey turned his attention to the baby in his arms. He stroked Malcolm's cheek and then touched his tiny hand, fascinated with his tiny fingers. His tiny fingernails. Tiny knuckles. Everything so tiny. Malcolm gripped Trey's finger with surprising strength. "You're going to be a master guitarist like your daddy someday," Trey told him.

Malcolm scrunched up his face and Trey laughed, totally enamored with Brian's son. The son born from the love Brian shared with his wife, Myrna. The son Trey could have never given Brian no matter how much he loved him. Trey took a steadying breath, kissed the baby's forehead, and handed Malcolm back to his father. "Here. I'll probably break him or something."

"Good-lookin' kid, ain't he?" Brian pressed a kiss to Malcolm's temple.

"Of course," Myrna said, love shining in her hazel eyes as she stared up at her husband and son. "He looks like his father."

"He has your lips," Brian said.

"And your hair."

Trey chuckled. Father and son both had tufts of black hair sticking up in all directions.

"I hope he has your brains," Brian said.

"And your talent," Myrna added.

"He's perfect," Trey said, unable to resist the impulse to smooth Malcolm's fuzzy hair with his palm. It did no good. The baby's downy black hair immediately returned to standing on end.

"You'll be his godfather then?" Brian asked.

Trey lifted his gaze to Brian's. As if he could deny him anything. "Yeah. I guess so."

Brian smiled. "I think you need to get busy, Mills—find yourself a nice girl and make Malcolm a best friend. You're already nine months behind."

"Ha! Like that's ever going to happen," Trey said flippantly, but something inside him wanted that. Wanted something he and Brian *could* share. Pride of their respective sons. He could almost picture Malcolm and Trey Junior playing together in the backyard, learning how to play guitar together, getting into mischief, growing. Trey *Junior*? What the fuck was he thinking? There would never be a Trey Junior. He didn't even like kids. Not even cute little shits who were cursed with the name Malcolm Trey. The baby cooed and Trey melted into a puddle of mush. Okay, so there was *one* exception to his dislike of kids, but only one.

"I should probably leave you three alone so you can bond as a family or whatever."

"You can stay," Myrna said. "You're part of our family."

He appreciated the gesture, but Trey knew better. Things would never go back to the way they'd been before Myrna had crashed onto the scene. He'd been sulking over it long enough. It was time to finally let Brian go. As agonizing as that decision was for Trey, he'd lost all hope of Brian ever returning his feelings. Brian belonged to Myrna. Belonged *with* Myrna. And Malcolm. Trey had been fooling himself into thinking Brian might eventually come to think of him as more than a friend, but now he didn't even want him to. He wanted Brian to continue to be a wonderful husband and an amazing daddy. Myrna deserved that. Malcolm deserved that. Trey couldn't interfere with something that important. It wouldn't be right.

"You know I hate hospitals," Trey said. "I'm going to go see what Dare is up to. Hang out with my big bro in his McMansion until we have to head back to the tour bus. You can call me if you need me to change a diaper or something."

"You're willing to change diapers?" Brian asked.

Trey chuckled at his startled expression.

Trey glanced down at little Malcolm who was making a face that led Trey to believe he was already cooking up a ripe diaper in his honor. "Nah, but I'm sure I can talk some sweet fangirl into doing it for me." He winked at Brian.

"You will not use my son as a chick magnet, Mills," Brian said.

Trey laughed and then bent over the bed to offer Myrna a hug. She met his eyes and cupped his cheek. "You okay?" she whispered, seeming to recognize that Trey was moving beyond his infatuation with her husband. Giving up on Brian. Letting her win. She'd been infinitely patient with him. And trusting of her husband. Because she'd recognized the truth far sooner than Trey had. Brian didn't love him—not the way he wanted him to—and he never would.

Trey leaned closer and whispered, "Love him enough for both of us. Okay? Just promise me that."

Her hand pressed against the back of his head as she hugged him close. "I will. I promise."

When he stood upright, he offered Brian a vigorous, one-armed bro hug. He met Brian's intense brown-eyed gaze steadily. "Good-bye." He could scarcely get the word out through his constricted chest and throat. Brian obviously had no clue that there was significance behind that single word of farewell.

"Later," Brain said. "If I don't see you before, we have a show tomorrow night."

"Wouldn't miss it," Trey said with a smile.

Brian's gaze shifted to his son's face. "Yeah," he said breathlessly. Trey could practically see his separation anxiety and pictured Brian onstage with a baby sling strapped to his chest above his electric guitar and tiny, sound-blocking headphones on Malcolm's fuzzy head. So not Sinners' style. But totally Brian's.

Trey kissed Malcolm's forehead. "See you soon, godson. Don't break too many hearts."

Brian chuckled. "Look who's talking."

Trey left the room, forcing himself not to look back at the scene of domestic bliss he left behind. He really needed to do something fun to take his mind off things. Something or some*one*. What he needed was sex. His drug of choice.

The pretty, young nurse who had woken him with smelling salts stood just outside the delivery room door. When he walked past her, she perked up and grabbed his arm. She'd been waiting for him. Too easy.

"Hey," she said breathlessly. "Hey, um, Trey, right?"

He offered her a crooked grin, and she flushed before lowering her wide blue eyes to his chest. He watched her, noting the submission in her stance, the way she swayed toward him slightly. The way her thumb stroked his bare arm just above his elbow.

"Um…" she pressed onward. "I was just about to take a break and wondered if you'd like to go grab a cup of coffee with me."

Trey's heart rate kicked up a notch. He turned and took her firmly by both wrists, pressing her back against the wall, their bodies separated by mere inches. He bent his head so his breath would caress her ear as he spoke to her in a low voice. "You don't want coffee."

Her pulse raced out of control beneath his fingertips. "I don't?"

"No, but I know what you do want."

"What's that?" Her dark blue eyes flicked upward to meet his. She'd already surrendered, and he rarely turned down a good time.

"A hard, slow fuck against the wall."

"Here?" she whispered, her eyes wide.

He didn't dare laugh. That would have broken his spell over her. "In that supply closet." He nodded down the hall.

He held her gaze in challenge, daring her to deny him. She tore her gaze from his and peeked around his body for witnesses before grabbing a handful of his shirt, racing down the hall, unlocking the supply closet, and dragging him inside. The instant the door closed, she wrapped both arms around his neck and plastered her mouth to his. He let her kiss him. Let her touch the hoop piercing his eyebrow and the ones in his ear. He'd show her the one in his nipple, but she was still a little skittish and he knew if he took the upper hand too quickly, she'd balk and either leave or pretend he'd taken advantage of her.

"You're so sexy," she murmured against his lips. "Why are you so sexy? I shouldn't be doing this."

By *this*, he assumed she meant unfastening his belt, tugging at his T-shirt, rubbing her firm breasts into his chest, biting his lip.

"I don't want you to think I normally do this kind of thing," she said, her hand slipping into his silk boxers to toy with his hardening cock.

He did this kind of thing almost daily, but he wouldn't make the mistake of telling her that.

"Take off your pants," he whispered.

When she obeyed, he knew she was in this until the end. Which he estimated would be approximately fifteen minutes in the future.

"Are you really in a rock band?" she asked.

Trey chuckled. Couldn't help it. Did she seriously not know who he was? It had been a while since a woman had jumped him without knowing he was notorious for this kind of thing. "Yeah, I'm really in a rock band. And I play an actual instrument."

"Guitar?"

He grinned. "How did you guess?"

The excitement in her eyes led him to believe she wasn't half-naked in a supply closet at work because she wanted famous-guitarist Trey. She was pantsless and submissive because she wanted bad-boy Trey. He was all about giving her exactly what she wanted. The walls were concealed behind floor-to-ceiling shelves, so he pressed her back up against the door and trapped her arms on either side of her head. She gasped when he lowered his head to kiss her neck. He nibbled, suckled, and licked the pulse point under her jaw until she began to fight his hold with impatience.

"You're driving me insane," she said. "Do you have a condom?"

"Are you in a hurry?" he murmured.

"Kinda. My fifteen-minute break is almost over."

"You're going to be late." He nipped her earlobe and released her wrist. Trey's left hand moved down her body and gave her breast a gentle squeeze before moving between her legs. She clung to his hair and then fingered the tiny hoops in his ear, then his eyebrow again.

"Do you like piercings?" he whispered. "I have a couple more."

"Where?" she whispered.

"I didn't wear the one in my tongue. Didn't realize I'd have a sweet pussy to lick this early in the morning."

Acknowledgments

Thanks to all of the musicians who inspire my writing—who make a bad day good and a good day better. Thanks to all of my writer friends—both published and aspiring—for their feedback and support: Wendy, Vivian, Jill, Lisa, Judi, Pat, Beth, and Dale, you rock! Thanks to my family for not disowning me no matter how bitchy I get during the writing and revision process. Thanks to all the reviewers and book bloggers who take the time to read my work and share their opinions with the world. Thanks to the hard working team at Sourcebooks for polishing my work—inside and out—until it's fit for human consumption. And a gargantuan thank-you to my fans, who always brighten my day. I have a major crush on every last one of you.

About the Author

Science professor by day, writer by night, Olivia Cunning combines her passion for naughty rock stars and erotic romance in a sweltering mix of sex, love, and rock 'n' roll. Her debut novel, *Backstage Pass*, has won numerous awards, including the Readers' Crown for Best First Book and Best Long Erotic Romance. She currently lives in Texas.